TIME DONORS WANTED

A novel by

Russell Scott

Virtue is meaningless in the absence of temptation; temptation, on the other hand, does just fine when virtue's nowhere to be found.

Gordon Middleman in <u>Observing Earth</u>

To my parents for teaching me the value of both art and science.

To my wife for being the great romance of my life.

CHAPTER ONE

2007

Jarvis Sloan moved purposefully as he made his way along the side of the room. It was one of those big amorphous spaces that hotels called ballrooms these days. Right now it was filled with seats, which made it an auditorium, but Jarvis wasn't terribly concerned with the subtle possibilities of the space he was moving through as he hurried towards the podium at the front of the room.

If he'd looked around him he would've noticed the eyes that tracked his progress as he made his way forward. Even then, he probably wouldn't have understood why. He wouldn't have recognized himself as different because the difference was subtle and had come on him gradually over the space of years. But there was something that set him apart from any of the other people that sat in little clusters scattered among the seats. It wasn't anything he would have been able to put his finger on anyway. It was kind of like seeing a hundred watt light bulb in a light panel full of forties. He was just a little shinier maybe, just a little bit more.

But Jarvis was only focused on where it was he was trying to get to. He scanned the seats on the front row until he found a series of blue cardboard signs bearing the words FEATURED SPEAKER taped to their backs. Finally he spotted them. They were all on the center aisle. He was on the side. That meant he had to go to the front row and across to get to there.

Only then, crossing in front of the stage, did he turn to look at the assembled physicians that occupied the rest of the auditorium. They filled the room in a sea of long hair, beards, checked sports coats, corduroy, and khaki. Jarvis, in his dark Brioni suit with a faint, chalk blue stripe, looked nothing like them and exactly like what he'd become, an extremely successful California businessman, tanned, perfectly groomed, and wearing a two thousand dollar suit, linen shirt, and silk tie. His dark hair, veneered teeth, and the little bit of work he'd had done around his eyes made him look ten years younger than his actual age of forty-five.

As Jarvis took his seat, the speaker on the stage was already leaning on the lectern finishing up with questions from the audience. Something about the questions made Jarvis realize for the first time that he was just a little bit nervous. The moderator nodded in his direction and rose from her seat to conclude the question and answer period. Jarvis took a deep breath and felt it shudder, almost imperceptibly, as it filed his chest.

He didn't have any reason to be nervous, he thought. He'd done this talk more than thirty times already, in one form or another, same slides, same spiel. This was just another run through, adjusted up a notch to fit an audience of his peers. Hell, he thought as a smile crossed his face, they should be glad for something a little bit different after two and a half hours of academic crap-ola. They should welcome a show, and Jarvis had a good show to put on for them. He'd paid a PR firm ten thousand dollars to come up with it. The material was good, and Jarvis was a pretty good speaker. He was one of those people who was always on-stage anyway, even when he wasn't.

Somewhere right there, something snagged on a little bit of worry that had started niggling in the back of his mind. It had been sitting there unformed, and suddenly it started to grow. The more he tried to push it away the more it opened up. As soon as he thought it, he knew, that was exactly what his detractors would hold against him.

The sound of his name snatched Jarvis back into focus. He took another ragged breath, centered his tie, smoothed the front of his suit jacket, and then walked briskly on to the stage. When he reached the lectern, he turned to face his fellow members of the California Psychiatric Association.

"Thank you for asking me to be here tonight," he said and smiled as he looked out at the audience. "Tonight I'd like to talk to you about something that I feel is going to revolutionize our profession... LifeSolutions Seminars."

He clicked the remote for his Power Point presentation, and a lightning bolt cut across a midnight blue sky on the screen behind him.

"Just like a flash of lightning can break the darkness in the dead of night, the Internet can be used to bring illumination to individuals and families that are hurting. We all do our best when we know someone's hurt. As psychiatrists our profession has always provided the care that we can to the patients and clients who come to us in their times of need and distress. But there are too many people who need help and too few of us to provide what they need. Which leaves so many out there who simply don't have access to help of any sort at all. What I've tried to create is a way to address that void. Our goal is to be able to provide information and guidance for anyone who needs it, any time, anywhere."

A map of the United States appeared, filling the screen behind him. Cities with small yellow halos around them emphasized the vast empty areas in between.

"These seminars can be a godsend for small towns and rural communities where counseling isn't readily available. People in need of psychological assistance no longer have to drive to a larger community to get the help they require; they can simply log on."

Jarvis looked out into the darkened room. The spotlight made it difficult to see much.

"Each script is based on a protocol which follows an individualized response thread. That way, each patient who logs on will see a response tailored to his or her own individual problem." Pressing the button brought a slide depicting the selection algorithm onto the screen.

And so it went for the next ten minutes, Jarvis clicking along through the slides just like he had the thirty times before without a hitch. He was most of the way through it when he heard a cough and the sounds of movement from the back of the room. Jarvis looked away from the screen and glanced out into the audience. He squinted against the light, trying to identify the source of the sounds that had disturbed his concentration. He could vaguely make out two small clumps of doctors that were standing in the back. As he watched they began ghosting toward the exits on each side of the room. That's not a good sign, he thought as the sounds of first one door and then the other slamming shut reverberated through the room, sending an unmistakable message. It was time to wrap things up. Jarvis raised the microphone and continued, determined not to let the distraction prevent him from coming to a coherent close.

"Sexual issues account for over half of the visitors that log on to our site," he said as he pushed the button again to reveal a young couple in bed, obviously engaged in intercourse, but tastefully concealed. He continued, summarizing the next few sentences of his script. "If you include the issue of procreation, and the emotional issues associated with that, the percentage increases...."

When a book flashed on the screen, Jarvis began his wrap-up. "I'm often asked, 'why online, why not write a book?' Writing a book would have been a lot easier. For the seminars, each section has to be completely self-contained. Since they're interactive in nature, it's impossible to predict in what order users will want to access the information. We've tried to make each seminar something that meets a specific need, to offer unique solutions to deal with life's problems. We believe we've succeeded in doing so. Thank you."

Jarvis stepped back, setting the microphone down on the lectern, and let the moderator take over. He was glad to have gotten through it without further disruptions.

"Dr. Sloan, how long did all of this take?" the moderator asked, as she reached to extend the microphone towards him. He returned to stand beside her so that they could share it more comfortably.

"It took a year to raise the initial capital to film the first eight seminars in Los Angeles, and using a format developed for video games, we developed an interactive lattice that allowed us to proceed." He paused.

"And then?" the moderator said, encouraging him to explain further.

"And then.... LifeSolutions was born."

The moderator brought up the house lights and turned to the audience.

"Are there any questions? Yes, at the second microphone."

Jarvis didn't recognize the thin, grey-bearded psychiatrist who cleared his throat and leaned into the microphone. "Interaction, Dr. Sloan, involves two people, not a person and a machine. Therapy requires the give and take of a patient and a professional drawing on years of experience." The man then abruptly turned and walked away from the microphone, having voiced his opinion without bothering to ask a question.

Jarvis was used to the critics. Earlier that summer LifeSolutions had blazed into the limelight, catching the attention of both the public and the press. It started as a local phenomenon. California was, after all, the self-help center of the universe. The creation of a new web site devoted exclusively to improving family life and sexual relations was just too much for the press to resist. Newspapers from San Diego to San Francisco had run stories on it. Jarvis was featured regularly on morning shows and health spots throughout the state. Within weeks the buzz in California began to catch national attention. Soon LifeSolutions, and Jarvis, as its inventor, showed up on USA Today, the Today Show, and the cover of Newsweek.

As expected the number of detractors grew almost as quickly. Before long any coverage started to include an opposing opinion as well, usually provided by one of his peers. Psychiatry, as a whole, seemed unimpressed with what the new medium offered. Some of his peers went so far as to make it personal, intimating that Jarvis was a charlatan or that LifeSolutions wasn't "real" therapy. So far he'd ignored them, considering them unenlightened. That wasn't going to be possible here. It was better to face it now, he supposed, and get it out of the way. At least he could try to answer their questions.

The moderator pointed to a young man. "Yes, the microphone in the back," she said.

"Your methods are quite unorthodox," the young man accused.

"I'll admit that," Jarvis conceded. "But if you can try to see the possibilities...."

It became rapidly apparent that no one in the room wanted to see the possibilities. The audience response seemed to go in two directions; most of them lost interest, drifting out between questions until all that was left were those who had an obvious bone to pick. And they moved to the aisles to line up behind the microphones.

It seemed that every person left in the room was determined to have their opinion heard and object to this new intrusion into their profession. They clamored to have their own views registered in the court of public opinion, fighting for a spot as detractor of the day on tonight's evening news.

Jarvis remained patient for about twenty minutes. By then no one even pretended to have a question any more. They'd take their turn at the microphone and jump straight to their accusations, often repeating verbatim the same sentiments as someone that had just spoken before them, as if they hadn't heard what had just been said and were thinking of it for the first time themselves. Jarvis wondered if this was some form of professional hysteria.

He needed to put this to a close. He'd had enough. He wasn't gaining anything by standing up here and being abused. He stood with the microphone hanging in his hand as a younger doctor launched a particularly virulent attack on his motives. When his attacker ended his tirade with, "You sir, are the very worst type of fraud," Jarvis pulled the plug.

He spoke through clenched teeth. "Perhaps if you could somehow get your collective heads out of your collective asses, you might see what can be accomplished. You're so worried that someone or something can do the same thing you do, for a fraction of the cost, that you're totally incapable of considering its validity! Keep your blinders on. Dig in your heels. I'm sure you can stop the future. It worked so well in the middle-ages."

With that said, Jarvis turned, and handed the microphone gently back to the moderator, who was clearly embarrassed for them both, her face as red as his. She opened her mouth several times to speak, but nothing came out.

"Don't worry about it," Jarvis said to her, as members of the audience huffed and harrumphed still milling around the microphone stands. As Jarvis left the stage and walked past them, several members of the audience fell into step behind him determined not to be denied their chance. Others he could see and hear, muttering "Well, I've never," under their breath as he passed.

Jarvis walked in a tunnel of his own making. A red curtain of anger enveloped him until he became impervious to the harsh words around him and unresponsive to any attacks directed at him. He moved with the same sense of purpose and deliberation that he had entered the room with just a few minutes earlier, but in the opposite direction. He was aware of the small group that trailed him as he walked up the aisle, through the door, and across the lobby toward the hotel bar. One of the jackals in the pack that was trailing him reached for his arm as he walked. Jarvis fixed him with a look that was so hard it melted the resolve of the whole pack and they dropped away, standing there in an awkward clump as he entered the bar.

Jarvis didn't know if he would have hit the man if he'd touched him, but he noticed his fist was clenched, and he had the vague sense of something shaking somewhere deep in his chest. He was halfway through his second martini before his heart rate dropped enough for him to start to think again.

"What did you expect?" he asked himself. They obviously hadn't invited him to speak because they liked the idea of what he was doing. He'd hoped when he got the invitation that maybe it was a crack; a chance to show them what LifeSolutions could do. That clearly wasn't the case, he realized now. Nope, this wasn't the chance to explain that he'd hoped for. This was an invitation to a lynch mob, and he wasn't here to be a part of the mob.

Those idiots out there didn't care what it had taken for him to get to this point. The years, waiting for the technology to come of age, years that he'd spent trying to grow a practice, just like they had. It wasn't like he'd started out rich. He knew what it was like to struggle to get going. There were bank loans for medical school and to open an office, then there were the rent payments, staff, malpractice insurance. Every time he'd turned around back then he was digging in deeper. They were mad because he'd found a way out and they hadn't.

They'd all had the same opportunities. They just didn't have the guts to do what it took to do what he'd done.

It had been hard as hell. To keep up with the overhead, he'd had to work more and more, which kept him from taking the computer courses he needed to. By the time the technology was ready, he wasn't anymore. That meant taking out more loans to pay for someone else to provide the technical expertise that he needed.

He'd ended up finding a software company in Mira Mesa to do the programming for his dream site. The software development costs alone had been more than he could ever have afforded without help. But to move forward he hadn't had any other choice. On the plus side, he hadn't really had to learn anything about programming at all. Hell, he hadn't even understood the mechanics of how the Internet or the servers he'd need to use worked when he'd started out. All he'd had to do was come up with some way to find the money.

That's where Sharon had come in. She was beautiful, she was rich, and she'd thought he was a genius sent to save the mental health of mankind. At first it had seemed perfect. So he'd married her. It took him a couple of years to realize that the financial costs were nothing compared to what he'd really ended up giving away to meet them.

What he'd really given up was his freedom, his contentment, and any hope for a happy future. He'd given them all away to get to this point. Even with all of the money he'd made, half of the time he still wasn't sure it was worth what he'd paid to get it.

"Simple-minded bastards," he fumed as he bit into an olive. They didn't care what he'd gone through to get here. They didn't care that there weren't enough of them to even begin to provide care for the number of people that needed help.

Jarvis almost jumped off his bar stool when a hand slapped him on the back and a voice close to his ear said, "...and remember, any landing you can walk away from...."

Jarvis's head spun around, and he found himself looking into the face of an old friend. "Qualifies as some form of success," Jarvis replied, completing the saying they'd used with each other since residency. It was a sort of shorthand, something they said when things were so fucked up there was nothing else to say. Jarvis smiled despite himself.

Rob, like Jarvis, had started as a specialist in family and sexual medicine. Unlike Jarvis, Rob seemed to be able to apply its lessons to his own life. Over the years, Rob had become the avuncular role model for a happy marriage, settling down, gaining weight, and starting a quiet practice up above Santa Barbara.

"Come and join us," Rob invited, sweeping his arm towards a table where the most beautiful woman in the bar sat in a light green dress.

The woman Rob had been sitting with smiled back. "Hi, Tanya, it's good to see you again," Jarvis said, perking up considerably.

"I didn't realize you two knew each other," Rob said, an unasked question in the statement.

"We worked on one of the point papers on conversion factors for Medicare reimbursement a few years ago," Jarvis answered and rose from his seat.

He didn't wait to follow Rob back to the table. He closed the space between them quickly and leaned over to give Tanya a hug and a kiss on the cheek.

She was not the sort of woman that was easily forgotten. She was a redhead, for one thing, but that was only a small part of what made her so memorable. Her eyes were so blue that sometimes they seemed to be clear. When he looked into them Jarvis would be struck by a feeling that he was going to fall in. When she spoke, the combination of those eyes and her sharp intellect hypnotized him.

During their protracted discussions on reimbursement Jarvis found out repeatedly just how potent that combination could be. Her logic drew him along and her eyes mesmerized him. He knew it put him at a disadvantage in their discussions, but he liked it, and it wasn't just him. She was the reason that they'd done as well as they had. Even bureaucrats found it difficult to resist her. They'd become immediate friends and over the years Jarvis had found any excuse he could to seek her advice, in person if at all possible.

"I'm sorry about what just happened at the meeting," Tanya stood and returned Jarvis's hug, turning her face for his peck on the cheek. "Rob and I left when it started to deteriorate."

"How'd you even manage to get away?" Rob interrupted. "It seemed like it was just starting up when we got out of there. There were lines down both aisles to get to the microphone."

"It was pretty simple, really," Jarvis explained. "I just insulted everyone left in the room and walked off the stage."

Rob chuckled, "Now, why doesn't that surprise me?"

Tanya shook her head. "As a whole, I think psychiatrists tend to be the most judgmental, neurotic group in the world."

Rob winked at Jarvis. "Well, I've been told that I'm judgmental, so that must make you neurotic."

Jarvis looked at Tanya and then back to Rob. "If we weren't neurotic, we would never have gone into psychiatry in the first place."

"So you think we went into psychiatry to solve our own problems?" Tanya asked, a smile in her eyes.

Jarvis shrugged, "Well to some extent, but tonight I think most of the psychiatrists in this building should have gone into proctology, if they wanted to help themselves." He added quickly, "Present company excepted, of course."

Rob grinned. "They clearly were inflamed, and the big red-faced guy did look a lot like a hemorrhoid, now that you mention it."

"Well he certainly gave me a pain in the ass!" Jarvis said, laughing for the first time, surprised at how nice it felt to have someone to complain to. That was probably why they all still had jobs anyway, and why computers would never replace them.

"I know him," Tanya offered. "He's from the Bay-area, I think Berkley..."

"I didn't mean to insult your friend..." Rob started.

"He's not a friend, but he is giving a paper tomorrow. I guess you could go to it and harass him back," she offered Jarvis innocently.

"What's it on?" Jarvis asked.

"The psychological benefits of paternal breast-feeding," Tanya answered her face still serious.

"That's not..." Jarvis started, and then stopped as he saw a smile was just barely beginning to form at the corners of her mouth. "Oh yeah, make fun of the guy that just got hit by a train."

"I think you held your own," Rob offered. "Are you going to stick around for any of tomorrow's talks?"

"You're kidding, right?" Jarvis answered, pretending to wince.

"Morrison has her talk on sexual dissonance at ten. You could leave after that," Tanya offered.

"Sure, just wear some jeans and a T-shirt. Nobody'll even recognize you without an Italian suit on," Rob teased.

"That's really what I came for," Tanya turned toward Jarvis. "I know you don't do direct clinical practice anymore, but this is what I'm seeing most of in my practice now. When I first started doing marital counseling, if couples came in it was for one of three things: technique, orgasmic problems, or one of them wanted to experiment and the other one didn't. Now, the number one problem I'm seeing is that one of the partners just doesn't want to be bothered to have sex at all anymore."

Jarvis nodded his head, relieved to be talking about something that would take his mind off of what had just happened. "I remember reading the article that started all this. This isn't a new problem. It's just taken this long to make it into the mainstream thought process. It was in the <u>Journal of Sex and Marital Therapy</u>. I think it came out in two thousand or two thousand and one by Basson? He focused on women's low sexual desire at that time."

"But I'm not seeing it as being restricted to women," Tanya said, shaking her head slightly

"It isn't just women," Rob agreed. "A lot of the career-obsessed guys I'm seeing say there's a decrease in their libido as well."

"All the books and articles a few years ago about 'the new celibacy' didn't help anything," Tanya added. "Self-professed experts pushing celibacy to help focus creative energy and clarify priorities."

"Look, by encouraging people to forgo sex for some intangible secondary gain, the guys writing these things are essentially giving folks tacit permission to unilaterally make the choice to hijack their marriage," Jarvis said, with a touch of anger in his voice.

"Without considering the fact that they're hijacking their partner's sex life as well," Rob interjected.

"Women have been doing that for years," Jarvis muttered.

"Whoa now, doctor," Tanya said sternly.

"I was just saying…" Jarvis decided to change the subject. "Anyone else want another drink?" he asked, raising his hand to get the attention of a passing waitress.

Jarvis tapped his glass and the waitress nodded and then turned to Rob who shook his head no. Tanya ordered another martini and returned to the discussion that had been interrupted. "That's a societal stereotype. You know that as well as I do. Women have a lot more stressors now. More women have to work outside the home just to make ends meet, and they still end up doing most of the household chores, as well as most of the child care."

"That's bullshit," Jarvis exclaimed. "It may be true in some cases. But how does that explain the men? I'd say at least half of the marriages in California are just suffering from some form of sexual starvation."

There was a moment of silence as the three of them considered the truth of that statement. Then Rob spoke up. "The easiest to help are the ones that come in with both partners claiming it's the other one's fault. All they need are communication skills. The hardest to help are the ones where one partner doesn't believe there's a problem at all."

"That's the story of my life," Jarvis muttered, just audibly.

"You're right, Rob," Tanya continued as if she hadn't heard Jarvis. "The frustrated partner always knows there's a problem. If you can't convince the other partner, the one with the lowered need, that there's a problem, it's almost impossible to work out a solution."

"The frustrated partner really only has three options; stay and be miserable, leave the relationship, or find someone else to meet their needs," Jarvis declared.

"There are more conventional choices," Rob argued.

"For chrissake, don't start talking about the three M's," Jarvis said, shaking his head.

"What are the three M's?" Tanya asked.

"Meditation, medication, and masturbation," Rob began.

"Give me a break," Jarvis interrupted. "None of those qualify as a happy outcome."

"And your options do?" Rob countered.

Jarvis shrugged. "As far as I can see, it's the three A's that are the only real choices…anger, adultery, or adios amigo."

"That's four A's," Rob pointed out.

"I was being polite," Jarvis shrugged.

Tanya studied the two men. This was obviously a conversation they'd had before. Then she turned to Jarvis. "You know, I just had a strange idea. Couldn't you could use your seminars to set up a registry of some sort?"

"It has a registry. That's how we keep track of who uses it," Jarvis answered.

"What if you used your registry to somehow pair up sexually frustrated men and women? You'd be doing everyone a favor. Maybe even save a lot of marriages that would otherwise fall apart."

Rob stared at her in disbelief. "Now you're suggesting that we should encourage our patients to engage in adultery? You're as crazy as he is. Can you imagine the lawsuits… malpractice… alienation of affections? You'd end up spending most of your time in court."

"That is one problem…" Jarvis started, already weighing the practicality of the idea.

"Besides, they already have those, 'have an affair tonight' websites all over the Internet. They even had a billboard on the five," Rob offered.

"Those are electronic whorehouses," Tanya spat.

"Someone must be using them. They can afford billboards in LA…money's coming from somewhere." Jarvis could see the possibilities. Rob interrupted his thought process by looking at his watch and standing up.

"Look, I really hate to leave such an interesting theoretical discussion, but I've got to go. I was supposed to meet Mary Alice for dinner fifteen minutes ago."

"You want us to come with you? I'd love to see Mary Alice…" Jarvis started.

"No," Rob answered as he pushed in his chair. "This is a date…you know…we have a house full of kids. We're away in LA…" He leaned over to kiss Tanya's cheek. "It's always good to see you." He smiled at Jarvis. "You never cease to amaze me." He gently patted his old friend's shoulder. "It's good to see you didn't let the bastards in the other room rattle your cage too much. It'd be nice if you tried to stay out of trouble."

"It seems to follow me," Jarvis offered. "Tell Mary Alice I said hello."

The two men shook hands warmly for a moment before Rob turned to go.

Jarvis and Tanya sat quietly and sipped their martinis until Rob was out of sight. Tanya broke the silence first. She turned to Jarvis and grinned. "I think we may have gotten outside his comfort zone."

Jarvis shrugged. "He's happily married. He's having a date night, for crying out loud. That's one of his limitations in this field. His knowledge of marital frustration and unhappiness is purely theoretical, no practical experience." There was more than a hint of bitterness in his voice.

He studied the ice cubes swirling in his glass for a long moment. "There has to be a way to make your idea work. Rob's right about the malpractice and all. It's not the kind of thing that a psychiatrist can recommend directly…but if it was a resource…something a patient could choose to use. That might work. The biggest problem would be keeping everything anonymous. Almost anything electronic can be discovered now. Eighty-five percent of contested divorces in California last year were based on electronic records. That's the biggest problem we'd have to get around."

Tanya shook her head in disagreement. "Not anymore. Not with some of the new technology that's out there. I've got a friend in San Francisco who's been working on something that solves that issue completely."

"What kind of thing?" Jarvis asked, leaning forward as he stared into her eyes.

Tanya responded, leaning forward as well. "She invented a new kind of server, one that can clear itself of any identifying information. Data can be traced to it, but there's no way to trace the connections that are made inside of it."

Jarvis stared at her, he thought for a moment and then raised a hand its index finger tracing some invisible pathway in the air, his eyes far away now. After a few swirls, his other hand joined it, moving independently, swirling in its own direction, until the two index fingers came together. As she watched, a light turned on somewhere behind Jarvis's eyes. "That's how to do it! To use your idea to make money, you have to have two servers. The first one's a standard server that you use to sell something…books, or shoes … or even seminars. Then all you need's a trigger, something that sends them to the erasable server when they buy it. We could do this. We just have to find a way that we can link this new thing to LifeSolutions, we just have to find a way to keep it outside of the main area at the same time."

Their faces were close now. Excitement blazed in Jarvis's eyes. When his eyes focused on hers again, at this distance, he had the overwhelming sensation of being pulled into that old vortex again, and he wanted it. More than anything else he could think of right now he wanted to disappear into those endless blue pools.

As he sat transfixed, almost as if he was stunned, he felt her place her hand over his. As she did, it was clear that the subject had changed.

Jarvis could feel the heat in that touch and it spread through him as fast as any electric impulse ever could. In all of the times he'd pursued her she'd never let him in, never given him an opening. Now she was obviously signaling something. He just wasn't quite sure what.

"Are you really as unhappy as you sound?" she asked softly.

"Well today wasn't one of my finer moments."

"I meant your marriage," she corrected.

"I have a lovely wife and I have two boys that I love more than anything in the world," Jarvis answered.

"Then why are you sitting there fantasizing about seducing me?" Tanya asked.

"What makes you think that's what I'm doing?" Jarvis replied sitting back, but only slightly.

"I could see it in your eyes when you looked up."

"I was just excited ..." Jarvis stumbled briefly.

"I know you are. Now answer the question. Are you fantasizing about trying to seduce me?" she pressed, looking intently into his eyes.

"Yes," he answered truthfully. "Do you mind?"

"I find it flattering really," she said. "But if you love your wife, why are you doing this?"

Jarvis thought for a moment. "As much as I love my wife, right now all I can think about is how exciting you are."

"No," she stated. "You have an erection that's not going to go away on its own and you want me to help you with it."

"That's true too," he admitted. Jarvis wasn't sure why but he felt like he needed to tell her the truth. "There is that... My wife's interest in sex died after our youngest son was born. She wanted two children…Then they were born, it got worse after…Two kids…it's just…just… an unfortunate situation. What about you? You're the one calling the shots. Why are you interested?"

"I'm attracted to you, that's a big part of it. Some of it may be because I'm trying to make you feel better after what you went through this afternoon… and some of it's because my husband's fifteen years older than I am… He was diagnosed with metastatic prostate cancer three years ago. They've put him on leuprolide. It keeps his disease in check, but it's essentially a chemical castration. It takes away everything… the ability and the desire." She looked into her lap. "What we do all day is hard, especially without a release. Listening to people tell you about their sex lives, their fantasies, their experimentation, it builds up pressure."

"We can help each other decompress." Jarvis said smiling.

"…and this is why you really do need to pursue the registry," she whispered as she stood.

CHAPTER TWO

Jarvis opened his eyes and found himself face to face with a soft red patch of well-trimmed pubic hair framed by two beautifully muscled thighs. Tanya was standing next to the bed. He took in a deep breath as he let his eyes rise and found her looking down at him.

"The dead has returned to life," she said as she continued to look through his wallet. "Scoot over..."

He slid sideways on his back, then rolled back up onto his side to face her. She slid her rear end onto the bed and leaned softly against him, her back resting against his stomach.

"Do you love me?" She asked.

Jarvis hesitated.

"You loved me last night. You loved me a lot as a matter of fact."

"You're right," he answered, unsure of what she was getting at.

"I loved you, too. I still do, right now. I have for a long time."

Jarvis didn't know what to say. This was the last thing he expected.

"But I won't tomorrow. I'll remember you, I may even want you, but I won't love you any more. Because I know you never felt anything back...all you can think of right now is how you get out of here. Don't you ever let yourself...feel?" There was a sadness in her eyes, they were closed to him now and he couldn't come in any more.

"Sometimes. I really do...with you," he stammered.

"But usually not. Unless someone puts you in this kind of uncomfortable position, then you say whatever you have to to shut them up," she hissed. Her teeth clamped together as she spoke.

He didn't know where this was going, so he proceeded cautiously. "Usually I don't let myself feel anything."

"So the women you're with, they're like blow-up dolls for you. Something to come in and then put away?"

"That's kind of harsh," he replied.

She held out one of the snapshots. "You have a beautiful family. That's Seth?"

"No, Paul," he answered looking at the picture of his son and immediately feeling awful.

"Why would you risk losing your kids for something so shallow, something you didn't even really let yourself feel? A healthy family, that's something worth fighting for not something you throw away. Not for something you don't even care about in the first place. Why not just jerk off…or buy a real blow-up doll? You can afford the best. Hell you could buy a silicone and latex woman if you wanted to. You could just rinse her out and shove her in the closet when you were done."

Jarvis held her gaze without speaking trying to see where she was going with this.

"Tell me about her," she asked holding out a picture of Sharon.

"There isn't that much more to say. I told you most of it last night…in the bar."

"You didn't tell me anything. You pretended to, but you didn't. That's the problem with this for me. I have to face what it is I'm doing. I'm cheating on my dying husband. And you get to pretend it's all your wife's fault."

Jarvis didn't know what to say.

"It's not. It never is. I can look at her picture. I can see her, but that's not who she is to you."

"Okay, what do you want to know?" Jarvis could play along.

"Where was the first place you had sex?"

"On the couch. In my office."

"Was she a patient?" Her eyes had become searchlights now, looking for any indication of deception.

He felt uneasy at first, but he told her the truth. "She was my secretary. She came along while I was trying to get LifeSolutions started. The secretary before her was married to a Navy pilot and her husband got orders to Norfolk. She was my only employee at that time, so when she quit I was screwed. I spent the next three weeks making my own appointments and answering the phone in-between patients. I didn't even try to file stuff. Every day sucked, all day long. I would've hired Attila the Hun in a heartbeat. Sharon was the first person that the agency I called sent over. She was beautiful and she had great work skills. At first it was just business. But we got close, she believed in what I was trying to do with the seminars, and her father was a manager for one of the big hedge funds in Los Angeles. It all just kind of worked out."

"You're a lucky man," she said. "I hope your luck holds out."

Jarvis felt her hand moving over him, going to his crotch. She tugged softly until he was ready. Then she lifted his tie off of the bedside table and leaned over him. He busied himself with first one of her breasts and then the other as she took his hands in hers and raised them over his head, pressing herself down onto his mouth. Slowly she slid her hands down his arms as she raised herself back into a sitting position. She drug her fingernails lightly across the skin of his chest, and then his stomach, until she was back to where she had started.

"I want you to think of her this time. This is what she should be giving you."

Jarvis thrust forward into her hand and groaned softly. Suddenly her hand clamped hard around his scrotum. He looked up in surprise. What he saw in her eyes was new, a kind of maniacal fire.

"I'm not going to love you like she does. I'm going to fuck you, like you do them." And she did. With the intense pain his erection began to fade, so she started on him with her mouth, and from the beginning it was too hard. When he winced and reached for her, he found that he couldn't move his hands. She had looped his tie around his arms at the elbow and placed the loop behind his head so he couldn't get them down. She shoved him back and pushed two of her fingers into him from behind. Her nails were sharp and he felt something tear as she did. There was no tenderness. There was no gentleness or love. It was violent, and it was hard. When she straddled him it was almost as if she were trying to kill him, that her vagina was a razor that she was using to slash him with. It was the best sex Jarvis had ever had.

"You have to know who you really are," she whispered in his ear, her hands wrapped around his throat, choking him, as he ejaculated inside her, seemingly forever, wave after shuddering wave, balanced on the edge of consciousness. "Who ...they are," she panted as she came herself.

Jarvis was perfectly sure that he didn't love her, and she didn't love him either. In a strange way it was better than that. Purer some how.

He came back from Los Angeles black and blue. He was bruised and sore and his wife never even noticed. It took him a week to get over what had happened physically, but he didn't even begin to mentally. She was all he could think about. He needed to call her. He needed to talk to her about moving forward with what they'd discussed. He was sure they could make it work. He needed to but he couldn't. He didn't have any idea what to say.

It took another week before the fax came. "It was good to see you again. Enjoyed our conversation. Hope the idea works out." Below that were a name and phone number, and it was signed Tanya.

In his office, Jarvis sat at his desk and dialed the number Tanya had sent. He sat up straighter as the ringing stopped.

"Hi, this is Brooke. Can I help you?"

"Hello, Brooke, this is Doctor Jarvis Sloan; I'm a friend of Tanya Reynolds."

"Yes, Tanya told me you might call. She said you had a project in mind that might be able to use my server to meet some unique security needs."

"Did she give you any details?" Jarvis hoped she had. It would make things easier.

"Not really, but if you could give me a feel for what it is you need, perhaps I can tell you if it's something I can help you with."

Tanya lay on a blue exercise mat in the workout room of her Russian Hill home. Exquisitely, slowly, she raised her body into the yoga position called down dog and breathed rhythmically, counting the inhalations. When the phone rang, she finished her breathing and wiped her face with a towel before putting the phone to her ear.

"Hello," she said.

"Tanya, this is Brooke. I've got to talk to you."

"Sure baby, what's up?"

"I just need to talk to you, but I don't really want to do it over the phone."

"I'm at the house; you're welcome to come over," Tanya offered.

Brooke hesitated. "Do you have time to get some coffee? I haven't had lunch yet."

"Sure, let me grab a quick shower," she replied. "Are you at your apartment?"

"No," Brooke said. "I went in to try and get some work done this morning; it'll take me at least fifteen minutes to get there."

"Perfect then, I'll meet you at Étoilés in thirty minutes."

As Tanya showered and dressed, she thought back to the beginning of their relationship. Brooke had been referred to Tanya for depression, but it wasn't depression that Brooke suffered from, just a series of unfortunate decisions, not the least of which was an affair with her thesis advisor. For him it had been sport, a quick fling with a younger lover. Unfortunately, Brooke had been naïve enough to think it was love. Her misperceptions were ripped away when, after they'd been together for six months, he published the majority of her master's thesis as his own work. For Brooke, the intellectual violation was as painful as the idea that he had used her physically. At least she'd consented to that.

Her complaint to the faculty council had turned into a "he said, she said," as it always did, and since he was a well-respected member of the faculty, her complaint was noted with no official action taken. Unofficially, it was suggested that she needed some counseling, maybe some medication and, if that didn't help, perhaps she should consider transferring to another program.

That's where Tanya had come in. By the end of their first session, Tanya was certain of one thing, medication wasn't what Brooke needed. She needed to regain her sense of self-worth, some self-confidence, and somehow she was going to have to learn to trust again. Taking a pill every day would have been a whole lot easier.

They started with sessions several times a week. Then, in place of some of their sessions, Tanya began taking Brooke with her to some of the different associations and clubs she went to. It wasn't long until the doctor-patient relationship softened and dissolved. The two of them became simply friends, and then something more, but that was much harder to define.

It was clear from the tone of her voice on the phone that Brooke had some reservations, and she should. Jarvis Sloane was just the kind of man she needed to stay away from. But she had to grow, and learning from life's mistakes was the only way to do it.

Sitting at a table in Étoilés Tanya smiled automatically when she saw her young friend come through the door. For some reason whenever she saw Brooke in person it always made Tanya think of sunshine. Her skin was the color of caramel, her face surrounded by a cloud of flying, curly black hair. She described herself as a second-generation hippie culture mutt. And wherever the genes came from that had come together to form her, it had worked out just fine. She wasn't classically beautiful, but if there was one word to describe her that word would be "radiant".

It was obvious that she was coming from the computer lab, plaid shorts, an orange peasant blouse, and those damned horrible cat's-eye glasses that Tanya had been trying to get her to get rid of for a year. Her look at work was almost always geek city. She even had a backpack. She was Bay area hipster perfect.

Brooke came straight to the table where Tanya sat licking the foam from a cappuccino off of her top lip.

"I started without you. I ordered us both one," Tanya offered, pointing to a steaming cup.

"Sorry it took me so long…how do you drink that? You know I only sip the foam when you get them for me," Brooke blurted as she plopped down, dropping the backpack beside her chair. "I don't know about your friend's idea," she said, abruptly changing gears.

"Jarvis you mean?" Tanya said, picking up her coffee cup.

"Yeah, we talked on the phone for a long time last night."

"And you have some reservations?" Tanya asked.

"<u>Some</u> may not quite cover it," Brooke said, raising her eyebrows.

"So what are they? Let's put them in words," Tanya suggested.

"Well…there are a couple of things. First, I'm getting a Phil vibe," she said, referring to her old advisor. "I don't want to get screwed again."

"Then make sure you don't," Tanya replied. "You're in control. You have something he wants. Use that. But you have to make sure he still needs you once he gets it."

"I'm not sure I'd know exactly how to do that," Brooke said.

"Think marriage…."

"Are you crazy? He's the last man in the world…."

Tanya laughed. "Not literally," she assured Brooke. "Figuratively. Marriage binds two people together to make it hard for either one of them to leave the relationship. You need to bind yourself to Jarvis so that once you develop what he needs, he won't be able to get along without you."

"And just how do I do that?" Brooke asked, clearly puzzled.

"One way would be to ask for partial ownership of whatever you develop."

"I don't think he'd do that," Brooke said, squinting her right eye.

"Sweetheart, you won't know until you ask. You have something he needs. You don't need to agree to anything until he gives you what you need as well," Tanya concluded simply.

"That's not the only issue," Brooke admitted. "I'm not sure how I feel about what he wants to use the servers for."

Tanya set her coffee cup down and leaned forward to look straight into Brooke's eyes. "Don't let naivety keep you from being a part of something that has the potential to help people."

"I'm not sure what he wants to do is going to help people. He wants to set up a foolproof way for people to cheat on their partners. His whole goal is to make adultery some sort of safe and palatable therapy-oid thingy."

"Nothing can be foolproof and adultery never ends up being easy," Tanya said flatly. "Look, he and I have talked about this. He's not setting up some swinger's website or anything like that. Did you look at his seminars?"

Brooke nodded. "I was impressed with the detail he's put into them. He's really made very innovative use of gaming technology. It makes the interface really workable."

"And does it seem to be the work of an amateur or someone who doesn't know what they're doing?" Tanya asked.

"It's not that. It's what he wants to do that bothers me."

"Brooke, Jarvis is just trying to do online what I try to do every day in my office. Keep marriages together that otherwise are probably going to fall apart."

"Well, if these people are all ready to cheat on each other, maybe their marriages should fall apart," Brooke answered, crossing her arms.

Tanya sighed. "Spoken like someone who's never been married. If marriage was that easy, I'd be out of a job. There are lots of reasons to keep marriages together. And a lot of people believe that fidelity and love aren't necessarily the same thing."

Brooke thought about that, chewing her knuckle, then looked up. "So you think I should do it then?" she asked.

"I think that's something you have to decide for yourself," Tanya answered.

"All right then I'll do it," Brooke huffed "It's not like I have any real choice. My grant money will be gone by the end of the semester, and I don't think I'm going to get a very strong faculty recommendation to get it renewed."

"That would be exactly the way not to approach this. You don't need to do it because you have to. You need to do it because you want to do it," Tanya suggested.

From that point on Brooke was clear and unwavering whenever she spoke to Jarvis about what she had in mind. To Tanya, she was a nervous wreck. With each counter offer he made, she stalled, texting Tanya immediately to ask her if she should give in yet, and each time Tanya just sent back a single word, "no". After the third offer, Brooke's nerves were shot. She couldn't do this by text. She needed to talk.

"How can I keep telling him no? Every time he calls back he comes up. He offered to make the down-payment on a condo if I'd agree to come by the first of the month," she spilled breathlessly into the phone.

"Because he still hasn't given you what you asked for," Tanya explained.

"What if he gets upset?" Brooke almost wailed.

"Then he gets upset."

"He called me a prima donna," Brooke explained.

"He calls everybody who doesn't give him what he wants a prima donna. Look, you didn't want to do this in the first place. What's the worst thing that can happen?"

"I won't get the money to develop my project. I'm calling him and saying I'll take it," Brooke wasn't able to face that possibility.

"If you do that you've created another Phil. Given another man permission to rape you intellectually," Tanya started, now the therapist, showing her patient for the first time what she'd been doing all along. "This is how you come to grips with this world. This is how you regain your self-worth. You have to have the strength to know what you're worth. Never, never compromise on that."

Two weeks went by before Tanya heard from Brooke again. Then without a call or text, she looked up from her desk to see a huge grin on her young friend's face as she leaned into the doorway of her office.

"You're not going to believe this," Brooke started.

"Jarvis gave in?"

"And, he gave me almost everything I asked for."

"Almost?" Tanya asked, frowning.

"Everything he could," Brooke assured her. "To get the developmental budget I wanted, he had to agree to split all of the profits with his investors. The rest we split fifty-fifty."

"For how long?" Tanya asked warily.

"That's the great thing. Essentially forever; we're married, just like you said."

"How?"

"Security," she laughed. "I just had to explain that everything we were doing depended on absolute confidentiality and that requires absolute security. One time would be all it would take. One blackmail scheme, one public posting and the whole thing collapses."

It was one thing for a virus to shut down LifeSolutions for a day or two, but it was another thing entirely for a hacker to threaten to post the identities of the people using the new site on the web somewhere.

Tanya didn't even try to suppress the wave of maternal pride that surged through her as she rose to embrace her young friend.

Despite the tedious negotiations he'd gone through, Jarvis was fairly pleased with the deal himself. In reality, Jarvis was his company's only investor. He'd bought out all of his original investors years ago, even his father-in-law. As it stood, he'd end up owning a total of seventy-five percent of the new enterprise, and seventy-five percent of something was a lot better than a hundred percent of nothing. He was thinking about how much money he was going to have to commit to the initial phase of the project when his cell phone rang. He glanced at the caller ID and saw a 415 area code.

"Hey Brooke, I was just going over the start up costs for the project," he said without introduction.

"I hear congratulations are in order," a soft female voice answered.

His face flushed and Jarvis had to swallow before he could answer. "I need to thank you for that."

"You need to thank me for more than that," Tanya answered cryptically.

"You're right. This started out as a joint idea. I guess I should have gotten back to you before now to talk about how to include you in the revenue stream...I mean, do you have any suggestions? I suppose you know the details of Brooke's deal. I wanted to wait until

I had the details of that worked out before I called." Jarvis was nervous, which was making him talk too much.

"I do, but I don't suppose that it was Brooke that kept you from calling me." Tanya offered. "Most men aren't used to being in that position. They don't know what it's like to not be in control, but it's something almost all women know at some point. You need to understand that if you plan to really go forward with this."

"I think you can count that as a lesson learned," Jarvis replied.

"That's good, because you're going to open Pandora's Box, so you'd better have some plan to keep the evils of the world under control when you do it. Brooke will think of a lot of it, but she's only twenty-four. She hasn't really seen the kind of evil that's out there. As one of the parents of this child, I don't want to be part of creating a monster," Tanya explained.

"I understand that. Neither of us does," Jarvis assured her.

"I want you to push her to exclude bad people. There are all kinds of databases to keep track of sex offenders. You need to run all of your contacts through those before you match them to anyone. You could run a FFL check too. You can do that for free through the Department of Justice. They keep track of everybody that has a history of domestic violence to keep them from buying guns."

"You've thought a lot about this," Jarvis said. He was silent for a moment. "So LA was all a lesson? It wasn't you? It wasn't something you liked?"

"No, I liked it. I liked it a lot. What I liked best was watching the fear wash away as you started to come. It felt so good that you were more afraid that I was going to stop than you were of dying. What could be better than that?"

"Well, for me, the night before was a lot nicer," Jarvis started. He was thinking of laying some ground rules in case they ever decided to try this again.

"That was for you. I was just trying to be polite, which brings up another thing you need to understand. We both know people carry a lot of things that they don't share around inside of them. Sometimes it's anger. Men don't expect that in women, but it's there. You need to be careful of them too. There will be a lot of men with families. Just like you. Do you understand what I'm saying?"

"I think so," he answered slowly.

"One more thing, Jarvis. Don't try to take advantage of Brooke."

"I know she's your friend, but I'm sensing there's more to it than that." A question hung in his tone.

"She's the daughter I never had. Maybe she's the chance I wish I had to rebuild myself into something better, if I weren't too old to change."

"Old isn't exactly how I'd describe you," Jarvis reassured.

"Old is relative, but there's something else you need to know, and this is a violation of a lot of things…confidentiality, trust, HIPAA regulations. She's a genius, and she's my friend too, but you need to know that she was my patient first. She's carrying around a lot of things, Jarvis. Things that, if you open them up, could make Los Angeles seem like a walk in the park."

"Oh shit," Jarvis muttered as he kneaded his forehead with his left hand. "What in the hell have I gotten myself into?"

What Jarvis had gotten himself into was a gold mine. Three months after she moved to San Diego, Brooke had her first functioning secure server. Jarvis already knew exactly how he wanted to use it; as a sub-site within the LifeSolutions framework. Now it was up to Brooke to figure out how to do that and how to maintain ongoing security. She'd convinced Jarvis that a static security system was totally inadequate for their needs. The only way for them to stay ahead of the rapidly changing tide of hackers, probes, and viruses was to make security their number one priority. Jarvis, to his credit, got it immediately.

TimeDonors was the working title for the project. Jarvis liked the way it sounded. LifeSolutions and TimeDonors, TimeDonors and LifeSolutions. There was a kind of symmetry in it, so the name stuck. Where LifeSolutions had been hard work from the beginning, the new site was a project that took on a life of its own, primarily because of Brooke. She was one of those people who had the ability to take a project from concept to completion with nothing more than permission and funding.

Placing TimeDonors inside the LifeSolutions framework solved all the billing issues and gave them the information they needed to run background checks before they paired new clients with anyone else. But the best thing was there was absolutely no electronic trail. They simply charged for the LifeSolutions access and gave TimeDonors away for free. Once a client paid the weekly seminar fee, they'd have full access to all of the seminars and workshops, including a new

CHAPTER THREE

The Present

Laura Dees whistled softly as she loaded the canvases she'd
finished over the last few weeks into the back of her silver Suburban.
She was careful to protect the face of each painting by laying a
blanket over it to keep the stretcher bars of the painting on top of it
from scratching the painted surface while she drove. Her back seats
were folded down to maximize her cargo space. That caused her to
have to stand on her tiptoes to get the paintings into position. She was
dressed a little nicer than she usually did for the trip down the
mountain. She still had on jeans, but they were nice jeans. There
weren't any paint stains on them, and she was wearing a new blouse.
Her long, dark hair was pulled back and tied to keep it out of her face
as she loaded. She usually tied it back when she painted too, but she
still found bits of hair matted together by brightly colored pigment
most nights when she brushed her hair before bed.

She picked up the next painting and, as she turned, she bumped
the edge of the frame against her son Cody's car seat. Cody was their
only child. She'd already dropped him off at school. Every other
Wednesday after she dropped Cody off at school, Laura would leave
the car seat by the wall in the carport so the babysitter could stop by
and get it on her way to pick him up in the afternoon. Then she would
load up her car and drive from her studio in Sedona to the gallery
down in Scottsdale where she sold most of her paintings now. Kent,
who owned the gallery, would pick out the paintings that he thought
would sell well in the Phoenix market from what she'd brought down.
At first, he'd only kept about half of what she brought, but lately he'd
been keeping more and more. That was a good sign.

She liked Kent. In fact, they were best friends. Some of it was
the business. Kent sold more of her paintings, for more money, than
any of the other galleries she showed in. That was reason enough to
like him by itself, but it was more than just money. Kent was always
so much fun to be with. And if there was one thing she needed to
have more of in her life lately, it was fun.

She examined the edge of the frame. There was only a tiny
mark. She didn't think anyone would notice it. There wasn't any
reason to leave it here for Morris to look at. Morris was her husband,

if you could still call him that. Every one of the paintings she loaded, he'd framed, cutting the molding and fitting the edges. It was the only thing he'd have to do with the world of art anymore.

It hadn't always been that way. They'd met at the University of California in San Francisco in the Fine Arts program. They weren't friends back then and they certainly weren't lovers. They were rivals. For four years they'd competed to be the brightest star. Morris had the early lead. Students in San Francisco in those days tended to think that they were the avant-gardes. It fit his style of painting much better than it did hers. The other students loved his work. The faculty preferred hers.

While they were still evolving, each trying to find their own style, Morris studied the works of Mark Rothko and Jackson Pollock and became infatuated with abstract expressionism. The problem was that he was forty years too late. Everybody had seen it all before. What had been ground shaking in the forties was well beyond passé by the eighties.

Morris didn't deal with criticism well. It unnerved him. By the time they were seniors the disintegration of his confidence had already started.

At the Upperclassman's Annual Exhibit, in the fall, she'd won first and he'd won second-place. They'd had to stand up in the front of the gallery together and have their pictures taken with their ribbons. When she'd tried to congratulate him, he'd been a complete jerk. He'd made a rude comment about her switching to photography since she didn't really paint and walked out, refusing to even shake her hand.

A few days later, he found her in one of the studios and apologized for being such an ass. She'd felt bad for winning, for some reason, so she accepted his apology. He offered to buy her a beer. Biology did the rest.

After graduation, they moved in together and stayed in San Francisco for the next two years. Laura went on to get her Master of Fine Arts degree. Morris left school. He said he was sick of talking about how to paint and wanted to find his own way. He'd ended up working in construction during the day and painting in an old warehouse at night. He did some nice pieces back then. They just didn't sell. Morris had expected to awe the world with his brilliance. Unfortunately, about a thousand other kids had the same idea every year. It ate him alive.

By the time Laura finished her MFA he was done. The final painting he'd ever started still hung on the wall in Laura's studio, waiting for him to finish it.

The likelihood of his ever picking up another brush diminished with every painting she sold. Laura felt bad about it. She knew she was the reason that he couldn't paint any more.

A twenty-four-by-thirty inch landscape by Laura sold for around seven thousand dollars in Sedona, maybe fifty-five hundred in either of the other galleries. She got half. Even her signed giclees brought eight hundred. Morris had never sold an original painting for half that. Her successes in the galleries in Phoenix and San Diego were like nails in his heart, though, because he couldn't dismiss them as tourist junk anymore. So they never talked about it. He pretended that it didn't bother him, but it did.

Most of the money they lived on was coming from what she sold. He'd decided to start his own remodeling business a few years ago, so he wouldn't have to work for anybody else. That only made things worse. She guessed he was breaking even, but she wasn't sure. He kept all of his money in his business account. She didn't have any idea how much he had in there.

As Laura left Sedona, she headed south on Arizona highway 179, which ran right through the middle of the Coconino National Forest. The sun on the windows warmed and relaxed her. She thought about how many years she had been making these trips.

She'd started out in a small gallery in Sedona. It was gone now. The owner, Becky, had married a banker from Utah and moved up there. Kent was doing one of his scouting trips, looking for local talent, and saw her paintings. Becky was being sweet and gave him her number. She even let him use her phone. He called Laura from the gallery and asked her to do a show for him in Scottsdale.

That was when the trips started. Since then she'd become one of his biggest sellers. Then a few years ago, she'd gotten the opportunity to expand into a gallery in California.

Kent had been the one that arranged it. She had been kind of surprised at first, but the two galleries weren't in direct competition, so she'd assumed he was doing it for her benefit. She didn't find out until later that the reason that he'd done it was to impress his new boyfriend, James, who was the owner of the gallery in LaJolla. That was pure Kent in so many ways.

She smiled as she thought of the two men. Kent couldn't keep a secret if his life depended on it, but James didn't even try to. When Kent introduced them, he called James an out of town friend. James, on the other hand, was rather flamboyant. He'd proceeded to elaborate in great detail about the long-distance love affair that the two of them were carrying on.

It was funny to think about, but it made her sad at the same time. They both seemed happier with their relationship even now than she was with hers. Maybe the distance kept things fresh for them. They each had their own day-to-day life, but whenever they got together, as James explained, "It's always a Dom Perignon and chocolate-covered strawberries event."

As she drove, Laura fantasized about what that would be like to have a relationship like that, one where sex was entertainment and not an obligation. Her unhappiness with her own sex life had a lot to do with the fact that it was…well, crap. It was terrible from almost every standpoint. It was constant, unvaried, unfulfilling. The best thing about it was that it was becoming less frequent all the time.

Sex for Laura consisted of Morris grabbing her left breast, thumbing her nipple until he heard what he thought was a response, then pulling off her panties, and pounding away for five minutes. After a brief shudder, he'd roll off and murmur, "love you," just before he fell asleep, leaving her both aroused and frustrated at the same time.

It wasn't that she didn't like sex. She liked sex a lot, and she really liked orgasms, but for her this wasn't sex, it was just Morris masturbating. "Look Ma, no hands!" She, unfortunately, was left with the "hands on" technique, coming quietly so she didn't wake her sleeping husband.

The drive south to Phoenix was just like her sex life, straight, flat, and colorless. Nothing like the drive to Flagstaff, with its sharp sweeping turns and dramatic vistas. Driving south out of Sedona, toward Phoenix, was always a battle with falling asleep. She'd driven it so many times she felt like the car should be able to drive it by itself. It would be great to be able to lean back the seat and take a nap. But she couldn't lean the seat back anyway. There were paintings back there.

Besides, she thought as she passed the familiar white rumps of a small herd of elk. That would be the other of the major flaws in that plan. Sleeping in her car while she was driving would certainly endanger the local wildlife. Her car didn't seem to be able to recognize animals all that well. It was always flattening snakes, tortoises, and jackrabbits even when she was helping it. Hitting an elk, with several large framed paintings leaning against the back of the driver's seat, would undoubtedly end up acting kind of like a guillotine.

"Look Ma, no head!"

Not that the lack of a head would bother Morris. He never kissed her anyway and he certainly wasn't interested in anything she had to say. As for using it for anything else, she didn't think either of them had much interest in that anymore, at least not with each other.

For years she'd tried not to think about how unhappy she was. She had a son to think of. So that's what she'd thought of. She'd tried to keep from thinking about sex at all. To keep rolling it over in her mind was like picking at a scab; it just kept everything irritated and painful. It was a lot easier not to think about it. It wasn't that not thinking about it made her happy, but by ignoring it, at least she could stay numb, and being numb was better than being miserable.

Today was different, though. Today she was making a change. Today she felt like there was a kettle boiling inside of her. Each bubble that popped to the surface brought with it a new ache, a yearning for something better, something more fulfilling and complete, and not the sad, insufficient, half-measure her life and marriage had turned into. She knew it was her fault. Morris was always telling her that she was asexual, but if she was, it didn't feel like it today.

Today she knew that her unhappiness and frustration was, in reality, her own problem, not his problem, not their problem, her problem, to take on and do something about. She knew about Morris's extra marital affairs. He'd been having them for years. Why she continued to allow it for so long without saying anything she couldn't say. But she didn't guess it really mattered anymore.

He hadn't tried to keep it a secret. Sedona was too small a town to keep secrets like that. It started with the rumors, whispered conversations from the next aisle that she overheard at the grocery store. He had to know she'd find out, or he didn't care.

Of course, she did at first, but whenever she confronted him, he'd simply deny it and explain away whatever incriminating evidence she found against him. If she persisted, he'd accuse her of having an overactive imagination. What started out as whispered accusations rapidly turned into screaming matches that upset Cody. She'd grown up with that herself. She didn't want to put her son through it too.

So, for Cody's sake, she'd let it go. In some ways, it was for her own sake too. It was easier for her ego to accept that he wanted other women than to accept the fact that, more than anything else, he simply didn't want her any more.

Dealing with her unhappiness in any way other than by simply ignoring it had never really occurred to her. Doing anything else happened by accident, about a month ago, while she was having lunch with her friend Sue at a rooftop bistro on Prospect Street in LaJolla.

Susan Wong had been showing paintings in James Watson's Gallery for a decade when they'd met. The two of them had done a two-woman show a couple of years ago. It worked well. They sold a lot of paintings, but they also had fun together, anywhere, anytime. So whenever Laura was in town they hung out, picking one another's brains about shopping, art, and whatever life was throwing at them right then.

Their painting styles, and their personalities, were very different. But, for some reason, they complimented each other. Their paintings seemed to provide a sense of both balance and diversity when they were viewed together. So did their personalities.

Sue was a constant tease, and had nicknamed Laura "Rocky" for all the "damned rocks" she painted. Laura loved the jutting red landscape of her home in Sedona, and that was the defining subject in most of her paintings. Sue preferred to portray people and their influence on the landscape, rather than the landscape itself. In her words, "Who wants to paint naked dirt?"

They'd met at the gallery and Sue helped as Laura and James discussed how to hang the canvases she'd shipped to be there when she arrived. They would hang a painting. Sue would hate it there. So then they'd move it. They'd hang another painting, and another, each one changing what they thought about the paintings they'd just hung. Since the two women's suggestions were often contradictory and James was sick of being bossed around, he kicked them out so he could hang them, "wherever in the hell he wanted" by sending them to lunch. Well, it was more like, "You two bitches had better get out of here, before I have to hit you with a hammer. Go get something to eat."

Sue ordered a Cobb salad and Laura got the French Onion soup with a spinach salad. The rooftop view along LaJolla's high-cliffed coast, looking north to the glider port and Black's Beach below, was fantastic. Beyond that point, the cliffs curved away and out of their line of sight. All that could be seen was the blue-green of the Pacific.

"Look at these great rocks," Laura teased referring to the sheer cliffs. "They're even framed by an ocean."

"I'd prefer to paint the naked people at the bottom of them," Sue countered.

Laura arched her eyebrows. "What naked people?"

"That's Black's Beach," Sue explained. "It's a local 'clothing-optional' destination."

Waving her fork, Laura asked, "Are there many of those around here?"

"There's Black's, a place just below Camp Pendleton, and a couple of retreats out in the desert to the east of town," Sue recited.

"Have you ever been there?" Laura asked.

"Sure, Rocky. I live here, you know. It's a little tough getting down the cliff, but there's a pretty good trail. Getting back up's the hard part. It's not anything like you're thinking though."

"What do you mean?"

"It's not just the 'beautiful people,' it's just people. There are attractive people there, but there are plenty of hernia scars, droopy boobs, and cellulite-dimpled butts around too. The real pretty boys are all at the gay end of the beach."

"Why is it always like that?" Laura wondered aloud. "The guys you like to be around and have fun being with are all gay."

"Don't ask me. I liked gay guys so much, I apparently married one," Sue said bitterly.

Laura winced. She had forgotten the circumstances of Sue's divorce. "I'm so sorry. That was really a shitty thing to bring up."

"That's 'cause you're a shit," Sue said, beaning Laura in the head with a crouton. "Who knows? With heterosexual men you can never get around to liking them too much because they just want to screw you. Once they screw you, then they screw with you. So how can you ever really get to like them?"

"I'm sick of being married," Laura blurted, and then looked down at her plate. "I'm just a little tense."

"I'd guessed," Sue laughed.

"Sometimes I wish I wasn't... married that is... not tense. I know this sounds terrible, and I can't even stand myself for saying this, but sometimes I wish Cody wasn't even born. He's the best thing in my life, but if he wasn't there I could leave. Morris wouldn't care."

"Sure he would. You know he'd miss you if you were gone. You're just having a hard time right now," Sue tried to comfort her.

"No he wouldn't. Do you know what it feels like when your own husband doesn't want you? It's like when you go to the grocery store, and you're going to make something with canned tomatoes. But when you get to the shelf with the canned tomatoes, the only can left is all dented and bent. It doesn't matter that you really need those tomatoes. You're not going to buy that can. That's how you feel, like that can of tomatoes. Your husband doesn't want you. He wants other women, but he doesn't want you."

"Sweetheart, of course I know how it feels. After fourteen years of marriage Larry decided he was gay. I was tomatoes with botulism toxin in them. I was so bad I made him swear off tomatoes for life." Sue shrugged, "The truth is what it is, and sometimes it sucks, like Larry." She made a face.

"You'll find somebody else." Laura said quickly.

"I'm not going through that again. That's one thing I'm sure of. I'm always going to protect myself."

"With a gun or with a condom." Laura's attempt at a joke failed to get a response.

Sue shook her head. "With men, you're a lot less likely to get yourself hurt, and you tend to like them a lot better, if you keep them at a distance. So I have a rotating door policy. That's been my policy since the divorce. I have James for company. He's great to hang out when he's not being bitchy, so I just have to fill in the 'need for sex' thing. Doing it yourself is fine for a while, but eventually you'd like having somebody else there too."

"I'll give you my husband if you want. Then you can rotate his butt right out the door when you're done with him," Laura offered.

"No thanks, baby, you keep him. That's what I'm saying though. I don't want anybody to hang around. I have a great life. I've put up with a man making me feel like there was something wrong with me for sixteen years of my life, and I've come to the conclusion that I just don't need any more of that."

"So, explain the mechanics of the rotating door thing. How does it work?" Laura asked.

"It's simple. I want a man who will fuck me and then leave," Sue stated bluntly.

"For then, or for good? I mean, do you let them come back?" Laura asked.

"Of course for good, no I don't want them coming back," Sue said vehemently.

"Isn't that dangerous?" Laura was incredulous

"Well, that's why you actually do need the guns and the condoms," Sue laughed.

"You don't feel bad about it?"

"I like to think I'm performing a public service. I'm like a saint really. Saint Sue. Oriental patron saint of horny husbands whose wives are too tired, bored, or depressed to screw them."

Laura stuck her finger in her water and flicked it at Sue. "Shut up, I'm one of those wives."

A concerned look crossed Sue's face. "You're on antidepressants?"

"What are you talking about?" Laura asked.

"Prozac, Zoloft, Effexor, whatever. We're a depressed nation. All those depressed women get medicated and stop worrying about anything, including the fact that their husbands need sex."

"You're joking," Laura laughed.

"Not really," Sue said. "One of the side effects of the meds is that you lose your sex drive."

"Maybe that's what's happening to me; maybe Morris is spiking my coffee with Zoloft."

"Can't be. You're too depressed to be on Zoloft."

"Kiss my butt!" Laura spat. "How do you know so much?"

"Brushstrokes, Rocky, tiny sad little brushstrokes. I haven't seen a bold or happy movement in your paintings in over a year."

"I'm being exact, careful, precise...," Laura offered.

"Depressed, unhappy, repressed," Sue countered.

"You know, you can really be mean!" Laura said, smiling.

"You can call me mean if you want, but you know I'm right, and you know it's true. Auntie Sue knows just how to fix what's wrong with your pretty little butt. Before you go home, you'll love me for what I'm gonna do for you."

"What are you talking about <u>now</u>?" Laura asked.

"Look sweetie, if you could have a one-time affair with someone you were never going to see again, and no one could ever find out, would you?"

"No one could ever find out?" Laura asked, furrowing her brow doubtfully.

"Nope, no way, no how," Sue assured. "Now answer the question."

"I mean…I guess…I would," Laura answered hesitantly. Then a broad grin spread across her face.

"That's what I thought," Sue laughed. "Then you better get ready, because tonight, we're gonna make you a saint."

The two bottles of Chardonnay they shared during the afternoon helped Laura get past her inhibitions and accept the fact that Sue was serious about what she kept calling her "initiation." Sue had arranged to meet a man through a website called TimeDonors. The man, it turned out, was quite pleased when two women showed up instead of the one he was expecting. How pleased was obvious by the tent that formed in the front of his trousers. Sue reached down and ran her index finger along the undersurface of the tent. "Now don't blow a gasket, just yet," she'd said. "We'll get to that in just a few minutes…you know my friend here's an expert in gasket repair."

CHAPTER FOUR

Kent loved every one of the paintings Laura brought through the door. The first thing he did was to arrange them along the wall where a group of her previous paintings were hanging on display.

"My God, what happened to you?" Kent gushed. "Look at these brushstrokes. These are the best paintings you've ever done. Even the colors are brighter."

Laura blushed slightly, "Thanks, they're a little bit freer."

Kent raised his arms with a flourish. "A bit? A bit? Now there's an understatement. Look at that impasto, its wonderful, much thicker use of paint." He turned back to face her. "I already have these sold. I'm not kidding. I could sell them all to one collector, but I'll probably limit them to one painting each, just to build up a little tension. These four are already out the door. What sparked this? This is a big change."

"I talked with Sue Wong some when I was out in San Diego," Laura said. "She showed me that I've been a little constrained lately."

"Whatever she said, she was right," Kent offered. "These paintings are so full of vitality and life. Juicy is what I'd call them. If I didn't know better I'd think you were in love." He paused and raised his index finger to his lip. "Wait a minute, the paintings, the little blush, don't tell me you're leaving that boring husband of yours for that brilliant and delicious Sue Wong."

Laura shook her head.

"How is Morris? Is he still the angry young artist, fighting to revive the past, or has he adapted to being just a resentful carpenter?"

"Morris is going through a tough time." Laura defended her husband; she didn't know why.

"Well at least he isn't going on about painting with guns still, is he?" Kent asked.

Laura remembered the conversation from a reception they'd had at the gallery a few years ago. It was the only time Morris had come to one of them and he drank too much and decided to become the center of attention.

Kent had his arm around her shoulder and hugged her. "Now don't get all mopey about stupid boring Morris. Where do you want to go to celebrate?"

"I can't," she said as she crossed the room to Kent's telephone desk and picked up the phone book, thumbing through it. "I've got to pick up a few things." Jotting down a number and address, she turned and started toward the door. "I'll see you in two weeks."

"Be careful, you're becoming one of those dreadful 'soccer moms,' rushing everywhere. You need to take the time to stop and enjoy yourself. You know, take a breath…chat…relax. You just got out of the car," Kent warned, waving his hand in the air for emphasis.

"That could be because I am one of those dreadful 'soccer moms'," Laura said, feigning anger.

"My God, how can Cody be old enough to play soccer?" Kent exclaimed.

"That's how it is, they grow up too fast. One moment they're in diapers and the next, they're on a soccer team," Laura said with a tinge of sadness. "Not that I miss the diaper thing," she added quickly.

Kent kissed her cheek and followed her through the door, still talking as she got into the car. "More paintings, I need more of these wonderful paintings. Whatever's stirring you up, keep on doing it. Kiss Cody for me."

As she left, she looked back through the door at the paintings leaning against the wall and thought, "I guess that's what comes from stirring things up."

She drove west along Camelback, passing the ramp for 17 North, which is how she should have gone to go home, but she wasn't going home just yet. Kent had called the new paintings juicy. Juicy was how she felt, wet and juicy, but with butterflies in her stomach, a tremble in her hand, and so nervous that she felt like she had to pee about every thirty seconds. She was going to a motel to meet a man she knew nothing about, except that he wanted to have sex with her. It had been easier in California. She'd had the wine then. That helped. So did having Sue along to guide her.

The sound of a car horn brought Laura back to the present, and she looked up to see that the traffic light she was stopped at was turning from green to yellow. She pushed the accelerator and shot through the intersection. Elton John was singing about Mona Lisas and Mad Hatters as she pulled into the Shell station and stopped at the pay phone. As she got out of the car she sang a modified version of the song's hook, "She knows not if it's dark outside or light." How true, she thought, considering the modified lyrics, how true. She was in uncharted waters and she was tremendously apprehensive about what it was that she was going to do. Even if she was afraid, the one thing she was sure of was that she wasn't willing to stop herself.

It all seemed so foreign, dropping in coins, using pay phones. She knew she should put down the receiver, get into her car, and drive back to the interstate toward home. She dialed the motel's number. She'd looked it up in Kent's yellow pages before she left the gallery.

She swallowed hard when the motel operator answered and managed to ask for Mr. Butler's room.

When she was forwarded, she heard a man's voice answer, "Hello, Butler here."

"Hi, Mr. Butler, this is Scarlet. We talked…well, interfaced is a better word, on TimeDonors the other night."

"Well, I'm glad you decided to come, I wasn't sure you would." His voice had a Midwestern accent. "I'm in room 246. It's to the right as you come into the motel lot."

"I'll call you when I get to the parking lot…" Laura started.

"No electronics, remember? I left a card key under the passenger side windshield wiper on the car I'm driving. It's a maroon Taurus with Alamo plates at the bottom of the steps."

"Okay Rhett, I'll come up when I get there," she said.

She thought to herself, "Obviously you've done this before." The key thing was a great idea. She had to admit she was a little nervous about walking into the lobby to get the key.

"I can't wait. You sound very sweet," he replied breaking her reverie.

"Thanks," she said. "I'll be there in five minutes."

"Just use your key and come on in."

She hung up the receiver and regarded the scrap of paper with the hotel number in her fingers. It was just like the scraps of receipts and lunch checks with women's phone numbers on them that she found in Morris's jeans pockets on washdays. When she asked about them, they were always a skylight, or cabinet repair, or broken door. She carefully tore the phone number into five pieces and scattered it like confetti.

The flashing green lights of the electronic door lock signaled that this was, indeed, the right room. She turned the handle and slowly opened the door, not knowing whether to expect a Clark Gable with a martini or a drooling maniac. As she peered in, she made sure she had an open escape route just in case it turned out to be the latter. The room lights were off; only the bathroom light was on. Visible in the light from the bathroom was a man in the bed with covers pulled up to the middle of his chest. He was wearing a white tee shirt.

"Mr. Butler?" she asked.

He nodded, "And you must be Scarlet, I hope."

"I know I said time was a factor, but we don't have to hurry <u>so</u> much," she said, smiling as she entered the room. She let the door close behind her. It took a moment for her eyes to adjust after coming into the dimly lit room from a bright Arizona afternoon. As she crossed the room, she could feel his eyes on her, even without being able to see yet. Reaching the bedside, she studied his face. He returned her gaze, his eyes reflecting the same searching curiosity she felt. He was Caucasian, a very pale Caucasian with sandy blond hair, about 45-50 years old and somewhat overweight. An average guy, someone you see every day at the supermarket, the mall, or the PTA. No Clark Gable, but not obviously a drooling maniac either.

"You're beautiful, I mean really beautiful," he said in a low voice filled with conviction.

"Thanks, it's nice to have you notice." She sat on his side of the bed facing him. He slid over slightly to accommodate her.

"You're not from Phoenix are you?" she asked.

"No, I'm from Muncie, in Indiana." He was nervous and the words came in small rushes. "I travel a lot, for work I mean. I guess you're from here in Phoenix?" She nodded, offering no further explanation. "I see you're married," he said looking at her left hand. "Unhappily I take it."

"You take it correctly, and you?" she replied.

"The same," he said. "Unhappily enough to try TimeDonors, but not quite unhappy enough to leave I guess."

She rested her hand on the rounded bulge of his belly and felt it recoil suddenly under her hand. Then, she understood. He was already in bed because he was self-conscious. The extra weight, she thought. He was probably anxious about her watching him undress. She, on the other hand, had no such inhibitions. Suddenly, the thought of undressing slowly in front of this man, a man she didn't know, had never seen before, and would never see again, began to make her very excited.

"Will it make you nervous to watch me undress?" she asked.

"No...I mean...yes, no's what I mean...I mean I'd really like that...." he babbled

Laura reached over and put her finger to his lips. "Shhh," she said, "Let's not talk. You just lay there and watch." She turned on the radio of the bedside alarm clock and adjusted the tuner until she found a song that made her want to move. Then she stood, and took two steps back from the bed into the shaft of light from the bathroom. She slipped her feet out of her sandals and as she did, her hands moved to her hair. She untied it and let it fall free. Her hands dropped to the top button of her blouse. She undid each button one by one, swaying slowly from side to side as she did, watching his face intently as it registered his own mounting excitement. She was encouraged by the increasing bulge in the covers at what she estimated was crotch level. When she reached her jeans she continued her performance, making a show of the snap and zipper. With the final buttons of her blouse now undone, she shrugged it off her shoulders and let it fall. She turned sideways to the light showing her profile and, leaning forward, pulled the jeans down. Stepping out of them, she turned and walked back toward the bed, very aware of the growing wetness just beneath her Victoria Secret panties. She turned her back to him at the bedside. "Unhook me," she said hoarsely. When he did, she straightened her arm toward the floor, letting her brassiere fall. She wanted to tease him. She knew how badly he wanted to see her breasts, so she turned slowly, by degrees, drawing out the tension of the moment. First her head, eyes locking on his already flushed face, then slowly one breast came into his view. His eyes locked onto it as it eclipsed its twin, then the twin, in profile. Now his eyes darted between them. Too many choices, she thought, and raised her right hand to caress her right nipple. As she did, her left hand cupped the back of his head, pulling him forward, and his eager mouth went to work quickly on the left.

The shower had good water pressure and stung slightly as it hit her shoulders. She glanced at her watch. It was 3:10. She would dress quickly. She had gathered her clothing on her way into the bathroom. She would run the brush she kept in her purse through her hair and be gone by 3:20. With a little luck, she would be in Sedona to pick up Cody by 5:00. She'd have time to stop at Ralph's and pick up a salad and rotisserie chicken at the deli counter for herself and Morris. While she was there she would get some macaroni and cheese for Cody. He loved the deli's macaroni with tater tots.

As she crossed the bedroom on her way to the door, she glanced at the recumbent form of the man who called himself Rhett Butler, apparently asleep. "Men," she thought, "they're all the same." But an afterthought teased her, "just different enough to be interesting."

As she walked down the steps, she reached into her purse for her car keys and was startled to see the key to the room still there in the bottom of her purse. That was the kind of mistake she couldn't afford. She discarded it quickly into the trashcan at the bottom of the stairs and headed to her car and home, already back in "mommy mode."

CHAPTER FIVE

Willie Weeks didn't like it much but he was still the new kid on the block in the Homicide Division, still just trying to learn his way around, and having his share of trouble doing it. He'd changed assignments out of burglary a month ago. Homicide was the big time, and he'd wanted a shot at it to see what he could do. He'd put in his paperwork more than a year ago and it took that long to come through. It seemed like a good idea in theory, but at forty-six years old he was a little too old to have to play the FNG again.

FNG stood for, "fucking new guy." It was a term everyone in the Army knew. Soldiers were just like cops. They gave everything an abbreviation. The FNG was the guy that was always just "this much" out of step with of all of the other guys on the team. It was because they didn't know the routines. They didn't know the rhythm of the group. Rhythm was essential for success in any operation. Weeks had learned that lesson from spending sixteen years as a member of a Special Forces unit. That was where he'd learned how teams worked. It wasn't because everybody liked each other. It was because they'd all faced the same challenges together and had been forced by need to come up with some way to get things done together. The respect gained working together like that, over time, created the rhythm of the unit. That was what kept a team running like the Army's proverbial "well oiled machine." The FNG was the sand in the oil can, the one that moved too soon, or too late, and got himself or somebody else killed. Willie was having to learn that all over again.

Willie's early life had been a recruiting poster for the Army. A greaser kid from a tough neighborhood, he got in a little trouble in high school and had gone into the Army at seventeen to get out of an assault charge. Sure he'd hated boot camp, just like everybody else, but something about it changed him. He got a new found sense of place, a sense of belonging to something more important than a street gang.

It had all gone too fast though, he'd earned his green beret by twenty and been discharged on medical disability by thirty-five. It seemed like, in the blink of an eye, sixteen years were gone. He'd barely had time to see them go by. When it was over, all he'd accomplished was one tour of duty in Iraq and a tour of duty as a husband that had to be considered a couple of months shorter than the time he'd been gone, no matter what the paperwork said.

Being deployed to Iraq had come at a bad time for Weeks. He'd just gotten married when the orders came through. He wasn't too happy about the timing, but they didn't ask him. He was a soldier. When an assignment came, he went. He was at the height of his abilities. He'd spent his whole career up to that point getting ready to fight and never gotten to get in one. Nobody knew if there was going to be one or not, but everybody thought there might. Saddam was threatening the oil supply, and the Army thought it would be a good idea to have somebody go take a look and keep an eye on what was going on over there.

There was no big send off, just a flight into Kuwait City in the middle of the night. They were all out of the city, en route to infiltrate their assigned objectives, in three days. But the fight he'd gotten sent to wasn't exactly what he'd expected.

Instead of doing any of the things they'd been trained for, the team was split up, with each member going to an assigned location. He'd spent months in the desert in a hole in the sand with a sheet of plywood for a roof and more sand on top of that, so he looked like any other pile of sand in the desert. His position was on a hillside overlooking an airfield with a bunch of Russian surplus airplanes that just sat there. Nobody ever flew them, at least not while he was there. But he'd stayed right there and counted them day after day just in case. He'd stayed and stayed, fighting sand fleas and boredom, waiting to see if any other planes showed up, maybe from some neighbor who wanted to help Saddam. But none ever did. So Weeks just sat in the hole all day, living on MREs, only able to move at night if he needed to resupply. Their mission was to lay the groundwork, preparing for Operation Desert Storm.

When the war finally came it was over before he knew it. He never fired a shot. He'd guided in a bombing raid and a cruise missile attack. There were lot's of big explosions in the valley his little hillside overlooked. The planes he'd watched for so many days were reduced to smoking rubble. The airfield ended up looking like the surface of the moon, it was so full of craters. Before he ever got a chance to climb out of his hole the war was over. By the time the pick-up chopper pulled him out Saddam had surrendered. He'd fought the whole war with a range finder and a pair of binoculars. Some hero.

As quickly as the war seemed to pass for him, it was apparently quite a bit longer for his new wife, Denise. By the time he got home, after eleven months in the field, his marriage was over. Denise was three months pregnant with her new boyfriend's child, and Willie, after the initial fury cooled, just didn't care enough to fight about it.

They didn't have any kids and, after spending that many months in the desert, he didn't really feel like he needed anything that didn't fit in a backpack anymore. He tossed his clothes and gear into the toolbox in the back of his 1987 Dodge pickup, cracked the top off a new bottle of tequila, tossed the lid over his shoulder on his way out the door, and muttered his good-bye to Denise. "Adios mamacita," is what came out. What he meant was, "fuck off and die," but he was being polite for the sake of the kid. Who knows why, he didn't think the kid could hear him. It was just that his mom had always emphasized the importance of being careful of how you treated pregnant women, so he had.

As he left, he saw Denise's boyfriend sitting in his car halfway down the street. After the direction their initial discussions had gone, Weeks was pretty sure he knew why he wasn't interested in getting all that much closer, but he was over all of that now. He didn't have any interest in doing anything to the guy any more. Life would pay him back, sure enough. The poor dumbass had no idea the hell she was going to put him through. All Weeks wanted was to get out with what little dignity he had left.

He didn't know what he was thinking. Maybe he wanted some kind of movie ending or something. He turned so Denise could see his silhouette, tipped up the bottle, and then jumped into his truck and drove off into the night. He chuckled, remembering.

It would have turned out a lot more macho-romantic if that had been the end of it. It would have been, if he'd checked to see that the toolbox lid was latched before he drove off, but that would have spoiled the effect. Instead, as he sped off the toolbox lid popped open, and he drove away trailing socks and underwear behind him. Half of what he owned flew out on the road before he was out of sight. When he turned the corner and was sure Denise couldn't see him anymore, he stopped and closed the lid. He picked up some of the stuff near the truck, cursing himself for being an idiot, but he sure as hell wasn't going to walk back around that corner for any of the rest of it.

He'd left the Army in August of 2001. A bad wind on a training jump carried him into a rock outcropping on a mountain in North Carolina, leaving him with a concussion, a punctured lung, and his right leg broken in eight places. That was the end of his parachute qualifications. Instead of fighting to stay in and riding a desk to twenty, he took the medical retirement the Army was pushing on him. Then he called his uncle Lorenzo, who was a state senator, and he was able to pull a few strings to get him past the physical and into the academy for the Phoenix Police Department.

At fifty-six he'd have two pensions instead of one. Then he could do whatever he wanted, and the police pension would come with its own health insurance. That meant that he'd never have to end up being just another old vet dumped in the VA, spending the rest of his life filling out forms in triplicate just to take a leak.

So, as soon as he took off one uniform, he put on another. He served a few years on the street, riding in a patrol car. When he passed the detective's exam they put him into Burglary. It had been good there, and he'd done a good job for them, but he wanted something more so he'd asked to transfer to Homicide.

Things started out okay. The first murder case he rode on was an easy one. It was a drunken husband who shot his wife. The guy was pathetic. He handed Weeks a rusty double-barrel shotgun when they walked through the door. "Here, here, take it, don't shoot man. It was an accident."

"What kind of accident?" his partner, McBride, snorted at the old man. "The neighbor who called 9-1-1 said you two'd been screaming at each other for an hour before they heard the gun go off."

"Yeah, we were fighting. We always fight. I just got the gun out so she'd shut up," the man explained.

"She didn't shut up, so you shot her?" McBride only half-asked.

"No, it wasn't like that. See, I was just holding it. Then she got really mad and grabbed the gun by the barrels and pulled it toward her. Trying to get it away. I thought she was going to shoot me if she got it, so I tried to hold on. I don't know how it happened; the gun just went off by accident."

The splash pattern disagreed. The wife was face down on the floor. Blood and brains were splattered across the floor and wall in front of her and had stained the front of her clothes where she'd fallen forward onto them.

"It's pretty hard to shoot yourself in the back of the head by grabbing a shotgun unless you're double-jointed or something. Even then, you have to wonder how she'd know where the gun was to grab it. You want to try the truth this time?" Weeks asked.

The old man shrugged. "You don't know what it's like man. She's mean. When I say mean, I mean really mean. I had to sneak up behind her. Otherwise who knows what she would have done. I had to shoot her before she knew I was there. I put up with that shit for twenty years. It was self-defense…one of us had to go."

"Why didn't you just divorce her instead of using this thing to take the top of her head off?" Weeks had asked, motioning with the shotgun.

"I'm Catholic, man," the guy said holding up his hands.

"What in the hell does that have to do with shooting your wife in the back of the head?" McBride half-shouted.

"We don't believe in divorce or suicide," the man explained.

He didn't see where he'd had any other choice in the matter, as far as that went. The investigation was pure paperwork and forensics. It didn't take a lot of detective work.

The second case though that was a different story. The second case Weeks was assigned to was a gang-related drive-by.

"It's see one, do one, teach one around here. This one's yours all the way," McBride had explained.

McBride was on the slide. He was on his way out, and he saw his new partner as a way to avoid any more work than he absolutely had to do.

Weeks knew that everybody was going to be watching to see how he handled this case. He had one chance to make a good first impression, so he'd jumped right in and pushed hard, spending time in the neighborhood to try and find out what had really happened.

He figured something was up when he got the call that Captain Bryant wanted to talk to him. He knew that couldn't be a good thing. The Captain hadn't said shit to him since he'd checked into the division and that was the way Weeks would have preferred it to stay for as long as possible.

It wasn't possible any more. Weeks knocked on the door frame and stuck his head around it, since the door was open. "You wanted to see me?"

The captain was a big guy. Rumor had it that he'd been a lineman for Arizona State once upon a time. Now he was carrying way too much weight and had a red face that looked like he was always about to have a stroke at any minute. Maybe his red face was more noticeable because he had a head full of curly white hair. Right now it looked like a neon sign.

Bryant raised tired looking eyes. "Yeah, Weeks. Come on in here. I got a couple of things to go over. I'm a straight shooter, so let's cut the bull and get straight to the facts. See this?" He held up a Phoenix Police Department personnel file. On the front was stamped PC in large red letters. "Do you know what these letters mean?"

"No idea, Cap," Weeks answered.

"It means politically connected," Bryant explained, tapping the front of the jacket for emphasis. "This is your file, and what I need to know is who do you know that I have to worry about?"

"Really, it's nothing. My uncle's a state senator. His name is Sanchez. He just suggested I apply to the PPD when I retired from the Army," Weeks answered.

"Senator Sanchez, the head of the appropriations committee?" Bryant said unbelievingly.

Weeks nodded yes. Bryant threw the jacket down on his desk and leaned back heavily, his chair groaning under his weight. He pinched the bridge of his nose and took in a deep breath. Weeks wouldn't have believed it was possible, but his boss's face seemed to be two or three shades redder than it had when he'd walked in the room.

"Nothing. Just Senator Sanchez, the head of the fucking appropriations committee. Just the guy who fights to keep the rest of those bastards in the legislature from cutting our funding every year. Year in and year out. Just enough for the chief to crawl all over my ass if I manage to piss your uncle off. What great FUCKING LUCK," Bryant exploded, pounding his fist on his desk. "Look Weeks, I know you were a green beret and all that shit in the Army. I know you did a good job in burglary, but this is homicide. There's no room for you to screw stuff up."

Weeks didn't really know what to say. "I know that Cap," he started.

Bryant cut him off, "Look, I know McBride's a dick. He's just coasting until he can retire. I know he wasn't doing much to teach you, but you can't go around like you did on that dead gang banger, Assa."

"Captain, everything points at Munoz. The two of them hated each other before Assa took his girl," Weeks said. "McBride wasn't even trying. Besides nobody in that neighborhood was going to tell McBride anything."

"And they were all just happy as hell to talk to you?" Bryant asked.

"I don't know why McBride's so pissed. I didn't ask him to do shit, I just got to find the kid now," Weeks replied angrily.

"That shouldn't be too hard." Bryant offered.

"Why's that?"

"Well, one reason's because they just found Munoz with twenty-three holes in him, bleeding all over the sidewalk in front of his mother's house."

Weeks felt like he'd been punched in the gut. "Chinga me, you know it was Assa's posse, getting even. Let me work this. I can get these little bastards."

"Not only no, but hell no!" Bryant said, his voice hard, "You're off the case. You can't ask the kind of questions you did. You're the one that pointed the finger that got the Munoz kid killed."

"He killed Assa," Weeks argued.

"You don't fucking know that, detective. You're neither judge nor jury, and it sure isn't your job to be the arbiter of some kind of street justice. For all you know, you just got an innocent boy killed. Munoz was only sixteen. Do you know how that would look to the press, if it got out?" Bryant hollered.

Weeks felt pretty bad about the whole thing at first, but in a strange way what had happened did make sense. He knew that wasn't what Bryant wanted to hear. "Like shit," he offered.

"Like shit on a stick," Bryant agreed. "I need to put you with somebody who can teach you something. You're done with McBride. I'm putting you with Kinney."

"Shit. Please Cap, not Kinney. He's the most pompous, arrogant, preppy...." Weeks started to argue.

Bryant didn't even let him get started. He got up out of his chair and moved around to sit on the front edge of his desk, then leaned forward into Weeks's face. He suddenly seemed a lot bigger than he had behind the desk. Standing between the two chairs, Weeks had nowhere to move.

"I'm sure he's thrilled to be getting you, too. I want you to listen to me. I don't want any trouble out of you, the chief, or your uncle. So I have to pair you with someone who can teach you something, someone who can keep you from doing anything stupid that's going to end up killing anybody else. Ben Kinney is the sharpest cop I've got. I know he's younger than you, and I know you aren't in any hurry to start learning from a kid, but you had better start learning from somebody. So, until I say otherwise, you do what Ben says, and I mean you don't take a shit, unless he says shit. Got it?"

"Yes sir," Weeks said, knowing better than to try to object.

"You better. If you don't, I'm going to take this folder," he waved the file in Weeks's face to make his point, "and I'm going to take it to the chief myself and ask him to sort things out. You'll be lucky to end up a meter maid on the graveyard shift." Bryant slammed the file down onto his desk. "Now sit your ass down." Bryant walked to the door and leaned out into the hallway. "Johnson, send Ben in here," he ordered a passing detective, then returned to sit behind his desk. He looked at a hand-written note as he waited. Weeks just sat there uncomfortably.

"You wanted me?" Ben Kinney asked as he stuck his head through the door.

"Ben, come on in here a minute. I've got a new case for you. Go ahead and sit by Weeks," he gestured with his arm towards the empty chair. Kinney sat down stiffly, looking at Weeks like he had just stepped in something. "Ben, I want you to work with Weeks here on this case."

"Sure thing captain, but what about Wilson?" Kinney asked.

"I'm partnering Wilson with McBride for now. I have a dead tourist at the LaQuinta on Camelback," Bryant said, glancing at the note he still held in his hand. "There are two black and whites there already, and the beat cops have already called in a forensic tech from the Medical Examiner's Office. The preliminary is that a maid goes in to clean up the room and finds its occupant face down on the floor, naked, blood everywhere. I want you two to get down there and sort out what's what."

"Sure thing," Kinney said and then turned to Weeks. "We can take my unit, since you were riding with McBride. I'll meet you in the garage in a few minutes."

"Sure thing," Weeks said looking at the captain to judge his response before he got up and left the office.

Bryant nodded towards the door, so he didn't really have much choice.

When Weeks was out of earshot, Kinney turned back to Bryant. "Captain, you can't really partner me with him, and for God's sake not on a real case. Everybody knows what happened with that banger."

"What part of what I just said did you not understand, Ben?" Bryant asked, anger boiling just beneath the surface.

"It's not that. It's just that I don't want my reputation hurt by some commando asshole," Ben replied, unaware that he had pushed too far.

"Then you had better do this right, hadn't you?"

Ben pointed at Weeks file still sitting on top of the desk. "Everybody in the department knows he's just here because he's got some kind of family pull in the Hispanic community."

Bryant picked up the folder, "Look Ben, you're from a family in Washington that has more connections than a beltway hooker. You and Weeks aren't that different. You just got a few breaks early on. You went to college at Georgetown. Weeks went into the Army. Weeks's age is working against him here. He isn't getting the kind of help you got starting out. He doesn't look like a fresh-faced kid that needs a break, so nobody, including you, gives him one. I talked to Captain Connor, his old boss in burglary. Connor says Willie's a good, smart cop. He's someone with the potential to be a big asset, if we can show him how to do things right. Do me a favor, show the man what you can, OK?"

"Yes sir," Kinney said, and turned, heading to collect the excess baggage waiting for him in the garage downstairs.

Watching Kinney's retreating back, Bryant massaged his temples, and reached into his top desk drawer for his blood pressure medicine.

CHAPTER SIX

As he opened the driver's door of the unmarked Crown Victoria, Kinney faced Weeks across the car's roof. "I'm not any happier with this than you are, but let's get the rules straight, right from the start. For now, I'm in charge. Don't do or say anything until we talk about it. All right?"

"Sure thing, junior," Weeks snarled.

"Don't start off fucking with me, Weeks, and don't even think about trying to go around me with the Hispanics, like you did McBride. I know Spanish," Kinney came back, matching Week's venom.

"Well that's gonna make things easier. I won't have to bother with English then," Weeks said sarcastically.

"Look, everybody already knows about what a great job you did for Mac," Kinney replied threateningly. "I don't want you doing or saying anything that's going to flush my career down the toilet. It didn't matter for Mac. He's done in six months, but I'd like to get somewhere. I don't want to be a detective the rest of my life."

Weeks's face tensed, and the muscles of his jaws clenched. "Everybody knows your story too, kid. Highbrow Washington family, you had it all, the doctor slapped your ass and stuck a silver spoon in your mouth the day you were born. You were a golden boy, good grades at Georgetown, headed for Law school. But you choked on the admission test …three times. So its good-bye law school, hello police academy. So, if your life doesn't turn out like you want, it's your own damned fault, not anything that has anything to do with me."

Weeks slammed the door and sat dead still, facing foreword. Kinney got in behind the wheel fuming, but just as determined not to talk. Kinney slapped the shift lever down, only to have the engine rev wildly while the car sat motionless. He shot an "eat shit" look at Weeks, who only barely let a smile turn up the corners of his lips.

Infuriated, Kinney reached abruptly for the shifter, knocking it down into drive, jolting the car forward until the bumper met cinder block.

"Don't say a fucking word!" Kinney hissed through clenched teeth.

"At least I can see why you're driving," Weeks smiled. "You need the practice...try to remember R means reverse, not rev."

Kinney's face may have, at one point, gotten even redder than the captain's had earlier. His ears looked like they were on fire. That's about all Weeks could see, because his new partner was just sitting there staring out through the front windshield. Weeks hoped he'd calm down enough to look in the rear view mirror before he found reverse. Weeks figured that he'd said about enough for now, so for the next few minutes the two of them just sat there. Weeks didn't mind screwing with Ben but he was pretty sure he didn't want to end up in a gunfight inside of a police car in the precinct parking garage. That wouldn't do either one of them a whole lot of good.

When he got finally did get the car into gear, Kinney accelerated too hard and squealed out of the lot. From there on, he drove staring intently through the windshield, apparently trying to pretend that Weeks wasn't there. The stony silence didn't bother Weeks. He needed to digest all of this a little anyway and try to figure out where he was.

Maybe he would just let this case be a fork in the road for him. If he was able to pull it together on this case, he'd stay with homicide. If not he was going to have to try and switch to anti-terrorism or something. Maybe he'd just go back to Burglary. One thing he was sure of was that if he was going to spend all of his time for the next couple of years being Kinney's flunky, he was gone as soon as possible. It didn't matter where he had to go.

Anti-terrorism still had a lot of money being put into it, and it was probably a better fit for him, anyway. He'd tried to go into it when he came out of the police academy. Every day somebody was plotting some bullshit or another, and it was only a matter of time before it spilled across the southern border with the illegals. A coyote could smuggle a terrorist cell just as easily as he could hustle a family of Mexicans across the border, and that would put the fight right in his own back yard. Not in New York or Washington, but right here in Arizona.

New York or not, September 11, 2001 had been a wake-up call. The attack on America had been hard for him, just like it had for anybody who had ever worn a uniform. It didn't matter if it was a cop, a fireman, a paramedic, or a soldier. The country they'd sworn to protect had been attacked, and he couldn't really let that go. He'd wanted to do something. When it had first happened, he'd called his old unit at Fort Bragg. The new commanding officer was a kid he'd known as a First Lieutenant back when he was OIC of a team. The kid, who was a major now, had broken the news to him gently that it wasn't going to happen, saying, "Weeks, if we need a fat, old, crippled guy who can't run or jump, you'll be the first one we call." That had depressed the hell out of him. He'd spent his war hiding in a box buried in the sand, and then when his country needed him he was too old and broken up to help.

He'd even tried to go and help out as a volunteer, but the Phoenix P.D. needed cops on the street. Some of the guys had been sent to help out in New York, but they weren't going to send a guy just out of the academy, even if he had been in the Special Forces. The guys who went all had some expertise, dog handlers, search and rescue, explosive ordnance disposal, and Willie didn't fit the needs as the brass saw them, so Willie stayed home and did his job here.

Maybe it had been a mistake to ask to move over to homicide in the first place. He'd done a good job up to now. He had a good case clearance rate. In any other division as long as he kept a respectable clearance rate he was golden. Nobody expected anybody to find everything, so if he lost once in a while, so what? These guys didn't play that way.

Weeks figured he'd better pull his shit together. Pissing off Ben wasn't going to do him a bit of good. After getting his last suspect bumped, Captain Bryant wouldn't be too happy with anything but hard work and cooperation. He figured he'd gotten the only break he was going to get. If he kept acting like a dick, it could be he wouldn't have a choice about leaving, and then there'd be no telling where he ended up. Probably, like Bryant said, as a meter maid working the night shift downtown. He better turn down the volume on being an asshole, at least for the time being.

The big, dark blue Ford rolled into the parking lot of the La Quinta Motel. Weeks could already see the yellow crime-scene tape at the door of an upstairs room, to the right of the entrance. There were two uniformed cops leaning on the rail outside the door. Looking around he spotted two more, taking statements near the entrance of the lobby. He wanted to be sure to find out who they were. He didn't want to miss something that might be important because he didn't listen to the cops on the scene.

As he entered the motel room, the first thing Weeks saw was a crime scene photographer snapping pictures and a broad back with a Phoenix Cardinals football jersey with the number 78 stretched across it. The man wearing the jersey was hunched over the torso of an obviously deceased white male.

"Hey Ruiz, what you got?" Kinney asked.

"Looks like a dead guy to me, detective," the man responded without looking up.

"No shit. No wonder you're such a good forensic tech man. You're a fuckin' genius," Weeks said.

Kinney shot Weeks a dirty look. Mole` had finally looked up and caught the look of consternation in the younger detective's glance.

"Don't sweat it Little Ben. Dance King and I are old friends, and he's new, so I'm gonna give him a break about trying to walk on my crime scene without any shoe covers on. Both of you go back out and try not to make my job any harder by tracking in extra shit for me to have to go through as evidence," Mole` said, standing up. At six feet, six inches tall and three hundred and twenty pounds, he dwarfed Weeks by comparison.

"Sorry, bro. Thanks," Weeks said sheepishly, turning back toward the door, where he saw Kinney was already slipping a white surgical shoe cover over an expensive loafer.

Ben looked at Weeks and ordered, "Gloves too," as if he himself hadn't just been busted for screwing up.

"I promised mamacita I'd look after you," Mole` said. The big man's real name was Gustavo Ruiz, but he had nicknamed himself Mole` after the sauce made of a mixture of chocolate and chili. As he told anyone who'd listen, "it's because the ladies think I'm so hot but sooo sweet." Hearing him talk, most people thought the big man was a real player. Weeks knew better. Mole` was a good Catholic boy who'd moved back home to take care of his mother after an automobile accident had killed his father and left her with a complete paralysis of her left arm. Mole` sat with his mother at Mass every Sunday. In fact, they met at church. Father Joe had introduced the two policemen.

Weeks should have known to look out. Everything the priest did, he did with what he called a higher purpose. Weeks called it an ulterior motive.   Father Joe loved sports, and he loved helping kids. Only Father Joe could have come up with an outreach program for poor kids that involved fifteen sets of season tickets for every professional baseball, football and basketball game in the city.

It was part of the priest's "big brothers" program. The two unmarried policemen fit perfectly into the plan. They were strong role models without any valid excuse not to help. So, it wasn't long before they found themselves taking underprivileged Hispanic kids to Diamondbacks', Suns', and Cardinals' games, along with Father Joe.

Father Joe always joked that Phoenix had two of the perfect sports teams for a Catholic, "the Sons, get it boys, sons with an 'o,' and, of course, my next job 'the cardinals'." "What about the Diamondbacks?" one of the boys asked once. Without a pause the priest answered, "We must always be there to keep a sharp eye on serpents, in case Satan tries to show up as one of them again."

For the last two years Weeks had stopped on the way to whatever ballpark they were going to and picked up Mole` before they met Father Joe and the kids.  Each time, before they left the house, Mole` would make sure that his mother was settled and had everything she might need while they were gone. Every time, Señora Ruiz would tell Mole`, "Watch out for Willie and the children, and you listen to Father Joe," and every time Mole` would answer, "Yes mamacita, we'll be back soon."

"So, why do you call him Dance King?" Kinney asked Mole`.

Ruiz smiled, "I had to give him a new name. Who ever heard of a Chicano named Willy Weeks?"

"My mother's Hispanic, not my father," Weeks directed his explanation toward his new partner and shot a withering gaze at his friend.

Mole` continued, totally unfazed, "When he's born, his dad names him before his mama even wakes up from the anesthesia. She wakes up and there's 'William' on the birth certificate."

"I still don't see what any of that has to do with 'Dance King'," Kinney persisted.

"W-W," Mole` explained, as if that alone were enough. When Kinney obviously still failed to grasp what he was getting at, he finally spit it out. "W. W., the Chicano Dance King, you know like the movie?"

"I don't have any clue what you're talking about, but I'm going to leave you two to talk about it." He turned toward Weeks. "You stay here and write down everything your large friend says. I'm going to talk to the uniforms and check the security cameras."

When Kinney was safely out of the door, Mole` looked at Weeks and raised his eyebrows. "What in the hell are you doing partnered with Little Ben?"

Weeks shook his head. "It's a long story. I asked too many questions and a kid got whacked in a drive-by. Bryant was so happy we didn't have to bother the D.A.'s office that he gave me Little Ben as a reward."

"Couldn't you just have asked him to take one of your cajones or something? You'd a still had one left," Mole` said.

"Just about anything would be less painful than having to put up with that prick, but forget about Ben. I need you to keep me out of trouble, kinda make me look good." Weeks said, looking at his friend, who returned a barely perceptible nod, indicating his agreement.

"So, what have we got here? The evidence is what's gonna keep you out of trouble. Stick with that, and you'll be okay," Mole` instructed.

"All right, what do you know so far?" Weeks questioned him.

"So far, the dead guy here is named Harold Butler, and he's from Muncie, Indiana. He's forty-six years old, and he's married," Mole` recited.

"Shit, man, I'm impressed. You already made all that?" Weeks said incredulously.

"Don't be. I knew all that just from looking at the bedside table. His driver's license was in his wallet, which was sittin' there with $1,200 in it. So were his watch, wedding ring, and two entry keys for the room."

"I guess robbery's out," Weeks stated flatly.

"Looks like it. Anyway, he's taken a shower and he's coming out of the shower when somebody must have stepped out of this closet and clobbered him in the back of the head." At this point he indicated a laceration on the right occipital region of the victim's scalp.

"Damn, he bled like a stuck pig," Weeks exclaimed, looking down at the halo of blood spread out on the motel carpet.

"Scalp wounds always do," Mole confirmed.

"But that didn't kill him did it?" Weeks asked. "This did," he said pointing to four or five small purplish holes in each flank.

"See, you're not as much of a screw up as everybody says. That was a pretty good pick-up for a burglary cop," Mole` said, smiling slightly, then quickly turned back to the job at hand. "I really won't know until the autopsy, but I think you're right."

"It looks like a sentry take-out," Weeks offered.

"So now you're gonna start teaching me my job?" Mole` asked with mock consternation. "Go on professor. What, pray tell, is a sentry take-out?"

"The sentry take-out gets taught to just about every Special Forces operative. Knife into the kidney, jerk back and forth vigorously, lacerate the kidney, cut the renal artery, and the victim bleeds to death internally. They call it a sentry take-out because it's so painful, the victim can't even holler. It lets you take 'em out and get into a camp without waking the whole camp up," Weeks instructed.

"This wasn't a knife," Mole` said authoritatively.

"What, maybe an ice pick?" Weeks asked.

"I don't think so, Dance King. The diameter's too big. See the little edges, the nicks on each side of the puncture? It looks like a mouth. I think a small flat bladed screwdriver."

"Oh shit, that would hurt," Weeks said emphatically.

"Lucky for him, I think he was still unconscious from getting hit in the head. It doesn't look like he thrashed around too much. He just laid there and bled to death."

"But that doesn't make any sense," Weeks said, rubbing his chin.

"Why use a technique that's supposed to keep somebody quiet if they're already unconscious?" Mole` completed his thought.

"I thought you were gonna tell me," Weeks replied.

"That's why you're the detective. My job is how, your job is who and why. So, I guess that's something you're going to have to figure out on your own. But remember what I told you. Stick with the evidence," Mole` warned.

An hour later, Ben returned holding two VHS tapes, "Well here's what we have so far. <u>Not Jack Shit!</u> Nobody saw or heard anything. The guy arrives from Indiana yesterday, rents an Alamo Taurus, drives here, checks in at 1:00 p.m., and gets two keys...."

"They're both right there," Mole` offered, pointing at the bedside table.

"So I guess he kept both of them. Anyway, he gets a phone call about 1:20, makes several calls to area gas distributors around 3:30 p.m., and he's found dead by the maid the next morning."

"Did you call all the numbers?" Weeks asked.

"Gosh, I didn't think of that," Ben said sarcastically, "but you can get on that first thing when we get back to the office."

"What about the maid?" Mole` wondered.

"I talked to her," Ben replied. "Name's Ramon. Doesn't speak much English, but as far as I can tell she doesn't know anything. She walked in, saw a body, ran out, and called 911."

"Let me go talk to her. Maybe she'll remember something," Weeks offered, knowing that if Ben talked to her in the mood he was in, he got very little, if any, information. As soon as any Latina got a look at Ben in his Brooks Brothers with his fifty-dollar haircut and pissed-off attitude, she wasn't going to be able to speak a word of English.

"Suit yourself," Ben said. "Here are these numbers. I'm going back to the office to look at the videotapes from the security cameras and see what I can find. Whoever did this should be on it."

"Okay Ben, I'll stay here." He turned toward Mole`. "Are you gonna be here a while?"

"About an hour. I have to bag his hands and finish the trace collection," Mole` answered.

"Can you give me a ride back?" Weeks asked.

Mole` smiled. "This will be your first time riding in the deadmobile."

"You boys have fun." Kinney said sarcastically and started out, but stopped just outside the doorway to pull his shoe covers off. He looked behind him, frowned, and came back through the doorway. He leaned over and whispered harshly to Weeks. "I'm warning you, don't go and do anything without talking to me. Just stay here with Ruiz, write down whatever he finds, and come back to the station. You got that?"

"What if I gotta take a piss? Do I have to call you for that?" Weeks growled.

"Nah, you can ask Ruiz. He won't let you piss on the evidence," Kinney said, turning and walking out of the room.

"Yeah, well I'd rather piss on you," Weeks said to the empty doorway, his voice raising to be sure his new partner didn't miss the insult.

With Ben's departure, Weeks felt the tension level drop by half. "I'm going to have to kill him eventually," Weeks said, pointing toward the door Little Ben had just gone through.

"Well, do it somewhere outside the city limits so I don't have to work the case," Mole` suggested.

"I'll keep that in mind when I finally snap," Weeks said with a frown to indicate that his snapping point may not be all that far away. "I'm going to try and catch the maid before she gets off. You think she really can't speak English?"

"Hell, around Little Ben, I can barely speak any English," Mole` laughed.

"That's okay, he knows Spanish," Weeks said, making quotation marks with his fingers when he said "knows Spanish."

Weeks made his way to the motel office. On the way, he stopped to check out the motel security cameras. There were two fixed cameras; one at the drive-in/check-in area and another behind the desk, to record the faces of anyone approaching the desk. There were also cameras on the pool and at the exits on the main building. Nothing on the lot entrance or the parking lots in front of the individual units. He didn't think Ben was going to find much on the security tapes. No one at the desk remembered seeing anyone, so they probably never entered the lobby or office area. Without a view of the parking lot in front of room 246 or the entrance of room 246 itself, it wasn't likely that the videotapes would solve the case. He asked in the office how he could speak to Ms. Ramon and was told that she was working again. He and the assistant manager located her in room 117.

"Ms. Ramon, could I please speak with you? My name is Detective Weeks."

"Dije ya todos," she replied.

"Señora, por favor, sometimes we remember things better after we have time to think."

"Señora Roberts, ya dije al otro policia todo que se`," she implored the assistant manager.

"Por favor señora, un taso de café y solamente preguntas pequeños," he said, trying to relieve her.

"Okay, si," she replied.

Sitting in the restaurant over coffee, he leaned over the table and just started talking to her. She wasn't going to tell him anything right now if she thought he was questioning her, so he just talked.

He found out that she was from Tecate', the town made famous by the beer. She'd been in the U. S. for six years but had never become a naturalized citizen. She had three children, the oldest of whom was twenty-three and was in dental school in Tucson. Mr. Ramon had died of a heart attack about six months ago. Things were tough at casa Ramon. She made it clear she needed her job and couldn't afford any trouble. None of it had anything to do with the case and everything to do with finding out what it was that she'd really seen.

"How could anything you saw in the room cause any trouble?" he asked her.

"Sometimes things we do for good can bring us trouble," she replied.

"What have you done for good? Tell me and I'll do my best, I promise, to keep it from bringing anything malo," he promised.

"I was thinking about my Ernesto when he died. He got chest pains at work. They called the ambulencia, but he died before they got there. They tried, they took him to the hospital, but his friends at work told me he died before they ever got there. He just collapsed onto the floor. Such a thing is too sad to think about. It is all the pain a woman can stand, to lose her husband after twenty-six years. She doesn't need anything else to break her heart."

"Tell me, mujer, what was it you did?"

"The man was dead. I saw his wedding ring there on the bedside table with the condoms, two of them. They had been used. His wife did not need to lose her husband and the memory of her husband. To find that what she thought was true was not. So I took them, I picked them up with the rubber gloves. When I pulled the glove off so the condoms were rolled inside. I threw them into my cart and made up the bed. Then I went to the office."

"Are they still in your cart?" He asked.

"No, they went to the trash already."

"Well, I'll see what I can find and I won't tell anyone where I got this for now."

"Gracias Señor Weeks," she replied.

"Did you see <u>anything</u> else…anything?" Weeks asked.

"Solamente el pelo," she answered.

"What kind of hair?" He asked.

"Pelo de mujer."

"How do you know it was a woman's hair?"

She held her hands about eighteen inches apart.

"Dark or blond?" Weeks pressed, getting excited.

"Dark. Lo siento, I threw it away too. I didn't want his wife to know. The hair of the girl, it looked like it...she is Latina."

Willie left the restaurant and called up to room 246. When Mole` answered, Willie told him to check the bedclothes and look for bodily fluids and hair. Then he headed down to the dumpster. When he got there, it was already empty. Just his luck, his best lead gone, all because it was trash day. He decided to ask Mole` to run him downtown. He'd try to run down the phone numbers Butler had called before he died. If he pushed, he could check them all out before five.

CHAPTER SEVEN

The sound of the alarm clock in the soft pre-dawn darkness jerked Laura out of a deep sleep. Her hand fumbled out from beneath the covers and hit the snooze button, then retreated back under. She shifted and settled more comfortably, then drifted back to sleep. She repeated the routine two more times, until the first light of morning was undeniable even through the bedroom drapes. Now she was going to be behind schedule, but since the schedule was her own, she didn't guess it mattered all that much. The mountains would still be there when she got up. The light might be a little different, but she knew how to adjust that if she needed to.

Finally, she slid herself out from under the blankets. The stone floor was cool under her bare feet, cool from the night air. They didn't have the radiant heat on this late in the year. She stretched, then walked into the closet and closed the door behind her before she turned on the light. Morris slept on the side of the bed nearest the closet. If she didn't close the door first, the light would shine right in his face.

Laura pulled on her painting uniform, a pair of old blue jeans and a camp shirt. She brushed her hair quickly and fastened it behind her head. She clicked off the light, then opened the door and made her way across the bedroom. She drew the drapes to block the growing brightness of the morning sunlight and glanced at her husband to be sure she hadn't disturbed him. He hadn't moved a muscle.

Down the hall, she stepped into Cody's room and inhaled deeply, letting her nostrils fill with the smell of the sleeping boy. Then she scooped him up into her arms, carried him back down the hallway, and gently laid him on her side of the bed next to his sleeping father and pulled the covers up around him. She kissed his cheek and ran her hand through his hair before she turned and headed for the kitchen. Almost silently she closed the door behind her.

In the kitchen, she made a cup of coffee and stuck an English muffin in the toaster. Looking at the day coming alive outside her kitchen window she smiled. Laura lived for Saturdays. They were the only time she had the luxury of walking the countryside. It was her favorite part of painting. Just walking around trying to find the exact looks she felt the need to capture. It was something she preferred to do alone. That was a big part of the aesthetic. She needed the solitude. It allowed her to focus in a way she never could if anyone were there.

She'd tried to include both Morris and Cody at different times and once she even brought both of them along, but that had been a disaster. Cody had been bored, and Morris wasn't much help entertaining him. She should have known what was in store when Cody started crying that he wanted to be carried before they were more than a hundred yards away from the car. Morris put him up on his shoulders and gave him a trail ride, complete with galloping and sound effects. That lasted for another two hundred yards or so, before Morris twisted his ankle on a rock. So that was it for her walking, three hundred yards from the car. She was so aggravated by that point that she just turned around and picked out a direction, then painted quickly to get it over with

She'd been painting less than ten minutes when Cody stabbed himself with a cactus spine and started crying again. So she'd had to stop painting for that. It took ten minutes to get the sticker out and another ten to convince Cody that he was fine. Morris's patience had run out in less than an hour. Finally, after only thirty minutes of actual painting, she realized that this was hopeless. They left after she had finished nothing more than a rough sketch, which she'd tried to complete later in her studio. The end painting was a mess. She'd ended up painting over it.

Since then, Saturdays had become a day for Morris and Cody to share at home. Well, not at home so much as in town. They'd have breakfast at McDonalds. Morris would drink coffee and read the paper while Cody played in the play area. Next they'd hit the bookstore. Cody loved books and would entertain himself in the children's section, looking at books or playing with the Thomas the Tank Engine play set, for hours. This gave Morris time for more coffee and to shuffle through whatever books or magazines he wanted to look at. When they got bored with that, they'd go see whatever movie was on at the Sedona Six that looked good to Cody. Mostly they saw the cartoon type stuff. Morris didn't seem to mind.

By then she was usually finished with her painting. She'd call and check on them as she drove back into town and meet them for dinner at whatever restaurant they felt like. Usually, it was the Red Planet Diner. Cody liked the space ships. She didn't mind the decor. They had a decent menu.

Today she only took a short drive. She didn't want to waste her time in the car since she'd gotten a late start. She already had an idea of what she wanted to try to do. She gathered her stuff out of the back of the car and headed uphill.

Alone, Laura walked steadily toward Coffeepot Rock, keeping her eyes on the trail in front of her. Her easel folded into a backpack with her oil paints, brushes and a bottle of turpentine easily stored inside. Two canvases rode strapped securely to it with Velcro strips. Walking in was easier. On the way out the canvases would be wet. Her lunch and water were in a fanny pack, riding easily below the easel. On her belt was a .22 Colt New Frontier in a leather holster. She walked for an hour before she found what she was looking for.

A glint of sun reflected off the crest of a ridge. A large devil's tongue cactus made up the foreground. She laid out her specialized earth tone palate. It was designed to mimic the red rock coloration unique to this area. It saved time mixing colors from scratch. She unpacked her easel and fastened the first canvas. Then, she moved it ten times before she found just the right angle to get the look she wanted. Her mind drifted back to the when they'd first moved to Sedona.

It had been just the two of them. Morris had tagged along more back then. Those trips were never very productive. He'd already quit painting by then. For Morris, the purpose of days together in the field was simple, outdoor naked Olympics. She hadn't minded, she'd grown up a shy girl, too thin, and always worried about the way she looked. Morris had made her feel special. It was nice to remember and hard to reconcile with where they were now.

She and Morris were two people who had fallen out of love. Not quickly, but over time they'd both found separate lives. Now only a child bound them. They put all their energy into raising Cody. There was nothing left over for each other or themselves. It was as if Cody was the culmination of their passions, and then somehow the passion was gone, consumed by the creation, never to return, at least not so far. She didn't have any doubts that Morris loved Cody. He clearly loved Cody more than he did her, but becoming a father wasn't something he was looking for, not at first anyway.

She completed her sketch of the layout for the painting in burnt umber diluted down with turpentine. She placed the skyline one third of the way down the canvas. She wanted to focus on the rock formation and not the sky so much.

She felt bad that she'd told Sue she wished Cody had never been born. That wasn't true. She was just trying to give her an idea of how frustrated she was. She remembered the joy she felt, looking at the little plastic strip she had just held between her legs, pushing it into the stream of urine, splashing her fingers and inner thighs, not caring, anxious to see the little minus turn into a plus. The twenty seconds that it took had seemed like an eternity. When the plus came, she had been so happy she rushed to the drugstore and bought three more tests, then back home again, drinking apple juice both ways, so she'd be able to pee again as soon as she got home. They, too, were positive. She floated around the house for the hour and a half until Morris got home. Her feet never touched the ground. When he walked in, she threw her arms around him, two urine soaked plastic strips in each hand, and then, stepping back, she thrust the strips into his face. He blinked, "What's this?"

"You're going to be a daddy," she gushed.

It still hurt to remember the look of panic on his face. He looked like a wild animal that had been caught in a trap when it realizes it can't get out.

"Are you sure?" he asked.

"See, I did it four times," she replied.

"Hey, that's great," he'd said, then turned on the television.

His lack of enthusiasm had been the first crack in her heart, a wound she never mentioned but always carried with her. It was an open sore to press on alone, in solitude, just to reflect on the pain.

The problem was that no one was prepared for the way life really turned out. Everyone spent their whole childhood reading fairy tales where the beautiful princess and the handsome prince overcame whatever bad stuff got in their way and then spent the rest of their lives "happily ever after." That's what everyone grew up expecting. To be little princes and princesses who would live "happily ever after," as if that were possible. No one expected the reality of life, which was usually "unhappily after a while."

"Be happy your life's not like that," she said to the cactus.

The cactus didn't really seem to be all that interested, but she continued to speak as she used a nice dark terra green to rough it into place in the foreground. "Its like you aren't sure if your marriage is dead, so you watch it float around, face down, for a while until you know it has to be dead. Then, just when you're sure it's dead, it catches another raspy, ragged breath and at first you're so relieved that it's still alive, you smile and everything's okay for a while." She tested the easels stance, to be sure it was stable. "But it won't last. The whole stupid thing just starts over again and again until you can't stand it any more. You start to wish that someone would walk in, like one of those doctors on TV, and just say, 'I'm calling it. This marriage's time of death is eleven-o-two p.m.'. Just so you could bury the damned thing and get on with your life." She kicked a small rock angrily. She unbuttoned her sleeves and, biting her lower lip, she started to work.

She had already toned her canvas with a mixture of yellow ocher with a bit of burnt umber, applied with a turpentine-soaked, rag yesterday afternoon. So with the key elements of the painting roughed in, she picked up the number eight filbert brush and entered that state of concentration where time, other than as a race against moving light and shadows, lost its meaning.

With every painting, she felt the touch of history. She was painting the western landscape. Vistas unchanged since Bierstadt's images had ignited the imaginations of Easterners and European immigrants in the heady expansionist days of the mid nineteenth century. What would that be like, she wondered, to have traveled west with Lewis and Clark? The only modern parallel to America's westward expansion she could think of was space travel. She fantasized about being the first painter to record the Martian landscape. Would the skies be yellow, she wondered? She imagined that the colors of the ground would be very similar to the red rocks and sand around Sedona. She thought of Georgia O'Keeffe leaving New York and moving to Abiquiu, New Mexico, alone after her husband Alfred Stieglitz died. Was she brave enough, she wondered, to fly away to Mars, or move to a wilderness alone, just her and Cody?

As she considered the question, her eyes registered minute changes in shade and color, and her hands mixed the exact color needed, applying, refining shape, then stepping back to compose. When she was nearly finished with the first painting, she took several steps back to assess it. As she did, she heard a dry, scraping rattle that froze her and lodged her heart firmly in her throat. Without moving her legs, she slowly rotated her head, searching the rocks and brush nearest her for the shape of the coiled rattlesnake. As she looked, her right hand unsnapped her holster strap and drew the little Colt.

When she couldn't find the snake over her right shoulder, she reversed direction and slowly rotated her head left. Again, the rattle froze her. She realized now that she had been turning with her right hand extended, sweeping it around as she swiveled her head. She had to hold her arm still and turn only her head.

She knew the snake was over her left shoulder. It had rattled in response to the shadow of her arm moving toward it. Halfway around, she saw it. It was coiled about three feet to the left of the heel of her boot. It was smaller than she thought, about four feet long with a bulge showing about halfway down, the remains of a small bird or mouse that had been its breakfast. The snake had been there for a while, sunning itself and digesting. She'd stumbled on it, not the other way around. She drew her right hand in tight to her body and rotated her torso. This eliminated the shadow crossing the snake's eyes as her arm brought the gun around. When she felt her hand was pointing toward the snake, she slowly extended her arm, making the gun the closest thing to the snake. The snake reflexively adjusted its aim; it was genetically programmed to strike whatever was closest to it. If Laura pulled the trigger now, the bullet would strike the center of the snake's body, just below the lower jaw. Now that her leg wasn't the snake's target, she slowly drew her left foot away. Once she'd backed up ten feet or so, she lowered the pistol. She held out her hand and saw only a slight tremor.

Smiling, she addressed the snake, "Well, it looks like it's both of our lucky day. I didn't get bit, and you didn't get shot. You just stay here and digest. I'm going to move over here a little bit and finish up."

She holstered the old Colt, proud that she hadn't needed to use it. If she wanted to paint in the wild, she had to get along with the wildlife and tried to never shoot a snake that rattled. If it had been polite enough to give her a chance, the least she could do was to return the favor.

CHAPTER EIGHT

Willie Weeks sat at his desk. His feet were resting on the pulled-out center drawer. On his desk, and in his lap, he'd spread out everything that they knew about the Butler case. He picked up the autopsy folder and started to flip through it, taking time to look at each of the photographs and diagrams. Maybe if he just let it all sink in he'd see a pattern. He turned back to the report summary and started to read through that, trying to soak the meaning out of the words. As he'd expected, the cause of death was blood loss. The next line read, "due to avulsion of both renal arteries by a sharp object."

"What in the hell does avulsion mean?" Weeks asked Steve Johnson, who was sitting two desks over.

"What do I look like, a dictionary? How did they use it?" Johnson replied.

Weeks read him the cause of death aloud.

"It must mean some kind of cut or tear," Johnson reasoned.

"I'll have to remember to ask Mole` next time I see him," Weeks said.

"Or, you could use that big box on your desk. You know the one with a screen? It's called a computer. Look it up," Johnson suggested.

"You can do that?" Weeks asked, surprised.

Johnson just shook his head and went back to filling in the report he had been working on before Weeks interrupted him.

The instrument of death was listed as, most probably, a flat bladed screwdriver 5-7 mm wide. The deepest depth of penetration was 15 cm. The wound over the right occipital area had been made with a round object, most probably metal, but without any evidence of metal flaking, fragments, oxidation, or paint fragments. There were no organic contaminants in the wound, and the blow, although it lacerated the scalp, did not fracture the skull.

Willie got up, tossing the file on to his desk. He headed for the coffee pot, grabbing his cup off the desk. He didn't ever have to worry about anybody else using his cup. It hadn't seen a dishwasher in years. The interior was a dark brown. The stains were lighter at the top and much darker at the bottom, probably because he never finished a whole cup before something drug him away. It usually sat half-full of cold black coffee, sometimes for days on the weekend.

He would wipe it out and rinse it some if mold or mildew grew on it while he was gone. He wasn't gross.

It was a Northern Arizona University cup he'd gotten from a girlfriend when he was still a cop on the street. If he'd kept it clean and washed it, it wouldn't have been there the next time he pulled into the precinct. Somebody else who needed a cup would have used it. The stains were its protection. Most people saw the dark interior of the cup as a threat, a repository of germs and contagion. He saw it only as a protective covering. It was what made it his. It didn't bother him. If there were germs floating around in his coffee, at least they were his germs. The coffee cup was the only real constant he had in his life. The girlfriend was gone but the cup was still there. Over the years he'd switched apartments, cars, guns, and even his sunglasses, but never his cup.

He thought about Butler. Everyone he'd talked to had liked the guy. Butler had been a good fullback in high school but he'd obviously softened some with age. Even so, at five foot eleven and two hundred and fifty six pounds he wasn't a guy to be taken lightly. Whoever had killed him had taken his size out of the equation by sneaking up behind him and hitting him in the head. Which was probably why they'd done it in the first place. That brought up the question of what had been used to hit the guy. A crowbar or what, a tire iron? If they were old, they would have left rust residue in the wound, and if they were new, they should have left small paint fragments. He wondered if a woman could have done it. Either one of those, though, would have fractured his skull if the assailant took a full swing . So either a woman had hit him hard or a guy had for some reason hit him not so hard. Whoever did it made the move from assault to murder pretty deliberately. What would it take to look at a helpless man laying there on the floor and make the decision to stab him ten or twelve times in the back? That wasn't something that Weeks could imagine a woman doing.

He took a swig of the black coffee and headed toward Ben's desk. Nothing he had so far gave him much to go on, though. The only trace evidence they had was the hair. They'd found a few strands in the carpet, eighteen to twenty inches long, dark, brunette, and that could have come from anybody that had stayed there in the past week. Damn he wished he had the condoms.

"Hey Weeks," Ben greeted him without any enthusiasm, "your buddy have anything new on Butler?"

"Just what we already know...nothing," he replied. "You're the big star Ben, so what do we do now?"

"Well, right now, we don't have a choice. We have to go and brief Captain Bryant. He just called. I was coming to find you. Look, whether we like each other or not, it's not going to do either of us any good to walk in and say, 'Golly gee captain we just haven't found anything out yet,' or to be bickering with each other in front of him. Either one's bound to piss him off. So, let's go in with some sort of a game plan. We probably ought to start with you giving an overview of what you found out from Ruiz, and then I can go through the stuff from the calls, interviews, and videotapes. We'll finish up with you giving the details from the autopsy report. Okay?"

"Sounds like as good a plan as any. You want to do most of the talking?" Weeks asked hopefully. He was pretty sure he didn't want Bryant on his ass any more than was absolutely necessary right now. "Isn't he gonna notice that we don't really have much in the way of concrete information?"

"Sure, but what choice do we have? We've got to go. He wanted us in there five minutes ago. Now's not a good time to have him sitting around waiting for us," Kinney answered.

Weeks could hear the stress in Kinney's voice. It was obvious he was feeling some pressure too. Walking down the hall together, Weeks felt a twinge of regret for some of the things he had been feeling about the kid. Weeks was used to the role of fuck-up from his school days, but he'd also felt the pressure of being a star too, when he was still in the Army. One wasn't any easier than the other. Weeks was so engrossed in his thoughts that he almost ran into his partner's back when Ben stopped to knock on the frame of the captain's open door.

"Come on," Bryant ordered. "Go ahead and sit down." Bryant gave them a moment to arrange their papers and folders after they sat down, before continuing. "Let's have it, but don't take all day. Don't read to me, just tell me what we have."

Weeks started, like they'd planned. "The victim's name is Harold William Butler, and he was forty-eight years old. He was five feet eleven inches and weighed two hundred and fifty eight pounds. He lived with his wife and two kids, both girls, one's twelve, and the other's seventeen, in Muncie Indiana."

"Could we get to something useful? I want the condensed version, not the novel," Bryant instructed.

"He was here in Phoenix on a business trip," Weeks added weakly.

Sensing they were heading down the toilet, Kinney picked up the narrative, adding, "Butler was in the paper goods business, specifically, he distributed those multi-layer rolls of paper that are used in self-serve gas pumps to print out receipts. The calls he made from his cell phone, or the room phone at the La Quinta, were all to local gas distributors. They were all clients who knew him and had worked with him before. They all expected to hear from him. He'd made preliminary calls to arrange to see them before he left Indiana. When I talked to them they all said the same thing: they liked him, he was a great guy, and they couldn't imagine anyone wanting to kill

him. The only call we don't have a good feel for is a call he received.
It came through the front desk of the motel. The desk clerk
remembered that the caller was a woman who asked if they had a Mr.
Butler registered."

"Did you run the number?" Bryant asked.

"Yes sir," Kinney continued. "It came from a pay phone at a
Shell station, about three miles from the motel."

"Business or pleasure?" Bryant asked.

"I don't know that yet, sir," Kinney answered. "No one at the
distributorship that owns the station was scheduled to meet with Mr.
Butler. So who knows?"

"Maybe he got close to some secretary here, maybe it was a
hooker? He was nude right?" Bryant looked at the two detectives,
they both nodded yes. "Was there any evidence of anything like
that?"

Weeks looked at his shoes. He really didn't want to have Ben
hauling Señora Ramon in and running her through the Spanish
Inquisition.

Ben answered quickly, "We can be pretty sure it wasn't a
hooker. There was twelve hundred dollars left in the guy's wallet.
None of his personal items or credit cards were taken. Ruiz was the
forensic tech. There wasn't any semen found on the bed sheets. The
bed was still made. He hadn't even been in it yet. We got a couple of
hairs out of the carpet, near the bathroom, but who knows how long
they've been there? Five guests have stayed in that room in the last
week."

"There may have been some condoms, but neither Mole` or I
found any," Weeks offered.

Ben looked at Weeks in amazed fury. "Sir, I talked to
everybody that'd been in that room, and nobody said anything about
any condoms. Where in the hell did you get that?"

Weeks decided he might as well take the lumps himself. After
all, a promise was a promise. So he went on, as if he were unsure, "I
just heard it, maybe one of the uniforms said it. I'm not sure."

"Well nobody put it in a report," Kinney answered firmly.

"Knock off the bickering," Bryant ordered. "Weeks, don't tell
me stuff you think, tell me what you know. Ben, did the maid say
anything about any condoms?"

"No sir," Kinney answered.

"Sorry," Weeks offered. "I didn't mean to confuse things."

"All right, let's move on," Bryant sighed. "Hand me the autopsy
folder." Weeks handed the manila folder across the desk, keeping his
mouth shut. He was just going to answer what he was asked.

"Exsanguination. So he bled to death?" Bryant stated flatly.

"That's what the Medical Examiner said," Weeks answered
defensively.

"Don't get coy, Weeks," Bryant said exasperated. "What'd you see?"

"When I first went in, I was pretty impressed by the amount of blood he had around his head, but all of that was just from the scalp wound. All that means is that he lived for a little while after he got hit in the head. Which let him bleed a lot onto the carpet. But not many people bleed to death from a scalp wound. What killed him were the stab wounds in his back, right where his kidneys were. There wasn't much external bleeding from there because that blood didn't come out. When his renal arteries were cut through he bled into his belly. I guess he died of that pretty quickly."

"The ME thinks the instrument of death was a screwdriver," Bryant read from the autopsy report.

Weeks reached across the desk and flipped to the Polaroid pictures that the autopsy tech had taken for him at the morgue. He pointed to a close-up picture of several of the stab wounds. "See these, these little lines coming straight out on each side. That's where the blade of the screwdriver tore through the flesh as it was pushed in. The autopsy tech measured them and they're between five and seven millimeters across. The deepest wounds were fifteen centimeters deep."

"So, about a six-inch blade," the captain summarized.

"Well, Ruiz thinks it could be anywhere between five and a half to seven inches. The handle could have indented the guy's fat for about a half inch, any more would have caused bruising. They didn't really see any bruising, so it's probably a longer blade," Weeks explained.

"The Medical Examiner puts the time of death somewhere between four and six p.m. the night before he was found. That correlates pretty well with what we have. The last call Butler made was on his cell phone. He called a BP distributor at three forty-five. He made an appointment to come by the next morning at nine to demonstrate a new paper-drop system, so I don't think he was expecting any trouble."

"What we expect and what we get are two totally different things most of the time," Bryant said quietly.

Kinney continued, as if he hadn't heard, "I went through the security tapes with the motel manager. All of the faces we saw during that time period matched registered guests or staff. The only other guy on the tape was a linen delivery guy, but the same guy has been running that route for the past two years, so he's not really a suspect."

"Then who is a suspect?" Bryant asked.

"I don't know," Kinney answered.

Bryant turned to Weeks, who, knowing what was coming, was doing his best impression of a deer in the headlights of an oncoming car. "Willie, you got any ideas?"

"Well, no not really…." Weeks started. "I think probably the killer was a male who served in the military. He was probably a member of an elite unit, like Special Forces, Marine Recon, maybe a Navy SEAL… on the other hand I'm not so sure the killer might not be a woman."

"Where in the hell did you come up with that?" Kinney snapped. "This isn't the Army. Commandos aren't running around Phoenix, knocking off visiting paper salesmen."

"Ease up Ben," Bryant said. Even though his voice was mild, there was no mistaking the command behind the words. "Ben, just because you're supposed to be teaching Weeks doesn't mean you can't learn something from what he has to say. Okay, Willie, what makes you think that?"

"It's confusing. Most women, even if they're tough, aren't going to take on a two-hundred-and-fifty pounder. It's easy to think our killer's an operator, because you have to be taught to know how to kill like that. Most civilians aren't going to think of stabbing somebody in the kidneys. Your average guy might accidentally hit a kidney when he was stabbing someone, but our killer made multiple stab wounds in both flanks and every one of them made it into the kidney. He also knew to wrench the handle back and forth, to cut through the renal arteries. In Special Forces, we called this a 'sentry takeout,' and somebody who's been trained to do it right did this one. One thing doesn't make sense though."

"What's that?" Ben said, amazed at what was coming out of Weeks's mouth.

"Why go to all of the trouble to use that technique on a guy who's already unconscious?" Bryant answered.

"Exactly," Weeks said, pleased that the captain understood what he was getting at. "The guy was already down. He was really clobbered on the head. The skull was indented, but not fractured. That's another question I have. What did he hit him with? No paint fragments, no rust flakes, no wood fibers. The weapon was round, but the diameter was too small to be a baton or a bat."

"A tire iron or a crow bar," Kinney suggested.

"A tire iron or a crow bar would have left some trace evidence, rust, paint, something," Weeks said.

"What about a gun barrel?" the captain wondered. "Not a semi-auto, but an old long barreled revolver, like a Python, or a Blackhawk."

"That doesn't make any sense," Ben interjected. "If the killer had a gun, why use it to hit the victim in the head, and then go to all the trouble of stabbing him in the kidneys?"

"Noise," Weeks said. "If our killer had a gun he didn't want to use it because he didn't want the noise. Everything he did was to avoid any loud sound. That's the whole purpose of the takeout technique he used."

"Why hit him in the head at all then?" Ben asked.

"Your victim was a pretty big guy," Bryant said. "Weeks is right. Very few women could take a guy that size on face-to-face, but it doesn't matter how big you are once someone sneaks up and clubs you in the back of the head. That would also explain the gun, in case something went wrong. So, I still think that the killer could be a woman."

"I've talked to my brother about this sort of thing before," Kinney said with a sense of authority. "He's a Bureau Vice-Chief at the FBI. He's worked with a lot of profilers. He told me that women that kill almost always know their victims, most know them intimately."

"So we're looking for a pissed-off girlfriend?" Bryant asked.

"I don't think so Cap," Weeks said. "This is too violent. This is a pissed-off guy."

"A minute ago, you were talking about used condoms, now you're saying that you're sure the killer is a guy. So, I take it you're saying that you think this is a homosexual thing?" Ben asked.

"I don't think that we can rule it out. A guy like Butler, who travels a lot, might have interests he can't indulge in close to home. Something he only did when he was away."

"Any evidence support that?" Bryant asked.

"They didn't find anything at the autopsy. Ruiz admitted that anal tone is one of the first things that goes when somebody dies, but there's no evidence of anal trauma. When they find a naked guy face down, that's one of the things they check at autopsy," Weeks explained.

"Better them than me," the captain said. "So basically, we don't have a clue who did this."

"This is where being the new guy shows," Weeks admitted candidly. "I don't really know where we go from here. We can keep going over what we have, but without some new input, I'm not sure how we get to the 'who' part."

"What did you do before, when you were investigating a robbery and you didn't have a clue?" Bryant asked.

"Well, we asked around, waited for somebody to try to move the stolen goods, and then worked back from there."

"So that's kind of where we go now. We ask around. Who's bragging? Is anybody talking about it? Whoever did this is going to want to talk about it. A lot of times, somebody we pick up for something totally unrelated will try to use something they know to get the District Attorney's office to plea-bargain them out of jail time. Hookers, pimps, breaking-and-entering suspects, you never know where it's going to come from. You two get on it," Bryant said, dismissing them.

"I'm going to see if Mole` has anything else for us. I want to look at the head injury, to see how the pistol barrel idea fits. You want to come?" Weeks asked, as they walked down the hallway away from Bryant's office.

Ben was surprised by the invitation. "The written autopsy report really wasn't all that useful. I guess it could help to have you run through things verbally. It can't hurt anyway. You go ahead. I'm going to stay here. I need to get started on those phone calls Bryant wants us to make."

As he left, Weeks wondered if he shouldn't have leveled with Ben about the maid. He probably should have told him that she picked up the condoms and remade the bed, but he didn't want to cause any trouble for her. She was a good woman who had gone through some hard times. Weeks had two long-barreled pistols at home, a Smith and Wesson 686 and one of the cowboy clones with a seven-and-a-half inch barrel. Maybe showing them to Dr. Thomas, the Medical Examiner who'd examined Butler's case, would help them get a clearer picture of what had caused the head injury.

He tried to summarize what they really knew. So far, they had only incoherent fragments of information. The guy had sex with somebody, somehow, and maybe that somebody had hit him on the head with a gun before they stabbed him to death with a screwdriver, or maybe not. Maybe someone else had hit him with virtually anything.

There was nothing here to build a case on yet. He'd stop by his house on the way to the morgue and pick up the two pistols.

CHAPTER NINE

Jarvis was having a great day. He'd had a good run on the beach when he woke up, ate breakfast with the boys before they went to school, and now he was cruising along the highway with the top down listening to the news. He usually enjoyed the drive in to work. Traffic was never too bad if he waited to leave the house until a little after nine. Which is what he usually did, since it didn't really matter all that much what time he showed up at work. Who was going to say anything? He was the boss, and his job was to do whatever it was that he felt like he was supposed to do that day. Most of his appointments were scheduled anyway, so he just made sure that he never scheduled anything before ten-o-clock.

Brooke always kept things running smoothly until he arrived. She was usually his first appointment. She'd run through anything important that had happened in the preceding twenty-four hours. She was there an hour before anyone else showed up every day, running through the security parameters she wanted set that morning and looking for any attempts to hack the system. There had been several unsuccessful attempts in the last month, but Jarvis knew that he could count on Brooke to deal with them and keep everything under control. She was terrific.

One big advantage of having somebody as obsessive-compulsive as Brooke running the tech side of things was that she kept a constant eye on everything that had anything to do with running the company. If there was a question about anything, she'd be able to come up with the answer in less than twenty minutes. She could analyze anything and be ready to move on it at a moments notice. She didn't really have a choice. It was who she was. If she had a question, it was something that needed to be looked into. Her title was Director of Engineering, but she also handled the Electronic Security division.

It was usually Jarvis that went to her. If Jarvis asked her for a usage pattern, user profile, or just about any other variable he could come up with, she could come back to him before the end of the day with a graph and a report to explain her findings. Jarvis loved watching her intensity and her passion for her creation. Most of all, he loved her charts. They were something that always looked great in a PowerPoint presentation, but it was more than that. She shared his feeling that everything they were doing was something that was really important.

When she made a chart, she was looking to see who the people were that needed them. It meant something to her, just like it did to him. Something about the demographics were wonderful and touching when he thought about it. They showed how much they were helping people, making a difference in people's lives, not just sending endless streams of zeros and ones out into some vast electronic void.

From Brooke's reports he really, for the first time, felt validated in himself, and he'd begun to achieve a measure of professional validation as well. Take any insignificant fact, for example, say he knew that Thursdays were usually a high-volume day for the LifeSolutions computer, that volumes tended to peak from Wednesday to Friday for traffic routed to the TimeDonors server, or that subjects on managing depression were most often visited on Sundays and Mondays. He could generate enough numbers on any one of these factors to generate a statistically significant study on the subject in a matter of days. It didn't have to be original thinking.

Say he looked at the numbers on depression, which matched published psychological profiles on the occurrence of depression. It didn't matter that he was just repeating what other people had already thought. He had the numbers to prove it was true, and to date no one else really had.

Jarvis had begun to write some articles based on the data they'd collected three years ago. Several of them had already been published in monthly "throw-away" journals, but his influence was growing, and Psychology Today had picked up his article on Patterns of Usage for Childcare and Education Seminars last month. It was a good study. He was able to show that young women usually visited those kinds of self-help sites in the morning or early afternoon on weekdays. The pattern was exactly what anyone with half a brain would have expected but no one had ever described it before. It wasn't rocket science. It simply corresponded with the times that young children were in school, periods when young mothers had free time to be on their computer.

TimeDonor's traffic was similarly close to what Jarvis would have predicted. Use was greatest during the latter part of the week, peaking from early Wednesday until Friday at five in the afternoon. There were two high-volume peaks daily. The first occurred during the workday from nine to five. The second was from eleven p.m. until two a.m., when the spouse and kids had gone to bed. He knew from personal experience these were the times when there was least chance of being interrupted by a family member walking in unexpectedly. He didn't suppose he was going to publish anything on those particular statistics.

One of the things Jarvis liked to see was how their network continued to expand, as the electronic highway helped them spread out across the country. So he'd asked Brooke to keep track of and monitor the area code patterns. Zip codes would have been just as good. It was a personal choice. Area codes just seemed more personal to him for some reason. Maybe it was just because he knew where most of them were, at least the biggest ones.

The demographics showed that the use of the seminars was occurring in pretty much a nationwide distribution. They were starting to get some international penetration as well. If that trend continued they were going to have to consider offering the seminars in additional languages at some point. They'd already talked about a Spanish language version. That one would get a significant amount of usage here in the United States as well.

The TimeDonors usage was a little more constrained. At the last review there was activity occurring in twenty-eight states and the District of Columbia. Most of the use was still in California and the adjoining states, but they were making inroads in New York, Chicago, and the nations capitol. Jarvis had always wondered if the TimeDonors activity in Washington was due to politicians who got acquainted with it at home and carried the habit with them when they went east and were away from their wives and families. Elected officials screwing the public wasn't a new concept. He did know that D.C. usage was clearly tied to the congressional calendar. He'd been able to look at that by a simple pattern overlay. He'd wanted to look at that one a little closer to see if he could determine which of the parties was a better customer, but Brooke had convinced him that asking people for their political affiliation was going to be a problem.

Jarvis was humming to himself as he parked his car in a slot with his name on it and walked into the building. He smiled at the receptionist and turned to look at the woman sitting in a chair in his reception area waiting to see him. When she looked up from the magazine that she was reading, he found himself looking into a pair of bottomless blue eyes framed by a cascade of auburn hair.

"Hello Tanya, how wonderful to see you," He said without waiting for any introduction from his receptionist.

"I was just in town checking on Brooke. I've been doing some traveling since Walter died and wanted to say 'Thanks' for the flowers you sent to the funeral," she answered without rising.

"I was sorry to hear about his passing," Jarvis said earnestly.

"Well, it was hard to get through, but it wasn't unexpected," Tanya said, looking down, anxious to get away from that subject.

That was clearly not what she was in town for.

"Let's go sit down. Would you like something to drink? Coffee…tea?"

He turned to his receptionist briefly as they went through the door into his office and whispered, "Ruthie, would you get some tea and some little cookies or something? Cancel my eleven-o-clock with Tom and hold my calls. "

"Do you want me to reschedule your appointment with Mr. Dugan?" Ruthie returned his whisper.

Tom Dugan was the head of the financial side of the company. If there was such a thing as an anti-Brooke, it was Tom.

"No. Just tell him to stay on track until I get back from Africa," Jarvis answered.

"He's not going to be happy about that," Ruthie warned.

Jarvis waved his hand dismissively. "Then tell him I said that this was his chance to show me what he can do on his own. I'm going to decide something…who knows…something important…just make something up, when I get back and I need to see how he handles things for the next few weeks on his own. What in the hell does he need to talk to me about all of the time anyway? It's always the same crap moved ten feet forward. I know, tell him I want him to put together the budget figures for the Spanish version of the seminars, and I want to see it when I get back. That should keep him busy." The last bit was said as he closed the door.

The main side effect of LifeSolutions' success was that Dr. Jarvis Sloan had become a very rich man, and to a lesser extent, as his only remaining partners, so had Brooke and Tanya. That couldn't be what she was here for. He made sure that they each got their share of revenues deposited to their accounts on the first of the month, every month. Since TimeDonors didn't have any income, it was a complicated arrangement. They had structured the agreement so that they each got a percentage of revenue based on the number of accounts that accessed TimeDonors after paying their LifeSolutions fees. And that was a still lot, so they were fine with that.

But the nature of the arrangement kept them out of LifeSolutions, which was where the money really came from in terms of revenue stream. They never had full access to the raw numbers. They only saw what was left after operating expenses, which included the half of the revenues paid to Jarvis's non-existent investors. That was the part of the stream that flowed steadily out of the company and into various projects Jarvis initiated in his wife or children's names. Just in case something went wrong. "You can't tell where a lawsuit might come from," he'd explained to Tom when he'd started. He never told Sharon about the money though, because you can't tell where a divorce might come from either. There were risks to everything, but if someone were going to end up with all of his money, he'd prefer it was Sharon and the boys rather than a bunch of lawyers. He still loved her, if only for where they'd come from to get here.

"Have you missed me?" Tanya asked as soon as they were alone.

"As much as you've missed me," Jarvis replied.

"You seem to be doing quite well for yourself. LifeSolutions must be doing well too," she offered without inflection.

"Well, it pays for itself and TimeDonors keeps the doors open," he answered.

"How's your family?" Tanya asked moving to another subject she seemed equally disinterested in.

"Sharon's doing well, the kids are ready to be through with school, but we still have a good way to go before the year's over. The usual."

Tanya nodded, then crossed her legs and leaned forward. "I see you've given up on medicine altogether now. Do you ever miss it?"

Although he still maintained his medical license, Jarvis never saw patients any more. His office was a luxurious corporate complex near Torrey Pines State Park, just past Scripps Hospital in LaJolla. LifeSolutions had an 11,000-square-foot office block overlooking the Pacific Ocean.

It was a long way from the cramped space he'd started out in when he first hired Sharon to be his secretary, two small rooms downtown over a barbershop. The rear room had been his office, the outer room was filled with mismatched chairs and a small antique cherry desk that he'd refinished himself. That was the combination reception area and waiting room. If patients were standing by the desk, they were in the reception area. If they sat down, they were waiting. He had done ten fifty-minute sessions a day in that little space. In some ways he did miss those days. Those were the days when Sharon had been the epicenter of his world. Now this was-the office, the business, and here he was in this room with a woman that scared the shit out of him, trying to figure what it was she was really here for. All he could do was play along and see where she was headed.

"I do miss seeing patients sometimes, but I think what we're doing here is in some ways just as important," he answered.

"Avoiding getting caught is always something we consider important, isn't it?" She asked.

A flash that passed across her eyes gave Jarvis a hint that she was upset. Her body language said she was getting to what she was really here for. Tanya hadn't been his first affair, but she was the one that had made it clear to him that he could never be too sure of himself. And here she was, like a tigress, and he was pretty sure that he didn't want to be the prey. He didn't know what it was she intended to do.

"I hear you're a satisfied customer of the product, too," Tanya said almost too casually.

"That implies that you've tried it," Jarvis answered.

"I have."

"And was it okay?" Jarvis asked, his concern momentarily overwhelmed by a mixture of pride and curiosity.

He knew he'd been rationalizing when he convinced himself that, as the architect of TimeDonors, he should believe in it enough to try it himself. His first affair had taught him how exciting it could be to have sex with someone different. . Tanya had taught him how frightening it could be if it went wrong. But those were just affairs. TimeDonors was bigger than that. TimeDonors was a scientific achievement. There was nothing tawdry about the pride he felt in what he'd done in the creation of it.

"I've used it some," she answered. "But I'm more curious about you. So tell me, was TimeDonors the answer to all of your problems? It has to be. You have unlimited access to women who deliberately make contact just for the sole purpose of screwing you. That, in itself, has to carry its own excitement," Tanya pressed, her voice clinically devoid of emotion.

What Jarvis would never admit to anyone was the disillusionment he'd felt following those first meetings. He couldn't think of much that was more repetitive and less satisfying than banging away on a woman that wasn't especially attractive, or interesting, and that he had absolutely nothing in common with. What initially sounded ideal, unbelievably, left a lot to be desired.

There was no preamble, none of the subtle foreplay that went into seduction. Both parties knew what they were there for, and there wasn't any mystery about what was going to happen. No titillation of "will she or won't she?" Pretty much, she was going to. The other thing that bothered him was that he cherished the idea that every woman was different and that making them happy required an effort to learn what it was they wanted. With TimeDonors all of that pretty much went out the window. Everyone had to come in knowing what it was that they wanted and guide their partner to get it. There wasn't any time to wait for them to figure it out.

Consequently, a pattern developed, a recipe; do this, get them to do that, you do this, then this, then that, then this. The vessel differed slightly but the potion remained the same. Sex had become less interesting than watching cooking shows on TV. There was, unavoidably, a great sense of disappointment when Jarvis realized that he needed more than TimeDonors was going to be able to provide him.

He didn't know if he'd failed his invention or it'd failed him. He just knew it wasn't good enough for him. He convinced himself that he was different, that he needed something more. Maybe he'd just set his expectations too high. It was still a valuable service, and one that generated a great income, so he wasn't too inclined to globalize his own reaction. He was picky, not a moron. And, it did beat jerking off.

"Is it enough for you?" he returned, refusing to be analyzed.

"It has its limitations. You know my…proclivities…they can be hard to indulge in such a limited format," she answered.

"It didn't seem to limit you with me," he replied.

"That's because you're special. You have the capacity for understanding. That's why I've missed you. I even think I could love you. I've told you that before, haven't I? You have so much to learn. Imagine what I could teach you."

That was what Jarvis was afraid of.

"Tell me about your last encounter." Tanya persisted, her eyes those searchlights of truth again.

"Shit, shit, shit Brooke had spilled everything," Jarvis thought. Now he was going to have to find a way to deal with that, and Tanya wasn't someone that he could bullshit on motives.

On the last encounter that he'd arranged he was supposed to meet a young woman in the late afternoon. Afternoons were best for him since he pretty much had unlimited flexibility in his office hours. He had a travel account he'd set up through the office to arrange the hotel rooms he used when he arranged TimeDonors encounters. They were, after all, product testing. It only seemed reasonable that they should be tax-deductible as a legitimate business expense.

He'd arrived ten minutes early and mixed himself a drink from the mini-bar. He'd just settled down at the desk with a vodka tonic and turned on the television when he heard the knock. Not wanting to appear too anxious and rush to the door, he took another sip of his drink before he pushed away from the desk and moved slowly to the door. He was hoping that this would be better than the last time when he heard what sounded like two women giggling from the outside it. What the hell was going on he'd wondered. He'd thought that maybe it was the maid or room service so he peeked through the peephole to find out.

To his surprise, there appeared to be two slightly drunk but very attractive women standing there, instead of the one he'd expected. He wondered why they were there. Were they both there for him? Or was one of them dropping the other one off or something? He tried to remember the details of the arrangement. He was pretty sure that this wasn't something that they had discussed on the Internet. It wasn't something that he'd asked for, but he didn't mind. In fact, it was a fantasy he'd had a lot but had never quite been able to arrange. Now it had been arranged for him. He tried not to smile too much when he opened the door.

The next few hours were, if not magical, then staggering, just because of the number of possibilities they'd explored together, and it felt as if they had barely scratched the surface. As exciting as it was for him, it seemed to be just as stimulating for each of the two women. There was no awkwardness. Things simply began to flow until the sex took on a life of its own, fed by each of them, but controlled by none of them. This was something Jarvis wanted to try again, but not with just anybody, there was something special about these two women, somehow they went together. That was part of the magic.

Thinking with the wrong head, Jarvis decided to take a step he could never have imagined taking, a step that was in complete disagreement with the fundamental concept TimeDonors had been founded on. He decided he had to somehow find those two women. That he had to see them again. That they had something that they had to finish and the only way they could finish it was together. The assurance that every encounter would remain anonymous was intrinsic to why they had created the site in the first place. He knew that he shouldn't ever even consider it, but somehow Jarvis convinced himself that this one time it would be worth the risk. That he was the one person that the rules didn't necessarily apply to, because he understood the reason for them. Somehow he could find a way to make it work for them.

That night he went straight back to the office and made two phone calls. The first call was to his wife. He told her that he wouldn't be home until later in the evening. He made up an excuse about having some production problems on the newest seminars and that he and the engineers from Los Angeles were going to meet for dinner to work through some of the problems. It was an excuse she'd heard before. His second call was to Brooke Werner. He told her that he needed her to come back in to help him with something.

Brooke was in Coronado, so it was going to take her a while to get there. Jarvis figured he had about forty minutes to kill, so he drove back to the motel room to take a shower and change clothes. He never went home without changing back into the clothes he'd left home in that morning. He always wore something different to a "meeting", something he could easily send to a laundry from his office. The last thing he wanted was to show up at home smelling like some other woman or wearing lipstick on a collar he hadn't noticed. There was no need to take chances.

On his way back to the office he grabbed a hamburger at a drive-through, then drove straight back to the office and used a restricted password to gain access to the engineering section. When he opened the door, the lights were already on in the hallway, so he carried his dinner with him to Brooke's office. He found her in her unlit office sitting behind her computer monitor, her face bathed in blue light.

"Want some fries?" he offered, holding out the grease spotted box.

"Haven't you ever heard of trans-fats?" she asked, shaking her head.

"'No, thank you,' would have been fine," he replied, smiling. "Thanks for coming back. I really appreciate it."

"So, what's the big emergency?" Brooke asked.

"What are you working on? How can you be working if you don't..."

"It has to be something to do with the appointment you arranged this afternoon. I was just running down the details on that to see if the details had erased yet," she explained.

"How do you know about what I arrange?" Jarvis asked, he wanted to get angry, but knew he couldn't. He was going to need her help.

"That's part of the job," Brooke smiled.

"Well, had they?" Jarvis asked, anxiously.

"Had they what?"

"Been erased," Jarvis snapped.

Brooke waved her hand. "Oh, I don't know. I just got here right before you walked in."

"Can you find out?" He was losing his patience.

Brooke drew her keyboard toward her. "I guess I could, but I'll need the screen name and password you used for the arrangements. Please don't tell me they're expired yet, because if that's the case, you can forget it. We'll never be able to trace her. Her details will have been wiped on the end-of-the-day cycle on the day they expired."

"No. It expires tomorrow. That's why I called you tonight," he explained.

"Good thinking," Brooke murmured as she manipulated the computer screens expertly, going quickly to the TimeDonors site, and entered the information that Jarvis had given her.

"What went wrong? Did she rob you or something? We can lock her out with no problem if she's a head case," Brooke rattled as she worked.

"Nothing like that. I just want to find her," Jarvis explained.

Brooke suddenly stopped and looked up, her eyes narrowing suspiciously. "Jarvis, I invented those servers just so something like this couldn't happen."

"I know why we developed the servers. I'm just asking you to help me do it," he replied tersely.

"This isn't a dating service. The people on here aren't looking for a steady boyfriend, you know? Are you sure you want to cross this boundary?"

Jarvis nodded.

"Here she is, citygirl322. The trick isn't following you in, it's following her back out. Now we have to use the screen name she used with you to access her account name." Brooke switched screens, moving to her restricted programming access screen. She typed in citygirl322. That gave her a LifeSolutions screen name. She then entered that screen name into the LifeSolutions billing computer to get a name and mailing address.

"Alright, the name's Susan Wong and she lives just down the road in Del Mar. Wait a minute, the mailing address is a post office box. Want me to see if I can trace her phone number?"

"I guess so. What else am I going to do, stand around a post office box and wait for her to show up?"

"That's no good either. The phone number she listed as her home number is 619-111-2222. That's a fake number. This is obviously a dead end. Sorry boss."

"Is there anything else you can think of?" Jarvis asked dejectedly.

"That must have been one heck of a date," Brooke observed. "I guess since we know her name we could Google her and see what shows up. That might work, if she used her real name."

"Might as well try." Jarvis wasn't hopeful. If she used a fake phone number, what were the chances she was using her real name? She was probably married anyway, and being a dumbass was only going to get him shot or something.

Brooke logged onto the Internet. "Okay, let's try Susan Wong, San Diego," she said, typing.

On the first page, an entry for the San Diego City Guide listed a Watson's Gallery on Prospect Street in La Jolla, which was featuring the artwork of a Susan Wong. Brooke clicked on the hyperlink and got forwarded to the gallery's website, where she selected Susan Wong from the artist's biography heading.

"Is this who you're looking for?" she asked.

When Jarvis looked at the screen, there she was. He grabbed the mouse and began to look around the gallery's website. Under the highlights of recent shows was a 2006 entry listed as Wong/Dees Two-Woman Show. His pulse rate quickened when he clicked on the entry icon and the faces of the two women he had just spent the afternoon with filled the screen.

"Thanks, Brooke. I really owe you one," Jarvis said, his face still flushed from the excitement of finding both women.

"Since you owe me, I want to talk about something else," Brooke said.

"You name it," Jarvis offered, then added nervously, remembering negotiating with her for the secure servers, "within reason."

"Why are you putting Dugan in charge when you go to Africa?" she asked.

"I've got to put somebody in charge," he answered.

"I'm just saying why Dugan? He's a pain in the ass. He already thinks he's in charge of all of the administration stuff, which is bad enough. Now he's going to think he's in charge of engineering too."

"He's just an administrator," Jarvis responded. "Besides, what do you care?"

"I don't want him thinking that he's in charge of what I do. I know, we agreed not to tell anybody at LifeSolutions exactly what TimeDonors does, or that I'm a partner in it, but how can you leave him in charge when he doesn't know that the company's main source of income even exists?" Brooke demanded.

"Let him have his delusions," Jarvis smiled conspiratorially. "If he doesn't know anything, he can't hurt us."

"If security's the issue, why aren't you putting me in charge? You trust me to do all of this kind of crap, but you don't trust me to run the place while you're gone?" Brooke argued.

Jarvis put his hand on her shoulder. "Why do you want to do the administrative garbage? You're brilliant, you run engineering, and you get a good chunk of the money TimeDonors brings in. Isn't that enough?"

"I just want some more responsibilities," she said. "It's time for me to grow."

"I talked to Brooke," Tanya said, smiling. "And I want to make sure what happened the other night can't ever happen again. I told her to find a way to keep anyone, including you and me, from tracking anyone ever again,"

"Who do you think you are?" Jarvis started indignantly.

"Your partner. Not just a partner, a partner that wouldn't hesitate to tell your wife everything we've done together, and how much you liked it. How you whimpered and begged me…"

"You've made your point" Jarvis interrupted.

"Not to stop," she pressed.

"I said you made your point," Jarvis conceded.

"As far as what you're doing personally, it's not for me to judge. When it comes to TimeDonors, it's the subscribers who's trust you're breaking by screwing around and giving yourself personal exemptions," Tanya said, anger evident in the sharpness of her tone.

"You don't have the right to judge me on any of it. You've had all of the same impulses I have." Jarvis was trying to defend his decision by going on the offensive.

"I'm not the one who just broke the cardinal rule we've followed since we started this thing. TIMEDONORS REMAINS ANONYMOUS. You had to blow that off and track down one of our members' identity without her knowledge or permission."

"Stop making a federal case of this. You're starting to sound like my wife," Jarvis said to shut her the hell up.

"Not your wife, your conscience," Tanya corrected.

Jarvis had a sudden thought. "I think you're jealous."

"There are two things that allow me to be quite sure jealousy isn't an issue," Tanya said with a little laugh.

"What two things?" Jarvis asked.

"You're an immoral sleazebag who's incapable of fidelity," she added, smiling to take some of the sting out of her words. "And so am I."

"Don't be so judgmental," Jarvis said. "I've spent years of my life staying in my screwed-up marriage, and now I'm staring down a half-century cliff. I'm standing right on the edge, looking down at the ocean, and I'm scared to death of the rocks and waves in front of me. Is it so wrong to want to have some enjoyment before I have to face things like impotence, prostate cancer and Alzheimer's?"

"I'm not the one to talk to about that. My problems were real not melodrama," Tanya reminded him.

Jarvis looked straight into her eyes so she couldn't avoid the truth of what he was saying. "The older you get, the more melodramatic life gets. Little by little, it robs you of the things you thought made up who you were. You saw it watching your husband die. I just want to use what I have left before it's gone too. Is that too much to ask for?"

Tanya cupped his cheek gently with the palm of her hand. "In this case, Jarvis my love, it is."

CHAPTER TEN

Laura was not having a good morning. Cody had crawled in bed with them at six and, when she put her hand on his face, he was burning up. She carried him into the bathroom and sat him on her counter while she tried to take his temperature.

"Do you want to do it under your arm or under your tongue?" she asked

"Under my arm. It hurts when you put it under my tongue," he wined.

She shook the thermometer and put it under his right arm. "All right, just hold still." She instructed. I'm going to get some alcohol to wipe it off when we're…"

As soon as she turned around Cody reached for her and, when he did, the thermometer under his arm fell out and shattered all over the bathroom floor. Barefoot on the tile, she had no choice but to pick up her now-crying son and carry him out of the bathroom. As she did, she felt the crunch and stabbing pain that informed her that she had found at least one of the fragments of the broken glass.

"Shit!" she exclaimed as she hobbled on one foot and the other heel out of the bathroom. Cody, of course, began to cry even harder. "Morris, get up. I need some help."

"Whazzit?" Morris mumbled out from under the pillow he had placed over his head to block out the noise coming from the bathroom.

"Cody's sick and he dropped the thermometer…" she started.

"I didn't drop it on purpose, it was an accident. It just fell when I tried to tell mommy my ear hurt," Cody wailed.

"Just take him a minute. I stepped on a piece of glass, and it's stuck in my foot," she said, lying Cody on the bed beside Morris and flipping on the lamp on the bedside table.

Morris shaded his eyes with his left hand as he reached out with his right to draw the sniffling Cody toward him.

Laura pulled her foot over and began to try and fish the piece of embedded glass out with her fingernails.

"You're bleeding pretty good," Morris observed.

This started Cody to crying again.

"I'm sorry you cut your foot," he wailed.

"You're getting blood on the sheet," Morris offered.

"Well I don't have much choice," Laura snapped. "The tweezers and tissue are in the bathroom that has glass all over the floor, and I can't put on a shoe because I already have a hunk of glass in my foot."

"If you wanted me to go get the tweezers, you could have just asked. You don't have to get all hysterical," Morris returned defensively.

"Would you please...?" Laura fumed.

The look on Laura's face clearly told Morris this could go nowhere constructive. He quickly hopped out of bed and slipped on his jeans and a pair of sandals. Cody was already engrossed in the hunt for the glass shard and barely acknowledged Morris's departure. After fetching the tweezers, Morris walked to the kitchen and returned with a broom and dustpan. "You want me to run to the drugstore and get another thermometer?" he offered.

"That would be great," she replied, checking the time on the alarm clock. "They should be open in another ten minutes."

"Okay, I'll be back in a little bit," Morris said as he slipped on an old shirt that was lying on the chair. "I turned the coffee pot on."

"Look, I'm sorry I snapped at you," Laura offered.

"No big deal. Bad morning, that's all," Morris said and leaned over to kiss her shoulder. "I'll be back in a minute."

When Morris returned, the new digital thermometer said that Cody had a fever of a hundred and three degrees. This started a whole new series of disasters. Laura knew she needed to get his fever down, and she knew she needed to get some Tylenol in him to do that. Unfortunately, even on a good day, Cody didn't like to take medicine, and with the fever and earache, he wasn't in any mood for it this morning. After carefully measuring out the liquid medicine three times, only to have it spilled, spit, and refused Laura gave up and poured the Tylenol into a cup of apple juice. He drank it easily, while she sat with him on her lap watching TV, bathing his neck and chest with a cool washcloth. With everything under control, Morris went on to work.

Unfortunately, twenty minutes later, Cody threw up. Laura had no idea how much of the medicine he'd had time to absorb or how much was left in his stomach. She had no way to know how much she could give him to make up for what'd been thrown up.

The last thing she needed was to be a walk-in at the pediatrician's office. She knew they tried to get everyone seen as quickly as possible, but if she went in as a walk-in, it was pretty much going to be an all-day affair. She'd hoped this was going to be one of those things she could take care of over the phone, but when she called the pediatrician's office, the nurse who answered the phone suggested giving him half of the original dose and bringing him into the walk-in clinic to see if they could find a reason for the fever.

"Great," she said to herself as she hung up. "Just great."

By the time she got Cody and herself dressed, he had gone from cranky to combative. When they finally got out of the doctor's office, it was two-thirty, and Cody was crying continuously. He didn't even want to be put down long enough for her to write the check at the receptionist's desk. The injection he'd gotten hadn't done anything to make him any happier. At least the Tylenol had taken effect, and his fever had dropped. Sick and cranky she could take. What scared her was sick and floppy.

Every time Cody had a high fever he got like a wet dishrag. Whenever it happened, she was reminded of the time when he was two and had gotten a bad stomach thing. They hadn't been able to keep anything down him. The fever, along with the vomiting and diarrhea, had caused him to get dehydrated in less than twenty-four hours. Before she knew it she was sitting in the hospital holding her son with fluids running through tubes and into his veins. He couldn't eat or drink anything at all. He hadn't been able to keep anything down at all. He'd been so little then. All he could do was lay there melted over her lap like a watch in a Salvador Dali painting. Not even trying to move or cry. Just lying with his little ribs poking through his skin as she bathed him with a cool washrag. Cranky and fighting was definitely better pale and floppy.

She called Morris on the way home to get him to run by the store and pick up some more Seven-up and popsicles, but he didn't answer. It wasn't even worth asking him where he'd been. He'd say he was drilling, or using a power saw and hadn't heard the phone. She'd heard it too many times before. She didn't really want to hear it again. So why ask?

It took him two days on antibiotics before his ear infection got any better, and with Cody home from school, he was all she was doing. She was spending more time diluting Seven-up and fetching Popsicles than getting any work done.

Morris wasn't much help during the day, but he had been more than happy to sit in the recliner in the evenings with Cody in his lap, watching cartoons, each of them with a Popsicle in hand. At least this gave Laura time to get a little work done. The paintings she finished were going to have to dry for a couple of weeks before she could put a light coat of varnish on them anyway. Then the varnish would still need to dry for a couple of days before Morris could frame them. This was the drawback of painting with oils. It was a slow process, but no other medium could give her the depth and brilliance that came from oil painting. Laura looked at the two framed paintings she had finished. They were resting against the south wall of her studio. She was planning to run down and take them to Kent next Wednesday and to bring down a couple of her older paintings that had been hanging at the gallery here in Sedona for a while and see if she could sell them there instead. Now maybe she would wait and bring a couple of the paintings down with her in a few weeks to make up for her break in production. That's what Morris had called it. For him her painting might as well be factory work. She wondered how many production breaks he'd taken himself with his bored housewives this week. At least one she was pretty sure of.

Looking through the doorway of her studio, she could see Morris and Cody silhouetted against the television screen in the den at the other end of the hall. Morris held a diet soda in his left hand, Cody a cup of apple juice in his right. They were both resting their drinks on the arm of the recliner on their respective sides. That was a picture, a picture that conveyed contentment, physical bonding, and unconditional love. Why did they have to be so screwed up? What had Cody ever done to deserve two such messed up parents? The words wouldn't come. What kind of parents would endanger the happiness of their child to satisfy their stupid, petty lust?

It was too easy to blame Morris, to justify her behavior based on his. Looking at the outline of her child and his father, rationalization of her infidelity was much more difficult. Even as she berated herself for what she could only see as stupid destructive behavior, she knew she wasn't going to stop. She knew that she'd go ahead and do it again. Why? She couldn't say. No, that wasn't true. She knew the truth. She didn't want to say, but she knew.

She needed it, and she'd needed it for too long to stop right now. Motherhood was wonderful, fulfilling, meaningful, and every other description found in the parenting and motherhood magazines, but she needed more. She needed to be something other than a mother sometimes. Maybe if Morris could see her as something other than just Cody's mother, she wouldn't need other men, men who didn't know she had a child, men who didn't care, and could see her as a woman first and foremost, men that would be happy to see her as simply a sex object. The hell with political correctness; she wanted to be objectified. She wanted her breasts, her vagina, and her mouth lusted over for what they could be, objects of desire that needed, and wanted, to be used. Not for what they had borne and nourished. Just for the sheer pleasure of it. She needed to be both sides of the paradox that was a woman, the Madonna and the whore. As Madonna only, she would never feel whole. Both sides needed to be fulfilled. Neither one was going to go away. What started in San Diego was growing, and she didn't know what to do about it. So she'd just have to worry about her child and feel awful for what she knew she was going to keep on doing until somebody or something made her stop. For now she couldn't see who or what might be able to do it. She only knew that she couldn't.

Later that night, after Cody had been put to bed, she reached out to Morris out of a sense of guilt, trying to heal things somehow.

Maybe there was still some way for them to repair the rift that sent them both to other people. She wished they could be the kind of family they were when something went wrong. She wished that they could be that way all of the time. Why couldn't they work together and help each other out like that every day instead of the way they were. All she wanted was to be in love with her child's father.

She reached across the pillow between them and cupped Morris's cheek gently with her hand, using her thumb to stroke the skin next to his eye. Immediately, she felt him pinching her nipple through her nightgown.

"Slow down, baby. Make me want it, tease me a little," she coaxed.

"C'mon baby, look at the clock. It's already midnight. I have to get up in the morning," he complained.

"Mission failed," a military voice in her head announced. "The flight to ecstasy has now been canceled," an airline hostess's voice followed. "All passengers will now lie back. Today we will be traveling on the Monotonous 180." The 180 is so named because it is a piston-driven engine that only works in the 180-degree plane, commonly known as the missionary position. "So, please lie back and spread your legs as we travel to today's destination, the grocery list." Morris came inside her just as the vegetable needs had been compiled. By the time she got to dairy and cheese products, Morris was snoring.

She slipped softly out of her bed and headed to the studio, closing the door as she switched on the light. She frequently painted at night, breaking down and repainting unsatisfactory areas she had painted in the field. Tonight it wasn't a paintbrush but a keyboard that would occupy her fingers. Quickly, she logged on to the Internet and navigated through the screens that sequentially presented themselves to her until she reached the "TimeDonors Wanted" screen, reading again the entry screen as if there were some hidden clue in the words themselves.

"Many couples have differing levels of sexual need." They had differing levels of fulfillment. Frequency wasn't an issue. She and Morris had the same needs for sex, it was just that his needs were fulfilled, and hers were sublimated, subservient to his. Yes, she enjoyed the penetration and thrusting, but she needed more than that to climax. He could pump away all night, but that was about him. Her achieving orgasm required putting her needs first, and with Morris, that just wasn't ever going to take top priority. Any discussion of it resulted in hostility.

"Why can't you just come normally, like other women?" he'd accuse.

"Because I'm Abbey," she had said once after having heard that particular question one time too many.

"Who?" Morris asked angrily.

"Abbey. Abbey Normal," Laura dropped the Marty Feldman punch line from the movie Young Frankenstein, but neither one of them laughed.

That's who she'd be tonight. Abbey Normal, the insatiable, degenerate slut who dared to need direct clitoral stimulation, and time, and somebody who would at least pretend to care what she wanted. She was reasonably sure that, somewhere inside this web site, there was some man in area code 602 waiting to fulfill her abnormal needs. Her eyes returned to the screen and she continued reading…. "If you are willing to donate your time to meet the needs of others click here."

It wasn't the mystery man's time she wanted him to donate, it was his penis… and his mouth… Well, it wouldn't hurt if the mouth was appropriately placed on a rugged handsome face. It would also be okay if his penis were on the large side and appropriately placed on a muscular body with a firm butt.

As she clicked to enter, she knew there were no selection criteria for any of those things. Rhett Butler had been none of those things, and it had been nice with him anyway. She entered her new 72-hour password and selected male and area code 602. For age, she selected the three five-year increments needed to indicate 35 to 50 and for race, she selected Caucasian. "Wasn't that racist," she thought, and changed it to no preference.

"This is hard enough. I'm not ready for any cultural differences," she argued. She returned it to Caucasian and quickly pressed enter before her more liberal thought processes could be offended.

She got up from the computer desk, walked to her drawing table, and opened a sketchpad. Using a charcoal, she shaded in the outline of a man. Shading and blending she defined muscle groups. He was standing facing away from the viewer but turning back toward his left, so that he was looking back at the viewer over his left shoulder, his left arm swept back and foreshortened, so as to appear as if it were projecting off the page. All this she did from imagination, coupled with the years of life drawing classes. The effect was dramatic, but still, the face was blank.

She flipped back a page to her previous sketch and looked at the two Janus-like faces on a loosely defined body. The emphasis of the previous drawing had been the faces, each looking in a different direction. One was distorted and cruel, spittle streaming from the corner of its mouth. The other face was quite familiar. Clark Gable, a martini to his lips, winking with his right eye.

CHAPTER ELEVEN

Jarvis began to visit Watson's Gallery fairly regularly, and over the course of the next week. He spent some time almost every day studying the two paintings by each of the women he'd had sex with. He took his time, looking at each painting in the idealized light of the gallery, trying to see the imprint of the woman in the work she'd produced.

The gallery owner was overjoyed, and Jarvis quickly realized that the best way to ensure James Watson's help was to appeal to his natural merchant's desire to sell more of his product. Jarvis instigated his new plan by buying first one of the paintings by Dees, she was the one with the deeper needs, she was the one that wanted to be opened like a flower to find out who it was she wanted to become. He could see the need in her barren landscapes. Wong, on the other hand, painted just like she made love, without reservation. She'd be the key to making this work.

Jarvis had a plan. It started with inviting James to lunch on the pretext of discussing further acquisitions for his corporate art collection. James, smelling money, was quite eager to be of help in any way possible.

"What I'm looking for," Jarvis began, "is to have a work of art created to display in the entryway of our corporate office. You know, something that would exemplify the company's motto, 'Helping people to deal with life's hardships'."

"I think that would be a wonderful idea," James said. "Art can create an emotional context, to emphasize what it is you're really trying to say with a motto. To take it beyond just words."

"That's exactly what I'm talking about. Do you think that either of the two artists I like, the ones we talked about, could do it? I mean, would either one of them be interested?" Jarvis continued.

"I'm sure either one of them would be thrilled," James offered. "It's a wonderful opportunity."

"How would we do it? I don't really know what it is I want. It's something that's going to take…communication. Do you think I should meet with them, you know, to kind of tell them the general idea I had in mind?" Jarvis asked.

"Really, I think that's essential," James replied seriously. "That's really going to be the only way for you to convey the scope of the project you have in mind."

"Well, what would be best? Should they just come to the office to see the space, or should I meet them at the gallery first? How are these things usually set up?" Jarvis continued.

"Don't you worry about a thing, Doctor Sloan," James reassured. "That's exactly what I'm here for. Sue Wong'll be the easiest to set up quickly. She lives here in LaJolla. She's always in and out of the gallery. I can set up a lunch meeting where we can talk, and afterward we can ride up to Del Mar and visit her studio so you can see the kind of things she's working on now."

"...and the other one, Dees, is it? I'd like to consider her too," Jarvis said matter-of-factly.

"That's going to be a little more of a challenge. Her studio's over in Sedona. She only visits San Diego a few times a year. The problem is she was just here," James replied.

"A fact I'm acutely aware of," Jarvis added under his breath.

"It may take some special arrangements to get her to return so quickly," James offered, leading the conversation back to his favorite subject, money.

"What do you mean?" Jarvis played along, faking naivety.

"There may be some costs involved...." James left the suggestion hanging.

"Well, I guess that wouldn't be a problem," Jarvis started, "but let me get back to you later in the week to finalize some arrangements."

"Wonderful, I look forward to hearing from you," James concluded. The two men stood and shook hands briefly.

As he sat at his desk the day after his lunch with James, Jarvis considered his options. Should he pursue a meeting at all? Did he really think they could recapture the intensity of what had happened between them? He knew intellectually that there could only be one first time for anything, and that some things were best left as wonderful memories. The last thing he wanted to do was to add layers of disappointment, obscuring and diffusing the original memory that was so wonderful right now.

He shouldn't meet with both women right away. It would probably be best to meet with Sue Wong first, alone, to try and get a feel for her willingness to proceed. She had clearly been the ringleader, often coaching and directing her friend, Laura. Laura was the one that clearly had both the deeper needs and the greater reservations. Who knew? Maybe he should try to arrange to meet with both women at once. Maybe they'd be less intimidated at being re-contacted by him if they were together. He rolled these questions around in his mind like a cats-eye marble, trying to see the intricacies of each possibility.

The professional side of him realized that everything Tanya had hammered him on was true. Repetitive contact would develop into emotional attachments, which certainly could erode his marriage and endanger his family. But when he thought about it, the likelihood that such a long-distance arrangement, requiring three people, would present a real danger seemed low. The risk was more one of getting involved with one of the women individually. He decided to limit himself to a single meeting with Susan Wong. He wasn't going to try and seduce her. He was just going to make a suggestion and try to assess her willingness to jointly pursue the process they had already begun together. With that decision made, he picked up the phone and dialed the Watson Gallery.

Sue Wong drove along the coast in her red Saab convertible. The back seat and trunk were permanently stained from the years of loading up and hauling around wet oil paintings. Sue was always impatient to see how her paintings looked in the gallery. She liked to get a painting about ninety percent done, then take it to the gallery so she could get an idea of how she wanted to finish it.

Most artists, especially en plein air painters, got used to having to transport wet paintings. Some used blankets or towels to protect their cars. Some used racks or boxes. Sue just tossed them in there. Actually, in some ways, she liked the spots. They made her feel productive. Today's load would leave permanent reminders of Alizarin crimson and a yellow ocher/burnt sienna mix on the carpet of her trunk.

Her car was already four years old. She didn't think the paint spots would depress the trade-in value too much. Besides, she didn't plan on getting rid of it anyway. At least, not until the California sun had destroyed it. There was a normal progression of car decay in Southern California that was different from most other places. There wasn't any rust, just fading, oxidized paint on the outside and cracked and shredded interiors. Unfortunately, she'd chosen the worst combination possible, a red exterior which was now fading toward orange and a black interior that would maximally absorbed the sun's ultraviolet radiation and take on all of the characteristics usually associated with a waffle iron. The second was by far the greatest pain in the ass, literally speaking. If she did get a new car, it would be white with a tan interior. She was sick of doing the little "I'm burning the shit out of the backs of my thighs" dance every time she got in wearing a skirt or shorts.

Maybe, if the corporate big shot she was supposed to meet for lunch liked what he saw, she could get a little Porsche Boxter. But then, where would she put her paintings?

Oh well, she thought as she pulled up to the back door of Watson Gallery. She called James on her cell to ask him to open the back door and retrieved the two wet paintings from the Saab's trunk. James held the door open and smiled to see the paintings that he knew at this moment were smearing paint onto Sue's thumbs and lower palms.

"Let's just set these down here," he said, handing her a paper towel. "You could let them dry first, you know."

She set the paintings down against the wall and looked at her hands to see that both had several multicolor stains.

"Thanks," she said, taking the paper towel and wiping at her hands. "You know I'm too impatient for that. Besides I'm never sure about how I'm going to finish them until I see them hanging and lit."

"Why don't you set up a little viewing area in your studio, like a mini-gallery?" James suggested. He took her hand in his and began to wipe the paint off her right palm with a clean paper towel. As he did, he leaned forward and whispered, "He's here already. Poor form to stain up a potential patron on your first handshake."

"What's he doing here? I thought we were meeting him for lunch in about thirty minutes," Sue replied in a stage whisper.

"I guess he's just an eager beaver. Maybe he's anxious to meet the famous Susan Wong," James teased, "or maybe he's just seen that cute little butt of yours wearing the tight shorts from that shot I put in your online bio…The one I took of you painting last fall. See, I told you action shots were a plus."

"Oh God! Not some artist-obsessed pervo," Sue said, her voice rising.

"Maybe just a little," a voice said from down the hall.

"Oh shit," she giggled punching James in the chest. "It looks like we broke the ice without any awkward moments, at least."

A man a few years older than herself, wearing a red polo shirt and khaki pants, stepped into the hall. Sue experienced a sensation of déjà vu. She was sure she knew him. It was the sensation she felt when she ran into a person somewhere she didn't usually see them, kind of like seeing her gynecologist at the skating rink. She knew him, but she didn't know where or why. She just couldn't remember the name that went with the face.

"Hi," he said extending his hand. "I'm Jarvis Sloan."

The name was of no help.

"James said you were in computers, a software designer or something," she stalled.

"Well, it's more an on-line educational company," he replied.

"I'm available to teach drawing and painting….for a nominal fee," Sue led.

"Well, we're not exactly a direct education program; it's more of a self-help series of seminars."

"Well, what's your company's name?" she asked.

"LifeSolutions," he replied and smiled.

In an instant, she knew. A floodgate opened and contrasting feelings of fear, attraction, panic, and desire poured across her mind.

She struggled not to avert her eyes, to avoid looking overtly panic-stricken. Time bent and slowed, her mind racing a million miles an hour. After what seemed like an hour or so, she replied, "Well, that sounds interesting. Do you like these?" she asked, sweeping her arm, rather than trying to point with the paint stained paper towel still hanging limply from her hand. It was a motion that was supposed to indicate the paintings hanging on the wall but came off like an exaggerated pose from a men's magazine.

"Very much," he replied, looking at her breasts and not at the pictures.

"I meant the pictures," Sue said obviously flustered. "Just a little wet," she said lifting the two new paintings, again smearing paint on her hands.

"I assume you're talking about the paintings again," Jarvis said, smiling at the double entendre. "Really, no kidding. I'd love to have those, when they're ready…I'm talking about the paintings too. Do you have anything else I could see, at your studio, perhaps?"

"Well, let's head off for a bit of lunch," James suggested, smiling and shaking his head.

Thank God, Sue thought. Just what in the hell am I supposed to do now? She could remember holding his head in her lap, her breast in his mouth, watching sensations ripple across his face as Laura, her hair cascading down so that it formed a small privacy curtain, moved slowly then rapidly, then slowly over him. She could not however, for the life of her, remember any words that had passed between them.

Sue lived in her studio. There was no way to take him to see the paintings there without him finding out where she lived. Initially James would be there, so it would be okay. What worried her was that there was no way to be sure he wouldn't come back when James wasn't there.

That was supposed to be the whole purpose of TimeDonors, to never see the person again. Now here she was, obviously being pursued by some kind of weird millionaire stalker, using his money to make her come to him. It was like a kind of reverse stalker thing.

She couldn't deny that the idea that he'd spent so much effort just to get to see her again appealed to her. It was quite flattering, really. Maybe this could be a good thing. She'd just have to wait and see how lunch went before she panicked and ran for it.

Lunch turned out to be a very pleasant and businesslike affair, punctuated only occasionally by a wistful look or a minor panic attack. James was good at what he did, and moving oil-covered canvas was what he did best. This time, however, it wasn't terribly difficult. He was aided immensely by the fact that Jarvis Sloan would have gladly sawed off one of his legs to be alone with Ms.

Susan Wong. Over lunch he negotiated the sale of the "nice pair" she'd come in with.

Jarvis seemed to sense Sue's growing apprehension as lunch came to a close. The longer they talked the more distanced and businesslike he became. She was afraid that he was losing interest. She had to admit that she felt a stab of disappointment, along with the relief she felt, when after they had finished their coffee, he stood and apologized that he wouldn't be able to visit Sue's studio today. An unavoidable commitment had come up right before lunch, and he very much wanted to see it sometime in the future, but perhaps it would be more useful for her to come and see the LifeSolutions offices in order to have a better idea of the space and surroundings she'd have to work with.

He's laying out a trail of money, knowing I'll follow it to him, she thought when he made the invitation. The problem was there was something inside her that couldn't wait.

"Here, James," Jarvis said. "You already have my business card; here's one with my private cell number on it. Here Sue, I'll give you one too."

"Thanks, but why?" she asked.

"I'd like you to call me," he said turning towards her with a wink, "so we can arrange for you to get a look at our office."

Very sly, she thought…very, very sly. This gave him a legitimate reason to expect her to call.

"Well Jarvis, I'm so glad you could join us for lunch," James interjected. "I hope we'll be able get something for you to look at very soon."

"So do I," he replied.

"If you'd like, I can come over and measure the entryway to your office so we can work out some estimate of cost," James offered.

Jarvis rested his hand on Sue's shoulder. "I don't think cost will be an issue. Let's let that wait until after I've had a chance spend some time with Sue and get an idea of what it is she has in mind. Anyway, I have to run. James thanks for a lovely lunch. Sue, I hope we can work together. I'm very attracted to your style and execution. Please call me fairly soon, though. I'm scheduled to take my family on vacation to Africa shortly, and I'd like to have some idea of what you have in mind before I leave," he said, then turned and reached for the door. As it opened he turned back to look at Sue.

"Would you be interested in doing something jointly with Ms. Dees again?"

Sue's mind froze up. Why in the hell would he say "again" in front of James? She looked quickly at James's face, but if anything registered, it didn't show. "We've never done a work together," was all she could think to say.

"Like the joint show you did together a few years ago?" He went on smiling.

Damn him, he'd done that to throw her off balance. "It's something I might consider. But we're a long way from agreeing on the details of something like that," she said suddenly serious.

Jarvis nodded slowly, then turned and left without saying anything else. After Jarvis had let the door close behind him, James turned back to Sue. His eyes were wide. "What are you doing? Don't blow this by getting all egotistical on me. My God, Sue, this is so exciting. You know you can work with Laura. You're wonderful together."

Yeah, apparently more wonderful than I ever realized. She thought to herself. She was trying to think this thing through some, but James was raving.

"A project like this will be sooo big. You were brilliant, starting that slutty, flirting thing back at the gallery."

"First, how much money is there in 'sooo big'?" she asked. "And secondly, that wasn't slutty flirting. It was more like a series of nervous disasters."

"Well, the money will be more than you've ever made for a single piece, but it'll be a lot more work, too. You know, it'll be different than any of the commissions you've done before. You'll probably have to come up with a couple of different ideas. You need to try and sell him on the idea you want to go with."

"I think that should be do-able," Sue answered thoughtfully.

"What am I talking about? The way he was looking at you the whole lunch, you could probably sell him the bridge to Coronado, if you wanted to. You need to take this seriously. It could end up getting you great exposure. Even better than your little arm motion." He swept his arm back in a pantomime of her awkward pose in the gallery. "You simply have to remember to do that whenever we have a straight client. I wish I could stick my boobs out and sell two paintings without saying a word."

"I don't have any boobs to stick out. Yours are almost as big as mine." She reached over and pinched his nipple. "Try it on your next gay client. If you stick out your crotch too, you might sell three."

James stuck his tongue out at her.

She reached to pinch his tongue. As he turned his head to avoid her fingers, she turned serious. "There's no way I can pass on this, is there?"

"If you do, it will be my duty as your official representative to go to the courts and have you involuntarily committed," he said with a smile. "You have no idea what you're being offered."

Yeah, I think I do, she thought, but aloud she just said, "I guess I'll just have to trust you." It was herself she was wondering if she could trust.

Later at home, Sue sat on the sofa holding her portable phone. She knew the unspoken rules. If she were going to contact Jarvis, she would have to wait until Monday. The weekend was strictly off limits, family time. She wondered if she should call Laura. Laura would be a good sounding board. She'd been there too. Maybe she would have some insight that could propel Sue one way or the other. She knew Laura would have picked up Cody by now. She'd wait and call her tomorrow. It would be a Saturday phone call from a long-distance girlfriend.

CHAPTER TWELVE

Morris ran through a maze of bushes and undergrowth, carrying Cody in his arms. He ran as hard as he could. He wasn't sure if he was chasing Laura or running away from her. It seemed as if he was doing both things at the same time, running like crazy to catch her and terrified that she'd catch him before he could get to her. Suddenly, he was crossing a rock ledge along the side of a steep drop. He couldn't turn back. He moved closer to the edge, shifting the squirming child in his arms. Keeping his back to the rock, he leaned back as far as he could, trying to ease along the ledge. Cody, frightened by the height, stiffened and began to slip from Morris's grasp. What was that sound? He tried to hold on to the boy, but the harder he tried, the more the child slipped. Was that ringing?

Morris sat straight up in the bed with a muffled groan, soaked with sweat, as the phone continued to ring. Crap, now he'd never know how it ended. He looked at the red numerals on the alarm clock beside the bed: 9:45. He looked at Cody, still curled asleep next to him. Cody stirred briefly, and he hurried to pick up the receiver. The caller ID had a 619 area code with "private residence" listed, instead of a name.

"Hello," he said trying not to sound like he just woke up in case it was a client of Laura's.

"Hi, good morning. Is Laura there?" a woman's voice asked.

"No, I'm sorry. She's out in the desert, painting. This is her husband. May I take a message?"

"Not really, there wasn't anything specific," the voice responded.

"May I tell her who called then?" Morris asked. Obviously she didn't know Laura very well. Anyone who knew Laura at all knew she painted in the field on Saturdays.

"Sure, that would be great. This is Sue Wong. I'm another artist Jimmy Watson represents, here in San Diego. Jimmy has a project in the works that he'd like us to collaborate on. I thought I'd talk with her about it. Tell her I just needed to talk to her about a joint project. Okay?"

"Sure thing," he said, ready to get off the phone.

"Just tell her to give me a call, if you would."

Suddenly, several things about what the woman has just said seemed unusual. A joint project? What kind of joint project? It was also kind of strange that he didn't remember anybody named Sue Wong. Laura hadn't mentioned her when she got back from San Diego. Morris decided that maybe he should prolong their conversation to try and get some clues about this project she was talking about.

"So this new project, is that why she's changed the way she's painting?" he asked, fishing.

"No, the idea of the project hadn't come up yet," Sue explained. "So we didn't get a chance to discuss it."

"Well, something's really transformed her painting style," he said, almost to himself, as he considered the implications of that statement in view of his wife's recent behavior. He'd thought that something was going on, but he wasn't sure what it was. He felt awful about it, but he'd sat on a hillside about a mile from their house, spying on Laura through a pair of high-power binoculars as she got ready to go to Phoenix the other day. He'd just wanted to be sure that she really was going and not just spending the day with some guy. He knew it was stupid. She had to be going down there. She was doing something with all of those pictures he framed and the money had to be coming from somewhere.

It was funny. Watching her through the binoculars, he saw her from a new perspective; not physically but like painting, emotionally. Removed from himself, he saw her like other men saw her. It was as if the binoculars provided distance from his anger and from the guilt that he felt about screwing around on her so much. He didn't mean to. Or maybe he did, who knew? The women he screwed were always bored housewives in the middle of a remodeling project. They'd start off trying to improve their marriages by improving their homes. Then they'd end up deciding to spice up their lives a little more than just changing the kitchen cabinets.

Watching her was alive in his mind. Maybe it was the dream, or maybe it was because he wasn't fully awake yet. He let the scene replay itself like a movie across his mind. He could see her like he was looking at her right now. He could see her removed from the guilt of his own failures, as an artist, as a husband, as a father, and all the other areas of life in which he had failed to live up to her unspoken expectations. The failure that stabbed at him every time he saw her painting, knowing he was too strangled by her success to ever stand at an easel again. At home these things killed anything he felt for her, but through the ten-power binoculars he knew how much he'd wanted what he saw. From a distance the subtle looks of disappointment weren't discernible, only her beauty was. Her brunette hair was pulled back with a tortoise shell comb. What he couldn't really see, he filled in from memory. Who in the hell knew what was really holding her hair back, but for now she was like his painting, he could make her be whatever he wanted her to be. The graceful profile of her face, with its upturned nose, green eyes and long eyelashes, belonged on a canvas, not loading them. As she leaned forward, he focused on her graceful body, and her beautiful round butt covered by a pair of jeans. That was a work of art unto itself, the way the jeans hugged the perfect arc of the curve.

Why didn't he feel like this when they were really together? He knew other men enjoyed watching her, following her retreating form with their eyes, sometimes irritating the women they were with. It made him furious. No matter what, she was still his wife.

He watched as she slammed the lift gate down and walked around the far side of her car to lock the door of their house. As she came around the front of the car, she turned and looked straight at him, almost as if she could see him as well as he could see her. Then he noticed something different about her. She was smiling. She almost never smiled anymore. Her mouth had become a thin, hard line.

Morris had the uneasy feeling that things were changing between them, or more specifically, that she was changing. He couldn't put his finger on how. He just knew she was.

"What do you mean?" Sue asked.

"About what?" Morris asked. He had been lost in his own thoughts and had forgotten what he'd said last.

"What do you mean she transformed her painting style?" Sue asked.

"Oh, yeah…well I've noticed a real shift in her style, much looser, more passion, less control." He wasn't sure if he was talking about her painting or her behavior.

"That's interesting. Those are some of the things we talked about. You seem to know a lot about painting," she replied.

"The first time we ever laid eyes on each other was in color theory class at UCSF. We were studying Itten. We both got our BFAs the same year. I painted in San Francisco a few years while she stayed and worked on her MFA."

"That's interesting," Sue responded. "What sort of things are you doing now?"

"Wooden things," he replied. "I came to the point that I couldn't stand to paint anymore."

"So now you're doing sculpture?"

"Nope, carpentry. I kind of burned out on the whole commercial aspect of art. I hated the idea that people want you to paint the same thing over and over, just different enough that they're sure they have an original. Who needs that? I was just a craftsman and not an artist anymore. So I quit." He knew that at this point he'd shared enough. Attacking the gallery system to a person who made her living from it wasn't going to go over too well. "So how is it that just a lunch together brought on such a change in Laura's painting?" he asked.

"Because she already knew what changes she needed to make, in general terms," Sue said. "I just said I thought she'd gotten into a rut and needed to liven things up a bit."

"I wish I could have found a way to do that when I was still painting," he said almost wistfully. "I tried everything I could think of to reinvigorate my imagination. Nothing worked." The truth was, he missed the creative process of painting.

"Your wife's a talented woman. She didn't change her subject or her inspiration. She just altered the execution."

This wasn't really going anywhere, and he certainly didn't want to hear how talented Laura was over and over. He sensed that, although Sue Wong was answering him, she was still holding back more than she revealed. The name Wong bounced around his memory like a ball on a roulette wheel, eventually dropping into a slot.

"Didn't you and Laura do a show together a few years ago?"

"Yeah, I think it was 2006.... Well, tell her I called. She has my number."

"Okay, I'll let her know. See ya." Morris disconnected, then lay back, wrapping his arms around his still sleeping son. He let his mind wander over the conversation. She had a California accent. No real trace of an oriental overlay. She had been, not evasive but ... inscrutable, he thought, allowing the stereotype to apply itself. He wanted to see what she looked like.

He disentangled himself from Cody, being careful not to wake him up. He made a cup of Maxwell House with the hot water dispenser he had installed on their sink and headed to the computer. He went directly to the website for Watson's Gallery and pulled up Sue Wong's bio. She fit her voice. She was about Laura's age and very pretty, a bit small-breasted for his taste. He came across a photo of her in her gallery painting, tight shorts stretched across an asset that made up for any possible deficiencies elsewhere. This was a hot chick, not some old oriental matron.

"....and how, Ms. Wong, did you help her 'liven things up a bit?'" he asked her rear end on the computer screen.

He heard the soft sound of small footsteps coming down the hall and Cody's sleepy voice asking, "Daddy, are you in here? Daddy let's watch some cartoons." He rose, clicking off-line.

"I'm in here buddy. Want to see if Pokémon's still on?"

He finished his coffee watching Japanese animation with American voices, as he played the conversation over and over again in his head.

It was, in fact, right after she had returned from San Diego that he first noticed a change in Laura. It was her attitude and demeanor, the way she held herself that he noticed first. The differences in her painting style he had seen only later. He thought at first that she was pumped up from a successful trip, but when he checked the inventory list she kept, she had sold only two paintings in California, a fairly poor performance. If she was concerned about poor sales, that could have accounted for a change in her painting style, but it didn't explain her air of self-confidence or the new sense of distance that existed between them.

Two songs alternated, verses from each intertwined and combined in his head so they almost became a single song. "She's Already Made Up Her Mind," by Lyle Lovett kept winding itself into Paul Simon's "Graceland."

She's already made up her mind...as if I didn't know that, as if I didn't know my own bed…. Then there was the line about ghosts and empty sockets, ghosts and empties, or something like that.

He sure had a ghost traveling with him now, a suspicious ghost. Laura, of course, was the empty socket, empty, as far as he was concerned. There was no love light left for him. There wasn't even a bulb to give him the hope of light.

He didn't know where Laura was trying to go with all this. He only knew that, whatever it was that she'd decided, she was resolute, and he didn't see how anything he said or did could really change things anymore. What a mess. He hugged Cody a little harder and smelled his little boy hair, hoping that the outcome of what had already been put into motion wouldn't hurt this sweet child. Children needed two parents. That's the only reason he'd stayed so long, but Laura was calling the shots right now. She'd determine how it all turned out; all he could really do was continue to respond to what she presented to him. He knew she was screwing around and even though he did it himself, something about it made him feel miserable.

A Fine and Pleasant Misery. Who had written that? It described how he felt. He would try to find it later at the bookstore. He thought he remembered seeing it in the comedy section. A farce would be appropriate, he thought.

He felt like anyone could learn almost anything they needed to know, just by spending enough time to gain a knowledge base, then applying that knowledge to perform and perfect the skills you needed. That was how he learned cabinetry. Now he was going to need to spend some time learning the things he was needed to know. But marriage was an art.

Art was different. Art wasn't just skill. Morris knew what art, real art was. He recognized it. Creating it, however, was a different story. Laura didn't feel that pressure. She was happy to be a good, proficient landscape painter. She was free of the need to redefine, to expand the way people thought about art. It was enough for her to paint what she saw. Why not use a camera? What was the point?

The last really original artistic idea he'd had had to do with guns, but not using them on people. It was a concept he'd thought of right after they'd moved to Arizona. He and Laura had been on a day trip driving up the old Schnebly Hill trail to Flagstaff. As they drove through the city they saw what, to him, was the epitome of freedom…freedom pushed to the level of absurdity.

Black Jack Drive Thru Liquor and Guns.

They both had Arizona driver's licenses. This was something he had to do. He pulled up to the window and ordered a fifth of Jack Daniels Black, a two-liter Coke, and, after looking at several used pistols, a Colt .22 New Frontier for Laura and the long barreled Colt Bisley for himself. He'd looked up the serial number. That old gun was made in 1903. They'd only made three hundred and forty-two of them in thirty-eight/forty that year. Thirty-eight/forty wasn't a common caliber. It wouldn't take them long to find him if he shot somebody with that.

The experience of buying the gun, the first one he'd ever owned, seemed to rejuvenate his creativity. He had an idea that he felt was just the thing he was looking for. Painting with guns. He would use his woodworking skills to make a box, he would then line the box with canvas and suspend three balloons filled with liquid acrylic paint by string so that they were centered sequentially in the box and then shoot the balloons. Before the paint could stiffen and dry, he'd remove the canvas and stretch it centered however it would be most dramatic. He would start with the three primary colors, red, blue, and yellow. He had worked out the details on the drive home. It would create huge controversy, if he could get it publicized. Anti-gun groups would be protesting his art. It would allow him to make the point, that an inanimate object couldn't have a specific moral value. Guns weren't necessarily good or bad. They could be used as tools of creativity just as well as they could be used for destruction. It had been a white-hot moment of inspiration. Unfortunately, the heat burnt out too quickly, and the next morning, without the fortification of bourbon, it seemed just a little less brilliant. But he still wanted to try it just to see if it would work. After a week had passed without the necessary box being built, the plan was officially a stupid idea, tossed on the scrap heap of burned out ideas with a thousand others, to be picked up and rolled around his head when he was driving long distances alone or lying in bed unable to sleep. But this new art he needed to learn was a different thing, a thing that was going to require some study if he was going to do it right, and he wasn't sure he even wanted to. He just hated the idea of tossing his marriage onto that same scrapheap that held so much of his life.

"Hey daddy, I'm hungry," Cody said, interrupting his thoughts. Pokémon was over.

"Okay pal, let's get dressed. Do you want to go to the play place at McDonald's or eat some donuts?"

"McDonald's!" Cody exclaimed, jumping off the arm of the recliner onto the ottoman, then to the arm of Laura's chair, back to the ottoman, then on to the floor.

"Last one dressed gets a pinchy butt," Morris challenged before running down the hall, knowing he was going to lose by a shoe.

CHAPTER THIRTEEN

Jarvis Sloan stood in the back of the darkened auditorium, watching his eight-year-old son Seth's school play through the viewfinder of a brand new video recorder that he had very little idea how to operate. The play was about the coming of spring. On stage, several children, mostly boys, were dressed as forest creatures. Each child recited a garbled line in a singsong voice describing the hardships of winter.

Seth's role was that of a wise owl who reassured the animals that winter was nearly over and spring was on its way. Jarvis tried to stay focused on Seth's moving face, but his flapping arms, or the butt of the child playing a raccoon, frequently obscured it. The raccoon stood on an elevated "stump" made of cardboard and two-by-fours, dominating center stage. Jarvis would zoom in and out awkwardly, trying to get a better view of his son. Unfortunately, he usually made his adjustments at exactly the wrong time, just missing whatever it was that he was trying to tape. He knew he had plenty of shots of the raccoon's ass and the back of the head of the woman in front of him. In the play's big finale, as Seth the owl predicted, many other children, all girls, dressed as flowers danced across the stage in the closing number. Seth had of course been brilliant, certainly a second-grade prodigy. Jarvis hit the rewind button and re-watched the final number.

"Crap," he said under his breath. His wife and children would tease him later about his lack of video recording skills. They always gave him a hard time about it, but they always made him do the recording. It was a no-win situation. Getting Sharon to do it was out of the question. She wasn't very technically astute. Her recordings were frequently sound with a blacked-out screen because she had forgotten to take off the lens cap. He could have had one of the videographers from LA record it, but that might be just a bit much. What he ought to do was offer to have all of the school's activities videographed in the future and write it off as a charitable contribution to the school. They could distribute copies to the other parents, and nobody would have to fool with these stupid video cameras. The problem was, if the tape was for everybody, then the close focus on Seth would be lost. Amateur videos, even ones that sucked, still had a special charm that professional video couldn't capture. It was the goofiness and mistakes that made them special. As the lights came on and the children began to file off the stage, Jarvis moved down the aisle to stand next to Paul, his youngest son, and Sharon.

"Did you get it all?" Sharon asked.

"I think I did pretty well for a brand-new camera. These stupid mini-sticks only last a half hour, so the last ten minutes are on a different stick," he explained.

"You can fix that on the computer, if you want," Paul said, then added, "You're going to have to get better at that, 'cause I want some great videos of Africa so I can take them to school and show the other kids."

"Africa's all he's talked about for a week," Sharon said. "You two stay here. I'm going to go backstage and get Seth." She made her way through the crowd of parents and kids clogging the front of the stage.

"Hey Dad, I'm going over by the juice machines to talk to Matt," Paul said over his shoulder, already leaving.

Jarvis was standing alone in the middle of a sea of people when his cell phone rang. The only people who had this number since his parents died were Sharon, the boys, and his secretary, Ruthie.

"Hello," he answered.

"Mr. Sloan?" an unfamiliar woman's voice asked.

"Yes, can I help you?" he responded.

"Hi, it's Sue Wong. May I call you Jarvis?"

"I think we're well enough acquainted for that. I'm happy to hear from you so soon," he said, a smile spreading across his face.

"I have to admit that I nearly stroked out when I realized who you were last Friday," Sue said.

"You certainly overcame it well. You seemed to be a very self-assured woman. But that was pretty apparent the first time we met," Jarvis said as his voice drifted a bit, remembering.

"I guess I was the ringleader," Sue answered.

"That's an apt term. Certainly for some of the positions we found ourselves in. It was obvious you're an artist," he offered. "I assume you were my original Time Donor."

"Yeah, I was, but at the last minute I felt like my friend needed some help. I didn't think you would mind. You didn't seem to, anyway."

"Well, I'm always glad to help out a friend in need. You don't have to thank me," he joked. "It was hard work, but I'm happy I was able to help her out."

"Well you handled it very well. I just hope it wasn't _too_ hard for you," Sue returned lightly, then changed her tone. "But I do have to tell you, I'm kind of nervous about you just showing back up. I never expected to see you again, so I haven't processed things beyond the 'that was nice' level."

"I'm kind of in the same boat. I don't know ..." He saw Sharon making her way toward him, Seth, still in his owl costume, in tow. "Look Sue, I'm at a play at my son's school. Can I call you back when I get to the office, after lunch?"

"Oh sure," she said, exhaling like a balloon when all of the air is let out.

"I'll get back to you on that, after I have a chance to go over the paperwork," Jarvis said as he disconnected, all business now that Sharon was within earshot.

"Who was that?" Sharon asked.

"The producer for the new seminar; he says they're going to need more money," he answered.

"They always need more money," Sharon advised. "It's your job to make them stay on budget."

"Easier said than done, sweetie," Jarvis said, kissing her cheek. "Okay Seth, stand by your mom so I can get a picture."

The play was followed by lunch in the school cafeteria. Jarvis found himself sitting on a backless, shortened stool, which was impossible to adjust because it was attached to the table. Jarvis had to sit with his knees jammed against the underside of the tabletop. Students and parents sat together eating the school's new nutritionally enhanced food off trays that reminded him very much of his own days in elementary school. This was a clear pitch to the parents, to show them how much attention the school was paying to what their kids ate. As much as they paid to send their kids here Jarvis figured the school felt they had to justify it somehow. The food was pretty crappy anyway, nutritionally enhanced or not.

Jarvis grew up during the height of the health food craze in California. Every kid had a recycled brown paper sack filled with granola, yogurt, and occasionally organic carrot cake or zucchini bread. He remembered when they celebrated "Earth Day" every spring. They were all going to save the planet from the mismanagement of their parent's generation.

What a switch! Now he was one of the irresponsible generation, pretty much unconcerned about the ecology and quite willing to eat prepackaged, reheated meals for the sake of convenience. His sons were the ones watching Animal Planet and Discovery Channel, making plans to save endangered species. They were the ones who criticized his diet and encouraged him to eat more fruits and vegetables. They were the ones who decided that the family should go to Africa for spring break.

The rest of the school's week was filled with spring-related activities. There was even a big "spring fling" for families on Thursday night. Then the children would get off Friday at noon to start their spring break. For the Sloan family, spring break would begin with an eighteen-hour flight to Kenya.

When he and Sharon had asked the boys where they should go for spring break, both boys quickly chose Africa. Paul, the youngest, immediately started planning pens in the back yard to hold the various animals he was planning to bring back with him. Explanations that the customs officials would probably be pretty unhappy with suitcases filled with lizards, snakes, and crocodiles did little to deter his enthusiasm. Even Sharon was excited. She'd bought new digital cameras for each of them. That also had been the impetus for the new video recorder that he was still trying to learn to use.

He had to admit, he was pretty excited too. He'd never been to Africa. In fact, he'd never been much of an outdoor person at all. Because of that, he'd been doing quite a bit of research lately so he wouldn't look like too much of a geek in front of the boys. Now, he just had to conquer his natural aversions to bugs and reptiles. For the past year Paul had delighted in creeping him out with pet tarantulas and scorpions. Seeing the boys with the horrid creatures, walking around outside their containers, gave Jarvis cold chills down the back of his neck. Even now, without an animal in sight, the very idea made Jarvis shift uncomfortably on the cramped stool on which he was perched.

"I think Dad's way too big for this table," Paul laughed.

"I think you're right," Jarvis agreed, then turned toward Seth and asked, "Do any of the kids bring their lunch?"

The look of repugnance on his face answered the question before he said, "No, that would be gross." He looked at his dad in the same way he would have if Jarvis had just asked him if he wanted a booger sandwich.

"Well, you'd better get used to it," Jarvis advised.

"No way! I'm not bringing my lunch," Seth said emphatically.

"Then you're going to get really hungry in Africa. All of the photo safaris we're going on have sack lunches," Jarvis said, winking at Paul, who smiled, knowing his brother had stepped right in to their Dad's trap.

"He gotcha that time," Paul said in delight.

"That's not the same at all. You can't eat a regular lunch with a lion watching you. They might get hungry and attack," Seth explained as if the rest of them were a little on the slow side.

"You don't think a baloney sandwich is worth attacking over?" Jarvis teased.

Sharon reached up, messed up the back of Jarvis's hair, and said to the boys, "I think your father's the one that's full of baloney."

Both boys laughed in agreement, and then Paul chimed in seriously, "Dad's full of baloney because he never eats any fruit or vegetables. He only eats meat. That's how you get full of baloney." He nodded his head sagely.

"I think you're all full of baloney," Jarvis said laughing. He stood stiffly as he rose from the stool. When he was finally up, he looked down at his family and said in a ringmaster impression, "Tonight, after dinner, in the amazing and wonderful arena called the den, for your enjoyment and amazement we will present Seth Sloan and the Scripps/Palomar Academy second-grade class in a movie produced and directed by Jarvis M. Sloan. Spring is Coming."

"Dad, please stop. Everybody's looking at you," Seth begged. Sharon gave him "the eye."

He leaned forward and said quietly, "I guess, I'd better get back to the office. I love you guys." He kissed both boys' cheeks. Seth quickly rubbed his cheek, as if to rub it off. Then he air kissed in the vicinity of Sharon's cheek and started to leave. After he had taken the first step, he turned back to his family and asked, "Is it okay if I sing on the way out? I loved that song about spring."

"No," they all three shouted in unison.

After lunch at the school, he arrived at his office at 1:30. As soon as he got to his desk, he began to scroll through the received calls on his cell phone. There weren't many, so it was simple to pick out Sue's number, as it was the only one he didn't recognize.

"Hello," Sue answered.

"Hi, this is Jarvis Sloan. I was calling back. I was glad to hear from you earlier, but I couldn't hear."

"From the way you ended the conversation, I'd say it was more likely that your wife could hear," Sue said pointedly. "I know you're married, so let's not start off telling lies."

"It was more of a social convenience," Jarvis explained.

"Well, let's cut the convenience. In the future, I'd prefer the truth. So with that in mind, I need to know what is it you want with me?" Sue asked bluntly.

Jarvis decided to use a psychotherapy tool. He simply reversed the question, asking, "What do you think I'm after?"

"Sex is the obvious answer, or more precisely, more sex. Frankly, the more I think about lunch, the more freaked out I get," Sue said.

"I didn't mean to 'freak you out.' I just wanted a chance to sort out what happened. I don't really even know what I'm after. I just know what I felt when the three of us were together. It was the most exciting experience I can remember," Jarvis tried to explain.

"How did you even find me? I thought the whole purpose of TimeDonors was that there wasn't any way it could be traced, so no one could find you afterwards," she asked.

"It is," he replied, "but I own the system, so I used an engineering password to access my own file before the system purged it. From there, I just tracked it to you. Then I put your name in a Google search and the Watkins' Gallery came up."

"Why?" Sue asked. "You're obviously a very rich man. If you want two women, you could afford to have two professionals. Why go to all the trouble to track me down and use my art to make me come to you?"

"Because what happened between the three of us was special; it wasn't just two women. It was the two of you, the way you reacted, the way I reacted...I don't know, there were a thousand things that made it different."

"That doesn't answer my question. Why are you pursuing me, specifically?" Sue demanded.

"You're the link. You brought Laura, you're the artist that started this painting," he explained.

"Which brings up another point. How do you know Laura's name?" she asked.

Jarvis heard the apprehension in her voice as she asked; he adjusted his answer to soothe her fears. "James showed me a picture of you. Laura was in it and I recognized her. I asked him her name. I liked her paintings, so I bought two of hers, as well as the two of yours I saw on my first visit to the gallery."

"No wonder James is jumping through hoops. Look Jarvis, my art's for sale. I'm not, and neither is Laura. I've known her a long time. Her marriage is in a rough spot right now, but buying her paintings isn't going to get her to do something she isn't comfortable with."

"I'm not trying to buy anybody," he responded defensively. "I bought the paintings because I liked them; the fact that they were also a way to get introduced to you was an added benefit. Yes, I spent some money to achieve a goal, but the goal was to meet you, not to buy sex from you or force you to have sex with me. Like you said, I could have gotten professionals for that, for a lot less money than I've already spent, if that's what I was after. What I want is the sense of intimacy and exploration I felt when we were all together. That's all."

"And you think you can find that with me?" she asked.

"I want the three of us to find it together," he replied.

There was a prolonged silence on the line before she spoke. "So it's not me you're after? It's both of us?"

"It's what we had. Just for that moment," he answered awkwardly.

"Jarvis, what happened was a fluke. I'd never done anything like that, neither had Laura. I knew she was unhappy and frustrated with her husband. I was just trying to think of something fun and I just said to myself 'well, just bring her along.' It wasn't something I thought out. As it was, it took us two bottles of wine to get up the nerve to carry through with it. I really don't think what happened can be recreated. It's a great memory but it's gone. It's just a memory."

"I'm not saying it could be the same, but that doesn't mean it couldn't be wonderful. Have you ever tried to relive a moment from childhood, a walk, a visit to your parent's hometown, going up to Juliane for the apple festival? I'll admit it's not the same but it can still be a meaningful, fulfilling experience to add to your memory, in and of itself."

"You sound like a psychiatrist," she said.

"I am," he replied.

"You are what?" she asked.

"I'm a psychiatrist," he answered.

"I thought you owned LifeSolutions. I thought you were a computer guy."

"Actually I'm both. I'm a psychiatrist who developed LifeSolutions. It's really a group of self-help seminars designed to provide some guidance in dealing with different problems people might have. Have you ever been to one of the seminar sites?" he asked.

"No, not really," she replied. "A girlfriend showed me how to get to TimeDonors when I was just getting divorced so I wouldn't be lonely or have to resort to picking guys up in bars."

"Did it work?" he asked.

"So far it's worked for me. Until Friday, that is. Then some guy tracked me down and started to make me deal with a bunch of questions and complications. You're a psychiatrist. You can understand. I don't want any complications. That's what TimeDonors was for me. No 'can I call you tomorrow?' No messy rejection on either side. Just 'thanks, that was great,' and you walk out the door and back into your own life. No pressure to share it with anyone else."

"I'm sorry. I didn't mean to ruin it for you," Jarvis offered. "I just needed to find out if you and Laura were interested in seeing where this can end up. TimeDonors is something that works well for a lot of people. It's worked for you. It just hasn't worked out as well for me. I found it limiting. There's no chance for it to go anywhere. You were the last appointment I ever intended to make," Jarvis confessed.

"The creator loses faith in his creation," she said. "Artists do the same thing. I call it the thirty-day waiting period. I used to drive myself crazy until I felt like my paintings were finished. I'd put them in my car. I'd drive them to the gallery. I'd hang them up. Sometimes I'd even paint on them there. But then I'd freak out and feel like they weren't good enough, so I'd take them home and put them into the closet for thirty days, just to make myself quit fooling with them. I just couldn't get them where I thought they were good enough, good enough for me."

"So you don't do that anymore?" Jarvis asked.

"She probably wouldn't, but I'll talk to her and let you know if she's interested," Sue replied.

"Sue, please call me back whatever she decides, okay?" he asked.

"Jarvis, if she's out, I'm out. This isn't going to turn into you and me. You understand that?" she said earnestly.

"I understand," he said and heard her disconnect.

Well, at least it's a start, he thought.

CHAPTER FOURTEEN

Laura felt great as she unloaded the paintings she'd brought with her from the back of the Suburban. The grogginess she usually had to fight with on the drive down had been replaced by a sense of excitement and anticipation. Kent met her at the door, holding it open for her as she carried in the paintings. His excitement was obvious. He literally snatched the paintings out of her hands and hurried to put them on an empty wall usually reserved for her work.

"Where're the paintings that were there?" she asked.

"They're gone, girl. All of them, gone," Kent almost sang. "The two you just brought in, they're already sold. The three you brought in last time, gone in two days. Everything else on the wall, just G-O-N-E. Baby, you're hot right now. I talked to James over the weekend. He sold two of your paintings Friday. You've sold twelve paintings that I know of in the last two weeks. That calls for a celebration!"

"Like my grandfather used to say, 'you gotta make hay while the sun shines,'" Laura replied, not knowing what else to say.

"From what James says, you better buy a new baler," Kent said cryptically.

"What does that mean?" she asked.

"James was really excited about some really rich guy that owns a web-based company or something. His company has already bought two of your paintings for their corporate collection. Now they want to consider you for a big project, something designed to represent their company."

"A mural or something. I've never done a mural." For Cody's sake, Laura wasn't sure she wanted to take on a large-scale project away from home. Especially if it meant she'd have to be away from home for extended periods. She knew Morris would take good care of him, but Cody tended to get anxious if either of them was away for more than a few days. Maybe it would be something she could complete in Sedona and ship. Who knew?

Kent looked at her face and took her hand. "Can you stop worrying until we get the details at least?"

She and Kent quickly telephoned James and everything he knew sounded pretty promising. The only other artist being considered was Sue Wong. He wasn't sure yet about the dimensions or the space

involved. He just knew it was big, an entryway or reception area.
He'd know more in the next week or so.

Laura agreed to return to San Diego as soon as he knew the
details. She'd need to look at the space and hear exactly what the
company's representative was looking for before she could try to
come up with a proposal.

After their phone call, she and Kent jumped around, holding
hands like a pair of ten-year-olds.

"I told you, you were hot," Kent beamed, elated.

"Maybe you better write me my check now. Since you're in
such a good mood, maybe you'll feel generous," Laura said smiling.

"You do know how to ruin a moment," Kent said with mock
glumness.

"I'll tell you what. Since I'm the rich artist, I'll buy lunch," she
said, putting her arm around his shoulder.

They decided to eat lunch on the patio at Old Town Tortilla
Factory. Laura only ate half of her enchiladas verde, even though it
was one of her favorites, a tasty dish of chicken, tomatillo salsa, and
sour cream wrapped in a flour tortilla. She didn't want to overeat and
feel stuffed and sleepy all afternoon. She had plans, and those plans
didn't involve sleeping. As excited as she was about the plans, she
wasn't sure she'd go through with them. She'd immediately had
some hesitation about the arrangements that had been suggested by
the man who identified himself as "Doubting Thomas." Thomas had
suggested they meet at the apartment of a single friend of his who was
currently out of town. Although she couldn't see how, there was the
nagging suspicion that this could be more dangerous than meeting at a
motel or hotel. There was the chance of something unforeseen going
wrong. She couldn't imagine what, but that was why they called it
unforeseen, wasn't it? The apartment was just east of Old Town out
toward the Salt River Indian Reservation.

Rousing from her concerns, she realized that Kent was in the
middle of a long and complicated story. He continued "—so, I told
her, 'I don't care what your interior decorator says, the brighter colors
are so much more exciting.' I just told her straight out, 'it just
depends on what you value most, a wonderful work of art or that drab
ratty wallpaper you've had for years.'"

"And that's why you sell paintings, and I can't. I'd have said,
'Fine I'm not selling you the painting anyway!' If she's too stupid to
appreciate it, I don't want her to have it," Laura said vehemently.

"That's why you should stick to painting," Kent replied.

Her mind wandered. As she sipped her unsweetened tea and
chatted about art with Kent, she casually wondered if she would go or
not. It was like teasing herself. How much did she want it? As she
played with the idea, she began to realize that this was a part of the
excitement, that there was an excitement and eroticism that pervaded

the entire decision-making process. It wasn't the sex only. It was the act of choosing and the moments before it actually started, that were the most pleasing and stimulating.

Like lying alone in bed naked, hand resting on your thigh when you feel something down there star to warm and before long there's a slight tingle and an ache. Will you touch it? The more you delay, the more the tingle builds to a throb, forming a biologic electromagnetism that starts a soft movement, the barest brushing of fingers. The brushing must stir up the electrons or something, because you know then where your fingers will end up. It's the buildup, the slowness of progression that is the most delicious, the savoring of a delicacy. The orgasm is the food less tasted that feeds the hunger, the need to come. You wish, though, that the sweet tasty delicacy of anticipation could last forever, unrushed by the demands of hunger. That was something men must never get. They go straight to the food.

Her mental fingertips began to brush the tender neurons of her midbrain, teasing the more primitive portion of her consciousness. Would she? Wouldn't she? Would she? Wouldn't she?

"Oh crap." Morris said, looking at the GPS he'd literally stuck under the hood of Laura's truck. He wasn't much at electronics, but the instructions that came with the kit showed him how to plug it into the fuse box and turn it on. To fasten it to the car, he had just taped it there on the side of the engine compartment with some duct tape.

He'd used it to track Laura to the gallery. It was working perfectly then. He sat down the street and watched them through his binoculars as the two of them unloaded her truck. Then the two of them went into the gallery and stayed for fucking ever. When they finally did come out, he followed her to the restaurant where she was having lunch with Kent, and they took forever with that too. So he'd gone to the Burger King a few blocks west of here to grab a bite at the drive through. Driving back, the GPS never moved then without warning it just went dead. He was eating the hamburger and driving but he was watching it the whole time. He was tapping on the receiver, trying to get the signal back, when he turned the corner and a bunch of stuff fell out of his sandwich. A big blob of mayonnaise with flecks of chopped lettuce that had disgorged itself from the Whopper he was eating fell and smeared all over the leg of his pants. When he turned the next corner to drive in front of the restaurant, her car was gone.

He stopped near where she had been parked and, when he looked down, the GPS, with a tangle of wires hanging off of it, was lying in the gravel parking lot. He should have used more tape. He picked it up and started to turn it around in his hands as if somehow that might give him a clue as to where his wife was now. It didn't help. Pretty much the whole endeavor was hopeless now, with the electronics gone. Now he'd never find her. If he did, it would have to be by complete accident. He didn't even have any idea of where to start.

All he could think to do was to go home and forget it. Maybe he could drive around randomly and look for her for a while before he headed back north. There wasn't much chance he'd find her. If he did, he'd just have to hope she didn't recognize him as the driver if they passed each other.

There was no way Laura would recognize the truck he was driving. It belonged to Billy Denison, his helper. Laura'd never seen it. He'd been using it to meet up with some of the women he'd been screwing around with so he wouldn't get caught. He let Billy use the company truck on Wednesdays, when he sent him to do errands and small repair jobs. Morris always told everyone that he needed the day to catch up on paperwork and take care of invoices and stuff.

Billy would leave the keys to his own truck on the keyboard, at the front of the trailer they used as an office, so Morris could use it if something came up. What usually came up was Morris. He had a couple of old customers, other men's wives who had finished remodeling their houses but still needed Morris to tweak a few things while their husbands were at work. Now he was using the same truck to try and catch his own wife doing the same thing.

He hit the rim of the steering wheel with his palm when he got back behind the wheel. He held the GPS up and looked at it again like some dead piece of road kill. Then he tossed it onto the floorboard on the passenger side. He jammed the truck into gear and made two quick right turns to try and see if he could find her. What a clusterfuck.

A pickup pulling out in front of him made him hit his brakes hard.

"Why am I doing this? What in the hell am I doing here?" he asked himself. After all, he'd been having affairs since Cody was born. Actually his first affair had been when Laura was six months pregnant.

He certainly didn't want Laura following him around, trying to catch him with the women he slept with. Why couldn't he accept that she was just doing the same thing? He was sure she'd known about his affairs for a while. If she didn't know for sure, at least she had a good idea that it might be happening. But over the years, he guessed, she'd just accepted it. For the past few years, he hadn't even tried very hard to hide it anymore. She had more than enough reasons to leave him, but she hadn't. Why couldn't he let this go?

Morris knew the reason he couldn't. It didn't make any sense, but it was because he still loved her. His affairs were meaningless fun, just something different to take the sting out of the fact that he'd failed and she hadn't.

He knew how he felt about Laura. Other women didn't mean he didn't love his family. They didn't mean that he didn't care about his wife. Morris's main fear was that it was only a matter of time before Laura realized that she didn't really need him anymore. She certainly didn't need him financially. Now she was finding out that she didn't need him sexually either.

Women weren't like men. They got sex and love confused. They thought they were the same thing. He was afraid that if Laura started seeing someone regularly, she'd get all tangled up with all of that and that would be the end for Morris.

He felt like crying. He felt his eyes stinging behind the sunglass lenses. Morris had never been insecure before, and he certainly had never expected to be so insecure that he followed his wife around. This had to stop. He just needed to get everything out in the open and ask her to stop. She'd probably laugh or scream. He could hear her now. "After all of these years of you doing whatever you feel like, now you want _me_ to stop?"

Laura maneuvered her big car into the tight parking space on the street outside of the apartment complex. This was a residential area with small groups of apartments on both sides of the street. This was going to be a whole lot scarier than the motel. She'd have to be calmer, more controlled. She'd have to think things through this time and be ready to run at the first sign of trouble. She reached into her purse and made sure that her little Colt was on top of everything else, where it would be easy to reach if she needed it.

Laura followed the directions she'd written down. Right three blocks, second building on the left side of the street, apartment 1004. The building only had three stories, so she assumed that 1004 would be on the first floor, but that sure was a silly way to assign numbers. As she approached the building, the walkway led to a gated pedestrian entrance with a call box next to the gate. She buzzed apartment 1004 and saw the name "Busby" printed below the number.

"Hello? Hello? How in the hell does this damned thing work?" a man's voice said over the intercom.

"Hi, this is Esther. Can you buzz me in?" she asked. Staying with the biblical theme he had set in his choice of screen names, she'd identified herself as "Esther with an H" a dual reference to both the Old Testament heroine who had become queen because of her beauty and the adulterous heroine of The Scarlet Letter.

"I hope so. I think it's this button," the voice replied.

Laura heard the buzz of the electromagnetic lock as the current held the latch open. She opened the gate quickly.

"It's the fourth apartment to the right of the pool," the voice said from the speaker on the other side of the gate.

As she approached the pool area, she saw a sign that explained the numbering dilemma she had been wondering about. Apartments 101 - 114 were to the left of the pool and apartments 1001 – 1012 were to the right of the pool.

A red haired man with a handsome face, a good body and a big smile was approaching her along the side of the pool. He held out his hand and she took it as he fell in step beside her. They didn't speak. He led her to an open door he must have just come out of. It was dark inside. Some of it was her eyes. She had to start wearing darker sunglasses, so she could take them off without her eyes having to adjust. This was a risk thing, she thought to herself.

As she scanned her surroundings, the light disappeared as Thomas pushed the door shut behind him. Before she could turn around, he was against her from behind. He pressed his erection into her bottom from behind as he reached around her to grab her breasts. One hand dropped to her crotch, and he was trying to force it into the top of her jeans. It hurt just a little but she liked it. He was clumsy, but he was eager. She wasn't sure she'd want him for a regular lover, but it was okay for now, and now it was her turn. She turned to face him, pushed him back against the back of the couch, and then sank to her knees. She didn't even remember how she'd gotten his pants down, but she had. He wasn't very big around but he was long, like spaghetti. Each time she moved her head, she pushed him deeper and deeper into the back of her throat. She pulled away to take a breath then threw herself against him, pushing herself harder and harder. She tried to see just how far she could force him into her throat. As his body began to stiffen, she stopped. She was in control for once, and she liked it.

He moaned in disappointment, "don't…don't…oh no…don't stop now."

She repeated her actions three then four more times. Each time she brought him closer and closer to the edge, and each time she stopped before he could cross over. By the fourth time she was ready to take him in a new direction. She'd let him come, but not in her. She wouldn't give him that. It was a funny sort of power, one she never felt like she ever had with her husband. He came whenever he wanted to come. It was her that ended up feeling like she needed to beg for some sort of release.

"Now I'm going to manhandle you," she whispered, her voice hoarse from what she'd been doing. His body twitched and jerked spasmodically, and she took pity on him. She began to rub her palm gently up and down, over and under. She played, not letting him have the release he wanted.

"Please…please…," he started to whisper over and over with each movement of her hand. She moved behind him without moving her hand.

"Now?" she asked.

"Yes...now..."

"You want me to let you come now?" Her voice was hard and hoarse. With her free hand she grabbed the back of his hair and pushed him forward so both of his hands were grabbing the back of the couch

"Yesssss, yesss," he begged.

She jerked rapidly with her hand and pressed the front of her jeans against him from behind. She wanted to be the penetrator. She thrust against him as he splattered the back of the couch.

CHAPTER FIFTEEN

Willie Weeks was eating breakfast when his cell phone rang. He sat down his steak biscuit and opened the cell.

"Hola Muchacho," the voice of Mole` Ruiz greeted him.

"Hey bro," Weeks responded. "How've you been?"

"Not bad. A little busy, but that's why I get the big bucks," Mole` replied. They both knew that, in Phoenix, a forensic tech in the Medical examiner's office made less than a detective.

"Well, maybe you can get me on over at the M.E.'s office," Weeks suggested, "because nothing's happening over here."

"Well, that's why I'm calling Dance King. I thought you might need old Mole` to perk things up for you."

"It's too early for anything but coffee to perk. Want to grab a few beers later? We can have dinner and catch the ballgame tonight on the tube?" Weeks asked. "The Suns can still make the play-offs if they win."

"I'd love to, man. I hope they make it. Are you going with Father Joe and the kids Friday for the next game here?" Mole` asked.

"Yeah, sure. You want me to pick you up?" Weeks replied.

"Sure, man. Remember when we were always in the finals? We had it all back in what? 1992? Barkley, Ainge, Westphal as a coach. We even got a new arena that year. How many championships could we have won if Jordan had broken a leg or something?" That was one of Mole's favorite pastimes, the 'what if' game. "Now it's a big deal if we make it into the first round of the play-offs. I wish I could get away tonight. I'd love to watch the game, but I'm covered up in work. Shit, I almost forgot what I called for. Can you come down here?"

"That will perk me up all right, bro... a coffee with the stiffs at the morgue. Do any of them like basketball?" Weeks said.

"That's not what I had in mind," Mole` replied. "I mean now, this is business. I think I found something really weird."

"Well zip up your pants, and quit looking at it," Weeks teased.

"Chinga te," Ruiz cursed. "No, we've got a case. I think it ties in with the guy from the La Quinta two weeks ago, Butler."

"Another motel murder?" Weeks asked, excited at the prospect of a break in the Butler case.

"Not that I know of. The guy was found dead in a parking garage. It's the pattern, though, that makes me think they're related," Mole` explained.

"What do you mean?"

"I mean it's got the same feel," Mole` explained. "On the Butler case, the method didn't make sense. It didn't fit what was going on. I feel the same way about this case that came in yesterday."

"Has the ME's office called anybody in homicide yet?" Weeks asked.

"No, I wanted to talk to you about it before it got over there and got lost. If it just got sent over, I was afraid nobody would make the connection. If you think the cases are related, you can take it to Bryant and get assigned to the investigation. If you don't, I'll just let the clerk make the call over there, and nobody has to know you've ever heard about it," Mole` offered.

"I appreciate that. Until I think about it I kind of want to keep this away from Little Ben. Fucking Ben called his brother at the FBI about the Butler case. The brother's looking to see if the case falls in their jurisdiction. They're trying to make the case that, because Butler was from Indiana and got killed here, someone may have followed him out here to do it. It's a stretch, but Ben's pushing it so he can get noticed, maybe get a job at the Bureau. I shouldn't mind. That would get him out of my hair," Weeks said.

"Well, this is going to screw up that theory," Mole` said. "This guy's from here in Phoenix."

"I'll be there in twenty minutes," Weeks said, gathering up the debris of his interrupted meal.

When Weeks didn't find Mole` at his desk, he went out to the front desk and asked if anybody knew where Deputy Ruiz was. A thin, black woman with her hair done up in braids directed him to the autopsy room. This was something he was going to have to get used to if he was going to stay in homicide.

Up to now, he had stayed in the observation room, detached, watching on the video screen, asking the autopsy techs to use the cameras to show him what he needed to see. He was a little intimidated about going into the autopsy suite itself…the smells, the chance of putting his hand in God knows what. Just another thing to learn, he thought, and pushed the door open.

The nude body of a middle-aged man lay face-up on the table. The red hair was just starting to grey at the temples a little. The face that stared unblinkingly at the video camera above it was one of those youthful faces that looked like a kid until about forty. Then cigarettes and booze would catch up in a few years, and the face would start to look like someone made a leather mask of a kid's face. A rough, Y-shaped incision came up the abdomen and across the chest on both sides. The top of his head had been removed, and his scalp flapped loose where the skull had been cut away with a bone saw. Mole` sat at a stainless steel desk filling out paperwork.

"The job isn't finished…," Weeks started.

"I know, I know, until the paperwork is done," Mole` completed the old saying. "Man, this chain of custody for evidence is some tedious shit."

Weeks sat down at the chair on the opposite side of the desk and began to look through a stack of pictures.

"Know what you're looking at?" Mole` asked.

"Something in the brain. What's weird about it?" Weeks asked.

"Pretty good for a city cop," Mole` said. "Like I said, this guy was found dead in a parking garage. The cause of death was massive intracerebral hemorrhage. Look." He picked up a metal pan with the brain lying in it and opened up a cut the pathologist had made. "See that stuff that looks like grape jelly? That's a blood clot. He bled into his brain. We call that massive intracerebral hemorrhage. In a forty-four-year-old guy, the most likely cause of death, in a bleed like this, is a berry aneurysm."

"Choose English or Spanish, cause I don't speak medical," Weeks requested.

"A berry aneurysm is a little time bomb in your head that you're born with. Actually, it's a weak area in one of the arteries that form a circle at the base of your brain. Your blood pressure normally rises as you reach adulthood. As it does, the area bulges out and looks like a little blueberry or something. If the blood pressure in the arteries gets too high...POW. All the major arteries that supply blood to the base of your brain are dumping into that circle. You're dead before you know what hit you," Mole` explained.

"Holy shit," Weeks half whispered. "Wasn't he too young for this kind of thing?"

"No man, that's the saddest thing. These usually burst in your thirties or forties."

"Damn man, how can I find out if I've got one of these little bombs in my head," Weeks asked, truly concerned.

"Get an MRI, but you might as well forget it. There's no way the city's health insurance is going to pay for one just because you're neurotic," said Mole`.

"I guess you're right, Mole`. Life sure isn't fair," Weeks complained. "But how does a guy dying of a time bomb that was inside his head since the day he was born tie into the Butler case?"

"First time around on the gross examination they didn't pick up anything external. They drew the blood and fluid levels, ran tox, nothing. When the pathologist did the organ inspection, the heart and lungs were as healthy as a horse. That ruled out an MI or a PE...."

"Damn it Mole`, English or Spanish," Weeks pleaded.

"A heart attack or blood clot to the lungs. So next, they open the brainpan to look for hemorrhage and, bingo, blood everywhere. Everything was done, by the book, and Dr. Thomas was about to sign it out as a berry aneurysm. That's where I came in. Because the guy was so stiff from rigor and because of the position of his arms, they were having trouble rolling him over. Sadie, who was working the case, called and asked me if I'd give her a hand. When we rolled the body, she spotted two round burns on the left shoulder blade." Mole` led him to the body and tipped it up to the right, to point out the two small spots. "They missed these on the initial gross due to livor mortis. You know, blood pooling. Apparently, he'd been lying between the two cars for about six hours before anyone saw him. Sadie called Dr. Thomas. When he saw them, he knew what it was right away. Contact points from a stun gun," Mole` paused to let it sink in.

"So you think somebody stun gunned this guy."

"Harry Zell," Mole` corrected.

"What?" Weeks asked confused.

"The guy's name is Harry Zell. I know because his wallet, watch, and all his money were still on the body when we removed his personal effects. That's what I'm saying. Who sneaks up on a guy in a parking garage, hits him with a stun gun, and doesn't take anything?" Mole` asked rhetorically.

"But how could our perp, male or female, know this guy had an aneurysm in his head before they stunned him? At best, it was just a really bad break for Mr. Zell."

"No muchacho, no accident. You know Dr. T was at AFIP...."

"What's that?" Weeks asked.

"Just the Armed Forces Institute of Pathology, the Mecca of the weird and bizarre. Anyway, he starts going through the guy's hair on his neck. He has me get a magnifying glass, and we're going through just about hair by hair when he finds a small round hole just below the base of the skull." Mole` was excited; Weeks could hear it in his voice.

"So what does that tell us?" Weeks asked, still unsure of the importance of what Mole` was saying.

"It was murder, not an aneurysm at all." Mole` was talking faster now. "We looked at the base of the skull from the inside, and you could see it barely from the inside too, a tiny puncture wound. Not through the skull, though. Come here." Mole` led him to the head of the autopsy table and, with a gloved hand, flipped the loose scalp so that the hair was covering Zell's face. "Look here," he said, aiming a spotlight. Picking up a metal probe, he pointed as he talked. "We had to move the medulla, the area where the brain and spinal cord come together. It's like a junction box where all the wires get gathered up. The puncture is right here in the back. See right here, below the foramen magnum, this big hole in the bottom of the skull that the spinal cord comes in through. The needle, or whatever it was, came in through the back of the neck and went up through the foramen magnum into the brain, through the medulla. When whoever was holding it from the outside wiggled their end back and forth, the tip lacerated the vessels in the circle of Willis."

"So we're looking for a murderous neurosurgeon?" Weeks wondered aloud.

"No, Dr. Thomas was saying that this was an old assassin's trick from Mata Hari days. It was a way to kill that was usually used by female agents. They would have sex with their target and, as he was climaxing, pull his head forward and drive a hatpin into the back of the neck angling up, through the foramen magnum. The victim would be dead before they could get off, at least physically."

"Okay, so we're looking for a ninety plus year-old female spy who convinced a forty-year-old man to have sex with her in a parking garage?" Weeks was beginning to see the similarities in the cases. Mole` was right, this had to be the same person who committed the Butler murder. He needed to roll this around his head. Asking himself stupid questions always helped shape more direct questions.

"Let me talk to Captain Bryant and see if Ben and I can get officially assigned to this case. Looking into his personal life will be a lot easier this time, since he's from here in Phoenix. We may get a break, find some kind of lead," Weeks stated flatly. "We can really look at his life. That part of the pattern's different, though. Butler was a visitor."

"That's something else I needed to talk to you about," Mole` said. "The guns you gave me to look at; I compared the barrels with the photos of Butler's head injury really carefully. I see what might be a crease on the scalp wound that would correspond to an ejector housing. At the top, it looks like a half moon ejector creased the top of the wound. It's not the little bump Ruger uses on the Blackhawk, so it has to be a Colt or one of these SAA clones, probably a five to seven-and-a-half inch barrel."

"Could just hitting a guy with the barrel knock him out like that?" Weeks wondered.

"I asked Dr. T the same question, Dance King. See, great minds think alike. He said it was funny when you saw guys getting clonked on the head in cowboy movies. The fellow doing the clonking usually holds the pistol like a hammer. That would give a larger, flatter impact point. By hitting his victim with the barrel, like our boy did, the shape of the Colt's grip acts as a force multiplier, and because the contact point is smaller, it's more likely to cut or cause a linear fracture rather than the compression fracture we were looking for. Where he hit him, behind the right ear, he could easily have knocked him out for a pretty long time from the direct force alone. The contra-coup effect caused by the brain splashing hard against the opposite side of the skull added to the damage, so the short answer is, yes."

"I want copies of the pictures to take with me, okay bro?" Weeks said.

When Mole handed him the printed photos, Weeks sat back down at the autopsy room's little desk and picked up a piece of paper. He attached one of the adhesive labels that the coroner's office used to identify everything associated with a particular case. On it was printed the case number and pertinent information. He stuck a label on the back of each photo and paper-clipped them together with the scrap of paper on the front. He was trying to decide what to take to Bryant. He hoped the captain went with Mole`'s hunch. He wasn't sure the cases were related, but there certainly looked like there was a pattern. He picked up a pencil and tried to organize a list to present to Bryant and Ben. He wrote:

Similarities:
1. Both vics were incapacitated before killed
2. Both were men, approaching middle-age, caucasians
3. Neither victim was robbed, had their personal effects
4. Both were killed by a known assassination technique

To be sure he was being balanced, Weeks turned the page and began to write.

Differences:
1. Garage vs. Motel room
2. Sex vs. None
3. Pistol vs. Stun gun
4. Screw driver vs. Needle or Hat Pin
5. Visitor vs. Resident

There were more differences than similarities, but since he was only going to share four of the differences with Kinney and the captain, they came out even. On paper, it looked like there was a strong enough case to justify looking at it a little closer.

"Hey Mole`, thanks," he said earnestly.

"Por nada," his friend replied. "I know you've got a lot of pressure on you. Being the new guy's hard." The big man smiled and winked. "Even if you don't screw up your first case."

CHAPTER SIXTEEN

Laura was in her studio, revising the way a shadow projected on the desert at sunrise. She had to paint sunrises and sunsets as quickly as she could in the field. The changing angle of the changing light altered the appearance of the shadows amazingly quickly as the sun burst over the mountains. If she painted them sequentially over the course of an hour, it was easy to tell where she'd started painting when she began because the shadows would either grow or shrink, depending on the time and the angle of the sun. So she didn't bother to try and paint them when she was in the field. She concentrated on the quality of the light in the sky. That was what she had to capture to make a painting special. Then she would come back into the studio later and look at the on-site digital photos she took when she started painting to try and make sure the light and shadows she'd painted matched together for that particular moment in time. That way she wasn't fighting with a ninety-minute range of variations. It was a small detail but one she felt made a difference. She was concentrating on a particularly troublesome spot, where the shadow was obscuring a cactus she wanted to emphasize. It hadn't worked like she wanted it to originally so she had let the painting dry and was altering the shadow by glazing in the darker hue when the phone rang. Laura jumped, smearing the dark paint all over the cactus.

"Damn it. I have to remember to turn this stupid phone off." She threw her brush into the coffee can full of mineral spirits. It wasn't a disaster, but she'd have to blot off the glaze and start over.

She walked back over to her desk and looked down at the phone. The caller ID showed that the call was from a private residence in San Diego. There were only two people in San Diego who would be calling her at home, and Sue was the only private residence in the 619 area code that would be calling her. "Hey kiddo," she answered without preamble.

"Laura?" Sue's voice asked, slightly confused.

"Yeah, it's me. Sorry, I guessed it was you from the area code and just started talking," she replied. "How have you been? I've been meaning to call you since Wednesday. I talked to James about the project. Look, if you want it, I'll be happy to bow out. You know, I really don't like to be away from Cody too long."

"Well, that's part of what I called you about last Saturday," Sue said with a touch of pique in her voice.

"Last Saturday?" Laura asked quizzically.

"Yeah, I talked to Morris. Didn't he tell you?" Sue said.

"No. I spend Saturday's in the field painting. It's the day Morris and Cody spend bonding. There's no telling what they were up to. It probably slipped his mind," Laura explained.

"I don't know," Sue said doubtfully. "We had a pretty long conversation. It wasn't an 'oh, tell her I called' thing."

"Who knows?" Laura replied. "When Morris starts on a project he's completely obsessive compulsive. Whatever he's thinking about takes over, and everything else in life gets pushed to the side."

"Good thing neither of us is like that," Sue said laughing.

"It sure is," Laura agreed. "So fill me in on this big project we're supposed to be competing with each other for."

"Okay. First off, we aren't competing, but there's a really strange part to it. Are you sitting down?" Sue asked. "Do you remember much about the guy we surprised?"

"You mean my conversion experience to Saint Laura?"

"That's the one!" Sue replied. "That's the guy that's been buying our paintings. He's the owner of LifeSolutions. He invented TimeDonors. The project he's talking about is the LifeSolutions corporate office."

"How do you know all this?" Laura asked.

"Well, I went to lunch with him...well, James and him. His name is Jarvis Sloan, and we've had a couple of phone conversations since then."

"Are you...?" Laura started, not knowing how to ask what she was wondering.

"Screwing him?" Sue finished. "No. It's like the project. He wants us to do it together."

"Screwing him or painting?" Laura asked.

"Both."

There was silence on both ends of the phone line, neither knowing where to go from there. Finally Laura broke the silence.

"My first question is how in the hell did he track us down? All this is supposed to be untraceable and..."

"Like I said," Sue replied, "he invented it, so he knows how to look inside. It's really just as simple as that."

"I wasn't even in his computer then. How did he even find me? Besides, isn't that unethical or something?" Laura wondered.

"Probably, at least that, but I'm not sure any of us are on the moral high ground here. We didn't ring his doorbell to sell him Girl Scout cookies or anything, so ethical gets a little blurry," Sue answered.

"I guess you're right, but it kind of feels scary and it's creepy, and I'm married," Laura offered.

"I felt the same way at first," Sue confessed. "I was really, really nervous about it all, but after talking on the phone a few times, I feel like I know him. He's not scary or creepy, and he's married too. In fact, his life is a lot like yours. He's trapped in an unhappy marriage he's staying in because of his kids. He's just looking for something to make him feel special again, and you and I did that for him." A heavy silence hung on the line as both women struggled with where they were going. "The sad thing is, as pathetic as it sounds, I haven't felt that special in years myself," Sue continued.

"It was pretty good, wasn't it?" Laura stated as much as she asked.

"The best," Sue confirmed.

"So I guess you're interested in pursuing things, the project and the perks?" Laura asked.

"Well, I agree with James about the project. It will do more to push up the value of our paintings than almost anything else we could do. A large project like this would pay us pretty nicely, just in terms of direct reimbursement. But even if we threw that out, the real advantage of it is that when one large corporation begins to buy your work for their corporate collection, other corporate buyers are going to follow suit. Think about Mijani in Seattle. Nobody knew him until Microsoft started buying him up. Now his prints are all over the Internet. That's huge. You get a percentage of every print sold, and neither of us has ever been able to tap into that yet. That's more money and it's huge in terms of recognition. So yes, I'm interested in the project. I think you can tell by what I've already said I'm interested in the perks as well, but what I want is only part of the equation. Jarvis and I've talked a lot about it, and we both feel the same way. It's all or nothing. So the question is, how do you feel about it?"

"It seems like a really big step," Laura explained. "Just making the decision to try to change the way my life was going was a big step and, really, one I probably wouldn't have been able to make yet without a little push from you. I've tried TimeDonors twice by myself since then, and it's nice. The big thing for me, the main attraction, is that you don't know each other. You're never going to have to see each other again, so there's no reason to hold back. You can do whatever pops into your head. It's a freedom you can't have if you have to worry about seeing the person again."

"I agree," Sue affirmed. "The last thing I want is to worry about some doofus coming up to me at a party and saying," Sue affected a southern California male surfer voice, "Hey, didn't I do you off that Internet site a couple of weeks ago? You want to hook up later?" They both laughed at the impersonation. Sue continued, "You can't tell about men, but Jarvis is happily married with two boys he loves. He isn't going to talk about this. He has as much to lose as you do, more actually. California is a community property state, and at the very best, he'll lose half ownership of his company."

"I don't know," Laura started. "I don't want to get into something that pushes into my regular life."

"The big plus there is that we live in different states. There wouldn't be any day-to-day pressure. It would always be something that took some planning to arrange," Sue said, trying to assuage Laura's doubts.

"It sounds like you've thought it out pretty carefully," Laura said.

"I think I have," Sue responded.

"So, do you two have a plan?" Laura asked.

"A great plan," Sue answered. "I've wanted to expand my market for a while. I talked to James, and he called Kent. I was going to try to arrange a time to be in Phoenix to bring a few pieces for Kent to look at and see how things go, you know, if he wants to represent me. He seems interested, but you can't tell. He's seen my work on James's web site, and I sent him some slides of my newest stuff."

"I know Kent. He'll love your stuff. Do you want me to talk to him?" Laura offered, not yet realizing she had acquiesced.

"I'd love it, if you really want to," Sue said, her voice sounding unsure for the first time.

"Of course, I really want to," Laura said emphatically.

"You didn't seem that sure a few minutes ago," Sue said quietly. "You know I like being with you…."

"Oh you mean…," Laura started.

"I thought that's what you meant," Sue said just a little too defensively, afraid of being rejected.

"I wasn't…no, I mean…," Laura felt like an idiot. "Well, that puts two of us in the same city." Laura shifted gears, avoiding an explanation. "Now all we need is the third leg for our tripod."

"Well he's going to Africa for spring break with his wife and kids," Sue said, her voice bright and in control again.

"That doesn't seem like an 'unhappy family' type trip," Laura said thoughtfully.

"What is an 'unhappy family' type trip?" Sue countered.

"Anywhere Morris and I go," Laura said. Her voice dropped slightly.

"Let's not get all depressed. We're talking about us having fun together, not troubles. Anyway, his whole family is going to be flying back to Miami together. He's having his wife and kids fly on home to San Diego from there, and he's going to fly into Phoenix. Ostensibly he's planning to look at a housing development he's got investments in. But the two of us are holding all the assets he's really interested in. He should be in town Sunday night, the eighteenth. He's planning to stay in Phoenix for four days," Sue explained.

"Well, I guess you two were pretty sure I'd say yes, weren't you?" Laura teased.

"We just wanted things to be arranged in case you did. Besides, you forget I got to watch your face when you came, all three times. So you're right, I thought you'd say yes," Sue said, her smile obvious even over the phone.

"You are such a bitch," Laura laughed.

"Well, see what you can arrange right after the eighteenth and call me back in a few days. Now that Morris knows me better, since our phone conversation, tell him I'm in town for a few days to start showing at Kent's. We can spend a few days in Phoenix, and then I can come home with you to Sedona for a night or two. The best thing is it's all true. You're only omitting a few tiny details."

"As they say, 'the devil is in the details'," Laura said.

CHAPTER SEVENTEEN

There was only one Harry Zell listed in the Phoenix phone book. The address matched the one printed on the driver's license that had been found in the deceased man's wallet. Weeks called Cell West using the cell phone that Zell was carrying when he died.

"Hi, this is Detective William Weeks of the Phoenix Police Department. We're investigating a homicide, and we need the call activity for the number I'm calling you from...No, I'm not Mr. Zell, Mr. Zell's dead, that's why I'm calling you on his phone."

He pointed his forefinger at the side of his head like a pistol and dropped his thumb. Ben, watching him, nodded and smiled.

"I need you to fax it...here's the fax at my station...No I don't have a warrant yet, but if you want I can get one when I get back to the station...Yes, what's your name?...Okay Beverly McCord, transfer me to your supervisor and I'm going to ask him to keep you right there until I have a chance to get over there with the warrant and then we can go over those records together, so I don't miss anything important...one line, one call at a time. Then you and I are going to run every one of those numbers down...Sure, sure...I appreciate you wanting to be so helpful. Thank you so much."

Ben had been quiet until now, listening. He chuckled slightly as Weeks hung up the phone. "Good luck trying that with AT&T on his home phone number. You're going to be lucky if you're talking to someone in the U. S."

"Yeah, we may need to wait on the warrant for that one," Weeks admitted.

They had just started gathering the details of the case. Weeks shared what Mole` had told him after he had asked Bryant if they could handle it. Ben's initial reaction had not been terribly favorable. But his disappointment that the lead didn't come to him first quickly faded as he heard the details of the murder.

The idea that just about anybody could be walking around with some kind of time bomb hidden in their head was unbelievable. The fact that it was essentially undetectable in most victims before it killed them was what had everybody at the station talking. Ben hadn't ever heard of the assassin's technique that had been used to kill Harry Zell, but neither had the captain or anyone else, so he didn't feel too bad about that.

Ben understood all too well what solving these cases would mean to both of them. Ben wanted to get past it, to hurry on into the glorious future that had, so far, eluded him. He wanted out of the Phoenix Police Department and into the FBI. Weeks wanted to solve them every bit as much as Ben did, but he had different reasons for wanting to figure this killer out. Weeks wanted to stay a detective. His ass was on the line right now. Weeks was having to scramble just to keep his job. Ben didn't see anything wrong with Weeks wanting to push to solve these cases locally, Ben just wanted to make sure it didn't happen at his expense. He would be really happy to be half of a brilliant partnership. Hell, he didn't even mind playing Dr. Watson to Weeks's Sherlock Holmes. He just didn't want to be the scapegoat if things went wrong. He could already hear it. "We had him cold but those dumbasses did this, that, or the other, and the judge threw the case out." Ben was going to make sure the FBI knew everything he and Weeks knew. It was the only way for him to protect himself.

It was no secret that he'd done criminal justice at Georgetown as a pre-law curriculum, nor was it a secret that, even with decent grades, his desire to be a lawyer had been torpedoed by the law school admissions test. Weeks had thrown that in his face within ten minutes of Bryant partnering them. Everybody in the department knew what had happened, what nobody really knew was why.

It wasn't about choking. He'd thrown the thing. But he couldn't tell people that. It would sound too much like an excuse for not making it. Ben had just never had any political ambitions or the desire to be in a big law firm. His father had chosen the political route, and his oldest brother was on his way to becoming a senior partner in one of the most prestigious law firms in Washington. He'd even argued a couple of cases in front of the Supreme Court.

Neither of those things was worth wasting his life on, as far as Ben could see. To keep from spending the rest of his life doing something he never really wanted to do in the first place, he tanked the test, three times to be exact. The humiliation of having to take the admissions test again and again was pretty awful, but his father wouldn't let him quit.

He'd done it so he could follow in the footsteps of his brother Bill. Bill was three years older than he was. They'd shared a room as kids. Bill had known from day one what he wanted to be. He wanted to be a G-man, to work for J. Edgar Hoover wiping out crime. The two of them had spent their childhood watching Elliot Ness and his men go after Alfonse Capone and all of the other mobsters in a blaze of shotgun blasts and rattling Tommy guns. All through law school, while their father had been setting up contacts and making plans for Bill's future, Bill confided to him that he wasn't going to need any of them. Bill's plan all along had been to go to the FBI academy. He was in shape, motivated, and soon to be a lawyer. If he could just prevent their father from torpedoing them, his chances of getting into the academy were excellent. The reaction at the Kinney household when Bill finally informed the family he'd been accepted to the academy and was going to attend was slightly less devastating than a low-yield nuclear device, but not by much. Ben wouldn't have a chance of doing the same thing. His father would make sure of that.

The timing couldn't have been worse for him personally. When Bill was getting his acceptance letter to the academy, Ben was taking his LSAT for the first time. He hadn't even tried to answer the questions right.

The last thing Ben wanted to face was another standardized test, but his dad had sent him to prep courses. They were pretty good, but they couldn't make up for the fact that Ben would deliberately write down the wrong answers. After two more tries Ben enrolled in the police academy. His father never understood.

By the time he finished training, Ben was sick of trying to measure up to what his family thought he should do. He left Washington and moved west. It was only recently that he'd begun to see another way to get what he'd always wanted. If he couldn't get into the FBI one way, he'd try another. Solving a serial murder case with interstate ramifications would be bound to get him noticed.

Weeks looked across the car at Ben but wasn't willing to interrupt whatever it was he was thinking so hard about. He turned his eyes back forward and stared at the windshield. What he was really seeing was a small round weak spot forming in one of the arteries of his head. Just waiting to blow.

"I wish I'd never heard of a cerebral aneurysm," Weeks whispered.

Ben interrupted his worrying by laughing.

"What's so funny?" Weeks asked.

"You've just got to be sure and test yourself regularly," Ben offered.

"With our insurance…no chance," Weeks pronounced.

"Nah, just do a pressure test. See the captain, he knows he doesn't have to worry about an aneurysm busting in his head. His ass had been pressure checked," Ben offered with a smile.

"With his blood pressure, if he had a weak spot anyplace in his head he'd have been gushing blood out of his ears twice this week already," Weeks added, shaking his head.

"Especially when you told him about the second murder." Ben laughed again, and then added, "That was a good catch."

The visit to the medical examiner's office and the discussions with Mole` and Dr. Thomas gave them a lot of information, but it wasn't as useful as Weeks would have hoped. They knew a whole lot about how Harry Zell had died, but it didn't really tell him a damned thing more than he already knew about why Harry Zell had been killed.

Ben had a few insights and a couple of new questions, but they really didn't illuminate too much more, either. A lot of their problem was the evidence. The initial determination that Zell had died of an accident had made everybody lax. Zell's wife had picked up his car at the parking garage the day before, so anything they found in it had to have to do with somebody that couldn't have been in it since it was picked up. The murder scene had not been taped off for more than twenty –four hours. It would be hard to find anything that was even admissible there now. Too many cars and people could have come and gone in the interim, but what Weeks needed now was the feeling, an idea of where to go. He needed to feel what the killer had felt when he was hunting.

As they pulled into the parking garage, Weeks let his mind become the mind of the hunter, not a person who wanted to shoot a deer, but a different kind of hunter, a hunter of men. That mindset was part of the life he'd lived before, but it never went away. In less than a millisecond, he became the wolf. He was a wolf, looking at how he would have cornered his prey. His eyes narrowed, every sense focused. The first thing that had to happen was that the killer had to be ready to prevent his prey's escape.

That meant blocking in Zell's car so he couldn't get away. Ben stopped beside where the body had been found and got out of the car. Weeks let his eyes take everything in. The killer would have stopped behind him, or more likely, to avoid tipping his hand too early, he would have pulled just past Zell's car, just far enough to prevent him from backing out of the angled parking slot. There was a concrete support there that would have blocked Zell's vision, and it would have allowed the killer to approach Zell unseen as Zell was stepping out of the car. Weeks got out of the cruiser and closed the car door behind him.

The killer moved up from the left rear. That would allow the killer to get good and close before he was ever spotted. Weeks let his mind move like a soldier's, thinking through how he would have killed Zell, coming up from behind, stun gun ready but concealed in his right jacket pocket. As the head turned to look, the right hand jabbed out quickly, discharging the gun on the nearest body surface, the victim's left scapula.

Brushing by his partner Weeks got in behind the wheel and pulled the police car into the parking space, then got out, leaving the door open.

"Hey Ben, help me out here," he called to Kinney.

"C'mon Weeks, the victim's car's been moved. A thousand people could have walked through here since then. I don't know what you think you're going to find," Ben complained.

"Help me and you'll see," Weeks insisted.

"Okay, show me what you're thinking," Ben acquiesced.

"Stand here," Weeks said. He positioned Ben in the open door of the police car. "Now face forward, like you're getting out of the car."

Weeks backed away. He pictured how the killer pulled just past Zell's car so he could move quickly around the back of his own car without having to go around the door. That would make the getaway quicker too. As he approached Ben from behind, Weeks movements unconsciously changed. His hands came up to maintain balance, his pace slowed, and he rolled slightly on the sides of his feet to quieten his footsteps. When he was close enough, he jabbed with his right hand, just touching Ben's left shoulder blade.

"See, here's how I think it happened," he said. "Stiffen up when I push you, then relax, like you've just been hit by a stun-gun, and I'll ease you down."

When Weeks pushed forward, Ben bounced back off the open door. The angle of the door propelled Ben back toward the car, and his shoulder struck the roof.

"Just go limp," Weeks instructed. He grabbed the shoulders of Ben's jacket and let him fall back. He came to rest in a sitting position, near the rear tire of the car parked beside them. Weeks grabbed Ben's hair and gently pushed Ben's head forward, and there, just above Ben's hairline, was the inion or external occipital protuberance pointing down like an arrow. It wasn't easily seen but was very easily felt. He remembered Dr. Thomas's description to him and Ben earlier, "in the building moments leading to orgasm, the victim would never notice his lover's left hand feeling the back of his skull, while with her right hand, she would position the hat pin to enter one inch below the point she was palpating. She held the hatpin angled towards the eyebrows. Next she would slide her left hand up, grabbing her victim's hair, pulling his head toward her into a flexed position and drive home the hat pin as her victim climaxed. Violently moving the base of the pin from side to side would lacerate the arteries at the Circle of Willis; by moaning loudly she would mask the sounds of her dying lover. When he ceased moving, she'd roll him off, tell the authorities he collapsed during orgasm, and it was ruled death by natural causes. There were no external wounds, and if she held her finger on the wound as her lover died, often there wasn't even a single drop of blood."

This was a reverse of that technique. That was obvious. The killer was behind him, grabbed his hair and pushed the head forward to drive the weapon home. Willie could easily see from the angle at which he held Ben's head by pushing it forward the place one inch below the inion where the puncture wound had been on Zell's hairline.

Weeks wiggled his hand. "You're dead," he said. "For crying out loud, it can't be this easy to murder someone. This guy has to be a professional. How else could he know all this?"

Weeks looked at the floor and could still see the faint red that told him where Zell had died. The clean up crew had gotten most of it but there was still blood soaked into the concrete. The killer hadn't even had to move him. It was the agony of the pressure building inside his head that had caused Harry Zell to roll away from the car he was leaning against and grasp his head, to die lying flat on his back. This was the position he had been found in when the paramedics arrived, alerted by an older couple going out to their car the next morning.

He and Ben had taken statements from them both and they were exactly the same. There had been no sign of a struggle. He was simply lying on his back holding his head. The dependent pooling of the blood into the tissues against the floor had almost totally masked the marks made by the stun gun.

"Even if he isn't a professional killer, this guy's a serial killer now," Ben said. "I'm going to tell the captain that we need to turn this over to the FBI so they can bring in experts who are used to dealing with professional killers. This has to have something to do with drugs or organized crime. It's sure as hell too big for the Phoenix PD."

"Look Ben, lets just see if we can prove that the two cases are even related," Weeks started. Looking at his partner Weeks knew where he had to go if they were going to have a chance to get anywhere without Ben calling his brother. "The last thing we need is to cause some big stir and have the FBI prove the two cases aren't even related. We'll all end up looking like morons."

After visiting the murder scene, the two detectives drove out to the Zell household to interview Harry Zell's widow. Ben was agitated. What Weeks had said had worked, but Ben wasn't happy about it. For the first time it was obvious that they could end up in the toilet either way they went. Ben was on edge before they ever knocked on the door. When they did, it was answered by an attractive blond, slightly overweight, with dark circles beneath her eyes. Ben spoke first. "Mrs. Zell?" She nodded and he continued, "I'm Detective Kinney and this is Detective Weeks. We need to ask you a few questions about your husband." The result was what Weeks had feared, a virtual torrent of tears. Between sobs, she asked why the police needed to ask any questions if her husband died of a stroke.

"Mrs. Zell, we have reason to believe that your husband didn't die of a stroke, but that he may actually have been murdered," Ben explained.

"Oh my God!" was followed by a resumption of the sobbing. "Who could have wanted to murder Harry?"

"That's what we were hoping you could tell us," Ben said.

This was the part Weeks hated the most. She may have just begun the healing process, and here he and Ben came to rip the wounds back open. The remainder of that visit was more about answering her questions than gathering information.

"How do you think he was murdered?" she asked.

Ben answered truthfully, if not tactfully, "It looks as if someone may have stabbed a needle through the back of his skull to make it look like a stroke."

"Oh my God, how horrible. Was it painful?" she wanted to know.

Weeks started to say he wouldn't have suffered much, but before he said two words, Ben talked right over him. "There was a lot of pain at first, but after the pressure built up in his head, he probably passed out."

"Who could have done something like that? That's not like getting stabbed with a knife or shot," she said.

"We think it may have been a professional killer. Can you think of anyone who may have hired someone to kill your husband?" Ben continued.

"How would I know that? I was just starting to believe that Harry's really dead. Harry worked nights, so he slept during the day. When I get home from work, I'll be sitting here watching the television, and I still think I hear him rolling over, or talking on the phone in the bedroom." Her mood was shifting from despair to anger, and it began to spill out the more she talked. "Now you come in here with a bunch of bullshit suppositions and not a single damned answer to anything I ask you. If you really think someone killed my husband, then go and do your job and bring me some answers."

Ben responded to her anger with anger. "The first person we talk to in any investigation is the spouse. Does your husband have any life insurance?"

"Are you suggesting that I killed my husband?" Mrs. Zell exploded.

"No, we think someone hired someone else to kill your husband," Ben fired back.

"I want you two out of my house," she ordered.

"This is a murder investigation, if we have to...," Ben started.

Weeks reached over and grabbed his partner's shoulder. He could see that things were deteriorating and knew it was time to end it before Ben or Harry Zell's widow did something they'd end up regretting. "Ma'am I understand how upset you are, and we're terribly sorry for the loss of your husband. Please try to think of anything you can that would make our job easier, okay? We'd like to have a chance to go through your husband's car, if we could. That may give us a hint. Maybe the person who killed him took something out of his car. We can check back with you tomorrow and see if you've remembered anything, I'll bring someone to look at the car," he offered.

Mrs. Zell seemed grateful to be given a chance to process the unexpected bad news she'd just received. Weeks offered their condolences and hustled Ben through the front door. On the way down the walk, Ben exploded.

"Shit Weeks, why in the world would you offer to leave without adequately questioning a suspect?"

"C'mon Ben," Weeks said in his best calming voice. "She's not a suspect, she's a grieving widow who just found out her husband was murdered. That's a lot to swallow."

"Listen to me, Weeks. I've interviewed more widows than I care to remember. They always cry first, and then they lose their temper when you ask anything that might point the finger at them. You can't stop questioning a suspect just because they get upset." Ben pressed his palms into the sides of his forehead, making strange indentations in his expensive haircut. "In this investigation, everyone, and I mean everyone, is a suspect! Don't you ever do this to me again! I don't give a damn if they cry or not. Now we've lost the element of surprise."

Weeks spoke like he was trying to placate a difficult child. "Look Ben, she didn't do it. What we gain by being human and decent is trust. That's going to be a lot more valuable to us in trying to work through Harry Zell's life than surprise is."

"This is how you're going to fuck up, Weeks," Ben replied. "If she does have something to hide, you just gave her plenty of time to work out a cover story. That's one thing you need to remember, old buddy. Women are much better liars than men. They don't forget, they don't get tangled up. They think up the lie in their head, then when they tell it, they believe it's true because they heard it somewhere before. After that, it's carved in stone."

"Okay Ben, I'm sorry," Willie said, seeing no point to the argument. "I'm new at this, okay?" And just when we were getting along so well, he added mentally.

"All right, I just hope it doesn't cost us this case," Ben said sounding like a junior high school coach using the potential loss of a "big game" to motivate his charges. "If the FBI takes over these cases, our interview notes could make a difference."

"Ben your name's going to get in the report. Relax," Weeks offered.

"I don't want it in the report that Detectives Weeks and Kinney failed to conduct a proper interview of the primary suspect," Ben snapped.

Weeks had run out of patience. "Ben, for crap sake, why in the fuck would Mrs. Zell hire someone to kill Butler? Use your common sense," Weeks exploded. "Let's use this time to see what the folks at work thought of Harry." Weeks knew an argument wasn't what Ben wanted but knew if he gave it a few minutes, Ben would see that what he was saying made sense.

"Maybe Butler was her out-of-town boyfriend. How in the hell would I know? Maybe that's one of the things we need to be thinking about," Ben sputtered, then switched gears and resumed his tirade unfazed by reason. "You just let me ask the questions from now on, and don't try that decent human shit again."

Guess I'm benched now, for sure, Weeks thought.

CHAPTER EIGHTEEN

"Good day sunshine, good day sunshine." Jarvis Sloan sang the old Beatles song too loudly and very off-key. Fairly quickly, his wife Sharon punched him on the arm.

"You're singing out loud," she said when he removed the headphones and looked at her.

"I thought you'd like the entertainment," he said with a grin. "It's going to be a long flight." Sharon shook her head from side to side, and Jarvis made a sad face. "I'm going to remember this later when you're bored and start begging me to sing more."

"Oh, it's not me," she said. "I love your singing, but I could hear the other passengers, almost everyone in first class, plotting to stuff socks in your mouth and shove you into the baggage compartment with the other howling dogs."

He kissed her cheek. "Thank you for saving me from such an undignified fate, ejected from first class and landing as baggage. I wonder if I would have been quarantined by veterinary services. Probably not, but you would probably have been arrested for trying to smuggle in an exotic species."

"Who says I was going to come and claim you?" she said, raising her eyebrows.

This close, joking, looking into her laughing blue eyes, he knew why he loved her. He placed the headphones onto his neck, rather than returning them to his ears, and sat back, reaching over to hold her hand. The headphones were uncomfortable on his neck, so he tried to adjust them with his free hand.

"Would you like something to help you sleep?" he asked her, giving up and letting go of his wife's hand so he could put the earphones on the floor.

"Not yet. The boys just fell asleep themselves. I'm going to try to read for awhile and give myself a chance to unwind a little," she replied. The boys had been as excited as she'd expected and had been jabbering like magpies in the row behind them about everything they wanted to do in Cape Town since they'd gotten on the plane. Although she'd tried to read some, with them talking to the back of her head, she hadn't been able to concentrate much and kept re-reading the same paragraph over and over again.

A stewardess stopped next to her shoulder, holding a bottle of wine in each hand. "Would you care for some red or some white wine?" She had what Sharon tended to think of as an English accent, but it was, in fact, South African.

"The white please," Sharon replied and was handed one of the small bottles.

"The Riesling was nice," Jarvis answered. "I'll have that too." He had already had one of each since they'd gotten on board. That was one of the joys of flying first class on South African Airways. The service was several steps above anything offered on an American carrier. Really, that was such a shame, Jarvis thought.

"Cheers," Sharon said raising her glass. "Here's to a quiet family vacation, without any drama."

"Cheers," he replied, "but I thought that was the purpose of a trip to 'The Dark Continent'…adventure and the drama of nature."

"Well let's let the drama come from nature, not your nature," she said.

"Oh, I take it you are referring to the intercontinental mile-high club I offered to initiate you into earlier," Jarvis replied.

"That and the drugs you're trying to pressure me to take," Sharon said disapprovingly.

"I wasn't pressuring you," he retorted. "I was just telling you about the article I read."

"That wasn't all you were doing," Sharon accused.

"Damn it, Sharon, I was just suggesting that if the combination resulted in a dramatically increased libido, it might liven up our vacation," Jarvis responded.

"Well you certainly don't need any livening up, and I'm not willing to endanger my health for a quickie weekend." Sharon made a plea for reason, "I really don't want this to be an issue. I want us to enjoy each other without you sulking."

"If we were enjoying each other, I wouldn't sulk," he promised, raising and lowering his eyebrows in a pantomime of Groucho Marx.

"I meant all of us, as a family," she responded. "Look we're here with the boys. It's a family vacation. It isn't like I don't want to have sex too. We just have to arrange time alone, when the boys are occupied, and you have to promise not to get all weird."

"Weird? I'm a psychiatrist. I'm never weird," he declared.

"You know what I mean. Once is never enough for you. It's like uncorking a genie, hard to get the stopper back on the bottle."

"My stopper is hard and wants to get in your bottle," he suggested.

"Jarvis, this is exactly what I'm talking about," she said in an exasperated tone.

"I'm just kidding. We're on vacation, let's not fight," he said, realizing that he had gone too far, and now she was just going to get irritated.

"I'm not trying to fight," she said. "Why can't we ever just talk about this without you changing the subject?"

"I'm always willing to discuss our problems, but we have to discuss our problems, not my problems. You always pretend that this as a one-sided issue. You don't see yourself as having a problem. Until you admit that our marriage is sexually dysfunctional, we'll never make any progress. Hypoactive Sexual Desire Disorder is a real clinical problem, it's listed in the DSM-IV under Sexual and Gender Identity Disorders." Jarvis started his usual defense, and got about as far as usual.

"Keep your voice down!" she hissed. "I do not want the entire first-class cabin to know our personal business, and I certainly don't want to the boys to overhear you."

"I thought you said they were asleep," he said glancing back between the seats at the faces of his sleeping children.

"Well, you don't know, and I don't want their vacation spoiled worrying about us fighting about sex," Sharon started harshly, and then softened. "I just told you I wanted to make time for it. I really do."

"I'm sorry. I love you," he said, giving up. He reached down to retrieve the headphones. After so many years, he was a master at masking his anger and frustration. "I'm going to try and get some sleep. The wine's got me drowsy. Enjoy your book. The sleeping pills are right here," he said, moving his carry-on between them.

"We're going on a family vacation with the children, not on some singles cruise," she said to her unhearing husband. With the music blaring in his ears, Jarvis glanced at her moving lips and blew her a kiss.

"Why does he always have to be so difficult?" she asked no one in particular.

"Good night," he shouted over the music only he could hear.

"Sweet dreams," she replied and shook her head.

As Jarvis reclined with his eyes closed and Eric Clapton singing about Tears in Heaven, he knew why he hated her. This has to be how people with cyclothymic personality feel, he thought. I've gone from love to hate in fifteen minutes. Manic-depressive disorder wasn't so rapidly cycling, he thought, but the extremes were the same. Sharon couldn't be spontaneous if her life depended on it. He could just picture her, her little appointment book in her hand penciling in, "Boys - photo outing, Jarvis/me - sex." It might even be funny if it wasn't so sad. He tried to remember why in the hell he had married her. He hadn't even wanted a family back then. Now he was completely dedicated to trying to make having one work, even if he had to put up with his wife's OCD... but she had been great back then. He smiled remembering.

It was shortly after they'd left that first office, in the new office with the leather couch, that he and Sharon had gotten started on their family.

For those first two years downtown, all of their energy had been spent on either the office or mutual exploration, sometimes both. He chuckled to himself remembering. Back then, a lot of their exploration was at the office. They could be painting or filing charts one minute and lost on the couch the next. He remembered one weekend when she had come in to help him reset a toilet. If some of the patients only knew what had been happening on that couch just before they lay down on it they would've been aghast. Sharon was amazing. It was like being in a whirlwind. Then they were constantly probing for new boundaries. She had electric fences all around her now.

The explorations all ended suddenly one night, without warning, when Sharon's need to procreate showed up from somewhere and decided to express itself. It seemed to just materialize out of thin air, like a tiger in a Las Vegas magic act. There wasn't any discussion, no preamble. She just said, "I think we should have children."

And they'd started working on it. They'd just been going through the motions before, but after she'd reached her decision, she got serious. For two weeks a month she became a dynamo. That lasted for about six months, but as her periods continued to flow by as regularly as the tide, it was obvious to Sharon that they needed to give Mother Nature a helping hand.

First came the trips to the bookstore to decide what they were doing wrong, then came the basal body temperatures and the panicked sex to be sure that they didn't miss her ovulation. For Jarvis this wasn't suppose to be a sprint. He was fine with taking a couple of years to have kids. For his part, Jarvis was content to lay back and enjoy the race. He wasn't in any hurry to get to the finish line.

When two more periods came and went, Sharon decided they should go and see a friend of theirs who ran the infertility clinic at Scripps Clinic. This was the first thing Jarvis resisted. He didn't want to waste money on something that they simply hadn't given enough time. But his refusal was no match for the fine arts of sulking and recrimination, and Jarvis, resistant at first, crumbled like chalk. Within a week they were being evaluated at the fertility clinic.

When carefully timed intercourse failed to produce the desired result, they proceeded to in vitro fertilization, and Jarvis went from businesslike sexual transactions with his wife to romantic interludes with a specimen cup. This was the beginning of Sharon's view of sex as something that needed to be controlled and managed. This was a view that became more rigid with time and with the arrival of their two sons.

With two small children, Jarvis found himself in an increasingly sexless world. Between all of the requirements of raising the two boys, Sharon simply didn't have the free time or the energy to make room for it. To compensate, he threw himself into the development of his seminars. The first thing he'd had to do was learn to type. Sharon no longer had time to do that either, and he had new scripts to develop and new seminars to fill out. So at least he got better at something besides masturbation.

It was a difficult and frustrating time, but it allowed him to concentrate on something besides his growing sense of unhappiness. He pushed himself to make the best, most useful seminars possible, as if that would prove something (he wasn't sure what). Jarvis spent every night writing and refining his protocols and scripts.

Once Sharon and the children had gone to bed, Jarvis would sit down at his word processor and work doggedly, staring at the monitor until one or two in the morning. It was tiring, but collapsing into bed and dropping into the unconscious slumber of the chronically fatigued was better than lying there awake, next to his sleeping wife, hating her for being able to sleep so peacefully while he couldn't because he needed to have sex.

If he woke her, at first she was happy to comply, but she would be sleepy and she didn't put much energy into it any more. His unfulfilled need became a simmering cauldron of repressed anger and resentment that got worse every time she gave in and sex wasn't what he'd hoped it would be. She told him to come to bed earlier if he was so unhappy, but every night something would screw up and he'd try to fix it or he'd lose track of time, until she was worn out with him too. Fighting and unhappy, page-by-page, he created the scripts that would become the LifeSolutions seminars.

He'd been unhappy then, but even that looked good by comparison now. At least then he'd had the work to keep him occupied. Now, more and more of the work was being hired out. Now, he rarely even wrote or produced the seminars. These had been subcontracted to a production company in Los Angeles. His workday consisted of a few executive decisions that his administrative staff brought to him and counting his money, scanning his various holdings as they flowed across his computer screen. Both things bored him. In reality, he thought, he missed practice. The appeal of helping people face to face was undeniable. In addition to the altruistic element of helping couples and families stay together, there was always the voyeuristic element of seeing how other people lived, fought, thought, and had sex.

It had gotten to the point now that sex once a month was more than enough for Sharon, and, true to form, it had to occur under only the most perfect of circumstances, circumstances that were more often than not, never met. There were literally thousands of reasons that she couldn't get around to it more often. Sometimes it was the children: she was too tired from running them all over the place, she was afraid that they would come into the room, they had overnight company, whatever. If it wasn't the children then the reasons were health-related; complaints too minor to keep her from playing tennis or going shopping, but far too debilitating to allow her to lie flat on her back for the next ten minutes. The truth was, she simply wasn't interested and once a month was about all she was going to put up with.

He'd been stupid enough to ask her once if she'd rather go on a romantic weekend alone or go shopping. The answer didn't do much for his ego. The pattern was typical for Hypoactive Sexual Desire Disorder, which accounted for most sexually deprived marriages. As far as she was concerned, there wasn't really any problem. If there was a problem in their marriage, she believed it was Jarvis--he just had unreasonable expectations. It didn't help that none of her friends admitted to being any more sexually active than she was. Much of their conversation at dinners and at the club centered on this very subject, and hell, who knew, maybe they weren't. They were like some kind of pathologic support group.

Although he had successfully counseled a lot of couples with this exact problem in the past, Jarvis had no chance of getting Sharon to even listen to what he had to say. He was hampered by the age-old problem Jesus described so well when he said, "No prophet is accepted in his own village; no physician heals those who know him." The opinions of even the most brilliant doctors are regularly rejected by their own family. Wives, who abstractly believe that their husbands are wonderful physicians, lose all faith in their husbands' professional abilities when it comes to themselves or their children.

That's how it was with Sharon. She wasn't ever going to accept his assessment of normal sexual frequency. "It's not like you're going to overdose or something," he'd said to her once, a line he used frequently, with good success, with his patients. It had had no effect on his wife. For her the dose would always be too high. She used her girlfriends as a yardstick to measure normalcy, and that was that. Evidence to the contrary was totally meaningless and, for the most part, a waste of the breath God gave him. It didn't do any good to argue. It only raised his blood pressure and didn't do a damned thing to change Sharon's opinion.

How was he supposed to deal with that? Half the time, he felt like banging his own head against the wall, the other half he felt like banging Sharon's. There was one thing he was sure of though. He wasn't going to consider divorce. He loved Sharon, and he loved his children more than anything else in the world.

As a psychiatrist, he knew that divorce was something he would survive and would eventually recover from. His sons, on the other hand, would not. Many studies over the past three decades had clearly shown links between divorce and depression, alienation, underachievement, and a variety of other problems in the children of divorced parents that followed them all the way into adulthood. As a father, he refused to subject the children he loved to these kinds of risks. Now he really was depressed.

Maybe he should take the antidepressant cocktail he'd read about himself. He would be calmer, and he could time it so that his libido was maximally increased when he got to Phoenix. What struck him as funny was that the article in the Journal of the American Psychiatric Association was cautionary in nature. It warned the Association's members to be aware that following a short course of serotonin reuptake inhibitor antidepressants, which greatly depressed libido, with a newer type of antidepressant, which nobody really knew how it worked, but which acted as a central nervous system stimulant, their patients could experience an episode of manic hyper-sexuality. Cases of individuals having intercourse fifteen or sixteen times a night were reported. There were other unpleasant side effects reported as well, including prolonged erections, ejaculatory delay, vaginal tingling, and hyperesthesia, with increased sensation in the breasts, occurring in both sexes.

He thought of Marlon Brando in Apocalypse Now..."The horror, the horror." He could picture the carnage; sex fifteen times a night, accompanied by ejaculatory delay, would certainly result in spontaneous combustion, men and women bursting into flames at the crotch. Think of all those poor women with hypersensitivity of their nipples and vaginas, tingling, suffering orgasm after orgasm in a state similar to status epilepticus. No wonder the APA was warning against it. He would start the serotonin reuptake inhibitor tomorrow. At least that would depress his libido while he was in Africa with Sharon.

He tried to avoid thinking about Phoenix. The last thing he needed right now was an erection trapped on the inside seat next to his wife. He thought of the joke about the rich ninety-year-old man who had just married a twenty-one-year-old beauty. His best man pulls him aside after the ceremony and sagely warns that too vigorous an approach to sex on their honeymoon may prove to be dangerous. "I know," the old man said, "but if she dies, she dies." He thought abut the two women he would be with in Phoenix coupled with the effects of the antidepressant cocktail. Oh well, he thought. If they die, they die.

CHAPTER NINETEEN

One of the few constructive pieces of information to come from their meeting with Mrs. Zell was that Harry Zell had been a nighttime shipping manager for a company called Whitaker Automotive Distributions, a wholesale automotive supply warehouse. He and Ben agreed that the first person they needed to talk to there was Zell's boss, to get a feel for what the company did and to try to see if there was some link to the paper salesman from Indiana. Weeks made the initial arrangements over the phone, and when they arrived, a secretary showed them into a brightly lit meeting room with a glass door, asking them to have a seat. A short time later, a heavy, red-faced man wearing a royal blue golf shirt with a crown and the letters WAD embroidered in gold on the left breast opened the door and stuck out a chubby hand.

"Hello, my name's Royce Whitaker. What can I do for you gentlemen?" he asked.

"We'd like to talk to you about Harry Zell," Ben answered professionally.

"Yeah, a terrible shame, dying of a stroke at his age. Who would imagine? Me, everybody expects me to drop over at any minute with my weight and blood pressure, and everything. But Harry, he was in great shape, kept himself thin, spent a lot of the time at the gym. Who can figure?" the big man asked.

"Well, Mr. Whitaker..." Ben started.

"Royce," the man corrected.

"Excuse me?" Ben asked confused.

"Royce, everybody calls me Royce. When I hear 'Mr. Whitaker' I start looking for my dad," he explained.

"Does your father work here?" Weeks asked.

"Yeah, he owns the place. He doesn't come in much, anymore, though," Royce explained.

"Is he getting ready to retire?" Weeks went on.

"Nah, he'll never retire. He'll drop over dead here at his desk, if he gets his choice," Royce replied with a smile.

"That's the thing, I guess," Weeks said thoughtfully. "None of us really gets to make that choice. That's really what we're here to talk to you about..."

"The final autopsy report indicates that Mr. Zell didn't just fall over with a stroke. Somebody gave him a hand," Ben said gravely. "And that person may have been a professional."

"What do you mean a professional? Like a hit man or something?" Royce said, clearly surprised and a little nervous.

Ben nodded seriously.

"Look I can't have you spreading those kinds of rumors, getting the employees all upset. We'll have a panic on our hands. We work twenty-four seven. This is just going to get everyone all upset about security again," Royce answered.

Weeks could see that something more than his employees' security was bothering Royce, and he wasn't sure what it was. If it was, they might as well use it to their advantage. "Look, Royce, we have to have full access to everybody on this case, and I mean full cooperation, or we might have to start looking a little harder to see what might be going on that could get a professional involved. Maybe some money, maybe some inventory goes missing, who knows? With Harry working nights, maybe he sees something he shouldn't have, somebody follows him to the parking garage. We have to look at every angle."

"What do you mean, missing inventory? Are you making some kind of allegation?" Royce said, all traces of friendliness evaporated.

Ben looked questioningly at Weeks. "No one's making any allegations, Royce."

"It sure sounded like an allegation and it was obviously a threat aimed at me," Royce blustered.

"Could we speak to your father?" Weeks asked.

"I told you my father doesn't come in much anymore," Royce sputtered.

"Is he about seventy, balding, built just about like you, and wears a blue shirt like the one you have on?" Weeks asked.

"How would I know what he has on?" Royce continued.

"You could go out that door and take a right and look," Weeks suggested.

Suddenly Royce was all cooperation. "Look, go ahead and talk to whoever you need to. We don't need to start out on the wrong foot. I want to help you get to the bottom of this. A man I know, one of my employees, might have been murdered. Of course we'll all cooperate with the investigation."

"We appreciate your help in this, Royce. Just one more thing. Did Zell ever try to get on day shift? I know his wife worked days," Weeks asked.

"I think that was a big part of the reason Harry worked nights," Royce said conspiratorially. He got up and made his way toward the door. He turned as he opened it. "You boys want a soda or something?" He spoke to the secretary outside the conference room door. "Get these fellas a soda while I get them a list of who they need to talk to."

When the secretary left them alone in Harry Zell's office, Ben turned immediately to Weeks. "What was all that back there with Whitaker?"

"He was going to jerk us around," Weeks answered matter-of-factly.

"We could have gotten a warrant," Ben responded.

"Or we could have bluffed him, like I did," Weeks countered.

"How did you know he had something to hide?" Ben continued with open curiosity.

"Everybody's got something to hide. He's a fifty-year-old guy, his dad's still running things without a chance he's going to retire. That says the old man's worried about trusting his baby to junior. Royce was worried about having to beef up security. It just seemed like he had something to hide. I didn't really know what. That's a little burglary 'fishing tip'. I didn't know what was up, I just knew there was something fishy. He's the one who told what it was when he took the bait about the missing merchandise."

"But how did you know what the old man looked like," Ben asked.

"He looked in the door when he was going past. You were talking to Royce or you'd have seen him. He looked just like the son, just a little older. The shirt thing says something too. I'm pretty sure Royce, when he doesn't even want to be called Mr. Whitaker, doesn't want to go around dressed like the old man. The dad's running the place with a pretty heavy hand," Weeks explained.

"Looks like you learned something working robberies. I'm glad it worked," Ben said with a nod.

As they talked to the people who had worked with Zell, the two detectives learned that he was a pretty good guy and, for the most part, he was a fair boss that everyone liked and felt was a regular guy. No one said anything directly critical about him at all. He was a hands-off kind of manager. He let his people work and only stepped in if he was needed. His performance evaluations had been consistently superior, even back when he was starting out as a shipping clerk.

The only area of questioning that seemed to evoke some evasion concerned the happiness of Harry Zell's marriage. This was much more obvious in his female co-workers than in the men that they questioned. The guy's response was usually, "Oh sure, I guess so." The women were universally aware that Harry Zell had not had a very happy marriage. On a hunch, Weeks asked a particularly attractive young woman if Mr. Zell ever flirted with her.

door. "Get these fellas a soda while I get them a list of who they need to talk to."

When the secretary left them alone in Harry Zell's office, Ben turned immediately to Weeks. "What was all that back there with Whitaker?"

"He was going to jerk us around," Weeks answered matter-of-factly.

"We could have gotten a warrant," Ben responded.

"Or we could have bluffed him, like I did," Weeks countered.

"How did you know he had something to hide?" Ben continued with open curiosity.

"Everybody's got something to hide. He's a fifty-year-old guy, his dad's still running things without a chance he's going to retire. That says the old man's worried about trusting his baby to junior. Royce was worried about having to beef up security. It just seemed like he had something to hide. I didn't really know what. That's a little burglary 'fishing tip'. I didn't know what was up, I just knew there was something fishy. He's the one who told what it was when he took the bait about the missing merchandise."

"But how did you know what the old man looked like," Ben asked.

"He looked in the door when he was going past. You were talking to Royce or you'd have seen him. He looked just like the son, just a little older. The shirt thing says something too. I'm pretty sure Royce, when he doesn't even want to be called Mr. Whitaker, doesn't want to go around dressed like the old man. The dad's running the place with a pretty heavy hand," Weeks explained.

"Looks like you learned something working robberies. I'm glad it worked," Ben said with a nod.

As they talked to the people who had worked with Zell, the two detectives learned that he was a pretty good guy and, for the most part, he was a fair boss that everyone liked and felt was a regular guy. No one said anything directly critical about him at all. He was a hands-off kind of manager. He let his people work and only stepped in if he was needed. His performance evaluations had been consistently superior, even back when he was starting out as a shipping clerk.

The only area of questioning that seemed to evoke some evasion concerned the happiness of Harry Zell's marriage. This was much more obvious in his female co-workers than in the men that they questioned. The guy's response was usually, "Oh sure, I guess so." The women were universally aware that Harry Zell had not had a very happy marriage. On a hunch, Weeks asked a particularly attractive young woman if Mr. Zell ever flirted with her.

desktop that was tied directly to the warehouse computer, and all Internet access was controlled and monitored. It didn't look like there was anything but business and account information there. Ben found a leatherette briefcase inside a drawer in a side table. Inside the case was an Apple laptop. Ben checked the accessory drive and found what he expected, a cellular modem. This was the kind of set-up Zell would have used for things that he didn't want anyone else to see. Ben scanned Zell's desk. Its center was occupied by a desktop calendar. The top sheet of the calendar was covered with notes around its edges. Only its center was clean. Ben sat the laptop in the center of the clear area of the calendar and began to look closely at the notes around it. On the day Zell had been killed there were four words written. TimeDonors was written first and underlined. Under that were written three names, Rusty Z, Doubting Tom and Hester.

"What do you think they mean?" Weeks asked from the doorway.

"I'm not sure," Ben answered. "That's the day he was killed. TimeDonors sounds like a business or place. We can check and see if it's a company they did business with. The other three look like names. Maybe it's a place he was going to meet these three," Ben suggested.

Weeks picked up a phone book and looked up TimeDonors in the white pages. No dice. He flipped through the Rolodex on Zell's desk. None of the names were in it. Searching, Weeks opened the other desk drawers. They contained the usual office supplies, and the bottom right hand drawer had several pornographic magazines, mints, and several unopened condoms, but no clues about what the words on the calendar meant. Ben picked up the computer and put it back into the briefcase. He wanted to take it with them back to the station. As they were sealing the office with yellow "Crime Scene" tape, Weeks had an idea and pushed through the tape to grab the desk calendar. He folded the top page and shoved it into the briefcase, too.

When they arrived back at the department with the contents of Zell's office, Ben made a call to Chip Jeffrey. He was the resident computer expert for the department. Chip was a twenty-something with curly, dark hair and bad skin that looked like it hadn't seen the sun in years. The guy knew what he was doing, though. In addition to the modem, the computer had a wireless card. Before they began, Chip checked the hardware configuration to get the phone number for the modem.

"You want me to call the cellular provider and get the numbers he called from here?" Weeks asked.

"Nah," Chip answered. "They're all going to be to Zell's ISP."

"What?" Weeks asked, lost.

"Internet Service Provider. The only number that this modem is going to be used to call is going to be however he accessed the

Internet. Once we find out who that is, we can move around a lot faster if we just go ahead and use our own wireless network. Any kind of modem's slow."

The guy ran around the passwords like a running back going past defensive ends. He quickly followed Zell's footprints over the preceding week. He had several favorite porn sites and regularly visited adults-only chat rooms. But there were no e-mails indicating anything unusual. One site that appeared several times in the week before Zell died was a self-help site called LifeSolutions. It was a subscription service that required a password to sign on initially. Chip tried Zell's birth date, different combinations of his social security number and wife's name without success.

"Hey Chip," Ben asked. "This is something new for him, right? It's not something he had been to in the past?"

"Not that I can tell," Chip answered.

Ben left the room, returning with the sheet from the desk calendar. They spread it out next to the computer and sat the laptop in the center of it. Weeks pointed out the words on the murder date.

Entering the first line, TimeDonors, as a screen name with any of the other names got them nowhere either, but when Chip entered "rustyz" as the screen name with "doubtingtom" as a password, they got in. LifeSolutions Seminars looked like a thousand other on-line sites. Chip entered TimeDonors in the search box, and they found themselves looking at a screen labeled, "Managing Time for Sexual Intimacy Workshop." When Chip clicked on the TimeDonors icon at the bottom of the screen, they went directly into TimeDonors, following Zell's electronic footsteps. After entering the site, Chip clicked the box that indicated that they already had a screen name and a password. He entered each of the three names written on the calendar. None of the combinations they tried worked, but both "Doubting Tom" and "Hester" produced a prompt that indicated that the screen name had expired. This meant they had both been used previously. After trying all of the other combinations of birth dates, addresses, phone numbers, whatever that they could think of, they were stymied.

"Hey guys, I need a break," Chip announced. "Grab something to eat. I'm going to get a burger and make a few calls to some friends to see if I can find out anything. We're just beating our heads against a wall now."

"You guys get something to eat, then get back here and get me a few answers," Captain Bryant said as he entered the room. None of them waited for a second invitation. Ben and Chip made it to the door first, and each went in a different direction when they hit the hall. As Weeks started toward the door, Bryant stepped in front of him.

"You know I'm taking a chance on you with this one?" Bryant asked.

"I know cap, but you gotta understand, this is no sure thing," Weeks equivocated.

"There's no such thing. Just make sure you do it right," Bryant said, stepping aside to let Weeks by.

As he walked along the hall, Weeks saw Chip sitting at a desk with a phone to his ear. He waved as he went past without slowing. The door banged behind him as he left the building. "Just make sure you do it right," echoed in his ears. How was he supposed to do that? He had no idea of what it was he was trying to do.

Weeks got into his own car, a silver Camaro. He closed the door, softer this time. Whenever he wanted to let his mind rest, he drove. He pulled into the street and turned up the volume on his car radio. He needed to let the case go, to see if he could think of something else. He stopped and got an order of fried fish and French fries. He ate in his car, listening to an oldies station. It was strange. He still didn't have any ideas, but somehow he felt like that was okay. Nobody else had any either. Maybe they'd find something in the computer. He just had to wait and find the pattern. There had to be a pattern. They just hadn't found it yet.

When he got back, Chip and Ben were just getting started again. "So what'd your buddies say?" he asked Chip.

"That TimeDonors is a site where the unhappily married can go to arrange a little sex on the side," Chip answered.

"Do singles go there?" Weeks asked.

"I don't think so, at least nobody my age. It's kind of for an older crowd," Chip answered.

"How old?" Weeks wanted to know.

"Late thirties to early sixties," Chip replied.

"Oh I see," Weeks said smiling. "The ancient to the truly ancient."

"I didn't mean you were old," Chip stammered.

"If the shoe fits...," Weeks said with resignation. Even with all of the hints Chip had gotten from his friends, they could only get back to the same screen that they'd gotten to before. For the next three hours Weeks and Ben sat and watched as Chip crashed into the same barrier over and over again.

Finally Weeks stood up and stretched. "Look, guys, it's after one, and as much as I like spending my Friday night with you young guys, we're not getting anywhere with this. I'm going to go home and try to get some sleep."

"I'll swing by and pick you up around 11:00 to go to the Zell place," Ben offered.

"Listen Ben, can you come by around 9:30? I have an address I got in one of the interviews that I think we ought to check out," Weeks suggested. Ben nodded his agreement and with that, they called it a night.

Morning came far too soon for Weeks. Even after two cups of black coffee, he still felt dull. Ben rolled up at 9:20, and they rode along in silence in the unmarked Crown Victoria. First, he and Ben drove over near the reservation to check out 1004 at Parkway Apartments on Moya Drive. Before they arrived, Weeks called the apartment manager, Mrs. Alston, who quickly offered that a man named Fred Busby was renting that apartment. She offered to meet them at the entrance for the parking garage, and as they pulled up, they saw a prim-looking elderly woman standing by an automatic gate. She waved as they pulled up.

"Mrs. Alston, do you remember anything out of the ordinary happening on Wednesday or Thursday?" Weeks asked after they'd made their introductions.

"There wasn't anything, I can remember," she answered.

"Was there any evidence of one of the gates being forced?" Ben asked. "Things look pretty secure in here. You would think someone would notice a person trying to climb over the fence."

"That was a pretty good guess," Mrs. Alston replied. "The gate to the parking garage wouldn't open Wednesday afternoon. I had to call our handyman to look at the thing."

"Could we talk to him?" Ben asked. Mrs. Alston pressed a button on her cell phone and then handed it to Ben. After a brief discussion, Ben disconnected and handed the phone back to the apartment manager.

"He said someone pulled a cotter pin out of the hydraulic ram that opens the gate," Ben told them.

"Can you show us?" Weeks asked. They retraced their steps, Weeks taking note of the security cameras in the garage. Weeks wasn't too hopeful about finding fingerprints. The gate had opened when they pulled up. Obviously it had been repaired since then. A homogeneous layer of grease over the piston mechanism indicated that the repairman had done a thorough job and lubricated the ram when he reattached it. So much for fingerprints.

"Mrs. Alston, may we look at the security camera footage for last Wednesday?" Weeks asked. She agreed and led them back to 1004 and rapped on the door.

A thirty-five to forty-year-old white male who appeared to have just awakened answered the door. He was a skinny guy with reddish blond hair, freckles, and was wearing a robe from the Fairmont Hotel over a pair of plaid boxer shorts.

"Mr. Busby, these gentlemen have asked to have a word with you," she said to indicate that he was indeed Fred Busby, the occupant of the apartment, and turned to leave.

"Stop by the office on your way out, and I'll give you the latest videotape from the cameras in the garage," she said.

"I guess this is about Harry," Busby said. "Look, what happened to him is terrible, but tell that wife of his I don't know anything about what he was doing that day."

The two policemen produced their badges and identified themselves. After they'd explained that they felt Harry Zell had been murdered, Busby became a lot less hostile and a lot more cooperative.

"If anybody killed him, it was probably his wife," Busby declared. "Not that she didn't have a good reason to do it."

"What do you mean?" Ben asked, shooting Weeks a dirty look.

"The bimbos," Busby answered, confirming what they already suspected.

Busby explained that Harry and he were cousins and had always looked out for each other. They were closer to brothers. Weeks had to admit this guy looked a whole lot like Zell did, though not as old and not quite in as good of shape for his age.

"So Harry was older?" Weeks asked.

"Yep. I didn't have any brothers or sisters. Harry was the closest thing to an older brother you could have. Harry was eighteen months older than me. Our moms were sisters. They were real close. We spent almost every summer together that I can remember," Busby explained.

"So I take it you two were still pretty close. Had to be if you're letting him use your place to screw around on his wife," Ben offered.

"Charlotte and I never really got along...well, we did at first. When I was still married she got along with my ex- pretty well, so we ate together at holidays and stuff. I got divorced a couple of years ago, and after that, Charlotte never really had a lot of use for me. She believed everything Sadie told her about stuff. That was my ex-wife's name, used to call her Sexy Sadie. You know that Beatles song?"

Both cops nodded. They were just going to let him talk himself out and see what he told them.

"Anyway, she thought everything was my fault. But it takes two to tango, know what I mean?" Busby asked, looking for some sort of absolution.

"You screw around on her?" Weeks asked bluntly.

"Kind of. You can say we screwed around on each other. I just happened to be the one that got caught doing it. Anyway Charlotte never got over that, never had much use for me after that. But there was more to it than that. She knew Harry was cheating on her from the start, and she knew that I knew, so that made a bad situation even worse. She blamed me for it. If she was going to shoot somebody for it I'd have always thought it was me she would have shot." Busby rubbed the stubble on his chin. "Who can figure?"

Weeks shrugged, admitting that life was unknowable. "Did Harry have a key to your apartment?"

"Yeah, I gave him one right after I got divorced. At first I did it just in case something should happen. I didn't really have anyone else. No other family or such. I knew Harry used it sometimes during the day, while I was at work, to meet women. I never asked specifically, and he never said, but you know, that kind of stuff leaves traces. It wasn't hard to figure out."

"Was Zell here Wednesday?" Ben asked.

"I'm pretty sure he had a woman here. Some things were moved around but the sheets hadn't been changed," Busby replied.

"What makes you think there was a woman?" Ben asked.

"This sounds kind of weird..." Busby started, then stopped.

"I promise you, it's no weirder than half of the stuff we have to go through every day," Weeks assured.

"Well he shot-off all over the back of the couch and all over the carpet. I mean who does that without a reason? It had to be a woman."

"Do you mind if we take a look?" Ben asked.

"I already cleaned that shit up and I mean with disinfectant. Who knows what was going on inside there or where that stuff leaked out of? I was going to bust Harry's balls over it. But then he was dead," Busby shrugged.

"Who's Rusty?" Weeks asked.

"Shit, I haven't heard that in years," Busby answered. "It's Harry's nickname. It's what we called him as a kid."

"Do you know anybody called Doubting Tom or Hester?" Weeks pursued.

"Harry's mom used to always call him Doubting Thomas because he never believed anything you told him. I don't know anyone named Hester, though," Busby replied.

After a few more questions, they had just about finished.

"I have one more question," Weeks said. "Was there any chance your cousin may have been involved with another man?"

"You mean was Harry a homo? Hell no. Harry may have been a low life heel with women, but he sure as hell wasn't homosexual. Women were what he wanted, and he always got plenty of them," Busby declared with undisguised pride.

"And that, my friend, is probably what killed him," Weeks whispered.

CHAPTER TWENTY

An old Alfa Romeo Spyder, its once-black top faded to an uneven gray with a yellowed rear window, downshifted and slowed rather than braking on the interstate exit ramp. Weeks had to get on the Camaro's brakes hard to keep from rear-ending it. He'd spent the entire day yesterday beating his head against a brick wall, and now he kept running every detail through his mind, trying to find some kind of a solution. TimeDonors was like a brick wall. They couldn't find any way to get into it or get around it. There wasn't anyone who could tell them anything about how TimeDonors worked. Even if they could get into it there was no guarantee that he could use it to find a way to identify who Zell had been matched with.

The guy he had to talk to at LifeSolutions was the most obstinate bastard Weeks had ever had to deal with, and after all those years in the Army he had seen his share of obstinate bastards. He wasn't the boss, though, that was part of the problem. Apparently the real boss was in Africa, without a phone or any sort of contact number. The guy he'd talked to was a vice-president who'd been left in charge, a guy named Dugan. Mr. Dugan had said he wasn't authorized to make any decisions until the real boss, a guy named Sloan, got back. So, until a judge issued a subpoena or an official request of some sort was received from the district attorney's office, they were dead in the water. Dugan had made it clear that, until such time as he was in possession of one of those two legal documents, he couldn't even talk to him about TimeDonors. Even then, it would, of course, have to be reviewed by the company's attorneys before he could act on it. The fact that this was a murder investigation didn't do a thing to change his mind. Weeks understood the man's strategy completely. If he could just drag his feet long enough, the boss would be back. Who cared if another guy or two got murdered? He was covering his ass with both hands and his hat. Dickhead!

Even if Weeks could have gotten the court order squared away pretty quickly, Dugan was going to bury it in legalese for weeks. That way, there was no need to make any decision. Why risk doing something that could piss off the boss? Anything he did could turn out to be the wrong thing- "wrong" being not what his boss would have chosen. It seemed all the jelly-spined idiot could do was justify his unwillingness to help by repeatedly restating the company motto: "Confidentiality is the cornerstone of our company's credibility."

Something about all those c's pissed Weeks off. He didn't know why. Obviously Mr. Dugan wasn't being paid for his independent thought processes. This wasn't the kind of guy that a scam was going to work on over the phone. He'd just turtle up and pull his head into a shell of lawyers until he was safe- "safe" meaning until he was outside the decision-making process.

"Worthless bastard," Weeks said to himself as he slammed the Camaro's door. He continued to fume as he made his way across the parking lot and into the building.

On his way down the hall, Weeks stuck his head into Chip Jefferies workshop. It resembled some strange computer graveyard. Computers in various states of assembly or disassembly were on every flat surface. "Hey Chip, you get anything else out of Zell's computer?"

Chip looked up from the entrails of the computer he was working on. "I never got a chance. The guy from the FBI picked it up this morning."

"What guy from the FBI?" Weeks demanded.

"The IT guy from the local office. The IT guy wasn't one of the agents or anything, he's just a contract guy, but there was an agent with him, a guy named McCourey. McCourey said it was their case now, interstate jurisdiction or something. I didn't ask too many questions. I'm not getting in the middle of it," Chip replied nervously, suddenly unsure he had done the right thing just letting them take the computer without any paperwork or anything.

"BULL-FUCKING-SHIT," Weeks exploded. He spun, heading out the door and down the hall to Bryant's office. When he reached the captain's office, he knocked once and stuck his head through the door without waiting for an answer. Bryant was sitting at his desk, talking to Ben, who sat across from him.

"So, what is the FBI doing, suddenly taking over?" Weeks asked angrily.

"We can use all the help we can get," Bryant answered firmly.

"My brother called the local office and asked them to look into this," Ben admitted.

"Well, how are we supposed to do our jobs if they take the evidence we need away from us?" Weeks asked in frustration.

"They have more resources. They can look at the stuff that we already have and run it by their analysts. I don't see how it can hurt us. It's not like we were making any progress anyway," Ben argued.

"What you mean is it can only help you. You'd kiss their ass if you thought it would get you a job," Weeks said harshly.

Bryant slammed his fist on his desk like a hammer. "Shut up, Weeks. I sure as hell don't need you letting your personality get in the way of solving this case. All I want is this case solved, as soon as possible. I don't want this fucking albatross around my neck. The

160

mayor is giving shit to the chief, and the chief is therefore giving shit to me. You were in the Army. You want to take a guess where the shit is going from here? If the FBI wants to take the heat in these two murders, I say, 'please do.' Now I want you to do your job and let them do theirs. Stay out of their way and help them if they ask you to. Okay? What's it to you anyway? Why are you so upset about them getting involved?"

"Because this isn't your everyday psycho. This isn't a simple serial killer. This is the kind of shit I know about. This guy's a professional, either military or spook, and I don't know where he's from. What I do know is that he's learning and gaining confidence. The only thing I'm sure of is that the murders are going to get harder and harder to detect as he picks up his game. It's not going to be long before we start missing them, if we haven't already," Weeks fumed.

"That's why we need some help. Who knows what these guys were involved in? No one sends a killer like that after a paper salesman and a car parts supplier," Ben said earnestly.

"What these guys were into," Weeks said, "was getting laid." He turned and slammed the door behind him, mumbling as he walked away. "Little, suck-up prick…"

"Knock it the fuck off Weeks," Bryant shouted through the closed door.

Weeks stomped back to his desk and snatched up his coffee cup, spilling cold coffee across several folders sitting on his desk. He walked to the coffee pot and filled up his cup before grabbing a paper towel. Returning to his desk he sat down and began to clean up the mess. When he picked up Zell's desk calendar and started to wipe it off, he looked at the computer screen, and suddenly, it dawned on him. He didn't really need Zell's computer, did he? "Maybe I can do it from my computer," he said quietly to himself, as he typed www.ls-seminars.com into the Internet address line. The LifeSolutions home page filled the screen. He typed in Rusty Z as a screen name, then Doubting Tom as the password. He got an invalid password prompt, so he entered doubtingtom and got a screen that asked if he wanted to use the credit card he had on file. After deliberating a moment, he clicked yes. He entered TimeDonors into the search box, like he had seen Chip do the night before, but when he arrived at the TimeDonors entry page, this time Weeks requested a new screen name and password. He was immediately forwarded to a screen that asked if he were willing to donate his time to meet the needs of others. He clicked yes and was asked for his preferences in a partner. There were four questions: Male or female, area code, age-in five-year increments, and a group of ethnic descriptions. The last two allowed you to select as many as you liked or to choose "no preference." Weeks entered: female, 602, no preference, no preference and hit enter. From there, he went to a mailbox screen, which asked him to select a screen name and password. He typed in doubtingtom, just in case, and weeks as a password. This time, when he hit enter, a warning flashed, telling him that all arrangements must be completed within seventy-two hours because the mailbox, its contents, and his password would be permanently erased.

"Holy shit! I'm in," he whispered, then quickly shut-up as Ben appeared in front of his desk.

"You ever wash that thing?" Ben said pointing at the cup.

"I washed it when I got it," Weeks replied with a shrug.

"You ever worry what's growing in there?" Ben asked.

"Enough with the hygiene questions, what's on your mind?" Weeks redirected the conversation.

"I'm going back to talk with Zell's widow. You coming?" Ben said.

Weeks mind raced. He had to get rid of Ben before he saw the computer screen. He stood, sweeping up the coffee cup, and started down the hall to the coffee machine. Ben followed, like he'd hoped.

"Come on Weeks. You're not taking that thing in the car," Ben complained.

"No. I'm going to stay here and let you handle Ms. Zell, if you promise not to arrest her...I know you didn't like the way I handled her, but if you go at it like you did last time, you're going to end up talking to an attorney," Weeks replied.

"You sweet talk her then," Ben offered, trying to make up for what he had said after their last conversation with Mrs. Zell.

"Ben, she doesn't know anything. She didn't even know her husband was screwing around for sure," Weeks tried to explain.

"She called Busby didn't she?" Ben countered.

"She was fishing, that's all. Besides, I'm working on something here. I don't want to leave right now," Weeks offered and immediately regretted tipping his hand.

Ben missed the opening, staying with his argument, "How do you know she didn't hire somebody to kill him?"

"We've already been over that. Number one: why would Mrs. Zell hire someone to kill Butler too? And number two: why would a professional hit man take two jobs in the same city two weeks apart? It just doesn't make sense. The wives aren't suspects. I think it's somebody on the other end, somebody they're meeting to have sex with," Weeks explained.

"You can't prove either one of them had sex," Ben argued.

Weeks shook his head. "If they didn't, they managed to get themselves killed just before they got around to it. Somebody's setting these meetings up and then killing the guy who shows up. That's why it doesn't make sense. The victims are being picked at random by the TimeDonors computer. The only thing that's going to be similar is the criteria the victims are selected on."

"Do you think the person picking is the killer?" Ben asked.

"I don't know if it's the same person or not," Weeks admitted.

Ben shook his head and looked at the floor. "Look, I'm sorry they took the computer. I need you to help me with that Zell woman. You know she hates me."

"I don't see how you can say that," Weeks said, letting a smile break across a face that hadn't done anything but frown for two days.

Ben pressed, knowing he had the winning hand. "Look, I went along with you on the parking garage thing...."

"All right," Weeks acquiesced.

They sat in silence as they drove toward the Zell house, both occupied with their own thoughts. Ben wasn't looking forward to talking to Charlotte Zell again and was trying to figure out how he was going to get Weeks to do all the talking and still get the answers he wanted. Weeks was trying to figure out how to tell Zell's widow that her late husband had been involved in some kind of on-line wife-swapping site called TimeDonors and that he'd been routinely cheating on her with whatever women he could convince to meet him at his cousin's apartment. Thirty minutes later the big Ford sedan pulled to the curb in front of Charlotte Zell's house. Ben and Weeks walked up the sidewalk with downcast eyes and heavy steps, looking for all the world like two men heading for the gallows.

It was six hours before they got back to the station, and it was six hours of conversation with a woman who made six minutes seem like six hours. It had to have something to do with relativity.

Weeks rechecked his TimeDonors when he got back to his desk and found a new message waiting. He'd been paired with a woman in Flagstaff, and she'd left him a message, asking if he could come to Flagstaff on a weekday some time between ten and one. Just enough time for a quick screw, then tidy up and get in the carpool line to pick up the kids. Whoever was doing the killing wasn't doing it in Flagstaff. He typed back his response.

doubtingtom: Sorry, work keeps me in Phoenix during the week.

He thought that his answer would end this particular contact, since if she wasn't coming to Phoenix, she wasn't who they were looking for. To his surprise the woman responded almost immediately.

Foxy Lady: Meet in Sedona/ Thursday night or Saturday afternoon?

"Well, well," Weeks thought, "a Hendrix fan that won't take no for an answer." He might as well rule this one out completely.

doubtingtom: sorry only available to meet Phoenix/ Wednesday afternoons. Can you make it then?

Foxy Lady: Sorry. Can't work that out. Bye.

"At least she's not a suspect," Weeks said to himself. Both the killings, well at least the ones they knew about, had occurred on Wednesdays in Phoenix. He was surprised at how easily the system worked. Were there really that many unhappy wives out there? Thank God he was divorced.

If everything was wiped out in seventy-two hours they were screwed anyway. Even if Zell's first contact was made on Tuesday evening, the seventy-two hours was way past. Hell, it had been a week already. Could there really be a way that the LifeSolutions people wiped out all the records every seventy-two hours? How could they get paid? Wouldn't the charge card companies have to have some records of the transactions?

He needed to go through both victims' charge card records looking for any common charge location. They could label it as anything. He was pretty sure they'd have to disguise it some way. Divorce lawyers would have a field day with charges to a site that specialized in affairs for the married. The other problem was, he wasn't sure that even if they did have some common charges he'd be able to use them to link two specific individuals unless the charges were pretty specific. How many people charge stuff to places like PayPal every day? If they used something like that he certainly wouldn't be able to, at least not without more information. He had to get the inside story on both LifeSolutions and TimeDonors. LifeSolutions had to be the key. That's where he was going to find the answer. He just had to find a way to get around Dugan.

They already knew Zell had charged a TimeDonors seminar the Friday before his death. The TimeDonors computer would have erased his secure mailbox on Monday night. Somehow he had to tie this to Butler. He'd already requested all of Butler's charge account transactions for the two weeks before his death. It might not be much, as far as finding the killer, but it could strengthen the case that the two murders were somehow related.

"So how did Zell arrange to contact whoever he was paired with after that?" Weeks asked himself out loud as he tapped a pencil against the side of his head. He thought about the exchange with Foxy Lady. It may not have been necessary. If Zell had regularly used his cousin's apartment, he would have simply given her the address and had her ring the bell. No e-mails, no cell phone records, nothing to trace.

"But women aren't serial killers." Weeks reminded himself. He and Ben had already had that conversation on the way back from the Zell house. Ben had gotten a profile printout from his brother. Ben delivered it a lot like a lecture, but it was worth thinking about, even if it might not be anything more than a logical guess.

"The only female that's ever been identified in the United States as a 'male pattern serial killer'..." Ben had started.

Weeks stopped him. "You're gonna have to explain that one."

"It means that the killer killed people that they didn't already know. Anyway, the only one on record is this woman named Aileen Wuornos in Florida."

"Didn't they make a movie about that or something?" Weeks asked.

"About three years ago," Ben answered.

"I remember that Wuornos was a prostitute that was a dyke in her spare time. She went all around down in Florida robbing and murdering johns that she claimed tried to rape her," Weeks remembered.

Ben continued his lecture. "The experts didn't know if her choosing a masculine role in her love life explained anything, but murder profilers had a field day with it. There were certainly male homosexual serial killers. However, most of those were actually pedophiles. Jeffery Dahmer was the obvious exception, but none of these guys have been chewed on as far as I can tell, so who knows?"

Hmmm, Weeks thought as the tempo of the pencil increased. "There has to be a woman at the center of this case."

He didn't know for sure how she was involved. It could be a man pretending to be a woman, maybe a transvestite or just a killer using an assumed identity on-line. He didn't know if Foxy Lady was a thirty-five year old woman or a fifty-year old man. He'd just taken her word for it. It happened every day. Chat rooms were full of liars.

He had another thought. Was it possible for gays to use TimeDonors? There didn't seem to be a good way to do it the way the selection process was set up. If a guy indicated he wanted to be paired with another guy, he'd get randomly paired with whoever. He'd have to go through a bunch of heterosexual guys before he was paired with another gay guy, unless.... unless he didn't care, unless he wasn't going to have sex with them anyway, unless his whole purpose was to kill them.

That didn't work. Both of these guys had shot off, and Butler had even taken the time to use a condom. There was still the gay angle that he had to consider. Was there some way to play with the options, to kind of signal your intentions? Mess with the possible combinations? The age criteria ranged from less than thirty to over seventy. There really couldn't be that many unhappily married septuagenarians, could there? So select "over seventy." That could be paired to an ethnic group like Asian or Native American to reduce the likelihood of being paired to a straight guy. If someone came up with a formula like that, the information could easily get dispersed in gay chat rooms or web sites. To see what he could find, he ran an Internet search for the words TimeDonors and gay. Nothing came up that looked very promising. He did however find seven pages of hits for TimeDonors alone.

Weeks didn't really see it. Something was just wrong with the way these guys had been killed if that was the case. Neither of them felt right. They were too exact. They felt like professional hits. A professional hit man using a dating service to find his victims? He didn't get how sex fit into it, unless it was the bait somehow...or what? The Wuornos woman, in Florida, felt like she'd been a victim. She was sexually abused as a child. She wanted some sort of revenge against men to make up for it. She hadn't realized that robbing and murdering men along Florida's interstates wasn't an acceptable way to express her anger. So she used the promise of sex to lure them in and did it. That possibility couldn't be ignored either. Maybe men had abused their killer? Maybe as a child? Maybe she had an abusive husband? Maybe it was some bizarre form of revenge?

"Shit, that's it!" Weeks said aloud. "This is all about fucking revenge. That's exactly what this is... some kind of 'fucking...revenge'." He'd felt the same impulse himself when he came back from less than a year overseas to find Denise three months pregnant. He'd wanted payback. He went after her boyfriend. He'd even told Denise he was going to kill him. When he found him, Weeks had pulled a pistol and asked, "Can you give me one reason I shouldn't blow your brains out?"

The guy didn't beg. He seemed to accept getting shot as part of what he'd done. He just said, "Nope, I got nothing to say, except I love her...and her baby needs a father."

For Weeks, those were the right answers, but what if their killer didn't get the right answers? Maybe he couldn't cool off. Maybe he didn't even ask, he just killed. The precision of using the assassin's techniques indicated this wasn't the heat of rage he had felt towards Denise's lover. This fit the old saying "Revenge is a dish best served cold."

Their suspect could be one of the women's husbands or lovers, following his wife then her lovers and taking the time to methodically murder them. The techniques he used meant he could be a professional, maybe military, maybe law enforcement, but whatever he was, Weeks was sure of one thing. A man like this would be dangerous if cornered. The lack of publicity in both of these cases meant the killer probably felt like the murders hadn't been picked up.

He thought he was getting away with it. That had to be a bad thing. If the killer felt like he was getting away with the killings, it wasn't likely he'd stop or slow down for fear of getting caught. So far, the official position had been to keep the publicity down. No one in charge was sure the cases were related yet, and there was no chance Weeks was going to get them to release anything on what they had so far. The only chance of getting anything to the press was to link both men to the same woman and getting into the LifeSolutions computer was the only way he could think of to do that.

Weeks walked to the fax machine and checked the slot with his name above it. It was full of paper. He'd requested the charge statements from Butler's personal and business cards as soon as they'd found out about LifeSolutions. He was excited to see that they'd finally come in. Weeks started to scan the business card charges on the way back to his desk. There was the La Quinta charge and three other motel charges in three different cities, along with the restaurant and air travel charges one would expect for a traveling businessman introducing a new product. No LifeSolution charges.

He sat the papers on his desk, walked to Bryant's office and asked, "You heard anything from the district attorney's office on pushing LifeSolutions for some help?"

"Nothing. I called about forty-five minutes ago," Bryant answered as he continued to look through the stack of time cards in his hand. He scribbled on one of them with a pencil before he resumed. "They're not convinced the two cases are related. The DA said they'd call the LifeSolutions office and ask them to cooperate, but they weren't going to go to a judge yet to try and force the issue."

Weeks thumped his fist gently, obviously restraining himself against the wooden door frame. "So can you explain to me why is it that the FBI's convinced the cases are related, and the DA's office isn't?" Bryant just looked at him over the tops of his glasses. "That prick in San Diego isn't going to do anything until his boss gets back unless we force him."

"Then we're going to have to wait, unless you can find something else," Bryant replied.

Weeks turned with a shrug and returned to his desk. He was going to sift through every charge on every card if he had to. First he looked at the American Express charges; restaurant, car tires, music store, bookstore, and a shoe store. Nothing here. Butler's Visa charges were the same sort of stuff. The last account was a MasterCard. Weeks looked at it a minute before he noticed something different about it. The mailing address was a post office box, not his home like the other two. Weeks traced his finger down the list of Internet services charged to it. That's all that were on it. His finger stopped and Weeks sucked in a deep breath. There, the

Saturday before he was killed, was a charge by LifeSolutions. Weeks shook the paper above his head.

"Not related my ass," he said out loud as he gathered the papers and started for the captain's office. He'd grab Ben on the way. He hoped this would be enough to get a judge to issue a subpoena so they could get a look inside LifeSolutions' computer, even if it wasn't enough to go to the press with yet.

CHAPTER TWENTY-ONE

The ball game had been great, but Weeks hadn't really been able to enjoy it. The Suns had beaten the Trailblazers by six, but it was a two point game with a minute to go. Fouls made the difference. Portland had to foul to get the ball back, and the Suns made their free-throws. That was the difference in the game. Father Joe and all of the boys would be hoarse tomorrow from screaming. Mole` was beside himself. Weeks helped Father Joe round up all the boys and get them into the church van for the trip home. They were riding in silence, each savoring the moment of quiet that riding in the front seat of the van allowed them. Mole` drove, and Weeks sat beside him in the passenger's seat. One row back Father Joe was turned around, giving the boys the game's lessons, as he saw them.

"Hey Mole`, what am I going to do?" Weeks asked, breaking the silence. "It's like I don't know where to go with this now. Little Ben called in the FBI, and we lost Zell's laptop. Then I found the link between the two murders. I can prove that they both visited LifeSolutions Seminars a few days before they were murdered. When I found it, man, I was so excited I jumped up to try and get Bryant to get me a subpoena. I was half way down the hall when I realized I couldn't tell anybody without screwing myself…Zell's laptop was a Mac and the FBI's contract computer guy managed to drag Zell's hard-drive into the trash and wiped it slick as ice. There's nothing left, not that they were going to ever let me look at it again, anyway. That's my basic problem. If I go for the subpoena, the FBI will snatch both cases away from me, and then they'll run out to San Diego and screw up any chance I have of getting what I need to solve this thing."

"Best you didn't ask. I don't see Bryant sending you out there anyway. Even if you told him what you found," Mole` replied. "Even with the new stuff I have for you."

"What do you mean 'even with the new stuff'?" Weeks asked.

"Even with the hair and the genetic analysis." Mole` smiled. "I found two strands of twenty inch long brunette hair inside Zell's pants. The both had active root follicles. Something pulled them out. The genetics came back double X. Two X chromosomes, which means you're looking for a female."

"That explains the shooting-off on the couch," Weeks whispered but not quietly enough.

A hand came down firmly on his shoulder. "Willie is right, boys. It shows you one of the most important parts of the game is the shooting of the fouls," Father Joe said sternly.

"You're probably right," Weeks said in a barely audible whisper. "I guess I might as well tell 'em."

"You could always take advantage of being the new guy," Mole` suggested. "They already think you're a fuck-up."

Father Joe's head snapped around to give Mole` a harsh look as well.

"Sorry Padre," Mole` responded, automatically lowering the volume of his voice.

"Well, that really cheers me up. Thanks for pointing it out," Weeks said. They didn't say anything else until they'd dropped off all of their passengers at the church.

As they drove away from Father Joe in the Camaro, Weeks looked in the rear view mirror at the van surrounded by the children. Mole` backhanded Weeks's chest, making a hollow thump. "No, you're missing the point. You can use that in your favor. You've been so worried about not screwing up again, you can't see that you can use it to your advantage too. Haven't you ever heard the saying, 'it's better to beg forgiveness than ask permission'?"

"Heard it, hell, it's a way of life in Special Forces," Weeks said, finally getting where Mole` was going with this. "If things don't work out, I'll just do the mea culpa thing."

"Here's how I see it working out best," the big man started conspiratorially. "You leave a note for Ben to find later. When it's too late to stop you, or send the FBI, you call me. Then I'll help the note appear on Ben's desk, for him to 'find.' Date it today. Drive to San Diego in the morning. Go see the LifeSolutions people on Monday. It's not your fault Little Ben didn't check his desk over the weekend. By the time he 'finds' your note Monday afternoon, what's he going to do?"

"I'm going to end up chalking tires. Bryant already..." Weeks started.

Mole` interrupted him in mid-excuse. "Who cares? You've already got an Army pension. Retire on a meter-maid's pension too. At least you'll be an honorable meter maid, and that's if you're wrong. What if you're right? You can stop one of the scariest son-of-a-bitches I've ever heard of. If he keeps changing, using newer techniques, nobody's going to catch him. We're not going to get many more shots at this. If you find out something that has any chance of stopping him, we're talking about saving lives. It's that simple."

"Don't get all moral on me. It's easy to play that when you don't have anything at risk," Weeks said.

"You're a Catholic. Guilt and duty are the first two cards out of your deck. You're just like me; you're a sucker for 'em both. We both know you don't have a choice. I'm just offering to help you do what you have to," Mole` explained.

CHAPTER TWENTY-TWO

Tom Dugan, the Vice-President Willie had spent last week referring to only as "that prick," turned out to be much more easily intimidated in person. He started out with the same crap, but the fact that someone had been sent to San Diego startled him, so his set speech seemed somewhat half-hearted. "Dr. Sloan will be out of the country for the next two weeks, but I can assure you that he would strongly resist any attempt to identify any users of our seminars. He has always seen our role as an extension of the doctor-patient relationship. I'm sure you can understand, Detective, people don't want their problems a matter of public record."

Weeks nodded his head. "I can certainly see that, but I'm not sure the FBI is going to buy it."

"What do they have to do with this?" Dugan asked, obviously growing more distressed by the moment.

Weeks had rehearsed his argument on the drive over. "Use of the Internet for interstate commission of a felony is a federal offense. If I go back to Phoenix with a lot of unanswered questions, you can be sure that the FBI will be back to ask the same things, plus a whole lot more about why you won't cooperate with an ongoing murder investigation, and there goes any chance of keeping this whole thing out of the news."

Dugan was literally sputtering. "I didn't say we wouldn't cooperate. Honestly, I probably don't have many of the answers you want. It'll probably be best if you talk to our chief engineer." He pressed the call button on his intercom. "Lydia, get me Brooke Werner, right away." He turned back to Weeks. "She can answer any of the technical questions that you have. Would you care for a soda or some coffee?"

"Coffee, black," Weeks answered, knowing he had won round one.

As they waited Dugan, confided that he didn't really know how the TimeDonors part of the system worked at all. He'd always been involved with the financial aspects of seminar production, but only Dr. Sloan, the owner, and some of the engineers knew exactly what that part of the company did. As far as he knew, it was self-sufficient. They never did any updates or marketing like the LifeSolutions side of the operation. It was only after they had first spoken that Dugan had gone to the engineers and had gotten the general idea of how it paired people in a given area code, and its purpose was for the paired people to have sex. That part of it seemed to be a shock to him.

"Tom, are you saying that up until now you never knew what TimeDonors did?" Weeks asked.

"Not really," Dugan replied. "I thought of it as an off-shoot of one of the seminars we produced, an educational program on managing time for sexual intimacy. In fact we just updated the seminar that was associated with that subject on our side last year."

"You mean a 'how to' for couples?" Weeks questioned.

"You know, making sex a priority in your marriage, suggestions like make dates, block out specific times that are reserved for the couple only; no business, no kids. Those sorts of things," Dugan said.

"But TimeDonors is the workshop, not the seminar, right?"

"That's what I've come to find out over the past few days," Dugan confirmed.

"How do you bill people for using it?" Weeks asked.

"That's it, we don't. LifeSolutions bills everyone the same fee. Once that's paid, anybody is allowed to access any seminar they want for one week, the workshop included," Dugan explained.

"So there's no separate TimeDonors billing. But can you track what happens once the visitor enters the workshop area?" Weeks wondered.

"That's the ingenious part," Dugan explained. "You can discuss this in more detail with Brooke later, but when you enter the workshop, you exit the main computer completely. You go into a separate server, and each account in that server is on a clock with an account life span of only seventy-two hours. There's no need for a different billing system because the only way to get to the workshop server is through the main computer, and the client was already billed at the entry point."

"So each time you enter LifeSolutions you could have as many TimeDonors accounts as you want?" Weeks asked.

"Apparently so. There's nothing to stop one individual from starting two, or three, or even a hundred TimeDonors accounts, each with a different identifier, each one assigned to a different partner," Dugan said, clearly proud of finding out what it actually was that he was suppose to be taking care of.

"Even ten would be impossible to keep track of at the same time," Weeks said, "but theoretically an individual could be paired with two or three different partners to see who had a compatible schedule." That explained the interaction he'd had with the woman from Flagstaff. If she couldn't work it out with him, she could just start a new account. She had a week's worth of unlimited accounts. It would also make tracking who was doing this exponentially more difficult, if they weren't able to go back and look at Butler's and Zell's contact histories.

"Tom, I really appreciate all your help, but I guess it's Brooke that I really need to talk to," Weeks suggested.

Brooke Werner arrived at the same time as the coffee. She wasn't at all what Weeks had expected a chief engineer to look like. She was tall, young and attractive. She wore an expensive tailored suit and wore her hair pulled back tight. She looked more like a model than an engineer.

"You needed to see me, Tom?" she asked in a not too friendly tone. It was obvious that she wasn't happy to be asked to be here.

Tom was visibly relieved by her arrival. "Brooke, thanks for coming so quickly. This is Detective Weeks from the Phoenix police. He has some strange notions about the TimeDonors portion of our seminars. Please assure him that we aren't involved in anything that could result in someone getting murdered."

Brooke's eyes narrowed. She was immediately on guard. "Exactly why are you looking into TimeDonors detective?"

"You don't look much like an IT guy," Weeks observed. "Most of the information technology guys I know are, how should I put it? Well...guys."

"I'm also not really IT. I have a Masters in computer engineering," Brooke corrected.

"Brooke is really the chief of engineering," Dugan explained. "If you can tell her what you're looking for, I'm sure she can help, can't you Brooke?"

"Sure Tom," Brooke said. "Again, Detective, exactly why are you looking into TimeDonors?"

Looking at Dugan, Weeks began, "I hate to take up any more of your time, Tom. I really appreciate your cooperation. I'm sure your company doesn't have any real connection to the murders. It may all be coincidence. Maybe Brooke could just show me around, and I'll get out of your hair."

"Brooke, give Detective Weeks all the help he needs. We're going to deal with 602 access only though," Dugan instructed. "Detective, I'm sorry you drove all the way out here for nothing. Good luck in your investigation," he said, rising from his chair and offering his hand.

"Thanks Tom," Weeks said and then followed Brooke Werner out of the room.

Halfway down the hall Brooke stopped and turned to face Weeks. "You were pretty slick back there, getting me away from Tom. What I want to know before we go any further is why?"

"I sensed a lot of tension between the two of you. I didn't think I'd get a straight story from you in front of him, right?" Weeks explained.

"Let's just say you have a good grasp of human nature Detective, and leave it at that," Brooke answered.

"Look, Brooke, I need your help. I have two men murdered two weeks apart, and the only common element that I can find is that they both visited your site within days of their murders. I know one man visited TimeDonors specifically. The other one had a LifeSolutions charge, but I haven't been able to track it any further," Weeks said.

"I'm surprised that you got that far. Not many people could have. How did you do it?" Brooke asked pointedly, looking for a bluff.

Knowing better than to lie to someone who invented the system, Weeks punted, "The FBI did the analysis. I'm not a computer guy. I'm a question and answer guy."

Brooke stopped outside her office door. "Then ask me a question," she challenged. "Because I think you're full of crap. There's no way to prove that they entered the TimeDonors site. Beyond what that knucklehead in there told you, I don't even think you know what TimeDonors is."

"We know a little more than that. The FBI couldn't follow where they went after they entered their password on the screen that had all of that stuff about people having different levels of sexual needs and asking if they wanted to donate their time. But they followed them to that point, and then got into the system from there. They got to where they could look around, and I don't know the details from there, but somehow they lost them once they got paired up," Weeks said, weaving the lie into the truth.

Brooke was quite obviously shocked, "You're bluffing, there's no way...."

But it was too late. She'd already told him what he needed to know. "What I know is that TimeDonors is some kind of swinging or wife-swapping site that you've gone to extraordinary lengths to protect," Weeks accused.

"It's not that crude or vulgar," Brooke said defensively. "It's to help people to stay in troubled marriages."

"By helping them screw around on their partners. Excuse me if I think that that's still pretty crude and vulgar. Besides, people don't really need your help to screw around. They've been doing it since there was a third person within walking distance," Weeks said emphatically, then added, "Why are you involved in this?"

"I developed the servers Jarvis is using to run TimeDonors," she answered.

"So, why did he buy you and the servers? If you buy a server from Dell or Apple, they don't send you an engineer along with it," Weeks said. "I don't know a lot, but I do know that one of the things you're protecting is the system itself. If the FBI looks into this, it all becomes a matter of public record. How will that play out? Whatever it is that you use to erase all of the information on people's arrangements, well, it won't be a secret anymore. Anyone will be able to set one up. I don't see how that can do anything but make your job totally unnecessary."

"I don't respond to threats, Detective, and I don't like being misled," Brooke lashed out.

"I'm not trying to do either," Weeks said earnestly. "I know you can't see it, but I'm trying to protect your company and your system and still solve these murders. I'm the only white knight that's going to come along. Nobody else is going to let your company's concerns stand in the way of a multiple homicide investigation. So please, let's start over as friends. Can you help me understand how your system works?"

"Okay," Brooke said, offering her hand. Weeks shook her hand, holding it a bit longer than usual and looking intently into her eyes to try and instill trust. For the first time, he realized just how young she was. He noticed her face was slightly flushed as she continued, "I designed the system, and my servers cyclically clear on a preset frequency."

"Could you say that again, in either English or Spanish?" Weeks requested.

Brooke laughed, "You're pretty cute."

"Thanks, but I wasn't trying to be. I was serious," Weeks said, somewhat self-consciously.

"Don't get nervous, Detective, I'm not hitting on you," Brooke said smiling. "I'm around men all day who have one goal-- to prove they're smarter than I am. It's refreshing to see a guy who admits he has limitations."

"My limitations are one of my strongest points. I have tons of them. I also have another question. Is Dugan usually in charge when Dr. Sloan is away?" Weeks asked.

"Jarvis hasn't ever been away as far as I know," Brooke replied. "If Jarvis is away from the building, he's still running things from his cell phone."

"So that kind of explains why Tom is nervous," Weeks offered. "He doesn't seem to know much about how TimeDonors works."

"He doesn't," Brooke confirmed.

"What do you mean 'he doesn't'? How can he run the company if he doesn't know how it works?" Weeks asked.

"That's exactly the question I asked Jarvis before he left last week. I was after him for a month not to do it," Brooke admitted. "Tom doesn't know anything about how the place runs. He doesn't even know where the money comes from."

"What do you mean?" Weeks asked.

"He thinks it's about seminars," Brooke explained. "The seminars are just a cover now, a way to bill. The cash flow is all from TimeDonors."

"So TimeDonors makes a fair amount of the money?" Weeks tried to clarify. "What percent of the business comes from TimeDonors?"

"About 85 to 90 percent." Brooke was on a roll, proud of what was obviously her baby. "We generated seventy five million dollars last year, with thirty-two state penetration."

"How do you know that? I thought you couldn't recover anything from the TimeDonors server."

"That's my job. How many hits on the main versus how many hits on the box. Day in and day out nine out of ten people who log on to the main computer go straight to the box," she explained.

"The box, that's what you call TimeDonors?" Weeks asked.

"Jarvis started out calling it 'the black box.' In IT now it's just the box," Brooke said. "The LifeSolutions or LS guys, you know like Dugan, the advertising and the production people, don't call it anything because, up until now, they didn't know it was there."

"How can that be?" Weeks wondered aloud.

"Because," Brooke offered, "in this company there are two sides; LS and the tech side. Only Jarvis knows both sides."

"But why would you hide what the company does from half its employees?" Weeks asked.

"Think about it. You're a detective," Brooke said, sitting up and looking Weeks straight in the eye. "This is about married people having extramarital sex and not getting caught. All the charges are to LifeSolutions. What could be better? A divorce lawyer gets one of the LifeSolutions guys on the stand and they don't have to lie because they don't know anything."

"It seems like a lot of secrecy and a whole lot of money to spend on making seminars nobody's using," Weeks offered.

"Adultery is serious business. People aren't using this so they can get caught. They have to feel safe, so Jarvis does everything he can to guarantee that. People don't know how safe they are. I drive all the tech people here nuts, and myself too, trying to make a fail-safe system. LifeSolutions as a cover is an expense associated with the security of the system; an expensive decoy, but one that almost pays for itself. Remember, people do use the seminars. They bring in about eight point two million dollars themselves, and the operating costs for the whole LS set-up, including TimeDonors, are less than ten million a year. So, effectively, for an unbeatable security system where no one can track a dime spent to the box, it costs less than two million dollars in real negative cash flow. It's that security that gets you a net profit of seventy-five million dollars a year."

"Okay Brooke, enough economics. How do we catch whoever it is that's knocking off the Phoenix Timedonor Club?"

For the next hour and a half, Weeks went over the details of the two deaths with the engineer. She focused on every aspect, looking at it like an engineering problem.

"The hair and the sex prove it's a woman, right?" she asked finally.

"I'm not sure a woman could do this, Brooke. This is calculated assassination," Weeks offered.

"I could do it." She answered seriously. "It wouldn't be that hard, you'd just have to study how to do it and then be angry enough to carry through with it."

"Have you ever been that angry? Think about it. This isn't the sort of thing a woman would do," Weeks explained.

"She would if she'd been hurt badly enough." Brooke answered looking down at her hands.

"You haven't been to Phoenix recently have you?" Weeks asked in his most serious cop voice. When he finally smiled she punched him in the arm.

"Just for that you're buying me lunch," she announced.

They parked just off Prospect and were heading to an Indian restaurant just up from the oceanfront. The two of them were so deeply engaged in conversation that Weeks didn't notice the attractive, petite woman coming out of Watson's Art Gallery until they struck, her forehead bouncing off his chest. Reflexively, Weeks wrapped his arms around her to keep her from falling; she, in turn, grabbed his waist, her hand brushing the Sig he carried as a sidearm.

"I'm so sorry," he said, looking down into her startled brown eyes, his arms still around her.

"Sue, sweetie, are you all right?" the man from the art gallery was asking as he took her arm and pulled her toward the door and out of Weeks's arms.

"Again, really, I'm so sorry," Weeks stammered.

"No harm done," she replied. "In fact, it felt pretty safe in there with the gun and all."

"I'm a detective," Weeks offered.

"And you're a lucky girl," Sue said, winking at Brooke.

"Sue, honey, come in, sit down. Let me get you some tea," the gallery man was saying as they went into the door. The last thing Weeks saw as she disappeared was her smile and a friendly wave.

"That was really smooth," Brooke teased. "So that's how you get women in Phoenix. Just tackle them and then hold on."

"I didn't want her to fall." Weeks's face was beginning to flush in embarrassment.

"Don't blush, Detective, it worked. She was hitting on you; the smile, the wave. She was saying, 'Come and get me big boy.'" Her voice rose to a falsetto as they continued to walk. Several passersby glanced and smiled as Brooke continued her act. "Come on,

Detective, let me hold that big gun of yours. It makes me feel so safe."

"Okay, knock it off," Weeks protested gruffly. "I'm here for work, not women." Then with a smile, "But who knows, once this case gets wrapped up, I may need to come back out here. You don't know anybody who could help me get some computer classes, do you?"

Over Tandori chicken and curried lamb, they worked out details. With no way to look back at Butler or Zell's contact information they would have to utilize a prospective approach.

"So, you can route all of the 602 area code calls out of the secure server and back to the LS server where we can keep track of them?" Weeks asked.

"Sure, but that would be a lot to keep track of. What else are we looking for?" Brooke answered.

"Both of the victims were in their forties, white, and they both got killed in Phoenix on a Wednesday afternoon," Weeks explained.

Brooke tapped a chopstick against her front tooth, "That's pretty specific: area code, sex, age and ethnicity are already monitored because they're selection criteria. The best thing that I can think of to do is to just route individuals who match your victims for all four of these four criteria back out of the box. That would keep the records from being erased. Then I'll set the account I route them back out and into so that it monitors for the word 'Wednesday' in all of the ongoing communications. Then I can call you if anything pops up and give you the details of the arrangements."

Weeks took out a card and wrote a number on the back. "Here's my cell phone. The number on the front is my office number."

"I guess you're going to need my number, too," Brooke said and took a business card out of her purse. Turning it over, she wrote her cell number on the back. "Look, I need to know if there's a chance this thing is going to blow up in the press or with the government. Please."

"I'll do my best to keep you out of trouble," Weeks promised.

"Whoever you're chasing seems like they're pretty dangerous. You need to try and stay out of trouble yourself," Brooke said sincerely.

"I will, don't worry," Weeks assured her.

"You need to be less of a gentleman," she warned. "If your killer is a woman, and you treat her the way I've seen you treat women today, you won't stand a chance."

CHAPTER TWENTY-THREE

"Hey Kent, can you give me a hand getting these paintings out of the car?" Laura called through the door of the gallery.

"I hope you have enough that I'll need a forklift," he answered.

"Not quite. Two strong arms will do," Laura replied.

"Darn! I swear, if you did bring a tractor-trailer full of paintings, I really believe I could sell them all in a week or two." He reached for the paintings she held in her hands. "I appreciate you coming down a week early," he said.

"Not a problem. Just don't expect me to come down every week. I can't paint that fast. I brought down everything I had at the house that was anywhere close to ready." She turned back to get the rest of the canvases from the Suburban.

"These are the heaviest things I should <u>ever</u> have to pick up," Kent said hefting the paintings. "I didn't become an art dealer so I could spend my evenings shoving furniture around."

"What's got you so bitchy?" Laura asked, although she suspected that she knew already.

Kent and James were "temporarily" broken up. Kent was accommodating for his loss with a very young boyfriend named Trevor. Laura's theory was that lust couldn't match the passion that Kent had shared with James for so long, so he was compensating by throwing himself into the non-sexual aspects of Trevor's life.

"We're redecorating the restaurant. Next we'll do the bar. We're going to redo one area at a time. So now every day when I leave here I'm spending my evenings moving furniture and, of course, it's 'No I don't like it here, lets move it over there.' I'm too old for manual labor," Kent responded.

"Why do you do these things?" Laura shook her head. "You know he's just taking advantage of you."

"I like to be taken advantage of, that's the problem. Let's face it, I'm no spring chicken. I don't even want to have sex with somebody my age. I have to do something to keep him around. I'm desperate," Kent replied honestly.

"Just give it some time," Laura counseled.

"I don't need any therapy," Kent started and then switched gears. "But I do need a favor, if you can."

"Give you my secrets for hanging on to young boyfriends without spending money?" Laura teased, trying to lighten his mood.

She knew how prone he was to the darkest depressions. When Kent was depressed he had no judgment. He didn't care who he had sex with. He just wanted sex to make him feel okay about being alone. For the first time she could remember, she understood what that felt like.

"No, baby, I've had more cute boys than you've ever even seen," Kent laughed. "I need to borrow your Suburban to take one of the paintings to Mrs. Prill. I had to put her off last time because I ran out of paintings. She's having a cocktail party tonight and wants your painting hung by three so the florist can match the decorations to the painting. I wouldn't ask, but Trevor has my van at the club. You could come with me to deliver the painting." Laura made a face. "I'm sure the little old dear would love to tell her guests tonight that the artist herself hung it for her. We could stop by the club on the way back, and you could see the place and meet Trevor."

"You know I'm terrible with the meet and greet stuff. I guess I'm just hypersensitive," she said. "I need my delusions. I like to believe that only brilliant, enlightened intellectuals buy my paintings. I'd prefer not to have to face the truth, that they're primarily blue-haired southwestern matrons with conservative tastes and more money than sense. Besides, I have a hair appointment," Laura lied, thinking about the arrangements she had made to meet a man at the Super 6 Motel. She sure as hell wasn't going to let Kent drop her off at a Super 6. There was nothing else there, no bar, no restaurant, nothing but cheap rooms, thin sheets, and single-ply toilet paper. Maybe she should just blow this one off. She'd be with Sue and Jarvis next week. For some reason this one just seemed like a loser. Everything about it just felt really cheap and tawdry. There was nothing about it that made her feel sexy. "If you trust me with your Mercedes, I'll skip my appointment and meet you at the club after you deliver the painting." She shook her beautiful hair. "Besides, I don't really think I need a touch up yet, do you?"

Kent reached over and took her hair between his fingers. "A touch-up. I'm not sure your hair was ever touched the first time. If someone's been coloring your hair, they should be shot for impersonating a hairdresser. Let me make a call. I have a friend that could do something with those split ends. For God's sake, stay away from whatever butcher's been coloring your hair without trimming it. I'll see if you can get that done while I'm with Mrs. Prill." He reached over and dialed the phone. As his voice rose and fell, Laura thought about how much she would prefer a haircut to what she had originally planned.

What had happened, she wondered? Was the excitement gone already, or was it already becoming too routine, too much like work? Who cared? Anybody that called himself Little Boy Blue and wanted to meet in a Super 6 deserved to have to jerk-off.

She drove Kent's car the three miles to his friend's shop. The big Mercedes was comfortable and made the trip to the hairstylist seem even more of a luxury. She tried to picture the camel carpet covered with French fries and different-colored drink stains, like her car was. She couldn't really drive a nice car until Cody got older, she thought. For now, she'd just have to hope mice or roaches never colonized her own car. God knew they could live for years on all the crumbs and debris that had settled, like the sediment in a river, into the fabric of her car's carpet and seats. She had tried to shampoo it all out once. The liquid had just made all of the different components in the sedimentary deposits congeal and actually seemed to make things worse instead of better. She decided dry vacuuming, when the sediment obscured the interior's original color, would be good enough.

Unfortunately, she had a similar attitude when it came to her hair and clothes. She hadn't been to a hair stylist in months, and she couldn't even remember the last time she had a manicure or bought new make-up. Her clothing all made the same rotation, new, good, casual, work, painting, and then rags in her studio. She wondered if Morris would have found her more attractive if she'd paid closer attention to her appearance. Who knew? Maybe she'd buy a new blouse and see if that and a new haircut made any difference.

Morris picked up the movement of Laura's car fairly quickly. He wasn't in any hurry. He could just use the GPS to find her, but he had to be there fairly quickly after she stopped if he was going to see where she went. He'd almost lost her the last time. The Suburban traveled south into a fairly sedate neighborhood, bordering a golf course. He saw Laura's silver SUV parked behind a white Lincoln in the driveway of a house that looked a lot like every other house in the neighborhood, myriad repetitions of tan stucco and red tile roofs, this one made individual by the numbers 657 on the mailbox and painted on the rounded curb in front of the dwelling. He slowed as he saw a pair of legs on the far side of one of Laura's large pieces entering the front door of the house she was parked in front of. Morris parked where he could see the front of the house fairly well and began to scour the windows with his binoculars. He really couldn't see a whole lot. Engrossed as he was in trying to find his hidden wife, Morris didn't notice the electric golf cart with the word SECURITY stenciled on the front of it. The first he was aware of the guard's presence was a sharp rap on the window just behind his head. Morris almost jumped through the windshield, whipping his head around, his right hand shooting into his right jacket pocket. Morris found himself face-to-face with a security guard who was tapping the window with his pen. Morris took a deep breath and tried to regain his composure before he rolled down his window.

"This is a secured neighborhood," the guard said. "You have some business here?"

"Hey, I'm a contractor," he said, motioning to a toolbox on the seat beside him. "I got a call about a frame separating from its casing." Morris paused and picked up a small clipboard with several colors of receipts clasped in its metallic jaw.

"Here it is," he said, pointing to a sheet of paper with undecipherable writing covering its front. "Bryce Johnson at 657 Larkspur. I was just trying to see if I could see which window it was."

"Did you figure which one it was?" the guard asked, eyes narrowing suspiciously.

"No, I really couldn't," Morris admitted. "Johnson's a single guy. He won't be home from work until five, I just thought I'd see what size stripping I was going to need to tie things back together."

"I don't think looking at Mrs. Prill's house is going to help you much there. You're on Lakeshore not Larkspur. I don't even think there's a Larkspur in this neighborhood," the guard offered.

"I must have put in the wrong street name when I was entering the address. I guess that's how I got the wrong driving directions," Morris said, holding up the GPS readout that was indicating Laura's car in the driveway in front of him. "Are you sure Johnson doesn't live here?"

"Look buddy, you better call whoever it is you're looking for and find out where he lives because a widow named Prill lives there," the guard advised.

"Damn electronics. They're supposed to make life easier. One little mistake and now I'm probably on the wrong end of town. Shit, I guess I better do it the old-fashioned way and call. Thanks for your help," Morris said as he started up the truck. He waved as he pulled away, holding his cell phone to his ear. Morris drove to a gas station and bought a diet soda. What was Laura doing at a widow's house? He thought back to the two legs behind the framed landscape. That had to be it. She was just here delivering a painting. He'd just wait until she left and see where she went from there. He bought a sandwich to go with the soda and a car magazine. Then he went back out to the truck. He was halfway through a comparison of three new sport sedans when he saw Laura's vehicle begin to move. He sat where he was, knowing she wouldn't see him as she passed because he was parked on the far side of the building. He just hoped she didn't decide to stop. His luck was mixed. Laura's car zoomed by the station without slowing, but before he could pull out onto the two-lane road she was headed down, two large trucks wedged themselves between his truck and Laura's rapidly moving SUV. It was more of an inconvenience than a real problem. There was nowhere to pass the trucks in front of him, but he'd still be able to monitor Laura wherever she went. He tossed the GPS monitor up slightly and caught it. Even though he had pretended to curse it, there was no doubt this was one of the smartest little gadgets he'd ever bought. Hell, who knew? Without it, he might be following a car Laura wasn't even in.

Laura turned from side to side, looking at her multiple reflections in the three-way mirror, trying to see how the sheer little blouse she was trying on rode on the curve of her hip. She moved this way and that to be sure it didn't bunch or ride up. No one wanted to look like one of those women in the grocery store with their butts poking out like they could carry a sack of sugar on each cheek. Taking the time to try on clothes was something she almost never did. She usually wore t-shirts in warm weather and flannel shirts on cold days, ordered from Cabella's or L.L. Bean. She wasn't sure where she would wear this little thing outside the house, but she was fairly sure Morris would like it. It was the cutest thing she had seen today. As she began to unbutton the top button of the blouse, her cell phone rang.

"Hello," she answered.

"Are you gorgeous yet?" Kent asked.

"I don't know about that," she replied, "but I did get my hair cut, and I've found a 'girlie' shirt."

"They call them blouses. I swear, you're hopeless," Kent laughed.

"Did Mrs. Prill like the painting?" Laura asked.

"She thought it was marvelous. In fact she's considering donating it to the Guggenheim Museum," Kent teased.

"You're such a rotten liar. But she did keep it, didn't she?" Laura asked.

"She kept it for her party, but she's coming down tomorrow to see if there's a smaller painting that might fit her needs better," Kent said.

"The size was a problem?" Laura asked.

"No sweetie, not the size, the price. Your value has gone up considerably recently, and Mrs. Prill wasn't aware what a painting of that size would cost when she told me what she was looking for," Kent explained.

"I'm sorry. If she really likes it, couldn't we make some kind of a deal?" Laura offered.

"Absolutely not," Kent said firmly. "You paint, and like I always tell you, let me worry about the business. Anyway, I'm almost to the club. Trevor called, and of course he's too tied up with some foolishness to take care of business at the club. So I have to meet with one of the liquor distributors this afternoon. I'll leave your keys at the front desk. That way, if I get tied up, you can just drop my car keys off. I really appreciate your canceling your plans and helping me out with the car."

"You're more than welcome. That's what friends do. I've just got to pay for this blouse. I'll see you in a little while, if you're free, but I really need to get started for home," Laura said, glad to get out of meeting Kent's young lover. She liked James, and hated that the two of them were fighting. She knew that they'd had their share of break-ups, but none of them ever lasted very long. One of them, usually Kent, would be on to the "next big thing." Then, the next thing she knew, they'd be back together, and Kent would be trying to recover from whatever harebrained venture his latest fling had convinced him to sink money into. If Trevor was already ignoring the business, that wasn't a good sign. She just hoped Kent hadn't fronted too much money this time. She'd know when she got there.

Morris spotted Laura's Suburban parked right in the front of a club called The Bleu Onion. The parking lot was empty, and there wasn't really anything else close by. Morris knew he couldn't just walk in the front door without risking Laura seeing him, so he drove around to the back. A young guy in a sleeveless t-shirt sat on a couple of shipping pallets smoking a joint. He looked to be about twenty. Morris parked the pick-up and walked over to him. The young man nodded and offered Morris the joint. Morris accepted, not wanting to seem rude.

"You open yet?" he asked without exhaling, holding the smoke in his lungs for as long as he could.

"Naw, we don't open til nine," the boy said, retrieving the joint and putting it to his lips.

Morris finally coughed, blowing the smoke out of his lungs. "It's been a while. Looks like you've got one customer," he said, pointing at Laura's car.

"There's nobody inside," the boy replied.

"Is it too early to get a beer?" Morris asked, wanting to get a look inside and try to figure out what was going on.

"Not for you," the boy answered as he got up and headed to the door. Morris followed. When they got inside, the youth turned and draped his arm across Morris's shoulder. "Come on in this way," he instructed.

"Davey, don't you have some work you're supposed to be doing?" a middle-aged man with silver hair asked.

"Yeah, okay Kent," the boy answered. "I was just showing my new friend where the bar was."

"Come on in. Laura's on her way," Kent offered. "Don't mind Davey. He's something my new partner drug in. I'm not sure how we're going to get any work out of him. All he does, that I can tell, is smoke and take out the garbage. Laura said you'd stopped painting. Pity, you had so many exciting ideas."

"Hey Kent, I didn't recognize you at first," Morris said. "I saw Laura's car out front...."

"Oh, I borrowed it today to deliver a painting," Kent said.

Reflexively, Morris examined the trouser legs and shoes Kent was wearing. There was little doubt that it was Kent who had entered the widow's house. "What's Laura doing?" he asked.

"She has my car," Kent said. "She went to get her hair cut and to buy a few things."

"Clothes?" Morris asked incredulously.

"Blouses," Kent confirmed.

"Laura, shopping for clothes at a real store? You must be talking about some other Laura, not the one I know," Morris answered. "What are you doing down here? I thought you'd be at the gallery?"

"I opened this with a friend. I just had a meeting this afternoon. What are you doing here? Laura didn't mention that you were in town," Kent asked.

"She doesn't know. I...I...was going to surprise her," Morris stammered, not knowing what to do next.

"I'm sure she'll be surprised," Kent assured him. "She should be here in just a few minutes to bring my car back and pick up hers."

Morris was pretty much out of ideas. He could wait and try to con Laura into thinking that he wanted some time together and decided to meet her here, but why would he have come to this club? It wasn't on the way to the gallery, and he couldn't just say he saw her car. He was going to have to try something else. "Look, Kent...well...how can I say this? I don't want Laura to know I'm here. I couldn't believe that it was her car out front, but I came in the back door, just in case."

"Oh my God. Now it all makes sense. You're in the closet," Kent said, thoughtfully.

"Well, sort of on the fence," Morris answered hesitantly.

"That's why Laura thinks you're cheating and you're not interested. She doesn't know yet, does she?" Kent was in gossip mode, and this was just too hot.

Morris shook his head no.

"You liked it that she dressed like a guy. The poor thing is getting her hair cut and buying a blouse to try and liven things up," Kent concluded. "She's going completely the wrong way."

"I'm not ready to tell her yet. She's always thought it was other women. I just don't know what to do." Morris said putting his face in his hands.

"You poor thing. I know it must be torture," Kent comforted. "Is there anything I can do for you?"

"As a matter of fact, there is. You could help us both. Give me something exciting, something I can picture when I'm with her tonight," Morris said as he leaned over to kiss Kent's cheek. "Is there somewhere we could be alone?"

Kent hurriedly led Morris to a back office and locked the door. When they were alone, with only the light through the window, Morris put his hands on Kent's shoulders and pushed him downward. "I want to watch you first," was all he said.

Kent, knowing what was wanted, sunk to his knees and began to expertly unbuckle and unsnap Morris's jeans. Morris reached into the pocket of his jacket and withdrew the pick. He drew the back of his right hand along Kent's right cheek as he palmed the weapon. That allowed him to get it into the right position without Kent seeing it. Morris tugged at Kent's hair playfully with his left hand, getting a handful to hold on to. In one motion, he pulled Kent's head back and drove the pick up Kent's left nostril, aiming at the Circle of Willis. This time, instead of a back and forth motion, Morris ripped straight back. He felt the paper-like bones of the back of the nasal cavity crack and break against the blade as he applied force. He looked down to see the look of shock frozen on Kent's face. As he jerked the pick free, he pinched the bridge of Kent's nose to prevent bleeding to the outside. He held on tightly as Kent's arms and legs jerked spasmodically. As the limbs flailed, Morris noticed that Kent died sporting an enormous erection.

"I'm sure you made a lot of lonely men happy with that big boy," Morris said admiringly as the seizure activity quieted and the rest of Kent became flaccid. Yet even in death the erection remained.

Laura walked into the front door of The Bleu Onion and looked around critically. The décor was urban modern, lots of neon and chrome. At the front desk sat an empty chair. She looked on the desktop and didn't see her keys anywhere. "Hello," she called as she walked through the restaurant and into the bar. There was no one in either place. She walked through the swinging doors into the kitchen where she saw a very young blond. "Trevor?" she asked.

"No, I'm Davey. Trevor isn't back yet. Can I help you?" he asked.

"I was just looking for Kent. He was supposed to leave my keys at the front desk," Laura answered.

"Is Maurice up there? He probably left them with him," Davey offered.

"Has Kent gone?" she asked.

"No, but I think he's tied up in the back with a piece of rough trade," Davey answered.

"I'm sorry?" Laura said, having no idea what the young man had just said.

"A guy dressed like a lumberjack or something," Davey replied.

"The liquor distributor?" Laura asked.

"I didn't ask. I'll go find Maurice and see if he knows anything," Davey offered.

"Is Kent's office back here?" Laura asked his retreating back.

"At the end of the hall," Davey answered as he shouldered through the swinging door.

Just as he was straightening up and putting the pick back into the jacket pocket, Morris heard footsteps coming down the hall. Quickly, he grabbed Kent by the shirt collar and drug him toward the only other door in the room. Opening the door as quietly as he could, he saw that his only hiding place was a very small bathroom, a toilet with just enough room to stand in front of. He shoved Kent's head along the far side of the toilet and rotated his hips so that his legs were going up the wall. He stepped up onto the seat of the toilet and forced the door shut.

Laura knocked several times, with no answer, before she tried the knob. Gingerly she turned it and opened the door slowly.

Morris, standing on the toilet seat, heard someone knocking on the door. Then Laura's voice called out Kent's name several times. He could hear her entering the room, just beyond the door. She moved around the room slowly. Her footsteps came nearer and nearer. He could imagine he smelled her perfume. Her hand on the doorknob made it tremble slightly; she knocked. "Kent are you in there?" she asked.

Morris knew she would recognize his voice. He drew the stun gun from his left jacket pocket. It was the only thing he could do. He would hit her with the stun gun and hope she didn't get a good look at him. He pulled his t-shirt up over the lower part of his face. If he jumped down on her, maybe she wouldn't recognize him.

"Hey Lady," a voice he recognized as belonging to Davey called into the room. "Here're your keys. Kent left 'em with Maurice."

"Is Kent gone?" he heard Laura ask.

"Well, he's not in here," Davey replied.

CHAPTER TWENTY-FOUR

Mole` Ruiz almost let this one slip by him. He wasn't watching for anything unusual. He'd allowed himself to believe that the killer had a schedule. There shouldn't have been another murder until next Wednesday. Then, he'd be considering any dead white guy that showed up as a potential victim no matter what. As it was, when the owner of a gay club was found dead, upside down in the bathroom of his office, Mole` was pretty sure it was a murder, but he had no real reason to suspect that it was connected to either the Butler or Zell murders. His buddy Mark Ceres picked up the body. Fitz and Parker were the detectives from homicide who were investigating the case.

Not many gay club owners accidentally died upside down in the john, with their head shoved under the toilet so the question was who, not if. The autopsy was being done this morning. Mole` already had a backlog of cases he was working on, and he hated to waste time on something that probably wasn't connected to any of the other, but who knew what they'd find? Even though the victim was fully dressed, speculation was rampant on the cause of death and how the guy ended up upside down like that. There were as many theories as there were gay jokes. The only thing he was sure of was that it was strange, and the more unusual stuff you saw, the better you got at figuring stuff out. When he got to the autopsy suite, Mole` caught up with Anne, the tech who was assisting the pathologist on duty that morning.

"Hey, you beautiful thing," Mole` greeted her.

"Hey big fella," she replied.

"Have you started on the guy they found upside down in the john yet?" he asked.

"Not yet. He could be next, but it'll cost ya," Anne offered.

"Okay, so what'll it cost me?" Mole` asked.

"I was thinking of lunch, and I'm not talking about fast food either. Something good," Anne answered.

"How about a candlelit dinner for two?" Mole` offered.

"They'll be doing an autopsy on you tomorrow. My husband's a pretty jealous guy," Anne warned.

"Okay, then I guess pizza will have to do then," he conceded. "Who's doing the cases today?"

"Bell," Anne answered.

"Great. Ding-dong. Unless the guys got 'I've been murdered' tattooed on his forehead, he's not going to find shit," Mole` grumbled.

"You going to be in here, or you want to watch on camera?" Anne asked.

"I can stay in here, if you want the help," Mole` offered.

She tossed him a rubber apron. "I can always use a strong back to roll 'em. Bell's all over the place. Front-back-front-back, he thinks its like flipping pancakes, and he never helps. I guess that's because he's older than God," Anne said conspiratorially just as the wizened pathologist pushed the door open.

"Get the next case," he ordered briskly.

Mole` wheeled the stainless steel autopsy table with Kent Davis on it into position under the lights and cameras. The gross exam was unrevealing. Mole` looked closely but didn't see anything that looked like ante-mortem trauma. The examination of the abdominal and thoracic organs was likewise unremarkable, but when they popped the skull, they found the same collection of clotted blood along the base of the brain that Mole` had seen in the Zell case. Mole` heard Dr. Bell dictate his conclusion. "Cause of death: massive intracranial hemorrhage from a ruptured berry aneurysm."

"Hey Doc," Mole` interrupted. "This looks just like the Zell case from last week, the one Dr. Thomas ruled was a murder. He found a puncture wound through the foramen magnum where a weapon was used to tear the arteries. You could see it when we sectioned them. This has to be a murder. Look at how they found him. His head was shoved under a toilet."

"That could be why it ruptured. People aren't meant to be upside down for too long." Anne offered.

The old pathologist cleared his throat. "Ruiz, isn't it, you're going to find a hundred ruptured aneurysms for every crazy murder like that. Even though I always say, 'If you hear hoof beats, think horses, not zebras', just to be on the safe side let's see if we see some stripes." Dr. Bell pulled down the light source and began to examine the membranes near the foramen magnum from every angle with a magnifying lens. There was no evidence of any penetration or disruption posteriorly.

"I guess you're right, Doc, it looks like an everyday plow horse," Mole` conceded when they were done.

"Not quite. Look at the pituitary gland. It's almost totally avulsed from the stalk. It's just hanging there, barely attached. Somebody tried a trans-sphenoidal approach this time."

"What do you mean?" Mole` asked.

"Someone stabbed into the cranial vault from below. They stabbed through the softer sphenoid bone to lacerate the arteries," Bell explained.

"How could they do that?" Mole` wondered aloud.

"Only one way," Bell explained. "The killer had to shove something up Mr. Davis's nose, and when he hit bone, the killer just kept on shoving until he got to where he wanted to go. Then he shook the handle and lacerated the arteries. Just like before, but from the front this time."

"Damn, Doc, great catch," Mole` congratulated.

"It wasn't all that hard really," Bell said, winking. "It was tattooed on his forehead."

"Look Doc, I just meant…,"Mole` stumbled, not knowing how he had been overheard.

"Take an old man's advice," Bell offered. "Before you say anything about anybody around here, make sure the microphones and video are cut off. Now, go call your buddy over at homicide, and tell him he has another murder."

The investigation of the Davis case was a nightmare, as far as Weeks was concerned. Everything was in slow motion now. Nobody seemed to get that this guy was accelerating his pace. He was going faster, and they were going slower. That wasn't a good combination for anybody who might be a potential victim, because it almost guaranteed that there'd be more of them.

Fitz and Parker didn't want any part of bucking the FBI, so they handed over everything they had as soon as it looked like the case was linked to the other two murders. Ben was ecstatic. He was getting to work hand-in-hand with the bureau's investigation team. All that meant for Weeks was that they were treated like gofers. Whatever the FBI wanted, they had to "go fer." The FBI had now assumed the central role in the investigation. If he didn't find a way around it, Weeks would find himself further and further marginalized until he essentially would have no place at all in the investigation. Ben would thrive. He was happy to play the role of the underling, happy to learn at his idol's feet. Weeks had never been one for hero worship, and he sure as hell didn't want to be the errand boy for a bunch of smug pricks in suits. The problem was there wasn't anything he could really do about any of it. After his unapproved trip to San Diego, he didn't have a lot of room to complain. Nobody was too interested in what he had to say about anything right now, so he kept his thoughts to himself. It wasn't as if he was brimming with brilliant insights anyway. They ought to be looking at the gallery, getting a list of all of the patrons, looking at all of the artists. That's where the key was. The problem was the FBI guy's didn't see it that way. They were locked on the nightclub. He guessed that made sense. You were more likely to be looking for sex in a nightclub than in an art gallery, but that was the only thing in this case that had any logical ties to the other two cases.

The club owner's death pretty much shot down Weeks pet theory, that the murderer was a jealous husband. It could still be a jealous lover. Maybe Butler and Zell were bisexual. The only trace evidence they had was the hair, and the DNA there was female. Two of the witnesses described a woman with long dark hair as being in the club looking for Davis right after he was last seen. So whoever the mystery woman was in these cases, she was still there. But what was she doing in a gay club? No one they questioned had ever seen her before. Once again she showed up and somebody died, but why? Nobody had any ideas.

What they did know was that Kent Davis was exclusively homosexual. So it wasn't sex. Everyone Fitz and Parker had talked to at the club had confirmed that. Davis's boyfriend, who went by the name of Trevor Island, had a rock-solid alibi. He'd been in the company of a local liquor distributor at a restaurant, surrounded by a bunch of witnesses who could verify his whereabouts for the entire afternoon in question.

Weeks regretted that he'd forgotten to explore the idea that TimeDonors was being used as a gay matchmaking service with Brooke when he was out in San Diego. It was something he'd have to call her about. He didn't want to admit it, but he was happy to have an excuse to call her anyway. She was kind of young for him, but she was interesting and very cute. He was tired of dating airheads and dodging marriage. It would be nice to be with somebody he could talk to, somebody who had a life of her own, who wouldn't feel like she needed to get married to have an identity. Maybe he would go back out to San Diego, if they ever got this case tied up.

CHAPTER TWENTY-FIVE

If Africa had a soundtrack, Jarvis thought, it was the hum of insects. He was on the roof of an old Toyota sitting in the middle of a national park while the boys snapped pictures of a herd of impala. He was sick of antelope. Sure there were different sizes. Who cared?

"Ow, shit," he exclaimed sharply as yet another of those damned flies with a mouth like a railroad spike bit the back of his neck.

"Jarvis watch your language," Sharon said in a stage whisper.

"Dad, you're going to scare the impala," both boys whispered at once.

The trip to Africa had been both wonderful and terrible. The boys had loved it; Jarvis had wished they went skiing instead. He had been wary of spending any time in Johannesburg, so they'd flown into Cape Town. Cape Town was beautiful geographically, but its population had grown uncontrollably since Mandela was elected, and there were literally thousands and thousands of homeless and unemployed people in the streets. There were people living in cardboard boxes all around the airport. After leaving the airport, the family had gone directly to the bed-and-breakfast. They took a taxi down to look at the Cape of Good Hope and went to eat dinner near the waterfront. It was strange to see eland and kudu steaks on a menu. The next morning after breakfast, they'd returned directly to the airport and flown to Nairobi. Kenya was much more the tourist spot, it seemed. It may just have been that the guides who worked for the outfitter were better at managing tourists than the Sloans were at managing themselves in a strange city. The safari operation was very well-organized. It even allowed for some supervised shopping trips for souvenirs and trinkets before heading out to the lodge. At the lodge, they were escorted to a two-bedroom, family-size thatched bungalow just across from a swimming pool. After dinner, they watched as zebra and wildebeest wandered to the water hole that the dining room patio overlooked. Jarvis and Sharon had enjoyed several "Sundowners" as the boys swam. As darkness approached, Jarvis at first thought it was the concentration of the alcohol in the mixed drinks and the anti-depressants that were giving him the impression of objects darting above the surface of the pool in the fading light. He asked Sharon if she was seeing birds or something, when one of the staff replied, "They're bats. The insects that come near the water attract them. The insects are drawn by the pool lights and the bats are drawn by the insects."

"Shouldn't the children get out of the pool?" Sharon asked somewhat alarmed.

"No, no," Robert, the houseboy they had been introduced to when they were taken to their rooms, replied. "The bats have very good radar. They know the children are too big to eat."

That answer was not really as reassuring as it was meant to be. By now, the boys were watching the bats and calling out.

"Mom, Dad, look at these!"

"Man, they're bats."

"Cool. Mom, look at these bats."

"Jarvis, what should we do?" Sharon asked. In response, Jarvis ordered them both another "Sundowner" and sat back to watch the bats.

It wasn't long before both he and Sharon were ready for bed. By the time Sharon got the boys showered and into bed, the fatigue of travel, jetlag, and alcohol had taken their toll on Jarvis, and he was snoring loudly. He couldn't have slept long before he felt a thump on the pillow beside his face. Then, he felt something run across his neck. He went from inebriated slumber to full panic in less than a second. He heard something scrambling over the covers as he switched on the lights. There, on the bed, was a five-inch lizard. Sharon, awakened by the light, followed Jarvis's frightened stare and saw the lizard just inches from her left knee. She performed one of the most surprising feats Jarvis had ever witnessed outside of a cartoon. She levitated from the bed, landing on her feet ten feet away, against the thatched wall.

"What in the hell is that doing in here?" she demanded as if Jarvis had been keeping it in his pajama pocket.

"I think he was looking for you," Jarvis replied. "Mating season perhaps."

"That's not funny, dammit," she protested.

"I didn't think so either when it jumped on my head," he replied.

The boys, drawn by the light and commotion, quickly caught the lizard. Seth held it as Paul washed out a Cheetos container and poked air holes in the top.

"Put that thing down!" Sharon ordered. "It may be poisonous."

"Mom," Seth said in a tone, which in itself, indicated that he thought his mother was a moron. "Who cares if it's poisonous? We aren't going to eat it."

"No, what if it's bite is poisonous?" she said, restating her objection.

"That's called venomous mom," Paul said. "The only venomous lizard is the gila monster, at home."

"All right, but you're going to have to let that thing go in the morning."

"Okay Mom," the boys said in chorus.

"If you guys don't want more lizards jumping on you, not to mention mosquito bites, you better pull the mosquito nets around the bed," Paul said, placing his hand on the netting that was bunched at the foot of the bed. "Don't you remember what Robert said when we got here about unwelcome nighttime visitors?"

With the boys back in bed and the netting closed, Jarvis was awakened repeatedly throughout the night by the sound of lizards running across the netting and the high pitched whine of the mosquitoes they had closed in with them when they drew the netting. He spent most of the night smacking them. It was just before dawn when he finally fell asleep. Forty-five minutes later, a staff member rapped on the door and announced that breakfast would be served in thirty minutes. Jarvis was really glad he had begun taking the first anti-depressant on the plane. If it would just go ahead and kick in, he might survive for the whole vacation.

Laura woke up Saturday and dressed quietly before going to the kitchen to start coffee and breakfast. She'd stopped at the grocery yesterday and bought strawberries and blueberries. Mixed-berry pancakes with blueberry syrup were one of Morris's favorites. She washed, and then sliced, the strawberries before she mixed them into the pancake batter.

This was obviously a compensatory gesture. She just wondered if it was too obvious. She'd spoken to Morris about Sue's visit last week, and he'd given her a non-committal response. She'd mentioned it again last night, and he'd acted like a wounded martyr ever since.

"I guess I can make arrangements to have Mrs. Williamson pick Cody up from school Monday and Tuesday, if you're going to stay in Phoenix," he'd offered with the same degree of enthusiasm she would have expected if she asked him to move the Hoover Dam.

Mrs. Williamson was Cody's regular babysitter, so it seemed like a reasonable solution, at first. "I guess that would be okay," she started, but it wasn't what she expected. "You won't be able to pick him up?"

"Nah, that'd be tough," he answered. "My work schedule is pretty busy early in the week."

"Really?" she asked, her suspicions rising. He was being evasive; he probably had a divorcee with trim problems he needed to "help."

"I was trying to push things up in the week so I could spend some time with you when Sue came up," he replied. "Maybe we can get to know each other."

Instantly she realized how hypocritical her thought process sounded, even to her. She was asking him to help out so she could have a "ménage a trois" in Phoenix, and here she was acting like a jealous schoolgirl.

To make up for something, she wasn't sure what, she had decided to stay home and cook Morris and Cody breakfast instead of going out and painting. She would try her best to make it a relaxed and comfortable weekend. The pancakes weren't much, but they were a start.

Standing by the stove, she realized that she was going through a re-evaluation process. It seemed she had been closer to leaving Morris before than she was now. It was as if her own adultery had done something to her. It allowed her to appreciate Morris for who he was again, a pleasant companion and a good father. She was detached from his infidelity. It couldn't hurt her anymore. It didn't have the power to make her feel unattractive or unwanted. She knew other men wanted her. She could see in their eyes how attracted to her they were. When Morris ambled into the kitchen with just a pair of jeans on, she could see what other women saw in him, too.

"Is Cody still asleep?" she asked.

"Like a little log," he replied.

She closed the kitchen door, and as he was reaching for a coffee cup, she slipped up behind him, wrapping her arms around his waist and kissed the back of his neck. Reaching down, she unsnapped and unzipped his jeans. Kneeling, she tugged them down and, as he turned, an old friend bobbed in her face. For the first time in years he was relaxed and receptive as she took him into her mouth. She had missed this so much, the freedom with each other. This drove her on, and as she quickened her pace, she slipped her left hand under her gown, grasping Morris with her right. "The survival rule of a tall-ships sailor," she thought recalling a book she had once read. "One hand for the mast and one hand for yourself." She would have smiled but that was quite impossible right now. Morris pulled her to her feet and leaned her over the kitchen table, sloshing the pancake batter as he entered her from behind. He reached both his hands forward and grabbed her hair, pulling her head back. She had abandoned the mast, as it was doing just fine right now, and devoted both of her hands to herself.

It was the sound of the bedroom door opening that sent them scrambling. The sound of little feet coming down the hall lent urgency to their zipping and buttoning, so that, by the time Cody opened the kitchen door, his mommy was wiping up spilled batter with a paper towel while his daddy was pouring coffee.

"Good morning baby," his mom said in a funny voice.

"Ready for some pancakes?" his dad added, sounding like he needed to swallow.

On her flight from San Diego to Phoenix, Sue let her mind wander. She allowed her memories of Laura and herself with another man to flow over her, but in her fantasy, she replaced the fifty-two year old Jarvis Sloan with the younger and very attractive detective she'd run into in front of the gallery on Friday. Sometimes, James was so stupid. If he hadn't drug her away, she could have at least learned something about the man. Jarvis was nice and everything, but for two women, he lacked something in recovery time. A younger man would recover quicker and leave less dead time, not that even that wasn't enjoyable. Lying there with the softness of Laura's body against her own was very different from lying next to a man. There was none of the urgency that always preceded sex with a man. Nor was there any of the male post-coital fiddling, continuing to fool with the nipples and crotch randomly until he lost interest and fell asleep.

Neither Laura nor she had been ready for full-blown, girl-girl sex. Jarvis had been the sexual conduit that allowed them to touch and caress each other without feeling strange about it. She didn't know if she was ready to put her mouth on to another woman's lips or press her tongue to a clitoris, but when she kissed Jarvis after he had been doing just that to Laura, she was unbelievably aroused by Laura's taste and smell on him. She wasn't a lesbian; she liked sex with men too much for that. But here was an undeniable curiosity she felt about all of it, the whole experience. Maybe she was tri-sexual. Bisexual wasn't really enough. The addition of the man into the equation was part of what turned her on. It allowed her to explore in a way she couldn't otherwise. Jarvis had been that man when it started, and he had been as excited at the experience as either of them. But could the three of them re-create it together? Could Laura and she re-create it with another man?

She would get the answer to the first question over the next few days; the second would have to wait. As the plane approached the gate, she was happy that she and Laura would have a few hours together to shop, have lunch, and go to the gallery before Jarvis got there. She wasn't nervous, but she needed a little bit of normalcy first, and a few glasses of wine wouldn't hurt either.

Laura and Sue walked arm-in-arm down the hallway, each woman acutely aware of the points at which their bodies met and moved against each other.

"I really wanted to talk to Kent. I can't believe he wasn't there. Jimmy called last week and told him I was coming," Sue said.

"He's not usually like this," Laura explained. "But he has a new boyfriend, so there's no telling. We can call him and run by tomorrow. When we get up. What did Jarvis say when you called?"

"It was a sixteen-hour flight from Cape Town to Miami. He only had a two hour layover, but he said he got a nap on the flight to Phoenix," Sue answered.

"We can let him rest some. There's no big hurry," Laura suggested.

"He said he's already taken a Viagra, and after a week in Africa, he doesn't want to spend any more time in a tent," Sue reported.

Both women laughed as they reached the door of room 2417. Sue looked at Laura and arched her eyebrows. "Are you ready?" she asked, her hand poised to knock. Laura nodded, and Sue rapped sharply on the metal door. A clearly tired and haggard Jarvis Sloan quickly opened the door.

"You have no idea how glad I am to see you. You're both just as beautiful as I remember," Jarvis said, kissing each woman on the cheek.

"You're going to have to do better than that," Sue said, taking his face in her hands and kissing him deeply. His hands wandered to the mounds of her buttocks, and he began to knead gently.

"You look really tired," Laura said. "Don't feel like there's a lot of pressure on you to do this now. If you'd like we can just take it easy or come back a little later so you can rest up some."

"The pressure I'm feeling wouldn't be very restful if you left," Jarvis replied, slipping one hand between Sue's thighs, and reaching for Laura's breast with the other.

"I think I know just where the pressure valve is," Sue said, searching for it with her hand. When she had it firmly in her grip, she turned to Laura and winked. "If he's as tired as he looks, and we're any good at all, he'll be sleeping like a baby in twenty minutes."

"I wouldn't count on that," Jarvis said smiling. "Now let's get rid of these damned clothes."

And so it began again, but this time Jarvis was unfailing and unflagging. Afternoon became night, and night became morning, and still he kept coming back for more. By dawn, both women were sore, tired, and very much in need of rest. Jarvis on the other hand, although he looked as if he were dying, was still ready to go. They'd taken showers, they'd tried naps, but he couldn't stop, couldn't sleep, couldn't leave them alone for five minutes. It was only a matter of time before one of them had to kill him if he didn't knock it off. So they said goodbye, each woman kissing Jarvis's cheek and apologizing for needing to go to their own hotel and sleep for a few hours. He agreed, regretfully, but only after they'd promised they'd come back later that evening to order a room service dinner and start back where they left off.

As they left the room, a small piece of thin metal that had been positioned by the hinge side of the door fell inward. It was thin and malleable enough to be deformed to fit the shape of the door frame by the closing door, but just thick enough to keep the latch from engaging. Neither woman noticed. They were already exchanging a whispered analysis of the preceding night's activities.

"What in the world was that?" Laura asked.   "I thought Viagra lasted for four hours, not fourteen."

"I don't know," Sue replied. "Viagra, Cialis, Levitra, who knows? He was like a cross between the Energizer bunny and the Tasmanian Devil with a hard-on."

"The Viagra may have been part of it, but there was something else, some sort of stimulant. It seemed almost like he was on coke, or meth, or something. Morris tried that combination once and he was kind of like that, but he wore out after three or four hours. I didn't particularly like it then either," Laura admitted.

"I should have brought Mobil One instead of Astroglide," Sue said, fanning her crotch.

"Personally, I was worn out long before either of you were," Laura confided. "Just getting pounded away on is what I get at home. Even with artificial lubrication, Miss Ginny feels like somebody's been after her with some sandpaper. If I'm this sore later, I'm going to bow out early."

"Honestly, I don't think you're going to have to worry about it. As tired as he looked when we got here yesterday and with only five minute naps through the night, when our boy finally hits the ground he's going to be dead to the world."

CHAPTER TWENTY-SIX

Morris hadn't needed the GPS to tell him where Laura was going. He already knew that, but there were other features of the little gadget that had been pretty helpful. An alarm feature sounded if, after being at a constant position for more than thirty minutes, the transmitter began moving again. This allowed him to get a few hours sleep as the long night drug on. When it finally went off, the night had passed. Morris shook his head groggily in the front seat of the pickup, two blocks away from the Ritz-Carlton, where Laura and Sue Wong had met Jarvis Sloan the night before. Morris replayed all the details in his mind as he tried to shake away the cobwebs. It had all started with the tap he'd put on the phone in Laura's studio. His new Spy Ware line-tapper gave a really good recording of both sides of a telephone conversation. He had known Sue Wong was somehow responsible for the big change in Laura. Now he knew how. She'd introduced her to some kind of swinger's website called TimeDonors and gotten her involved her in the threesome that was obviously still going on.

"Shit," he said when he first heard the tape. "Why didn't she ask me? With that cute little ass, Laura could have brought Sue Wong home to bed anytime."

Once he knew the where and when, it was just a matter of getting to the Ritz-Carlton twenty minutes after Jarvis's plane had landed and sitting at a booth in the bar across from the check-in desk. He knew Jarvis was being picked up at the airport by a limousine, so when a limo pulled up and the bellman got the luggage out, Morris aimed a small parabolic microphone, a bionic ear, that he held discreetly under the table and listened in as the man checked in. "Reservation for Jarvis Sloan," the man said. "Bingo," Morris thought. Sloan informed the desk clerk that he was from San Diego and worked for a company called LifeSolutions. Then Morris heard what he had come for, the room number. Casually, he got up and walked out, avoiding the front entrance to prevent the possibility of accidentally running in to Laura.

When he got back to the truck and checked Laura's location with the GPS, she was still several miles away. He wished he'd walked across the lobby and gone out the front entrance just so he could've gotten a good look at the Sloan guy. From across the lobby, he looked a lot older and smaller than Morris was. Not that that would matter now. After the mess with the first guy, Morris had gone to a gun show in Prescott and bought the stun gun he'd used on the redheaded guy in the parking lot. Just a pull of the trigger and it didn't matter who he was, he wasn't going to be moving for five or ten minutes.

Morris ate dinner and went to see a movie before he checked on Laura's location again. Her car was still at the Ritz-Carlton. He slipped in and put the spring-loaded door jam that would keep the door from locking into place. From there he headed to a liquor store and picked up some pre-mixed Margaritas, a cooler, and some ice. He found a good, quiet spot in a lot between two other cars and parked the truck there. He'd have a few Margaritas and take a nap until it was over. He'd use the GPS's alarm to let him know when Laura was leaving. That's when the waiting began. Several times during the night, he wondered if it was a mistake to rely on the GPS again. It was amazing how the smallest thing, like switching the cars, could make such a mess. He'd ended up having to kill Laura's gay art dealer against his own better judgment because he couldn't think of anything better to do. God only knew what that was going to end up costing him in lost sales alone. He hoped Laura could get into another good gallery while people still liked the stuff she was painting.

He wondered what they were doing now. They could have had a few drinks and taken a cab back to their hotel. Maybe Sue had rented a car and they used it to go back. That was the problem with relying on the GPS alone. Without direct visualization, he had no way of knowing if both women would leave the hotel room at the same time. The last thing he wanted was to walk in on two people if one of them stayed behind. That could be hard to control. He wasn't sure he could get two people immobilized before one of them could get away, but there was no way to get in where he could keep an eye on things for long, too many security cameras. If he hung out acting creepy it would only be a matter of time before someone showed up to check him out.

He ran through that scenario several ways. It always came out badly. If he threatened them both with a gun, he ran the risk of provoking Jarvis into acting like a hero. If he threatened to shoot Jarvis, would Sue Wong care enough to risk her own life by sticking around, or would she bolt? He had to hope Laura would stay true to her life-long pattern. Since college, Laura would stick with her friends, and whether they were stoned, drunk, or puking, would find a way to get them home safely. He should know. He'd been the beneficiary of her loyalty several times before they were married. In fact, on one occasion, she'd been forced to appropriate a grocery cart to get him to her car after a concert. Eventually, after several hours worrying and three of the Margaritas, Morris fell asleep.

When a strange beeping sound aroused him from his sleep, he opened his eyes and found himself in a strange pickup truck. None of it made sense at first. He felt disoriented and fuzzy, but as the fog in his head cleared, he realized where he was. The idea of what he was about to do brought him to a state of sudden clarity in which he was totally awake and totally aware. He quickly walked the two blocks to the hotel, crossed the lobby, and took the elevator to the twenty-fourth floor. When he found room 2417, he knew not to turn the knob. No need to risk alerting good old Jarvis. He applied pressure to the door, and it pushed inward easily. As he entered the suite, Morris picked up the door jam and slipped it into his pocket. He stood still, listening. He could hear the TV and that was all. With his right hand, he grasped the stun gun but left it concealed in his jacket pocket. He heard something make a metallic sound in the bathroom, and he eased into the room, silently closing the door behind him.

Jarvis was sitting on the toilet when he heard the door opening. He hadn't heard a card being placed in the lock, and he didn't hear anyone turn the door handle. He just made out the tongue of the latch popping open as it slid off the latch-plate and the faint sound of the hinges as the door opened. He was about to say he didn't need his room serviced right now, to please come back later, when he caught a glimpse of a shadow through the crack of an opening he had left when he came in. As he watched the mirror he could see a man entering the bedroom. He was about six feet tall and fairly thin with brown hair. He wasn't dressed in a hotel worker's uniform of any kind. He was wearing jeans, work boots, and a work jacket. His right hand was shoved firmly into the jacket's pocket, so he had a weapon of some sort. Jarvis quickly finished up but didn't flush the toilet. He surveyed the bathroom for possible weapons of his own.

He poured his shaving kit out onto a towel, looking for anything he could possibly use. He decided quickly because there weren't that many options to choose from. As he assembled his meager weapons, he kept a close eye on the intruder's reflection in the mirror. He tried to figure out how he could maximize the effectiveness of what he had picked out, the five-inch pair of scissors he used to trim his sideburns and a can of aerosol deodorant. He needed something with a longer reach. He tried the bar of the towel rack, pulling down gently at first and then jerking until one of the mounting brackets let go. Luckily, he had eased the door shut before he jerked down because the sound of the bracket letting go made a loud crack inside the bathroom. He hoped it would startle the intruder into leaving. He positioned himself on the opening side of the door, deodorant in his left hand, towel rod in his right, the scissors in his mouth crosswise like a pirate boarding a ship.

"Hoo's aut dere?" Jarvis asked, his words garbled by the scissors in his mouth.

"Room service. I've just come to get the tray from last night," Morris answered.

"Go ahead then," Jarvis responded, every nerve tight, his heart pounding at a hundred-and-twenty beats a minute.

When he sensed the slightest outward movement of the door, Jarvis kicked out hard, his foot coming down in a forward fighting-stance he remembered from the Tae Kwon Do he'd taken years ago. His assailant was hit in the face by the edge of the door flying outward. Jarvis's left hand came up as he saw the man's right hand start around with some kind of electronic device. He pressed the top on the aerosol deodorant and shot a stream of it into the eyes of his attacker to blind him. With his right hand he slashed out hard across his attacker's face with the towel rod at the same time. He connected solidly with the man's left temple. When his hands came up Jarvis attacked the weapon.

Morris brought both hands to his eyes instinctively to protect himself. Jarvis brought the towel rod down hard, hitting the electronic device, knocking it from Morris's hand and breaking off a piece of its plastic insulation. Jarvis was suddenly aware of an intense crushing sensation in the center of his chest. What could it be? The device was gone; he hadn't seen or heard a gun. He looked down. There was no blood or obvious injury. He switched the towel rod to his left hand, throwing the scissors with his right, but the crushing pain affected his aim. The scissors struck Morris in the left thigh, the point burying itself in the dense muscle.

As Morris staggered back, the crushing pain dropped Jarvis to his knees. The lack of sleep, physical exhaustion, and adrenalin, combined with the stimulant and Viagra, had driven his heart rate to a point that his coronary arteries could no longer keep up with the heart muscle's need for oxygen. The area of infarction expanded quickly as Jarvis continued to try to fight. The dying muscle altered the electro-chemical physiology of Jarvis's heart and it began to fibrillate. His heart moved like a sack of worms unable to effectively pump blood at all. By now, Jarvis was lying flat on his back, looking up at the ceiling light in the bathroom as it grew brighter and brighter. Soon, it was the only thing he could see. He wondered what had happened to the attacker. This was the last conscious thought that Jarvis's brain would ever generate. Suddenly he was sliding into the light, this world sinking below him. He could see himself lying on the floor as he floated away. His attacker was pulling the scissors out of his leg and throwing them at the pillows, then grabbing up the device and hurrying out the doorway. Before the door closed, Jarvis was gone.

CHAPTER TWENTY-SEVEN

When Morris ran from the room, he knew he should take the stairs to avoid being seen with his cut face and bleeding leg. But the stab wound in his thigh hurt too much to walk down twenty-four flights. Besides, he didn't do anything. The guy had died of a heart attack. He was sure these kinds of things happened in big hotels all the time. He wasn't even sure Sloan was dead. He hadn't stayed around to find out. What if he was faking? Maybe it was all an act. Shit, he didn't want the police asking a bunch of questions about breaking and entering, either. He hadn't bothered to avoid having his face seen. Sloan would easily be able to recognize him. He turned away from the elevator and started back to the room.

"I've got to be sure," he said to his reflection as he started down the hall. "No, if he was faking, he's already called security by now. Anyway, I think I heard the door latch when it closed."

He couldn't remember closing the door. Did it close or not? If it had, there'd be no way to get back in. A housekeeper moved a service cart out of its storeroom in front of him. He turned quickly, back toward the elevator, turning before the housekeeper could follow her cart into the hall. He didn't want her to see his face or his leg.

He was so distracted when he got on the elevator that, instead of getting off at the third floor and taking the stairs the rest of the way like he'd planned, he rode straight to the lobby. When the doors opened, he crossed the lobby quickly and made his way to the same side door he'd used the day before.

Morris tried not to limp as he made his way across the parking lot, but the hole in his leg was throbbing like a bitch. It seemed like it took forever to get to the truck. He stashed the stun gun, the Colt, and the homemade assassin's pick in the toolbox. Then he stuck the toolbox and the GPS monitor into a cardboard box and pushed that up under the big toolbox in the pickup's bed, taping it in place with duct tape. There was no reason for the police to stop him, but the last thing he needed was a cop seeing a gun or a stun gun on a routine traffic stop.

He poured the remainder of one of the margaritas onto a napkin and cleaned his face. The alcohol burned, but it would kill any germs. He unzipped his jeans and crammed two napkins over the stab wound, pouring on a little of the margarita. When it dripped down into the open hole, it felt like he'd set his leg on fire. Morris kicked the truck floor with his right heel.

"Shit! Shit! Shit! Shit! Shit!" he repeated rhythmically as the burning subsided. He started the truck and headed north, being sure to obey all the traffic laws so he didn't invite any police attention. He was surprised at how hard it was to drive the legal speed limit on the open road. Apparently it was hard for everybody else too, because car after car flew past him. He started to become concerned about drawing attention because he was going so much slower than the surrounding traffic. He sped up enough that he fit the flow of traffic.

Morris arrived home just before nine-thirty. Mrs. Williamson had already taken Cody to school, so that was taken care of anyway. Cody was not something he could face like this.

Morris drove straight to the house. He got in the shower and washed the blood that had caked on this leg. It had dripped all the way down from his thigh to fill up his shoe. Then he tried to clean up his face as much as possible. When he got out of the shower he looked into the mirror and assessed the results of this morning's fiasco. There was a large bruise that had spread around the cut on his forehead and a noticeable lump under the cut on his left temple. There was no way Laura wasn't going to notice and say something. He would have to tell her he fell off a ladder or something. Maybe he could say some boards fell on him. He worked on the details of the lie in his mind as he sat on the edge of the bathtub and tried to put a dressing over the leg wound. There was blood all over the stone floor. He'd started to bleed again when he took his pants off. If he were going to lie, there was no reason to hide the bloody clothes. They would actually support his story. Besides, all the blood on them was his. He turned and tossed them into the clothes hamper. He soaked a washcloth with some cold water from the sink and used it to wipe the blood up.

He needed to get Billy's truck back to him. He was going to have to lie about that, too. That one wouldn't be too hard. He and Billy were always comparing notes about getting laid. He would just tell him that Laura was out of town, and he'd been too busy to bring the truck back last night. He could try the story about falling off the ladder on him and see how it played before he tried it on Laura, too. No sense having more than one story floating around anyway.

He called Billy on his cell to see where he was and arranged to meet him in twenty minutes for breakfast. He needed time to run by the office and put the cardboard box with the GPS monitor and toolbox in his desk.

"This is the last time," he told himself as he drove. "This is some crazy bullshit." He didn't know how things like this always happened to him. If the first guy wouldn't have been from out of town, he probably wouldn't have even had to hit him on the head in the first place. Hell, if he hadn't been so big everything would have been just fine. Today was even worse. He hadn't even done anything and the guy still died. He didn't even really have anything to do with it. The only reason Jarvis Sloan was dead was because he had a bad heart.

Morris decided he had to settle things with Laura. He'd tell her he knew what she'd done in Phoenix. He'd play her the tape from the tap he'd put on her studio phone. He'd accept his share of all the blame, confess that he'd had a few affairs of his own. They could start over fresh. They just had to forgive each other. He knew there was a risk. There was a good chance she'd want a separation, but that would be okay for a while. He could win her back. He knew he could. It would just take some work. With Cody, they had too much to just throw away. She had to forgive him eventually. By the time he met Billy, Morris had made up his mind. If Laura was willing to try again, so was he. He hadn't really tried very hard the first time, but he would do better this time. No more screwing around. If she could do it so could he. They just had to work together.

CHAPTER TWENTY-EIGHT

Mole` Ruiz called Weeks before lunch on Tuesday. "I think we have another one," is all he said before Weeks interrupted.

"Let me put you on hold. I want Bryant to hear this himself. He's all over my ass since the little San Diego trip. Can you hold on while I get this on a speaker?" Weeks asked.

"Sure amigo," Mole` replied and waited for the static that would indicate he had been transferred.

"Mole`, can you hear me?" Weeks asked a minute later.

"Yeah," he replied.

"Okay Ruiz," Captain Bryant cut in, "Weeks here says you have some new information to tie the Davis murder to the other two."

"No sir. I'm not talking about the Davis murder," Mole` said somewhat confused. "Besides, I don't see what more you could need on that case anyway, to link it to the Zell murder. Two people killed by exactly the same method, with the same type and size weapon. I'm talking about another murder, or attempted murder, that just happened this morning."

"Are you sure? The timing's wrong," Ben said emphatically. "It's been less than a week."

"The timing was wrong last time too. It's accelerating. This is just another wrinkle," Weeks began. "In each case, there's something different. That's why you can't look for a pattern with only two cases. As we get more murders, we have to adjust our analysis to find out what the overall pattern is-two weeks, a week, and now five days. Each time shortening the interval between murders."

"All right you two, let's let Ruiz fill us in before we take off in every direction," Bryant ordered. "Ruiz you still there?"

"Yes sir," Mole` answered.

"Let's hear what you have so far," Bryant asked.

"I'm at the Ritz-Carlton. At eight this morning a housekeeper noticed the door to room 2417 partially ajar. When she knocked, there was no answer. When she entered the room she found a nude, middle-aged white male lying on his back in the bathroom door. Any of this sounding familiar? Anyway, she called for an ambulance. When the ambulance crew got there around eight-fifteen, the patient was obviously deceased and had been so for a little while. At first they thought it was a standard heart attack. The toilet was full of feces. It looked like the classic case of a heart attack victim straining to have a bowel movement. The Valsalva effect that occurs during straining creates increased intrathorasic pressure, which reduces blood return and causes the heart attack. But the room looked like it had been trashed. The thing that really caught their attention was that there was blood on the outside of the bathroom door and blood on the carpet, but the dead man wasn't bleeding. So luckily for us, they called the Medical Examiner. I heard there was a naked dead guy in a hotel, so I asked to go. I've been here about an hour, and I think this was our killer, but something went wrong. This guy put up a fight. He was holding a can of spray deodorant and a towel rod with blood and hair on the far end. There's also a pair of bloody scissors on the bed."

"Just what we need, something weirder than the weird shit we've already got. At least we have some forensics that can help finally," Bryant said. "You have any idea about the cause of death?"

"Not yet, but we almost missed the last ones, even at autopsy. It may just be a regular old heart attack, but I've been reading about some of the more modern assassination techniques. They have powerful vasoconstrictors now that can cause a heart attack in seconds. They're absorbed through the skin. You just spray it in the victim's face, or anywhere there's exposed skin. We won't know about any of that until we get the toxicology screen. The only place you can catch some of this stuff is the vitreous. You know, the fluid inside the eyes."

"You suck the fluid out of his eyes?" Weeks asked, forgetting himself for a moment. No one bothered to answer.

"What's the victim's name?" Ben asked.

"A Dr. Jarvis Sloan from San Diego," Mole` answered.

"Holy shit!" Weeks exclaimed.

"What?" the others asked in unison.

"Jarvis Sloan is the guy who invented LifeSolutions and TimeDonors. He's the guy I wanted to talk to in San Diego," Weeks answered.

"Holy shit is right," Captain Bryant whispered. "And now he's dead. Dammit Weeks, didn't you learn anything from the Munoz thing?"

"I thought he was in Africa," Ben said.

"Not anymore," Mole` answered. "It looks like he got pretty lonely over there though."

"What are you talking about?" the Captain asked.

"Well, sir," Mole` explained, "I don't think the room got trashed by fighting. It looks like he's been going to town with another 'F' word, though."

"What makes you think so?" the Captain demanded.

"There are five or six used condoms lying around. There are three room service dinners still here, and the manager came by and said that two very pretty women came by and picked up a key he left at the front desk for a 'Ms. Saint' mid-afternoon yesterday."

"Okay you guys," the captain said seriously. "All of you, let's get this right. The FBI may be on this case, but when this shit hits the press, it's us that will take all of the heat. Our killer just made his first mistake, and we have got to capitalize on it before he starts killing somebody every day. Weeks, call the TimeDonors girl and find out why we didn't get a contact on this, or the one last week. Who knows how the gay art dealer fits into this now?

"Ben, I want everybody interviewed. I want the security camera footage and I want to know who those two women are.

"Ruiz, don't screw this up. I want chain of evidence that's iron clad, I mean unquestionable. I want to know everything you find; tox, saliva off the containers, semen and vaginal secretions from the sheets and condoms. I want to know if the blood matches anybody having sex or if it's from somebody else. See if the hair on the towel rod and blood match. I even want you to make sure that's the victim's shit in the toilet, if there's a way to do it.

"I want everybody sharp because this is going to turn into a media circus. You mix a serial killer, kinky sex, and a multi-millionaire, and you're going to have every news organization in the country tripping over each other. Remember, don't you guys talk to anybody from the press. I want everything to come through this office. If we figure this one out, there's plenty of glory for everybody, so don't go running your mouths, trying to play glory-hound. If we don't figure this out quickly, everything that's said's gonna come back to haunt us. Got it?"

They all nodded in agreement. "Good. Okay boys, go out there and make me proud. If you can't do that, at least don't screw up. I've got to take this to the chief. He's going to want regular updates, so keep me informed."

On the way to the hotel, Weeks called Brooke Werner on his cell phone. "Hey Brooke, this is Willie Weeks. Listen, something's happened here and it's kind of strange, but no one working the TimeDonors surveillance called to let us know that anybody arranged anything."

"Were the arrangements for today? It's Tuesday. We were watching for Wednesday as the keyword." Brooke said defensively.

"One was yesterday, the other was for last Wednesday," Weeks explained.

"It must have been a prior engagement," Brooke suggested. "I mean, it's only speculation but you've only been monitoring 602 for a few days. It was probably something that was arranged before we switched the routing."

"I guess you're right," Weeks offered. "Do you happen to know where your boss is?"

"Why do you want to talk to Dugan? He won't have any ideas," Brooke replied.

"Not Dugan, Jarvis Sloan. Is he back from Africa yet?" Weeks asked.

"Not yet, he isn't due back until later in the week. Why? Is there something I should know?" Brooke Werner apparently caught something in the detective's inflection that seemed strange.

"I'm not sure yet," Weeks answered. "I'll let you know when I know more."

"Come on Willie, I've been open with you, don't get all evasive on me," Brooke pressed.

"Look Brooke, I can't say any more than I already have. I'll let you know when I've got more information," Weeks said firmly.

"Okay, just don't leave me in the dark. I don't want Dugan making me look like an ass when Jarvis gets back."

"Don't worry about that," Weeks said truthfully. "Talk to you later."

Ben sat in the security office at the Ritz-Carlton, running the lobby security tapes on the VCR. He watched as Jarvis Sloan checked in and then fast-forwarded until he saw two women approach the desk. He slowed the tape and watched carefully. There was no audio. He reversed and watched again. The woman who spoke appeared to be of Asian ancestry.

Sloan's wife had called twice that morning and had left two messages. Hotel records showed she had called him last night as well, a few hours after he had checked in. This morning's messages were about family matters. The first was his wife saying the boys just wanted to say something before they went to school. Then the voices of the two young boys told their father thanks for the best trip in the world, the younger adding he couldn't wait to tell everybody at school about it. Ben was filled with sadness for the boys, remembering himself and his brothers as kids. By now the LaJolla police had sent a notification team to inform Ms. Sloan that it appeared her husband was dead and that she would need to go to Phoenix to identify the body. For now, they were just going to say that it looked like a heart attack. The chief had decided to keep things quiet until they had a suspect in custody.

He started reviewing today's security tapes. He made a note on a hotel pad, "desk cam. Sloan in 2 pm. Two women? 3:15," and scotch taped it to the first videocassette. He wished he knew what Weeks was up to upstairs in the room with Mole`, but Ben had decided to stay down here for now. He'd already interviewed the hotel manager and housekeeper. The hotel was calling the night manager back in, as well as the room service server who had delivered the food trays the previous evening, so they could interview them later.

"Whoa now!" Ben exclaimed. The footage he was watching was from the first-floor elevator bay. The time line read 07:18 as a lone male exited an elevator, limping. He had on no hat and made no attempt to disguise himself. As he rolled the tape back and forth, he could see the man was bleeding from his forehead and left temple. He was limping on his left leg, and the thigh of his jeans appeared to have a dark stain, also bleeding. He picked up the phone and called room 2417. Weeks answered.

"Hey partner, I think I've got our boy on the security tape. Have Mole` check elevator number four and the 24th and 1st floor elevator bays for blood. He looked pretty beaten up and was limping with what looked like a stab wound in his left thigh."

"I'll tell Ruiz. Stay there. I'll be right down," Weeks answered, obviously excited by the possibility of a break.

As he crossed the lobby, Weeks watched as an obvious FBI agent showed his badge to the front-desk receptionist. Two other dark-suited men stood nearby. Weeks continued to walk without slowing or looking their way. He had to get Ben out of there before they found him, or he'd end up spending the rest of the day standing around while Ben tried to be helpful. He dialed Mole` on his cell phone. "Amigo, you're about to be invaded by a herd of dark suits."

"What do you want me to do?" Mole` asked.

"Just try to keep them up there. I need a little time. I can't just grab Ben and say let's go. He'll know something's up, but I don't want to play step-n-fetchit for these guys all day," Weeks explained.

"I'll do what I can. Adios," Mole` promised.

As Weeks walked into the room, Ben was reviewing the video of the suspect, frame by frame. Before he had a chance to say anything, the manager on duty stuck his head in the door.

"Detective Kinney, the switchboard has a phone call for Mr. Sloan's room. We told her to hold like you said."

"Put it through to this phone please," Ben indicated.

The manager's head withdrew from the doorway, and in a minute, the phone between them rang. They glanced at each other and Ben nodded and pointed, indicating he wanted Weeks to take the call.

"Hello," Weeks said.

"Is this Jarvis Sloan's room?" a female voice asked. Weeks found something familiar in the voice, but he didn't know why.

"Yes it is, but Mr. Sloan isn't available. May I ask who's calling?" he asked.

"Just a friend. I'll call back later," she replied.

"Hold on, don't hang up," Weeks said quickly.

"Really, it's not important. I'll call back later. I know he had some business to take care of," she said.

Weeks mind was racing. He should have thought this out more clearly before he picked up the phone. He was a terrible liar so he decided to go with the truth. "I'm Detective Weeks with the Phoenix Police. Mr. Sloan has had an accident, and we would like to find out if you might know anything that could help us."

"Is he okay?" the woman's voice asked.

"Well, not really. He had a heart attack," Weeks partially answered.

"What hospital is he in?" she asked.

Weeks had been holding the phone slightly away from his ear so Ben could hear both ends of the conversation. He turned his head toward his partner, looking for guidance. Ben shrugged. There was only one way to go. "No ma'am. He's at the morgue," Weeks stated flatly. He looked at Ben who mouthed the words "very smooth" and shook his head slightly. There was silence at the other end.

"Ma'am are you okay?" Weeks asked.

"Yeah, I guess so," she said. "Just shocked, I guess would be the best word." He heard her whisper to someone else nearby, "Jarvis is dead, he had a heart attack."

"Ma'am if you're one of the two women who had dinner with him in his room last night we really need to talk to you both."

"He was fine when we left this morning," the woman said, revealing more than she intended.

"Ma'am, where are you? I'll be happy to come there and talk to you, or if it's better for you, I'll meet you somewhere," he suggested. He heard her confer with the other person.

"We're right down the street from The Melting Pot. We'll go there if you want to talk to us," she offered.

"I'll be there in about twenty minutes," he said before hanging up. Turning to his partner, he said, "We need three or four still pictures of our suspect. If I'm right, one of these women will know him."

"Okay Willie, let's get going," Ben said, then turning he punched Weeks arm. "You did really well. What you lack in tact, you made up for in results."

"Thanks partner," Weeks replied. "Let's get out of here. You get those pictures made. I'll run by and pick up what we have on file at the office. Whoever gets to the Melting Pot first can just buy time until the other gets there."

CHAPTER TWENTY-NINE

Laura and Sue each shed a few tears but Sue recovered quickly. Neither of them had ever had a man they had been that close to die suddenly. The memories of the night before were extremely hard to reconcile with Jarvis being a dead man this morning. It was difficult for either of them to equate the-out-of-control whirlwind of last night with the corpses they'd seen at the funerals of their family or friends. They tried to talk about it as they waited for the detective to arrive. All of it was so hard to put into words, a lot of the time was spent just sitting there thinking quietly, trying to find a way to accept it as being real.

Laura was less concerned with Jarvis right now than what this situation could mean to her. He was dead already. Nothing she did was going to change that. Almost anything she did next was probably going to change her life forever. The last thing Laura needed was her name linked as a sexual partner to Jarvis, or to TimeDonors and what it did. Certainly, neither of these possibilities would play well in a divorce court. Her biggest concern was Cody. She didn't want a divorce, but if it came, she assuredly didn't want to lose her son. She was also worried about Cody growing up with all this out in the open. He didn't need to find out his mother was a whore who screwed someone to death, and it would come out sooner or later and be used as a weapon against him.

"My God, what if this shows up in the news?" Laura said tearfully.

"Try not to worry until we know what we're worrying about," Sue suggested.

"Couldn't you just talk to them first and leave me out of it? Coconino County is really conservative. It's not like California. There isn't a judge in the whole county that would give me custody of Cody if this gets out," Laura pleaded.

Sue noticed him first. Laura was too absorbed with her thoughts to notice much of anything. She was surprised at first, but raised her hand to signal the detective she had run into in front of Jimmy's gallery the week before. She saw the look of recognition in his face and knew he remembered her as well. "I think it's too late for that," she said to Laura and pointed to the detective who was crossing the room towards them.

"Hello, I'm Detective Weeks," the policeman said, taking his badge and offering it to Sue to look at. Laura looked up, startled. She felt like a deer or something, all she wanted to do was jump up and run out of there. Run home. Run back to the life she had been running away from.

The detective sat down, took out a small tape recorder, and clicked "record." "I'd like to start by asking you your names," Weeks started the interview without any further preamble.

"I'm Sue Wong, call me Sue," she said. "Didn't we run into each other in LaJolla two weeks ago?"

Laura hesitated and said, "Are our names really important at this point? You said Mr. Sloan died of a heart attack. I'm not sure there's any need to include our names in a police report."

Weeks looked at her left hand and saw the wedding and engagement rings. "I take it you're from here in Arizona, and since you're wearing that ring, I guess you would prefer that none of the details of the last few days gets made public, right?"

"I can't see what difference that makes," Laura said belligerently.

"Ma'am, it's not our job to cause you any embarrassment or to include your name needlessly in a complex situation, but we're looking into a series of murders and we need to know how you may have been involved?" He continued to watch her face closely and saw the panic fill her eyes, then fade as she gained control of it.

"I thought you said Jarvis died of a heart attack," she accused.

"He did," Weeks conceded. "But it looks like he had the heart attack fighting off somebody who was trying to kill him. Sue, I seem to remember running into you coming out of an art gallery," Weeks recollected.

"That's right," Sue admitted. "I'm an artist."

"Do you know any artists or gallery owners here in Phoenix?" Weeks probed.

"Well, I know Laura," Sue said. Laura flashed her a terrified look.

"Anyone else?" Weeks pressed.

"Well, I came here to meet with Kent Davis, to see if he would be willing to represent me in this area," Sue explained.

"Did you get a chance to talk to him?" Weeks went on.

"No he wasn't open yesterday or today when we went by," Sue answered.

"Laura, when was the last time you saw Kent Davis?" Weeks turned the direction of his questioning. Laura sat silently and refused to respond. "Let me make this as easy as possible for you, Laura. The last time you saw him was last Wednesday. You lent him your car and then came to pick it up at the Bleu Onion about three-forty, right?"

214

"How do you know all that?" Laura asked, clearly shocked.

"Here are some sketches, described to our police artist by a Davey Little and a Maurice Wallby. Not a bad likeness, huh Sue?" Weeks asked, passing the composites to both Sue and Laura.

"It could be Laura," Sue admitted.

"Why do you have these?" Laura asked. "What happened to Kent?"

Weeks handed her the crime-scene photos of Davis upside down, his head shoved behind the toilet.

"Oh my God," Laura cried. "I knocked on that door, I tried to open it, and he didn't answer."

"It doesn't look like he was in much of a position to answer," Ben Kinney said from over her shoulder. "Those are going to be pretty lame excuses when we find your fingerprints on that bathroom doorknob."

"This is Detective Kinney, my partner," Weeks said. It was the only introduction he provided.

Ben handed Weeks the envelope he held in his hand, and Weeks began to sort through the pictures.

"So why should we buy your lame excuse for your being at two murder scenes in the last week?" Ben asked harshly, taking the "Bad Cop" role to Weeks's "Good Cop." "We know of two more before that. Do you want to tell us how many there are in all?"

Suddenly, she didn't even know why, Laura was crying again, her face buried in her hands.

"Look, we know this is hard to think about," Weeks said gently, "but I think you know who this man is." He slid five images from the security camera across the table toward her, along with the composite drawing rendered from the descriptions of the two witnesses at the club. "I'm not saying he's a murderer, but we do need to talk to him. The pictures I just showed you were taken at the Ritz-Carlton this morning at 7:18. We just need to find out what he was doing there, and why he was the last person to be seen with Kent Davis before he was murdered."

Laura looked up, defeated by the facts. "My name is Laura Dees. I'm from Sedona. The man in your pictures is my husband Morris, but he was supposed to be in Sedona taking our son to school at 7:15 this morning."

"Obviously he wasn't," Ben interjected.

"Mrs. Dees, would you mind looking at a few other photographs for us?" Weeks asked.

Laura nodded her consent, and Weeks pulled four photographs out of a file he was holding. The first were photographs of Butler and Zell, alive, given to them by the victims' families. The second two were post-mortem shots taken by Mole' at the morgue. Again Weeks watched Laura's face closely for signs of recognition, but it was unnecessary at this point. Laura was already shaking her head "yes" before she got to the post-mortem shots. When she reached them, her eyes filled with tears again.

"They're dead?" she asked. Weeks nodded that they were. "They were men I met and had sex with. I don't know their names."

"You met them through TimeDonors...on-line?" Weeks asked.

"Yes," she whispered.

"Is that why you were in San Diego?" Sue directed the question at Weeks. "Those men used TimeDonors?"

"That was the main reason," Weeks replied. "Is that how you knew Jarvis Sloan, from TimeDonors?"

"Yes," Sue said.

"No," Laura said at the same time. Weeks looked confused.

Sue explained, "I met Jarvis through TimeDonors, Laura didn't know about it. She met Jarvis through me."

"Is this something you two do regularly?" Ben asked. "The ménage a trois thing?"

"No," both women said.

"It's something that just kind of happened," Sue continued.

"Was this the first time it happened?" Ben asked.

"No," Sue replied. "The first time was in San Diego. Then Jarvis used his ability to get inside the TimeDonors computer to track me down. He wanted to try it again, so I convinced Laura to meet us in Phoenix."

"Mr. Sloan flew straight to Phoenix on his return from Africa," Weeks stated more than asked.

At first, Sue was surprised the detective knew about Africa, but if they were investigating his death, they would check his travel arrangements, she reasoned.

"Okay, let me see if I have this straight," Ben broke in. "You meet in San Diego, no problem, so you decide to try Phoenix. You two got here last night, went to the room, had a room service dinner, fooled around, went to sleep, got up and left. Sloan was fine when you left and neither of you saw Mr. Dees or knew he was in town."

This time Laura said yes and Sue said no.

"No?" Ben raised his eyebrows.

"We didn't sleep," Sue said. "I think Jarvis was taking something, maybe a couple of things, but he didn't sleep. He just kept going all night."

"No wonder he had a heart attack," Weeks whispered to himself.

"But neither of you saw nor knew about Mr. Dees being present?" Ben directed the conversation. When both women answered in the negative, he continued. "Mrs. Dees, you were previously sexually involved with Mr. Butler and Mr. Zell."

"Yes," she answered.

"Were you having an affair with Mr. Davis?" Ben continued his line of questioning.

"Of course not. Kent was gay, he was my representative, he was my friend, but there was certainly nothing sexual between us," Laura stated emphatically.

"Ms. Wong, were you involved with any of these men, besides Dr. Sloan?" he continued.

"No," Sue answered.

"Mrs. Dees, did you know about the deaths of any of these three men, Butler, Zell, or Davis, before today?" Ben drove on.

"No," Laura said.

"Mrs. Dees, are you sure you weren't in any way involved in these men's deaths?" Ben was pushing harder.

"I didn't kill them if that's what you're asking," Laura answered.

"You are the only person we can put with all of these men." Weeks said softly. "We have some trace evidence. Hair that looks a lot like yours was found at two of the sites. We can get a warrant for a sample from you now and we will be able to DNA testing to prove it's yours. We're going to find your fingerprints on the door knob of the bathroom Davis was found murdered in, and there's plenty of trace evidence over at the Ritz-Carlton to put you there as well."

Laura suddenly realized she was the prime suspect in all three murders, as well as the attack on Jarvis, as far as Detective Kinney was concerned. She knew she was innocent, but she couldn't prove it. She could easily end up facing three charges of premeditated murder.

"Detective Kinney, I didn't do any of the things you've asked about, but everything you've said is true." Laura didn't know what else to say.

"The problem we have Ms. Dees is that we can't prove anyone else killed them either and all of the evidence is pointing the same way," Weeks explained.

"What about my husband? You have pictures of him this morning where you found Jarvis dead," Laura sputtered.

"We can't prove he killed anybody on his own. He may have just showed up to check on what his wife was doing and gotten beaten up for his trouble," Ben continued. "Or he may have been a part of something else, we just don't know."

"I didn't kill those men," Laura reiterated.

"But did you arrange, plan, or participate in their murders?" Ben demanded, his finger inches from Laura's nose. "What I want to know is did you conspire with your husband to murder these men?"

Suddenly Laura saw that she needed to stop talking. "With the direction this interview is taking I'm going to need a lawyer before I answer any more questions," Laura stated firmly.

With that, Weeks turned off the tape recorder. Ben looked at Weeks and said, "I guess we'll finish this downtown." Turning to

Laura he advised, "You can call your lawyer and have him meet us there. Ms. Wong, please don't leave Phoenix, we may have some more questions. Mrs. Dees, you can ride with us."

"Do I have to?" she asked.

"Yes," Ben said flatly.

"Am I under arrest?" Laura asked.

"If I need to," Ben said.

Weeks stood up and took his partner's arm, leading him out of earshot of the women. They talked for a few minutes. Ben disagreed firmly with something Weeks said, then turned and walked toward the door saying, "I hope you know what you're doing." Weeks returned to the table and sat down. "Sue, you look like a good judge of character. Do you think Laura killed these three men?"

"Why would she?" Sue asked rhetorically.

"I agree with you Sue. I don't think she killed them either, and I don't think either of you attacked Dr. Sloan, but Laura is the link that connects the deaths of all four of these men, however unintentionally. I think she was the reason they were killed. Laura, is your husband a jealous man?" Weeks asked.

"I never thought so," Laura answered. "Morris knew Kent was gay. There was no reason for Morris to kill him."

"Can you think of anyone else who would follow you around and kill men you were having sex with? Is there someone else you're involved with?"

"No," Laura answered. "Every man I've had sex with in the last twelve years is dead, apparently, except Morris. But it doesn't make sense. Why would he do something this crazy? He's been having affairs for years."

"Because love almost never makes sense," Weeks answered, "and neither does murder. They're both more tied up with passion than a rational thought process. Laura, the only way we're going to get the answers we need is to talk to your husband. Ben's gone to run a criminal check on your husband and get both search and arrest warrants. He's not going to find anything is he?"

"Probably not," she answered. "Morris has never had anything more than a speeding ticket that I know of."

"How long have the two of you been married?" Weeks asked.

"Just over twelve years," she answered. "We have one child, Cody. He's five years old."

Sue sat forward. "We need to get to Sedona and make sure we have Cody when they arrest Morris," she said.

"Morris would never do anything to endanger Cody," Laura responded as if hurt.

"You didn't think he would kill people either, baby. I'm not saying this to hurt you, but he may try to run, and if he runs, he may take Cody with him. If he sees the police cars before they identify him, there's no telling how he'll react."

"I guess you're right," Laura said. "Detective, can I call my babysitter and see if she still has Cody? It's already 5:00. Morris usually picks him up by 5:30."

"Sure, but don't call your husband just yet. I'm not going to have the local police involved yet either, until we have your son in our possession. Sue's right. If your husband sees police cars around your house or his office he may get the boy and take off. Ben and I will go back up with you and coordinate things."

Laura dialed Renee Williamson on her cell phone. "Hello Renee, this is Laura. Is Cody still there? He is, good. I know this is a strange thing to ask, but I need you to do me a favor. I'm leaving Phoenix now. I need you to take Cody and go somewhere for dinner. I'll call Morris and let him know that I'm going to pick Cody up from you. Okay. Thanks. Bye. I'll call you as soon as I get to town." She turned to Weeks. "I have to call him. Otherwise he's going to track down Renee. He has her cell phone number. I need to tell him I'm going to pick up Cody and take him home." Weeks nodded and called Ben to see where they stood.

CHAPTER THIRTY

At 5:30 Morris was still sitting at his desk, going over purchase invoices for a small remodeling job, trying to make out a bill for the customer. He was going to pick up Cody as soon as he got finished. He was adding up a line of figures on his calculator when his cell phone rang. It was Laura's cell calling.

"Hey," he said. "So how did your visit with Sue go?"

"Well," she replied, "a lot's happened. I'll tell you about it later. Sue's here in the car with me. We decided to come back tonight instead of staying in Phoenix. How was your day?"

"It sucked," he said. "I fell off a ladder this morning and just about knocked myself out. I'm limping around, too, because the trim strip I was holding stabbed me in the leg."

"I'm sorry. Did you go to the doctor?" she asked.

"No," he replied. "I just got a tetanus shot last year. Nothing's really big enough to need stitches."

"If you feel too bad, she doesn't have to stay at the house," Laura offered.

Morris thought for a moment. "What are you going to do? She's already in the car with you. She might as well stay here with us."

"I can always get her a room," Laura said.

"No, don't bother. I've got a little more paperwork to finish up anyway," he replied.

"Why don't you finish up and go home so you can fix a drink and relax?" she offered. "I'll call Renee and have her keep Cody. Sue and I are almost there. We can get him and grab a bite to eat. You just relax, we'll be home later."

Morris ended the conversation. He let the fantasy of the three of them in the bed together drift across his mind but knew from the way his face looked and how much his leg was hurting that it wasn't going to happen. That in itself pissed him off. He hoped that Jarvis Sloan bastard was dead for causing him all of this aggravation and ruining his chances of getting to know Sue Wong better.

He opened the bottom drawer of his desk and took out the cardboard box with the toolbox and GPS receiver stacked in it. He clicked on the receiver. Laura's car was still in Phoenix, unless the stupid thing fell off again. No, that couldn't be it. The whole thing had gone dead when that happened. He'd ended up driving around like a madman. He never would have found her if she hadn't gotten caught in road construction, and he'd been able to make out Cody's soccer sticker on her back window from a distance. He'd switched to a side street and caught up to her. She'd stayed on the main road.

He went back over the conversation in his head. They had to know that the man they'd been with was dead. He assumed that's why they were coming back early. Maybe they just hadn't been able to get up with him, or he went to the hospital.

"Well, a lot has happened. I'll tell you about it later," was what she'd said. That could mean a lot of different things and didn't tell him much of anything. Did they go back to the hotel room? If they had a key, were they the ones who found him? Were the police involved? He didn't remember anyone seeing him when he got off the elevator. Who would know him anyway? He wished there was some way he could have asked her if Jarvis Sloan was actually dead. If it wasn't for that damned maid this morning, he might have been able to go back and be sure. The maid hadn't seen his face. At least he was sure of that. He had turned as soon as he saw the cart start through the door. From where she was, she could have seen the door to 2417. If he left it open, she would have seen the body.

The cut on his forehead and the stab wound in his leg had both bled pretty well. He wondered if she'd seen it on the carpet. He had to proceed on the assumptions that:

1. If Jarvis Sloan wasn't dead the police would be looking for him for breaking and entering and they might or might not have been able to identify him from the security cameras. He'd tried to keep his face down, so maybe not.

2. If he was dead, Laura had at least been questioned by the police, and

3. Once they linked Laura to this, there was a good possibility that they could link her at least to the first man he had killed at the La Quinta, maybe to the second man if they had figured that one out. Her fingerprints would be on the doorknob at the Bleu Onion.

If the police were involved, this could be bad whether Sloan was dead or not. They'd have blood to prove he was involved. He needed to hide the pick and the stun gun in Laura's drawer. That would take the suspicion off of him if it got that far. He'd put it in a drawer she didn't use much, that way he could move it again before she saw it if nothing came of all this. But with his blood at the scene of even a non-murder, it might implicate him as an accessory. One of them needed to stay out of prison, for Cody's sake.

If it all fell apart he'd have to say he was worried about Laura. That she was acting different lately. Even Sue Wong would have to admit that. He'd tell them that he'd seen the pick and the stun gun in her purse when she came back from Phoenix last Wednesday. When he checked them out, it looked like there was blood on the pick, and when he asked her about it she'd been really evasive, so he followed her last night. He had just gone up to check on Jarvis Sloan, to be sure he was okay, when Sloan attacked him. He hadn't even fought back, then Sloan had the heart attack and he'd run for help. When he turned around to check the room number, he saw that the housekeeper was already calling, so he left. It wasn't a great story. They'd never be able to prove it wasn't true.

All the physical evidence they had would point to Laura. When they got the computer records, that would probably be all they'd need to get a conviction. At least they wouldn't execute her. Arizona would never execute a young mother. They'd execute him in a heartbeat for something like this.

He was sure if they had any suspicions about Laura, it wouldn't be long before they showed up with a search warrant. He'd need to go ahead and put the stun gun and pick in her lingerie drawer. Later, when he got a chance to get her pistol out of her car, he'd put it in there with them.

He rechecked the GPS. Laura's car was still in Phoenix. He had at least an hour before she'd get there. He opened the toolbox and took out his Colt, shoving it crossways across the back of his jeans just inside his waistband. Just for good measure, he dropped the door jam from this morning into the toolbox, took a paper towel, and wiped each item free of fingerprints, then wiped down the toolbox itself and its handle. He picked it up with the paper towel and carried it out to his truck.

CHAPTER THIRTY-ONE

The unmarked Ford's big engine made it a quick trip from Phoenix to Sedona. Ben drove the police car. Weeks followed behind pushing the limits of the Suburban. The two women rode in silence staring out the side windows, into the dark.

On a hunch, Weeks had opened the hood before they left, and as he suspected, found the GPS transponder mounted to the inside of the wheel well, its wires plugged into the fuse box so that it continually received power. Her husband didn't even need to follow her. He could just wait until she parked and drive there. On the way out of town, they'd stopped at his cousin's car lot, and his cousin hooked the transponder to a spare battery so it would stay powered up until they had the boy safe and Dees in custody. If Dees were watching, there was no need to give him any more information than they had to.

As they approached Sedona, they pulled over and Weeks got out. "You drive from here," he said. When Laura got out, he slipped into the back seat and lay down. Laura pulled out first, Ben falling in behind. Laura called Renee Williamson, and they met her at her home. Laura thanked her and paid her for both the sitting and the dinner, with enough extra to cover the cost of Renee's meal as well. Then she quickly gathered up Cody's things. Sue and Weeks stayed in the car. Ben had driven on and pulled over three blocks down the street.

As they placed the boy in his car seat, Laura introduced Cody to Sue and Weeks as her good friend and her husband, then continued with a glance to both Weeks and Sue, "So did you have fun spending the night at Mrs. Williamson's last night?"

"Why is he laying down in the car?" Cody asked, focused on Weeks and not his mother's question.

"I get car sick, and I don't want to throw up," Weeks said.

"I used to get car sick, too," Cody offered. "That's why I hate car seats."

"Well, maybe you better stay in yours for now," Weeks suggested.

"Hey Mom," Cody said excitedly. "Can I lay down out of the car seat if I get car sick?"

"I don't think you get car sick any more. Besides, you never told me about spending the night with Mrs. Williamson."

"Well I didn't like it much. I missed you and Dad, but Mrs. Williamson did let me sleep with her." Turning his attention to Weeks, he continued. "She smells kind of funny though. She puts this pink cream all over her face. She smells like a big flower all night long." Ben's car pulled out behind the SUV as they drove past.

"Did Mrs. Williamson get you to school on time?" Laura asked.

"Yep," Cody responded. "We had French toast for breakfast. I wanted to go to McDonald's with Daddy, but he had to go on a trip too. I don't like it when you both go."

"Well baby, I'm going to stop taking any trips you can't come on," Laura promised. "Guess what? Since Daddy isn't home yet, we're going to pretend we are on a trip and stay in a motel. Wouldn't that be fun?"

They checked into a room at a motel just off Highway 179. Cody agreed to stay with Sue and watch cartoons while Laura picked up clean pajamas. He whined a little at first, but after Sue had wrapped her arms around him and promised him an orange soda and a bag of popcorn if he would stay so she wouldn't be lonely, he relented. Weeks got into the back of the SUV, with Laura driving and Ben following in the unmarked sedan. When Laura pulled into the driveway of her house, Ben stopped and rolled down the passenger window. "Mrs. Dees, which way would your husband usually be approaching the house from?" Laura pointed in the direction they had been traveling. "Okay," he said. "I'm going to turn around and park a few blocks down the other way, just to avoid making your husband suspicious." He drove away as Laura unlocked the front door.

"Laura, you know we have a search warrant, but I'm still asking, may I look around the house?" Weeks asked.

"Go ahead. I'll even give you the nickel tour," she answered. They talked as she showed him through the house.

"It's not really any of my business," Weeks said as he checked the kitchen trash, "but how did somebody so intelligent end up in the middle of all this?"

"I'm not sure," Laura answered. "I don't think anyone could have predicted that Morris would follow me around, killing people."

"I don't know, but it seems to me that jealousy is a pretty predictable emotional reaction." Weeks looked in the washer and dryer as they passed.

"I guess I didn't look past what I was doing," Laura answered.

When they got to the master bedroom and bath, Weeks found wrappers and pull tabs from band-aids in the trash can and a bottle of peroxide on the counter. "There's a passage I read once, when I was trying to get over my divorce. 'The bullet never looks past the point of impact.'"

"What does it mean?" Laura asked as Weeks looked under the bed.

"There are two parts to the meaning," Weeks said, opening the closet. "The definition of 'point of impact' is the point at which two bodies meet. In that way, a lot of people are like bullets. They can't see past the point of impact to be able to see the destruction that can come from it." He opened the clothes hamper. "Bingo," he said and held up a blood-stained shirt in one hand and a pair of jeans with a puncture hole surrounded by blood in the other.

"Now, all you need is a murder weapon," Morris said from behind them. They both spun around startled. Weeks's hand moved to the Sig, still resting in its holster. "But then again there wasn't a murder, was there? Just an old man with a bad heart that couldn't take the excitement of screwing my wife and her friend." Morris's right hand was holding a weapon of some sort behind him as he limped toward them. "I already found someone trying to break into my house tonight. He walked right by me while I was standing in the bushes. I don't think he even knew what hit him."

Weeks hadn't heard a gunshot or sounds of a struggle, but there was a pretty good chance he was going to have to do this without any back up.

"Mr. Dees, I'm only here to ask you some questions. We have a search warrant," Weeks started.

"Is that the search warrant that the man laying face down in the front yard had in his jacket, along with this arrest warrant with my name on it?" Morris asked. He had closed the distance between himself and the detective to about four feet. Without warning, he lunged forward, bringing up the stun gun he had just used on Ben Kinney.

Weeks saw the attack begin, and he knew he'd made a huge mistake letting Dees get so close. There was no time to draw the pistol or even get his right arm up. He brought his left hand around hard, striking Morris's forearm with an inside ridge hand block, then he punched hard with his right hand to strike the back of Morris's hand and knock away the stun gun. It hit the stone floor of the bathroom, knocking loose another fragment of its plastic insulation. Morris countered quickly by grabbing at the holstered Sig with his left hand. As it cleared the holster, Weeks kneed him hard in the injured left thigh and head-butted Morris to the face, breaking open the gash under the band-aid.

Weeks never saw Morris reach back with his right hand and grab the Bisley. The first time he was aware of it was when the barrel came into crushing contact with the left side of his head. Everything turned to sparks and fireflies for a second, and Weeks found himself on the ground his fingers near the stun gun.

Laura knew she had to do something. Morris had both guns and Weeks was on the floor. She hit Morris in the back of the head with a candle holder, and he dropped to his knees next to the detective.

Sensing that this was his only chance, Weeks grabbed the stun gun and shoved it into the center of Morris's chest, pulling the trigger as he did. Weeks recoiled in shock at the pulsating pain that quickly shot up his right arm and enveloped him, shorting out his neural circuitry. He flopped back like a fish, unable to move. He was only able to look straight up. He heard Dees laugh, "Well baby, it looks like your hero electrocuted himself." Morris shoved the Sig into his left front pants pocket and brought around the Bisley. As he turned, he saw Laura, both hands up and pushed out from her body, forming the triangle of the modified Weaver stance. In her hands was the little .22 Colt New Frontier he had bought her on the day he had bought the Bisley he now held, its thin half-nickel front sight perfectly between her breasts.

"Put the gun down, Morris," Laura commanded.

"Laura, baby, you're not going to shoot me with the gun I bought to show you how much I loved you are you? We bought these guns together to show we loved each other as much as we loved our own freedom," he said softly, hoping to calm her with his gentle words. He needed her to relax. He needed her to look away so he could get an opening to cock his own pistol. He could see that hers was already at the full cock position.

"I'm not kidding Morris. You can't just go around killing people, especially not policemen," she said sternly.

"We can tell them I thought he was an intruder, that it was an accident," Morris answered.

"No we can't!" Laura was at a complete loss. How could he think that made sense? None of this made any sense. "How did you even know how to do all this bad stuff? You're an artist. Artists don't know how to do these kinds of things."

"On the Internet. It's amazing what you can find out if you try. Besides, this is just another kind of art. It's the art of killing," Morris explained.

"You killed all these men to make some kind of artistic statement?" Laura asked incredulously.

"Not in that kind of way. You make it sound like I'm nuts or something. I just wanted to be able to take care of things if I had to. I wanted to be able to do it right. The first guy was an accident. He caught me in his room. I saw you throw away the key when you came down the stairs, so I went over and grabbed it. I was just going to teach him a lesson about fooling around with other people's wives."

"If anybody could give lessons about fooling around with other people's wives you would certainly be the one," Laura said losing her temper. "You cheat and you cheat and you cheat and when I finally get to the point that I'm sick of it and decide to find someone who thinks I'm pretty, you have to kill him?"

"It wasn't like that. I was just going to threaten him, so I slipped in the room. He was in the shower, but I could tell he was pretty big, so I was going to slip back out, but he turned the water off. I was afraid he'd see me so I hid in the closet, and whacked him in the head when he went by," Morris explained.

"And while he was laying there unconscious, you accidentally stabbed him in the back with a screwdriver a bunch of times?" Laura asked.

"I didn't know what else to do. I used my phone and went online to try to find out how to kill somebody without making a lot of noise, and that's what it said to do." Morris answered.

"It said to stab someone with a screwdriver to keep them quiet?"

"No, it said stab them in the kidney. A screwdriver was the only thing I could find in Billy's truck to stab him with. There were diagrams, but it was hard to see them on the phone. It would have been a lot harder, I mean, I don't think I would have been able to do it, if he wasn't knocked out," Morris admitted. "I only really meant to kill that second guy, the one I followed to that parking garage. Watching the way you were when you went down on him like that. I didn't really have a choice. I had to kill him. And that Jarvis Sloan guy, he was the one that went nuts and attacked me. I didn't even hit him. He was just knocking the shit out of me with that towel rod. I couldn't even see him because he sprayed that deodorant in my eyes. He would have killed me, but his heart just gave out in the middle of whipping my butt six ways from Sunday," Morris tried to reason with her.

"Why in the world would you kill Kent?" Laura felt defeated by the unreality of what Morris was saying. Clearly, his logic was part of the problem. All of the things he'd done made some kind of sense to him. That was the scariest thing of all. To him it all made sense. How could he have gotten so far without her knowing that he was losing his mind? If he was really that far gone, how could she even get out of this now that he was pointing a loaded gun at her? If he killed her now he'd be as justified in his own mind as he was with all of the others.

"I didn't have a choice. He caught me following you, and I couldn't reason with him. He was going to tell you," Morris lied.

Weeks groaned unconsciously, and Laura glanced over at him. It was all the break Morris needed. He thumbed the hammer back, it spelling out the name of its maker, C-O-L... It never finished. At the sound of the hammer Laura knew she didn't have time to look back and aim before Morris shot. Trusting in herself just as she had with the snake, with no option of backing away this time, her finger squeezed the thin trigger, which launched a hypervelocity 32-gram projectile. The bullet struck Morris just above his left eyebrow. It broke into fragments when it struck his skull, each fragment tearing in a separate direction through his brain. His motor control evaporated, and he dropped the pistol, still at the half-cock position, and fell. As the pressure in his head built from uncontrolled bleeding, the small entrance wound acted like a flap valve, keeping the blood from exiting his skull. He had a brief seizure before his midbrain was driven down and crimped, ending his respiratory drive. Morris exhaled his last, jagged breath.

Laura dropped, sitting on the end of her bed in her own bedroom, and looked at her dead husband. As a child, she'd slept with a nightlight on because she was afraid of monsters, monsters under the bed.

"The monsters you have to worry about aren't under the bed at all," she whispered. "The ones you have to be afraid of are the ones in the bed with you, lying right there beside you."

Laura's gaze shifted from Morris's face to the helpless policeman, who was only now beginning to stir, and returned to the man she had loved but not really known. Morris's face was peaceful now, almost angelic, surrounded by a spreading crimson halo. A sad smile flashed across Laura's face momentarily, and a small tear cascaded down her cheek and stopped at the corner of her upturned lip. "The saddest thing," she whispered, brushing away the tear with her hand, "is I'm not sure which of us was the monster."

EPILOGUE

Captain Bryant's assessment of the press's reaction to what was now referred to as "The TimeDonors Murders" had been right on target. Every major news organization was providing blanket coverage of every aspect of the case. For weeks on end, every new fact that was released was heralded as a revelation and presented to an eager public as breaking news. Every aspect of the case was discussed, analyzed, and examined on-screen by panels of experts of every professional persuasion. At first, there were the police and forensic experts, medical professionals, and the legal analysts. These were quickly supplemented by the psychological experts, sexual and marital therapists, and the financial analysts needing to explain the dynamics of Jarvis Sloan's corporate and financial holdings.

In what may have been the most bizarre interview aired, the curator of a corporate art collection was brought on screen to analyze the paintings of Laura Dees and Sue Wong. Every aspect of the case was turned over like a rock so the public could gaze on the bugs and worms squiggling underneath. The lives of every person remotely involved in the case became a matter of public debate. America loved it. The titillation of sex, money, and violence permeated millions of conversations daily. Office workers, hairdressers, housewives, mechanics, everyone wanted to make their opinion known on some aspect of the case, or another. Within three days of the first press conference called by the Phoenix Police Department to present the facts as they were known, uninvolved TimeDonors users were appearing on talk shows to present lurid details of their own personal experiences and to speculate on what could have gone so terribly wrong. The term "no shame" took on a whole new meaning. Marriages that were walking on an unhappy tightrope found themselves in freefall, as the desire for a brief moment in the limelight overrode any concern for their partners' feelings.

Sharon Sloan, the grieving widow, refused interviews at first, and in her early silence, was cast by the press in the role of an elegant, fragile victim fighting to protect her children from the storm that surrounded their father's death. Privately, she was surprised to find that Jarvis had left her with a hundred and seventy-five million dollars in publicly traded stocks and equities, outside of his corporate holdings. Within six weeks of her husband's death, she'd sold all interest in both LifeSolutions and TimeDonors to a group of businessmen and investors, led by Tom Dugan, for a fraction of what it was worth. She was asked for a comment after the sale, and indicated to the reporter that she found the business and what it did disgraceful and that she wouldn't be any part of its continued operation.

With all the press coverage, the TimeDonors site became a favorite site for teenagers, the curious, and sexual predators. The first lawsuits were filed within three months, and soon there were TV ads in the Los Angeles, San Diego, San Francisco, and Phoenix markets posing the question:

"Were you or anyone you loved injured by a contact made through TimeDonors.com or its LifeSolutions parent company? If so, then you deserve compensation. Contact the Law Offices of Babcock and Meyer LLPC and let us get the money you deserve."

At six months from the time of the first murder, the volume of pending litigation forced the new owners to file for bankruptcy protection, leaving the lawyers to pick at the carcass of the once-thriving enterprise.

Ben Kinney and Willie Weeks had a roller coaster ride with the press, alternately being portrayed as brilliant detectives who took divergent threads and wove them together to solve the murders, and then as buffoons who were rendered unconscious by Dees and had to be rescued by Laura. Despite the sometimes unfavorable press, Ben was accepted when he applied with the FBI. Unfortunately, his return to the Washington area was a brief one. After undergoing his initial training, Ben was transferred to his first field assignment at the FBI office in New Orleans. Weeks just tried to keep quiet. He was glad to be out of the doghouse with Captain Bryant and finished with the role of FNG. If there was one thing solving this case bought him, it was acceptance as a bona fide homicide investigator. Ben's departure also helped. Now, Ben's replacement was lower on the totem pole than he was and he got stuck with it. Weeks was really glad only Laura and he knew that he had actually stunned himself by spanning the broken insulator with the web of his hand. He would never have lived that down. Laura never mentioned it, and that was one of the things he would be forever grateful to her for.

Sue was okay with her perceived role as the slutty sidekick. She was happy to give interviews and received perhaps the most airtime of anyone directly involved in the case. Prices for her artworks shot up as she became a celebrity darling. Right now, anybody who was anybody wanted to have a Sue Wong original hanging on their wall.

Despite her careful business arrangements, Brooke Werner got screwed again. Jarvis had funneled most of the money TimeDonors made out of the company and into private investments. She was left with twenty-five percent of the thirty million dollars left in the LifeSolutions account. She and Tanya had talked about it and they both agreed that they had a really good idea of what was coming. The lawsuits were inevitable. Once they started, she'd be lucky to get anything. They both left LifeSolutions before Tom Dugan completed his buy-out. With the money she got and the LifeSolutions billing records, she'd sold her condo, packed up her car, and moved to Phoenix to start her own company, TD-too.

Despite her resentment toward Jarvis over stealing her blind, Brooke left San Diego with a smile. The entire fiasco had garnered her one unexpected bonus. She was in love. Although it had happened quickly, there was no doubt in her mind. She had a relationship with a man who didn't feel like he needed to compete with her. A man she knew she could trust. It seemed to be too good to be true, but she felt like everything was going to work out...if she could just get used to that damned filthy coffee cup he drank out of.

Everyone lionized Laura, the flawed heroine. Her courage in saving Weeks's life, and the tragedy of having to take her husband's life, were favorite conversations around the country. Laura gave only one interview, and in it she said she regretted everything except keeping Morris from taking any more lives. When the interviewer asked her what she wanted in the future, she quoted a line from the song Splendid Isolation by the late Warren Zevon, "I want to live all alone in the desert. I want to be like Georgia O'Keeffe." Shortly after that, she disappeared, with her son, to find her own Abiquiu.

Acknowledgements:

I want to take this opportunity to thank everyone I pressed into being my test readers for the various versions of this book, especially my wife who is well past sick of it. I really need to say a special thanks to my good friend and screen writing partner Kevin for showing me how to do this, and my wonderful former neighbor Mary who had the courage to ask me if this was supposed to be for other people or if I intended it to be just for my own entertainment. I want to thank Shawnassey for believing in me and the folks at IsoLibris for giving me this voice.

About the Author:

Russell Scott is a writer from Jackson, Mississippi. He is married and has three children. He served in the U. S. Navy in a previous career, and deployed in support of almost every type of operation in the military. *Time Donors Wanted* is his first novel.